The Best of
Heroic Fantasy
Quarterly

Volume 3

also available

The Best of Heroic Fantasy Quarterly, Volume 1
The Best of Heroic Fantasy Quarterly, Volume 2

The Best of
Heroic Fantasy Quarterly

Volume 3, 2013-2015

compiled by the editors of
Heroic Fantasy Quarterly

Copyright © 2019 *Heroic Fantasy Quarterly*

Founding Editors: David Farney & Adrian Simmons
Editorial Team: William Ledbetter, Barbara Barret, James Row, Arien Skiba
www.heroicfantasyquarterly.com

Cover art by Robert Zoltan
www.zoltanillustration.com

Chapter glyph from openclipart.org

Additional glyphs by Jennifer Easter
pages 8, 28, 72, 140, 290, 292

Internal Art:
pages 14, 30, 70, 146, 242, 286 by Miguel Santos
pages 26, 74, 268 by Simon Walpole
pages 36, 50 by Karolína Wellartová
pages 46, 118, 142 by Justin Pfiel
pages 78, 96, 162 by Garry McCluskey
pages 190, 214 by Robert Zoltan
page 218 by Richard Hartley
page 134 by unnamed artist

Design by Keanan Brand
www.keananbrand.com

ISBN-10: 1702182142
ISBN-13: 978-1702182140

Printed in U.S.A

DEDICATED IN MEMORY OF

Stephen Sandifer,
a boon companion if there ever was one.

And to the examples of
Barbara Barrett and Gretchen Hembree,
who made their saving throws.

Contents

SWORD AND SORCERY IS WHAT I MEAN WHEN I POINT MY (INSERT CUTLERY OF CHOICE) AT IT

So, what do we mean by "sword and sorcery" anyway?

We know where the term came from. Robert E. Howard never heard it, even when he was in the process of inventing what L. Sprague de Camp used to call "the sacred genre." Fritz Leiber wrote, in George Scithers's fanzine *Amra*, Vol 2, no 16, July 1961, on page 21:

"I feel more certain that ever ... [that this field] ... should be called the sword-and-sorcery story. This accurately describes the points of culture-level and supernatural element and also immediately distinguishes it from the sword-and-cloak (historical adventure) story—and (quite incidentally) from the cloak-and-dagger (international espionage) story too."

When that was written, Robert E. Howard's stories were over twenty years in the past and largely out of print, Sprague de Camp was publishing historical novels (some of them a bit swashbuckling), and the two chief practitioners of the nearly extinct sword-and-sorcery form were Leiber himself, whose Fafhrd and Gray Mouser stories had found a new home in *Fantastic* magazine as edited by Cele Goldsmith, and Michael Moorcock, who was just beginning to develop the Elric mythos in Ted Carnell's *Science Fantasy*. The Edgar Rice Burroughs boom was just about to happen. The Robert E. Howard explosion in Lancer paperbacks was five years in the future.

Since then, largely due to the cover artwork of Frank Frazetta, and later codified in the comic-book versions, a distinct Conan iconography has developed. The barbarian is a huge, burly man, wild-haired but clean-shaven, wielding sword or axe, scantily dressed in what is often a fur loincloth, and bare-chested, even if he sometimes sports a cloak. He also seems to favor enormously heavy, fur boots, which strike me as particularly implausible, since, if the climate is mild enough that one can run about in a loincloth, the boots would be unbearably hot, and ridiculous unless one descends to the level of suggesting that in a pinch all Conan has to do is remove the boots and stun his enemies with the smell. Robert E. Howard, quoting the *Nemedian Chronicles*, suggests that Conan more sensibly trampled kingdoms beneath his *sandaled* feet.

But in the popular imagination a sword-and-sorcery story is one in which a muscle-bound hero, so clad (or unclad) battles wizards, monsters, and the occasional dark god, not to mention crazed minions of same.

There are a couple points of reference we all very likely agree on. The first, is that there must be a supernatural element. Or do we? Is it enough to have the story set in a fabulous, non-historical setting? Otherwise the King Kull story "By This Axe I Rule!" is not sword and sorcery. No magic in that one. We know that Farnsworth Wright rejected it from *Weird Tales*, very likely for this reason (no fantasy), and when Howard rewrote it as "The Phoenix on the Sword," the first Conan story, he was careful to include a substantial supernatural element. But there still exists a substantial body of borderline cases, ranging from the novels of Leslie Barringer (the Neustrian cycle, beginning with *Gerfalcon,* 1927) to Elizabeth's Lynn's Chronicles of Tornor (1979-80) and beyond which take place in imaginary lands, feature plenty of sword-play, but lack any fantastic element other than the setting.

The other thing we agree on is that there should be no use of firearms. Really? Where does that leave Solomon Kane, who, being a contemporary of Sir Francis Drake, was certainly acquainted with gunpowder? But then the Solomon Kane stories are not set in imaginary lands either, even if Howard's African geography is as hazy as that of Edgar Rice Burroughs.

So, if we declare that sword-and-sorcery is a subgenre, as the hardboiled detective story is to mystery fiction, we begin to indulge in an elimination game. Does the hardboiled detective need his trenchcoat? Does he have to utter sardonic, clipped dialogue? Does his romantic interest always turn out bad? Does he always get the crap beaten out of him in act three?

So, if the detective does not need the trenchcoat, then the sword-and-sorcery hero (thankfully) does not need that (probably very nasty) loincloth, although the iconography was once so widespread on paperbacks that sported Frazetta or imitation-Frazetta covers that we used to indelicately refer to them as "fur jockstrap books." Howard's Conan had a more practical fashion sense, even if the *Weird Tales* illustrator for "Red Nails" dressed him in pirate boots and Bermuda shorts.

Does the hero have to be a barbarian? That was an important point for Howard, who made much of the virtues and strengths barbarians supposedly retain, which civilized men have lost. But Moorcock's Elric of Melnibone is very definitely a civilized man, and a pretty decadent one at that. Leiber's Fafhrd is a bit like the traditional barbarian, but the Gray Mouser is a creature of boudoirs and back alleys.

Does he have to wield a sword? Obviously not. Conan himself used an axe at times, and King Kull ruled by one.

Does the hero have to be big and brawny? I do not think of my own *The Mask of the Sorcerer* as a sword-and-sorcery novel, but I will admit that I deliberately teased the reader with this in a couple places. The protagonist is a short, skinny, 14-year-old boy, about as unimpressive physically as it is possible to be. One night a couple of burly, sword-toting "barbarians" come in through his window and demand to know the whereabouts of his father's treasure. Dad is a notorious sorcerer, you see, and so these two are burgling the house of a sorcerer in classic sword-and-sorcery fashion. They snap the boy's forearm like a twig when he resists, but Dad makes short work of them. So there was indeed a barbarian swordsman vs. sorcerer situation in this book, though it didn't even last a full page. Later the boy discovers there's a (possibly magical) sword in the attic. His father, in a period of denial as he was becoming a sorcerer, had actually joined a bunch of anti-sorcery crusaders called the Knights Inquisitor in his youth. Is this a sword-and-sorcery novel? It certainly has sorcery galore, and even a journey into the land of the dead. It was actually written on the rebound from my failed Conan novel, *Conan the Deliverer* (which Tor Books paid for but never published, back in the 1980s). I had taken Conan himself into the Stygian afterworld.

If you think of it as being like tuning a stereo, in *The Mask of the Sorcerer* I had turned the "sorcery" dial up to full volume but turned the "swordplay" down to a whisper. But all the elements are actually there.

Does the hero have to be the good guy? Certainly Karl Edward Wagner's Kane and much of the recent "grimdark" fantasy have shown us that is not the case. Conan had a certain basic sense of chivalry, but could be pretty amoral at times.

Does the magic have to involve sorcery? How about pesky gods? How about plain old monsters?

You see how this goes. You can take out this element, or that one, and it is still sword-and-sorcery, but if you take out *all* of them, somehow the "sword-and-sorcery" nature of the story disappears. Or maybe not. It is like the proverbial grandfather's axe. ("This is my grandfather's axe. My father replaced the handle and I replaced the head. My grandfather's axe.")

We might also observe that sword-and-sorcery, as opposed to epic fantasy on the scale of *The Lord of the Rings*, usually takes place on a smaller *moral* scale. A sword and sorcery adventure is often about one or two characters tangled up in something which has no longer consequences beyond their own lives. Well, we used to be able to make that distinction. George R.R. Martin seems to have made a hash of that notion. Most of the characters in *The Song of Ice and Fire* are self-serving scoundrels and we are never sure if any of the events in the very long story have any cosmic significance. All they have managed to do by the end (in the TV series anyway) is establish an orderly means of political succession. The defeat of the Night King and his army of zombies is no more than a distraction.

So, where does that leave us?

The "sacred genre" must address the subject of heroism. In this sense I do not agree with Fritz Leiber's insistence that it be called "sword-and-sorcery". "Heroic fantasy" works better. If the hero in Lost Atlantis battles vampires with a spear, is that …? It could be. We might take a hint from Douglas Winter, who once defined "horror" not as a subject matter but as an emotion. You know a horror story because it makes you feel a certain way. Perhaps we know a heroic fantasy a.k.a. sword-and-sorcery story because it makes us feel a certain way. The glamor of the pseudo-antique, imaginary past. Howard was heavily into that. ("An age undreamed of …") A fantastic element beyond the mere setting is certainly a good idea. The fantastic element should be something which is unusual even to the characters who live in such an environment, not just part of daily life. The story which is worth telling, in most genres, is that of the *extraordinary* event, not the routine one.

We more or less agree there should be no gunpowder. But that is not what matters. What matters is an atavistic feeling of primitive heroism, the same thing we find in *The Iliad* or *Beowulf*. Such fiction is by its nature artificial, because we do not live in a raw, primitive world, as the hearers of Homer or the Beowulf poet did. It is something we try to re-create. In this sense, the most perfect sword and sorcery story may actually be Howard's "The Valley of the Worm," which purports to be the ur-epic on which all subsequent tales of dragon-slayers are based. Incidentally, it has no sorcery in it, just that primordial worm.

The protagonist does not have to be a Herculean figure. I wouldn't disqualify Frodo Baggins on grounds of his stature. An ordinary person can find himself in a heroic adventure. But he should have a mighty struggle. My own *The Mask of the Sorcerer* skirts the edges of the genre, but its heroic conflict is more internal. The boy-hero inadvertently becomes a sorcerer himself, and soon finds his own head haunted by the ghosts of his father and everybody his father ever murdered. His struggle is to retain his own identity and to avoid becoming a moral abomination.

If we go farther and farther out toward the edges of generic definition, we may lose sight of that special thing we are talking about. I think we *do* know what we mean when we point at it, and there are definitely specific emotions associated with the sword-and-sorcery story, but it goes beyond the "grandfather's axe" paradox to being something more like a hologram image. It is created out of the intersection many elements. The more you take away, the fuzzier the image becomes. Add more and the focus becomes sharper. But you cannot say precisely when it becomes what it is. You just know that it has.

Like magic.

DARRELL SCHWEITZER *is the author of* We Are All Legends, The White Ilse, The Shattered Goddess, The Mask of the Sorcerer, *and T*he Dragon House, *plus nearly 300 short stories, which have appeared in venues ranging from* Fantastic, Realms of Fantasy, *and* Interzone *to Andrew Offutt's classic Swords Against Darkness series and all six volumes of S. T. Joshi's Black Wings. He has published books on H.P. Lovecraft, Robert E. Howard, Lord Dunsany, Thomas Ligotti, and Neil Gaiman. He was co-editor of* Weird Tales *1988- 2007, and remains an active anthologist (*Cthulhu's Reign, The Secrect History of Vampires, The Secret History of Vampires, That is Not Dead, The Mountains of Madness Revealed, *etc.). He has been nominated for the Shirley Jackson Award once, for the World Fantasy Award four times, and has won the WFA once.*

A Whisper in Ashes

by Charles Gramlich

*Down from the death-lands of snow
came a warrior with eyes
like scars.
No one knew his origins.
None could foresee his end.
He had no name.
The barbarians called him Krieg.*

I. The Black Tarn

The northern wind was quiet for once. The polished surface of the tarn shone like a black shield beneath the ringed moon. To water's edge came Krieg, on silent boots with a battle-axe of ebon steel sheathed over his shoulder. He lay flat on the earth for a moment, drank his fill, then rose to ghost along the shoreline.

A shadow jutting into the lake from the shore resolved itself into the fire-ruined wreck of a dragon ship. Krieg knew such tales. A hero fallen in battle had been laid atop a bier on his finest warship. The spoils of his greatest victories were piled around him. Perhaps his female went alive and willing at his side; perhaps she was chained at his feet. Soaked with pitch, the ship had been set adrift and aflame. It burned to the waterline. The remnant lodged itself here like a splinter in the flesh of the world.

Krieg studied the hulk, studied the bleak shore upon which it lay. Someone else had been here before him. Even in the dark his keen gaze identified naked footprints in the soft loam. They were small and slender, such as those made by a woman. There was only one line of prints, coming from the burned ship to the shore.

Intrigued, Krieg turned to follow them.

II. Scarlet Droplets

The tarn sat in a bowl cupped by mountains, and as Krieg climbed toward the rim of the bowl the snow on the ground thickened and the cold deepened. The ascent grew steeper. The footprints flitted onward before him. In time he followed them to a narrow pass squeezed between walls of bare granite. Blood dappled the snow there; Krieg's eyes narrowed but he did not hesitate.

A few paces farther on the spatters of blood turned to gouts of gore. Amid a welter of torn up slush, Krieg found the slaughtered form of a white bear. Its belly was ripped wide, its intestines spilled on the ground like a miser's hoard. Its head was missing.

Beyond the ruined bear, the line of narrow footsteps reformed as if from a void. A rain of scarlet droplets marred the snow beside them.

Krieg followed.

III. Fire Eyes

Crossing the high point of the pass, Krieg started downward into a valley where legions of pines stood like dark sentries beneath their dustings of snow. From within the valley rose smoke, and the smoke led him to a stockade of raw posts hammered into the earth. The footsteps he'd been following disappeared just outside the stockade gate into the turmoil caused by the passing feet of many humans and their animals.

Krieg stopped. The gate was shut and archer towers stood to either side of it where men with bows watched him. Other men walked the wall itself. One wore a helmet, and armor finer than the rest. He called down to Krieg.

"What do you seek here, stranger?"

Krieg considered. Then, "I would speak with your Jarl."

"Jarl Tovar does not visit with just any stranger who begs audience."

Krieg smiled, and the helmeted man did not seem comforted. "And what of the last stranger to arrive here?" Krieg asked. "Perhaps a day ago. Perhaps less."

"None such have arrived for weeks now."

"Truly," Krieg said, primarily to himself. Then louder: "Not even a woman?"

"You speak as a fool," the helmeted one said. "I told you none have come here."

Krieg frowned. Finally, he called out: "Then let me be the first. I would take sup and a bed for the night. I have coin. Tell your Jarl I have come from the black tarn beyond the pass and would speak to him of a strange thing. If he will not see me, I will be on my way tomorrow."

"Granted," the man called down, though he seemed reluctant. "Fresh coin is always welcome. But draw no weapon while in our city."

The gates opened and Krieg entered. The "city" encompassed no more than thirty longhouses and their outbuildings, and from one of those buildings Krieg sensed he was being watched by eyes other than those of the warriors on the wall. These eyes burned.

IV. Night Visitor

The "city" was called Tovaris, after its Jarl, and there were no public inns available. For a few copper coins, a woman with braids of blonde sold him a rich stew of rabbit and wild onions, and filled for him a large flagon of mead. She showed him to a hay loft where he could spread his blanket.

The summons he expected from the Jarl did not come, and when the early dark of the northlands fell he burrowed into the hay and found it kind. He laid his axe under his right hand; his left curled around a dagger. In moments he was asleep, for he had learned long ago not to pass up opportunities for food or rest.

The cold deepened but it was not the cold which brought Krieg to wakefulness toward mid-night. A smear of gray had formed in the air a few steps away from him. Scarlet flakes swirled within the gray, and tendrils of some darker material trailed from the shape like the ribbons of a tattered cloak.

Krieg did not rage to his feet but remained still and kept his breathing easy. Only the tightening of his hands on his weapons revealed his readiness to move. The "gray" drifted toward him, but just as he prepared to spring up and strike, it paused. A rustling sounded in the straw. Then Krieg was alone again. He rose, moved toward where he'd heard the rustling.

Some brutish shape had been left behind by his visitor. Krieg bent closer, made out the grisly head of a snow bear. He thought it likely to be the head of the beast he'd found slaughtered in the pass above the black tarn. Blood had coagulated around the mauled neck like a circlet of rubies. The eyes had been replaced with winking coals from which smoke still curled.

Krieg knew he'd been warned. He didn't allow it to disturb the rest of his night.

V. Steel and Lace

At dawn, Krieg awoke refreshed and climbed from his loft to find a man approaching.

"The Jarl will consider your request now," the man said, and Krieg nodded and accompanied him to the largest of the village's longhouses. At the threshold the guards demanded his axe and daggers. He gazed at them until their demand turned to a request, then handed over his weapons and entered.

A long table of scarred wood ran through the center of the building's main hall, and just beyond sat Jarl Tovar in a chair of carved oak so old it was nearly black. At his feet lay a massive hound, also black, except for yellow eyes that recalled its wolfish ancestry. To the Jarl's left and right stood twin blond warriors wearing helmets and breastplates of steel. They stretched nearly seven feet in height and held warhammers at the ready. Krieg understood the threat.

At a smaller table behind the Jarl's chair sat a woman with mother-of pearl eyes above a veil of ivory lace the same color as her silk gown. Her hair tumbled silver-gray to her shoulders, and though it might hold the hue of the aged, it held the luster of youth. She watched Krieg, and he was less sure of this threat.

"You wished to speak to me?" Tovar asked.

"To you, and you alone," Krieg said.

Tovar smiled. He was younger than Krieg had expected, no more than thirty years. His hair and beard were blond, his irises blue as the agates of Norambia. His muscles corded beneath his sleeveless jerkin and he did not appear to be afraid of the black-eyed warrior before him.

"I am not a particularly wise man," Tovar said. "But I am not so much a fool as to allow a warrior of unknown talents easy access to my throat."

"Then bring your guards," Krieg said, gesturing toward the two blond giants with their hammers.

Tovar nodded as if he were considering, then glanced over his shoulder toward the woman in ivory.

"And my spaewife," he added, turning back to his visitor.

"I would prefer only the guards," Krieg replied.

Tovar laughed. "You fear a woman more than warriors?"

"When it is warranted," Krieg agreed.

Tovar nodded again. "Perhaps you are wise enough to speak with after all."

He stood up, gestured to his guards, and strode toward a corner of the longhouse hidden behind curtains of hide and fur. The hound rose as well, trailing its master, and after went the blond warriors. Krieg glanced toward the spaewife; her eyes were as expressionless as coins. He turned and followed the Jarl.

They passed through the curtains and into Tovar's bed chamber. The walls were bare and the fireplace cold. The bed was sturdy but not ornate. A table made of linked shields resting on a framework of oak was large enough to seat eight or more. Tovar sat, and the hound curled once more at his feet. The guards stood between Krieg and their Jarl.

"Speak," Tovar said.

"In the black tarn beyond the pass I found a funeral ship," Krieg said.

"That seems unlikely. There is no ingress from the sea into that tarn, and no villages nestle along its shore. Where would such a ship have come from?"

"Perhaps from hell," Krieg said, shrugging. "I know only that the ship had burned itself out but that a survivor came ashore from the ashes. I followed the footprints and they were those of a woman. She came here."

Tovar drew a long breath as he leaned back in his chair.

"Falk, Ivar," he said, and the guards glanced toward him. "Leave."

The two did not even attempt a protest and Krieg's respect for Tovar rose. The men left, and now only the hound stood between Krieg and the Jarl. The black-eyed warrior did not discount the power of the beast.

"A few days ago I would have laughed you from my presence," Tovar said.

"But not today," Krieg added.

"Yaris. My witch woman. Though she looks younger than I, she advised my father. Now she advises me. Three days ago, in a trance, she spoke of blood and water mixed with ashes. Two nights ago a guard on the wall disappeared and has not returned. Last night a mother found blood in the water she intended for her child. The worst of it is that Yaris is afraid. Not of any woman, but of a thing."

Krieg nodded.

"Yaris also spoke of you," Tovar added then.

"Did she?"

"She said that perhaps you could aid us. And—"

"What?"

"If we live through the next few days I will tell you," Tovar said.

VI: Hunter and Hunted

"Foolishness!" Tovar shouted, louder than perhaps was necessary. "You waste my time with fairy stories."

Krieg did not respond as he pushed through the furs surrounding the Jarl's bed chamber and into the main part of the longhouse. Tovar followed, held up his hand as guards moved to confront the black-eyed warrior.

"Do not accost him," Tovar said to the approaching men. "Return him his weapons but make sure he leaves our walls. We have no need of his superstitions here."

The crowd parted like waves to either side as Krieg moved through them like the prow of a dragon ship. His weapons were returned and he strode from the building and down the trodden path to the stockade's gate. The gate shut behind him with a clatter but he did not look back.

He moved up the mountain toward the pass he had so recently come down, but travelled only a few hundred paces before the somber pines closed around him and he was lost to the sight of the guards on the walls of Tovaris. He found a place to camp where two fallen trees had snared a thick shield of ice and snow behind them. There, he built a fistful of fire and melted snow in a wooden bowl he took from his pack. Dried meat added to the water cooked into a broth which he drank for his breakfast.

After, he set snares amid the pines and then gathered firewood for the night ahead. He used a length of dead tree limb as a shovel to pile up snow around his encampment so that on three sides he had shelter. Or perhaps a defense.

His weapons were sharp but he sharpened them again, and later took two birds from his snares and cleaned and ate them smoking from his fire. As soon as evening's shadows began to flow around him, he lay down in his blanket as if to sleep. Then he waited for a death he could not name to come seeking.

VII: The Benighted Dark

With no warning snarl of threat, the first wolf came through the opening of the snow shelter and leaped at Krieg's throat from across the smoldering fire. Had the man been sleeping, the beast might have had him. But Krieg was ready beneath his blanket, his hands solidly gripping the haft of his double-bitted axe. With a twist of his body, he snapped the weapon upward in a killing blow, and such was his strength and the sharpness of the black steel that the wolf's neck sheared through.

Blood sprayed the snow walls of his shelter, sizzled in the embers of the fire. A second and third wolf followed the first, but Krieg was rising to his feet. He drove the steel-reinforced haft of the axe crossways into the mouth of one beast, smashing away teeth and tearing loose the jaw, then brought the heavy blades around to hack away half the head of his remaining attacker.

From amid the pines outside, the shouts of men and the howls of beasts arose, and he heard the twang of bows and the hiss of arrows. He crushed the skull of the wounded wolf with a heel and leaped out into the snow. Fire bowls flared to sudden life, revealing struggling shadows. A man screamed only a dozen feet away as a lambent-eyed wolf savaged him. Krieg's hand flashed to his hip, came up with a dagger that he hurled into the attacking beast's side. The wolf leaped back, crouched, snarling, and two war-bladed arrows tore its life away.

The howling died. Men ran from the woods. One bent to check on his wounded fellow. Others milled about, as if unsure whether the threat was over or from where the next attack might come.

"Krieg!" called a voice.

"Here," Krieg answered.

Tovar strode over to him. "I saw nothing of the thing. Did it come for you as we had hoped? Did you kill it?"

Krieg shook his head. "It sent the wolves. It didn't come itself. Somehow it learned of our plan to trap it."

"Impossible! No one who knew would tell." Tovar gestured around. "These men did not even know until we were outside the gates. They could not have whispered it to friend or lover."

"What of Yaris?" Krieg asked.

"Certainly, I told her. In case she should foresee something of import. Gods, man, she cannot be the thing we seek. I have known her since I was a child."

Krieg jutted his chin toward the wolf carcass lying nearly at his feet. "Then how do you explain these beasts. And not the one we sought? We offered it my death. As one who might pose it a threat. And that offer was spurned."

"I cannot answer," Tovar said, his voice gruff with anger.

From where the stockade lay, a dazzle of sudden lightning leaped into the black sky. Thunder rolled on its heels like a thousand copper bells being crushed. The people of Tovaris began to scream.

VIII: Ashes and Embers

They ran—Krieg and Tovar and Tovar's men. They tore through the pines and into the clearing around the stockade. Orange flames climbed the sky from something burning inside the walls.

Tovar shouted at the gate and it was flung back. One guard met them, clearly frightened.

"What has happened?" demanded Tovar.

"An explosion!" the man cried. "I think at the spaewife's hut. Then fire everywhere. The others went to see. Since then, screams. I—"

Tovar did not wait to hear the rest but ran in the direction of the fire. Krieg and the others followed. They found the Jarl's longhouse burning fiercely, and another building's roof aflame nearby. Men and women and children beat at the flames. Tovar ordered those who had accompanied him into the forest to join that fight, but then turned himself and rushed toward where Yaris's hut stood. Krieg followed.

The spaewife's small house lay destroyed, but though some of its planks smoldered, it had been no fire that ruined it. It was as if some titan had burst it from within, sending the shards flying in all directions.

Tovar pushed into the rubble, frantically searching for his witch woman.

"Any sign?" Krieg asked.

"No," Tovar snarled. "Could you have been right about her?"

Krieg said nothing.

A high pitched scream punctured the darkness and both Krieg and Tovar spun toward the sound. This time, Tovar followed Krieg as the dark-eyed warrior raced in that direction. In an alley between two longhouses they found the body of a man. It recalled for Krieg the killing of the white bear above the tarn. Here, too, the head was missing. This time he could see no blood trail to follow.

"Whatever it is we seek," Krieg said. "It is on the loose in your village."

Cursing, Tovar drew his sword with a rasp from its sheath. "I will slay this monster or die," he snarled.

"We hunt as two," Krieg said. "Trap it between us. Remember, it is a thing of fire. Use no flame against it."

Tovar made no response but stepped over the cooling body before him and moved down the alley. Krieg went to the right, around the longhouse on the other side. He came upon a circular opening between buildings. A well stood there, lit by the lurid fires that still ate greedily at the bones of the village. Upon the wall of stones surrounding the well sat three grisly offerings: a man's head, a woman's, and a child's.

With scarce a pause, the warrior strode to the well and bent to look within. In almost the same instant, he spun back around, drawing his axe from over his shoulder. Out of the shadows from behind him came flowing some mist-like thing bearing the shape of a woman burned to ashes and embers. The face was a hole darker than black.

Most warriors would have wasted a moment on fear; Krieg swung his axe. The heavy blade hacked into the swirling mass and tore through. The mist roiled madly and to Krieg's ears came a thin shriek like the wind howling over pack ice. The thing hesitated an instant and Krieg struck again. Once more his weapon cleaved a gash through the shape. Again came the shriek, but this time the monster pressed forward.

Tendrils of the thing's mass solidified around the haft of Krieg's axe, tried to tear it from his grasp. The warrior and the monster struggled for possession of the weapon but neither could move the other.

The creature's empty face began to grow texture, began to sprout a muzzle that glinted black with teeth. The mouth struck at Krieg and he narrowly jerked his head aside. A tendril of gray tissue whipped from behind the thing to encircle the man's legs and lock them together. The monstrous muzzle split wide, sprouted a scabrous tongue that wove in the air before him like the head of a snake.

Krieg let go of his axe with one hand, grabbed a dark dagger from his belt and slashed across at the tongue as it began to form the shape of a spear blade. The dagger cut through, sent a sliver of flesh hurtling away. Krieg reversed the weapon in his hand, slashed downward to sever the tendril binding his legs.

The thing reared back in apparent agony, and Krieg thrust the dagger savagely into the side of its newly formed jaw. Steel caught on something that grated like bone. Whatever the creature was at its core, Krieg realized, when it took on form it became that form—and became vulnerable.

Falling back from the source of its agony, the creature suddenly turned and darted away, losing coherence as it moved, becoming once more a mist full of ash and coals. It took Krieg's dagger with it.

"Here!" Krieg shouted, hoping Tovar would hear. He ran after the monster, but it was swift as a river rushing toward a falls. He lost it amid a maze of sheds built to house chattel and store harvests.

Hunting through those outbuildings, Krieg found only slaughtered goats and cows. A sound of footsteps brought his head around. At the opening to the shed where he searched stood Tovar. With him ran his black hound. The hound bared its canines and let a low growl rumble from deep within its chest. The man held a drawn sword in his right fist and the urge to kill lived in his gaze.

"I found Yaris," Tovar said, in a voice cold and hard. "The hound led me to her."

"And?" Krieg inquired.

Tovar opened his left hand, showed a black dagger lying across the palm. "She was not decapitated like the others. She'd been killed with this. I'm sure you recognize one of your own knives."

A twisted smile curved Krieg's lips.

Tovar snarled, dropped the dagger and came charging.

IX: In Battle Lies Truth

The fires that still burned in Tovaris set the Jarl's greatsword aglitter as he leaped toward Krieg. Krieg's axe refracted only blackness as he brought his weapon up to block. Steel sang on steel. The sword rebounded.

Tovar spun, bringing his blade around like a scythe to reap Krieg down. The dark-eyed warrior twisted aside, tried to hook Tovar's leg with the haft of his axe to trip him. The Jarl was too quick.

The weapons clashed again. Again the sword rebounded. The Jarl tried to circle Krieg, hoping to open him to an attack from the hound crouched waiting and snarling by the shed door. Krieg did not allow the strategy, and in the confines of the building Tovar could not force it.

Now, Tovar began to use his blade to thrust rather than slash. The axe should have been slower than the sword, and perhaps it would have been in the hands of anyone but Krieg. Once, twice, again, the Jarl drove in for the kill and was forced back. Then Tovar saw an opening. He launched a thrust, and as Krieg went into a crouch to block that blow the Jarl converted his attack into a shoulder-high slash.

The blade came slicing down, but Krieg was not as out of position as he seemed. He snapped the haft of his axe up just enough to deflect the sword over his head, then powered forward and up from his crouch, slamming his shoulder into the Jarl's midsection and rising to flip the lighter man over his back.

The Jarl crashed into a hayrick that shattered into splinters, and in the same instant Krieg lunged toward the black hound, which had finally seen its chance and leaped to the attack. The beast's eyes flamed yellow; its mouth was a raw, red wound of savagery. Krieg was faster.

The half-moon blades of the dark axe thrust the muzzle of the hound aside, and Krieg freed one hand to scoop up the dagger Tovar had dropped. The hound twisted like a lion to lunge at Krieg again, and the warrior brought the dagger down with enough force to drive the blade through the thing's skull and into the frozen soil beneath.

A half-lost howl rasped from the beast's mouth; its paws scrabbled at the dirt. And Krieg came to his feet and swung his axe in an arc that ended with a spray of black ichor and the hound's head rolling free.

"No!" shouted Tovar, as he rose from where he had fallen. He still held his sword and made to rush against Krieg, then froze as the dead hound erupted with sudden flames that seared away fur and flesh to reveal first the shape of a burned woman, and then a writhing mass of ashes shot through with scarlet streamers.

Krieg lowered his axe, stood watching the Jarl, who watched what he had thought to be his dog melt away like mist into the earth.

Tovar looked up at Krieg. "My hound?"

"Likely killed when this thing replaced it. The same night the first guard disappeared, I warrant."

"How did you know?"

"Only the hound was present when we spoke of trapping the monster in the woods. Too, you said it led you to Yaris, who had my knife in her. Moments before, I stabbed the creature with that blade and watched it carry the weapon off."

Tovar's shoulders slumped. "I tried to kill you," he said.

"I am unharmed."

"And the monster is dead. By the Gods, what was it?"

Krieg made no reply.

Tovar straightened, sheathed his sword. "I must aid my people against the fires that still burn," he said.

Krieg sheathed his axe. "I shall as well."

The two went side by side from that place.

X: Leave Taking

They stood at the gate of Tovaris, Krieg and the Jarl.

"Do you wish to know what else Yaris said about you, Krieg?" Tovar asked. "After she told me you might be able to aid us?"

Krieg gazed for a moment at the Jarl. "It matters not," he said. Then he turned and strode from the town.

Tovar shook his head, smiling, then shouted after the black-eyed warrior. "She said you could aid us because you were far more to be feared than the creature we hunted. She spoke the truth."

Krieg gave no indication he had he

CHARLES GRAMLICH *writes from the piney woods of south Louisiana. He has authored the Talera fantasy series and the SF novel* Under the Ember Star. *His stories have been collected in* Bitter Steel, Midnight in Rosary, *and* In the Language of Scorpions. *He also writes westerns as Tyler Boone. His most recent releases, under his own name, are* Farhaven & Other Stories, *a collection of kids' tales, and* Out of Dreams and Nightmares, *which are retellings of some of his most memorable nightmares in story form. Charles' books are available at Amazon, Barnes & Noble, Wildside Press, or through the author.*

Don Quixote's Quandary
by Colleen Anderson

He had studied flags, kites and pinwheels
knowing them for the harmless fry of monsters
they would soon become his duty
for all his tilting at windmills
everything looked skewed

An enemy of state
of mind he sought the source
of untamed, wanton might
not just to cage a beating heart but to fire
engines whether of giants or turning, wooden sails

They bided their time or wasted his
aware they could outlast his futile forays
into imagination flickering like a candle's flame
fanned not to burning novas but guttering
in the breeze, thoughts bending this way and that

Unwilling to give a hint of their endless energy
the windmills creaked unceasing, deep
belly laughing millstones about his neck
he'd hung his hopes and dreams on discovering
something as mighty and invisible as a breath of wind

COLLEEN ANDERSON *is a Canadian author writing fiction and poetry and has had over 170 poems published in such venues as* Grievous Angel, Polu Texni, The Future Fire, HWA Poetry Showcase, *and many others. She is a member of HWA and SFPA and has performed her work before audiences in the US, UK, and Canada, and has placed in the Balticon, Rannu, Crucible, and Wax poetry competitions. Currently she is working on two poetry collections. Colleen also enjoys editing, and co-edited Canadian anthologies* Playground of Lost Toys *(Aurora nominated) and* Tesseracts 17, *and her solo anthology*—Alice Unbound: Beyond Wonderland—*was published in 2018.* A Body of Work *was recently published by Black Shuck Books, UK. Living in Vancouver, Colleen keeps an eye out for mold monsters and mermaids, and will be guest of honour in 2020 at the Vancouver Creative Ink Festival. Keep up with her at www.colleenanderson.wordpress.com.*

A Lonely Grave on the Hill

by Cesar Alcázar

Anrath yanked the reins of his horse as a piercing scream broke the silence of the night and startled the animal. After regaining control of the steed, the mercenary from Connacht examined the darkness in an attempt to find the source of the noise. Travelling at night did not please him at all. On the other hand, he was eager to join the men of Niall mac Eochada, King of Ulaid. Niall was gathering troops to plunder Dublin, and offering a payment he couldn't ignore.

The horse stirred again. Not far from there, Anrath spotted a shadowy figure running among the trees. Barks and snarls could be clearly heard. Moments later, the warrior realized it was a man being chased by wolves. The fierce creatures would catch up to him at any time.

With a swift movement, the mercenary's sword tore the icy air of early winter as it was removed from its sheath. He spurred his horse and it advanced reluctantly. Then, the wolves jumped over the prey who, to Anrath's astonishment, was a very old man.

Realizing the horse would not approach the scene, the warrior leaped to the ground, sword in hand. The animals noticed him, and attacked. Sharp and ravenous jaws tried to reach his flesh. Striking precise blows, Anrath eliminated two of the beasts. The remainder of the pack split: three wolves continued to attack the original victim, while three others faced the mercenary. Lying on the ground, the old man fought for his life in despair.

The largest of the wolves stuck its teeth into Anrath's arm, which was luckily protected by the chainmail. The animal made him lose his balance and spin; such was the ferocity of the attack. Struggling to stand, Anrath shook off the wolf, but the beast rushed towards him once more. An instinctive blow interrupted the assault, and the head of the wolf spun in the air before touching the ground.

Perceiving the pack leader's defeat, the remaining wolves receded. They looked at the mercenary with lowered heads, snarling in threat. Anrath, in turn, stared at the animals in the eyes without fear. He lifted the sword, which reflected the eyes of the beasts, and prepared himself for another combat. However, the wolves fell back a few steps, only to disappear among the trees seconds later.

The old man remained lying down and groaning in pain, his clothes bathed in blood. It had been a heinous struggle. One minute longer and the wolves would have torn the old man apart. Anrath wasted no more time and rushed to help him. The warrior, whose long dark hair almost covered his melancholic face, kneeled down beside the old man, who said between sobs:

"Thank you, my friend."

Anrath examined the man's injuries: the thigh was torn and bleeding abundantly, among other minor wounds. There was no way of saving him, because the artery had been severed.

"Don't thank me," said the desolate mercenary while tying a tourniquet above the ghastly wound to stop the bleeding, "I didn't arrive on time."

"I know that my condition is serious, don't worry. At least I may still live long enough to do what I must; and I owe it to you. My name is Fearghal mac Artie."

"Anrath of Connacht."

"Well, I thank you, Anrath. If it wasn't for you, those wolves would have eaten me for sure!"

"Why is a man of your age walking by yourself at night in these woods?"

Fearghal's eyes filled with tears, and he answered with difficulty in a mixture of emotion and pain:

"I wanted to see the battle—"

"Battle? As far as I know there is no war going on around these parts."

"I refer to the Battle of Tara, my friend."

"But that battle happened a long time ago!" exclaimed the mercenary.

"Yes. More than forty springs ago."

"Then, what did you expect to see?" Anrath asked, wondering if the old man wasn't delirious.

Fearghal gazed at the mercenary. The old man's countenance was overwhelmed by a nostalgic expression. Then, in a gentle tone, he began to explain:

"Our heathen ancestors used to say that, during Samhain, the boundary between the world of the living and the Otherworld became tenuous, thin. Following the arrival of winter, plants and animals died in abundance, opening a gate for the dead to walk the earth again. I never wanted to believe this, because I am a Christian."

Old Fearghal paused, and the wind blew a sad melody. The night fog seemed thicker. Anrath finished tying the dying man's wounds and listened to him sigh deeply before continuing:

"Listen, young man, I fought in the great battle at Tara. Now, every single man who fought by my side on that glorious day is already dead. I am the last one, but I will never forget our victory. The King Máel Sechnaill, of the Uí Néill, had just risen to power of the Kingdom of Mide and managed to secure the support of Leinster and Ulster. Only then we were able to face the Norsemen of Olaf Cuaran, King of Dublin. The armies clashed not far from here, on the Hill of Tara. I can still feel the excitement of combat. I can still hear the screams and the thunder from the clashing of steel against steel."

Fearghal looked at the fog shrouded sky and sighed again. Anrath stood there in reverent silence. Then, the old man asked:

"Do you have an idea of what a great battle is like?"

"Yes, old man, I fought in the Battle of Clontarf years ago."

"You? But of course, that's why I know your name. You are Anrath, the Black Hound! However, I cannot believe. The Black Hound I heard of is a cruel and bloodthirsty traitor, not a man who would help someone like me!"

Anrath frowned. His past would never cease to haunt him. Born a Gael, he grew up among the Vikings. Even his garbs were an amalgam of both cultures: wolf hides, typical of the wild men of Connacht, blended with the chainmail wore by the Norse warriors. Fate made him a renegade, a man condemned to wander between two cultures without belonging to either.

"I have never refused help to anyone. I did things in my past I judged as correct. I fought alongside the Vikings at Clontarf because they were my family. I am a murderer, yes, but I'm not the monster of the drunken stories they tell in the taverns."

The old man looked at the dark countenance of his benefactor, a face of harsh features like an axe carved image, and said:

"Would you fulfill the last wish of an old man who is about to die?"

"What are you talking about?"

"The inhabitants of this region say that, during the first night of Samhain, it is possible to see the dead of Tara, warring throughout eternity in the Otherworld. I wanted to see the magnificence of that battle once more. That's why I came here. Now, I ask you: take me to the Hill of Tara, Anrath."

"How I am going to take you there in your condition? You will die on the way."

"I beg you, Anrath! I want to relive that glory. The seasons pass, great feats pale, men forget. At least I want to remember. Please, let me see the Battle of Tara again."

"But this is madness!"

Given the mercenary's reaction, Fearghal stammered through tears:

"In a few hours a new day will rise, and I will not be in this world anymore. What happened at Tara will be lost forever. Before I die, I want to be with my companions."

Anrath thought for a moment. He could not put the old man on the horse, because the gallop would kill him in no time. He could not risk it, even if the Hill of Tara wasn't far away from there. He punched the ground and sheathed the sword, muttering under his breath. Then he made his decision and said:

"Old man, don't be afraid. I will take you to Tara."

The mercenary tied his horse to a tree. After that, he held the old man in his arms and lifted him off the ground. He was careful not to cause Fearghal more pain. In this manner, Anrath took the first steps towards Tara. Fearghal, despite the intense pain showing upon his face, remained silent.

Anrath walked through the forest at a leisurely pace, observed only by occasional nocturnal animals. After about half an hour, they reached a glade. Not very far from there, Anrath sighted the Lia Fáil, known as the Stone of Destiny, where the High Kings of Ireland used to be crowned on days long passed. The mercenary placed Fearghal carefully on the ground and said:

"We have arrived, old man! Look yonder; there is the Hill of Tara!"

Fearghal looked at the vast undulated terrain. The green fields were shrouded by the mists of the night, which flared with a blue luminescence due to the brightness of the moon. Everything was quiet in that landscape. There was no sign of life. Even the wind wasn't blowing anymore. The two men stood there, watching the bucolic scenery.

From the moment the mercenary had raised him from the soil, the old man had not said a word. He didn't let the soaring pain make him sob or moan either. He bravely endured every step taken by his new friend while he was led to his final destination. Now, the emptiness of the green hills afflicted his heart. Would it have been all in vain? Would he die without seeing again the glorious image of the past which he craved?

The old man felt his life slipping from his body like the sands of an hourglass. Then, something awakened him. A dark shadow moved in front of him and soon transformed itself into something magnificent. Fearghal finally exclaimed:

"There they are! It's wonderful. Can you see them, Anrath?"

A flash of lightning lit up the hill and, just for a moment, the mercenary was able to see thousands of fierce men fighting under the dense fog. The clamor of the clash of arms resounded through the winds. Swords, shields and helmets emanated a spectral radiance in the dark night. Amid the chaos of combat, Anrath spotted a man who closely resembled the old man who now lay in his arms. The resemblance was astonishing, although the warrior from the ghostly vision was much younger.

Within seconds, the apparition faded, and silence fell again over the Hill of Tara. Anrath looked down at old Fearghal. A slight smile marked the old man's still face and his gaze was fixed on the horizon. He was now in the Otherworld.

"Rest now, Fearghal. May Macha, Morrígan and Badb receive you!"

The mercenary rested the old combatant's head on the ground. He stood up and begun to gather stones for a cairn. Fearghal deserved to be buried at the site where the most important moment of his existence took place. The one moment he didn't want to forget. Over time, that land and Fearghal would become one.

It was dawn and the mists were dissipating when the task of covering the body was completed. Dew droplets accumulated on the cairn shone like crystals at the first rays of sunlight. To Anrath's eyes, it was a resting place fit for a warrior. A monument for generations to come.

Fearghal feared that which Anrath desired the most: oblivion. The mercenary who lived under the stigma of being the Black Hound of Clontarf, traitor of two races, glanced once more at the pile of stones before leaving. Men are no more than shadows passing through time, he thought. Yesterday, this place was the stage for the greatest of battles, a battle even greater than mine. Now, all that is left of it is a lonely grave on the hill.

CESAR ÁLCAZAR is *a Brazilian writer, translator, and editor. He is the author of the Tales of the Black Hound series of short stories and novellas. The Black Hound stories have also been the source for two graphic novels. He edited the anthology* Cronicas de Espada e Magia, *and translated to Portuguese stories from authors Karl Edward Wagner, Robert E. Howard, and George R. R. Martin.*

CORINTH

BY GERALD HENSON

They hounded me through the streets of Corinna. They had surrounded the crumbling barn where I slept and thought to catch me unaware, but even then I knew to listen in my sleep. I knew not to close my eyes long enough to dream.

The Antonine Empire had failed a generation ago, but the massive and fractured body was long to die. Only the coming of the Burning God had closed the throat of the gasping corpse. The Burning God had stopped the slowly beating heart of the Empire and ended the old ways even in this distant province far removed from the core of the realm. Antonius had not stepped within a thousand leagues of remote Corinna in his lifetime centuries ago, but his roads of stone, his marble gods who held all the virtues of men, his metered armies, and the bloody circles of his empire spanned the known world.

I lay panting in the Circle of Corinth, bleeding. My wounds were many, but mostly light. My pain was great, but time would soothe me. I would have been dead a dozen times, but the mob wished to cause pain before the kill. Each of them wanted to kick me, stone me—a mere child of the empire's blood. They wanted to club me with their fists or gouge me with their raking fingers. They wanted to slay the Empire in their god's name.

I was stabbed once, a glancing strike across the ribs, but some conductor among the carnage pulled the knife-wielding man away before he could end my life and spoil the sport for the rest of them.

I saw the man with the blade; he was Weldi whom I thought a friend. I knew not if he sought to vent some new religious wrath upon me, or if he wished to spare me from the Burning God's mob, but I took that disruption of the crowd to flee.

Only one who has been close to death could understand the strength reaching my undernourished, fourteen-year-old limbs as I fled. I was desperately panicked and my heaving flesh ready to collapse from the effort, but I moved with the Zephyr's haste and made my way to the circle, seeking sanctuary among the accursed and the damned.

A stone struck my head, and I stumbled several steps inside the circle before crashing to the ground.

I heard the shouts and curses of the crowd from beyond the high stands around me. They gathered at the breaks in the stone walls, the openings where quarrymen unmade the architecture of the old structure to erect haphazard things of thatch, waddle, and stolen stone. I thanked those thieves of history, for without their vandalism, I would never have reached the safety of the arena's interior.

To think that the arena became a place of safety is strange to me even today, half a century later. The great stone circles of Antonius were places of execution, places where the innocent and guilty alike were sent to die. The denizens of Corinna were loathe to enter such a place, thinking it tainted, haunted by spirits. It remained taboo to set foot within the stone walls even while those of the old Empire, who condemned so many, were themselves dead.

I remember sinking into a black sleep.

I remember the red and angry sky shepherding me into darkness as the mob burned the Antonine relics of old Corinth. They cleansed the city of its history and its name. It became Corinna in dedication to the Burning God who dwelt in flame, smoke, and rose from the ash.

I was so very close to death then.

It was not simply from my injuries, from thirst and starvation, or from any threat of my life passing, but I was so very close to the thousands before me who had passed in that place.

I breathed dust chipped from cobbled stones as spatha and axe clove through flesh to strike the ground beneath numberless bodies. I breathed the musk of voxen and panthers, the metallic tang of the chains binding the beasts, and the fearful stench of their victims before tusk and claw savaged their lives away. I lay among the grasses fed by the blood and bile of countless torn men, and I sprawled in the same shadows where noble equestrians and vulgar masses sat in horror and glee to watch their fellows die.

And in that black sleep, I did dream. I watched the deaths of so many, but I did more than watch. I felt the death blows delivered an infinity of times. I saw each strike by a myriad of blades and felt each agony.

First I was naked but for rags, starved, accused of a crime by the invaders, the Antonine. I did not know their tongue as the crime was announced, and in my heart I knew that there was none. I was simply an example for others of my barbarian kind. I remember a death for stealing bread from my master's kitchen, and death as a woman for refusing to submit to my master's touch. These deaths were horrible, savage, and clumsy, but there were other, older deaths.

When the marble of the arena was new, when the stones beneath my sandals were sharp and square, unmarked by time, I remembered a warrior's death. I remembered the struggle with a man my equal, not with a beast sent only to destroy. I died then for honor, for the glory of battle. I died for the Empire, and I died a thousand times.

I fell to sword and spear, to a dagger beneath my breastplate a dozen times. I died by javelin and garrote, and by fists and fingers, and in those times I knew what it was to walk in the shadow of Antonius. I knew what it was to serve our true gods, to master steel and warfare, and to bring a wild world within the reigns of a great civilization.

And knowing the last deaths here in the Circle of Corinth, I knew the error of ancient arrogance. I saw the decline of the Empire as the warrior became merely an executioner, and I could see at once the rise and fall of the new world under the Burning God.

What I saw last, before the sun rose in the east and I climbed from black slumber, was perhaps Antonius himself. He looked down upon me, eyes bright green even in the predawn dark, old as time, but as strong as the mountain. He was a warrior in leather skirts and plate. He was a hero with his helm removed in salute, and his knee bent.

"*Stá difícil dematar,*" he said in a tongue like ringing steel, and I did not know then what the words meant. I knew the word *fullonica* in Antonine. This word and the soiled clothes of better men were my only inheritance.

I felt something cold in my hand. Cold and as rough as his calloused touch when he patted my bare chest.

"*Agor mais difícil.*" With those words he vanished, or walked away, or I fainted once again.

The dawn was fully upon me when I woke. It was not the light in my eyes that woke me, but once again the voice of the mob. I sat up and blinked in the light, gathering myself, and intending to check my wounds. I found my tunic, little more than a slave's cloth, wrapped around my torso as a bandage. My mouth was dry, but not as dry as my thirst had left me in the night, and there was a strange taste lingering on my tongue like raw cinnamon. Strangest of all was the sword now in my hand.

It was an old, rusted relic. It was hilted for the use of two hands, once of great length and weight, but what remained was a broken thing, broken like the Empire. It was jagged where there was once a cleaving tip; pitted along the thick and dull blade. The thing had survived decades left in the dirt, beneath the weather in some lost corner of stone. This was once a great weapon. It was a sword of the old quality, a ruined legacy, I somehow knew, from the time of Antonius.

I rose up, strengthened from my rest and from the draught the man must have ministered while I slept. I looked around the arena that was the great Circle of Corinth, and I saw the history of my Empire. I saw the glory as warriors did battle to honor their martial art and warrior gods. I saw the shame as women and the innocent were torn apart in a spectacle of slaughter. As I watched the crowd churning at the open gates and guarding the breached walls, I could also see the death of the last martyr, Banoien. His death brought the riots and the fall. Banoien it was who ascended upon the prayers of his followers to become the One God. The Burning God was but an aspect of the One who dwelled in seven parts.

I closed my eyes and forced away the memories from beyond my young flesh. The centuries weighed upon me, but I carried the burden of my own years.

* * *

I was nothing. Nothing to hold high and nothing to scorn. I was a fuller, a laundry boy, and but for my father's eyes I would have never known the sword.

My father's eyes were green, Antonine green, but my mother was of the Selgo horsemen. Her hair was black as coal, her eyes midnight blue, and her colors remained true even when the sickness came again. The sickness had taken Father before I could know him, and on its return, it took my mother. Father left us with a partnership in a laundry shop, a *fullonica*, but what share could a woman or babe at breast wrestle from an unjust man?

By the time I was old enough to understand injustice, theft, I had already grown accustomed to a life of little more than slavery. I gathered the urine to fill our vats. I stomped and paddled filthy tunics in the buckets. I rubbed my hands raw working cloth against the boards and through the river stones. I ate little better than the slaves, often less, for they were many and shared their meager gains while I only had my sickly mother.

But Mother was satisfied. She said that for a Selgo, once fierce raiders and rebels, to wed the Antonine was a sign of the changing world. She spoke of better times in another life to the west where the sun departed and carried the day's woes into the sea.

It was godspeak.

It was the word of a priest carried on by the faith of sheep. Mother knew well the words of many gods, and to her, each day was a chance to take life anew, cycling away the troubles of the world as the sun bore them across the sky.

She did not know the terrors of my night.

I will not speak of this, but know that Weldi came to me. He knew, and together we burned my father's stolen *fullonica*. The lecherous thief's soul was sent to his god upon a missive of smoke and ash.

By then my mother was gone, and she did not have to share my life of dust. I was less than a slave, starving but for the scraps I could beg and what Weldi left on his *vestibulum*. In secret, he fed me like a dog, and I did have to be quicker than the curs of the street or my few meals would have been lost to feral teeth.

How could they hate such a one? Could such pain and fury be all for my father's eyes?

* * *

I took up the sword and stumbled toward the main gate. Faces peered through every gap in the arena wall, but I moved for the thickest of the mob. I sought the Primus, the godspeaker controlling the masses.

A poor and homeless thing I was, but in my blood was the blood of the Empire. For all I knew, the smoldering town was cleansed of everyone of my thin lineage and I was last of the Antonine to remain on the continent. I would fight as my forefathers did. I would die as a man of stone and steel though I was yet merely a boy.

I surged forward into the stink of wood smoke and sweat. An arm reached through the rusted bars near the main gate, brick in hand, and hurled it at my head. I batted the brick aside with the clumsy blade and hacked into the man's arm, bludgeoning and breaking bone more than cleaving, but effective. As he screamed in pain, the chipped corner of my broken blade drove into his throat to silence him.

He was the first man I killed that day, but by the legends, the single blow felled a score.

A hail of stones flew from the walls, passing over me as I moved toward the fray. A man blocking the gate hammered a blow into my hand, crushing several bones. I gripped the sword with both hands and pushed it up into his belly, somehow piercing the thick cloth, and somehow ripping through flesh.

His painful screams echoed into the roaring madness and bloodlust of the mob, terrifying and silencing those near me, and bringing doubt to those who heard.

A tiny space of shocked inactivity surrounded him for half a breath, and I used the freedom to rush through the gate and hack a deadly arc of steel at those around me. The crowd pressed back even further, stones hanging in paralyzed hands.

I remembered the martyr.

"Stones!" I yelled. "They stoned Banoien and you pray to the Stoned God for justice. What crime am I guilty of, but for having green eyes?"

A stone struck my brow, tearing a flap of skin loose, and a man stepped forward, possibly to speak, possibly to strike. I rushed him and smashed the hilt of my sword into his mouth. He reeled backward, I ducked another stone from the mob, then drove my knee into his stomach, doubling him over. A backhand slash tore into the cheek of a man who came too close, and I swept low to duck a kick and break the leg of that attacker.

I came up panting, blood dripping into my eyes.

"They shattered his bones and you pray to the Broken God! They tortured him and you pray to the God Upon the Wheel for the strength to endure. I have that strength!" I yelled loud enough for them all to hear. "And he is the Hanged God who sees the truth beyond the veil—"

"You dirty Antonine scu—" Weldi began, but as quick as the wind I clove the sword through his forehead, nearly splitting it in two, then dashed the brains from the men to either side of him in rapid succession.

The crowd stumbled back from me, fleeing the gore, guilt or death at my hands.

The life's blood and viscera of my only friend clung to my scrawny, wasted form. I would have fallen from grief or exhaustion but the sword held me up like a crutch. Like eagles' talons reaching down from the open sky. Through history.

Another man stepped forward from the crowd, and I took the look from his eye. I had seen it in the arena, upon the face of the executioner.

"You come to me for murder," I said. "Murder in the name of the God Who Was Burned."

"The Burned God seeks vengeance," he assured. He was tall with closely-cropped hair. He had the look of the soldiers from the faded mural on the wall of the civic hall. He was as broad as any man, wore a leather jerkin, armbands, and was the only person carrying a functional sword. "I will take vengeance in the name of Primus Naventi, and in the name of the Burned God."

He moved with confidence, like a fighter, which I was not. He had the bearing of so many men of the circle, like so many of the warriors who took my life those countless times as I dreamed the thousand deaths in my black sleep.

The man made a gesture and the crowd opened around us, forming a wide circle of flesh outside the stone Circle of Corinth. Worshippers, miscreants, whatever the mob was composed of, they gathered around to witness the drama of my execution.

Primus Naventi stepped forward, and I saw the flaming sword in his hand. "In the name of the Burning God I bless you, Arben, and bid you to do what must be done," the priest said. He touched his sword to the warrior's blade, and that too burst into thick, rolling flame.

The crowd began to chant his name: Arben! Arben!

Blessed Arben turned toward me, waving the sword before him, a sly and hungry smile upon his face. I had seen that smile a hundred times, and fangs that were much more savage, eyes far more than terrifying. After a thousand deaths, the loss of one life seemed the smallest matter, but I would fight for mine regardless. The small life to be worthless would be his.

Arben swung his sword from side to side casually, but he suddenly used the momentum to whip the blade in an overhand slash to unbalance me. He followed it with a quick thrust meant to spear my chest.

I had been killed in this way before, once, twice, perhaps twenty times, and twenty was enough. As he thrust forward, I stepped forward also, but just to the outside of his striking blade with my own sword held shoulder high. Its corroded edge easily sawed through his throat as I stepped past him.

The crowd's chanting instantly ceased.

Arben's blood fountained from his neck to spray me and mingle with my own dripping blood and the blood of the few who fell to my broken blade. The spirit of empire had honed its edge. The memory of sharpness was like razor steel. I spun around and hacked down, fully decapitating the man.

His flaming sword fell to the ground, still burning as more blood gushed to puddle at the fallen corpse.

"The burning martyr was drowned to quench the flames, my mother told me, and the Drowned God became the god of peace." I kicked the sword into the pooling blood, and flipped it in the gore to extinguish the flames.

"Banoien is now the One God of seven aspects," I said, moving toward Primus Naventi, and no one dared to stand between us. "Stoned. Broken," I began the litany. "Stretched upon the wheel."

"Hanged," a woman in the crowd intoned.

"Burned. Drowned," the crowd chanted with her.

"Can you tell me, priest," I said raising a bloody hand, "the last remaining aspect of the One God?"

The sword slipped from the Primus' hand, but he did not retreat from me. "The God in Seven Parts," he answered with what I now recognize as resignation.

"The god of salvation, and redemption," I agreed, speaking my mother's words. Then I took my sword to the Primus, beheading him, quartering, and castrating him to achieve the seven parts.

The crowd of worshippers watched in religious awe and holy terror as the strange sacrifice was made. After some time I rose up from the corpse, panting, delirious, still expecting to slaughter more of them before they took my life, but I didn't really care.

"The Empire is broken, and the Burning God has had vengeance," a strong, heavily accented voice spoke. His words were like steel. "The hungry flames have drowned in blood, and the One God is now whole."

"He is whole," the woman said.

"It was an offering," said another.

On that last day of the Antonine Empire, a new Kingdom of Corinth was born. I was the first monarch of the land, and as the mob now surrounds me again, I may be the last.

That sword has remained with me as a talisman, a trophy from the first battle that I fought and won. I clutch it now, and despite my great age and the number of enemies within this very throne room, I am smiling.

I remember what that strong Antonine voice first told me when he tended me in my sleep of death.

Stá difícil dematar. Agor mais difícil.

"You are hard to kill," he had said, then he gave me the relic. "Now even harder to kill."

I hold that broken sword in hand, and I face death with ease. Not my own death, but the deaths of all my enemies. I hold history in my hand; legend and fate. This is my palace, and there is stone beneath my feet. Stone that was once the Circle of Corinth.

G. J. HENSON *has been a technician for over twenty years, an amateur philosopher, and a last generation soldier of the Cold War. He has always enjoyed telling tales, none of them true, and decided to start writing them down. He is a husband, a father of two, and his family are happily living tales of their own.*

THE REGION LINUIS

BY LORNA SMITHERS

*'Then it was that the magnanimous Arthur, with
all the kings and military force of Britain, fought
against the Saxons… The second, third, fourth and
fifth (battles), were on another river, by the Britons
called Duglas, in the region Linuis.'*
– Nennius, *History of the Britons*

In the region of endless water
I see blazoned in blue stillness
A raging sky of crimson
And a thousand crashing spears.
The host of Arthur's war band
Reap their slaughter of the Saxons.
In spirals scream the ravens
Round the deep and bloody lake.
Fierce the red maned chargers
Through the blue and flashing sword thrusts.
Quick their dancing footfalls
Through the thick and blood stained mud.

Harsh the clash of iron on iron,
Unheard the shriek of cloven flesh,
Unmarked the final rattling breath
When ravens scream over blood.
Dead the barren battlefield,
Empty the skies of ravens and red,
Silent the stars that shine in the staring
Eyes of slaughtered men.
Sad the song of the marching shades
Departing this land to the afterlife.
Still the blue and crimson lake.
Silent the blood stained sky.

LORNA SMITHERS is a poet and author based in North West England. She has published three books: *Enchanting the Shadowlands*, T*he Broken Cauldron*,and *Gatherer of Souls*. Her work has appeared in *The Dawntreader*, *Eternal Haunted Summer*, and *New Myths*. She blogs at Fruits of Annwn (https://lornasmithers.wordpress.com/).

The Last First Time

By Colin Heintze

Every time I went to Karkil I stopped for coffee. I had always enjoyed K arkil's brew, a great deal of my enjoyment coming from the fact that no living lips had tasted it for two hundred years.

From my seat on the café terrace I heard the ass braying. I smiled. It made me smile every time I heard it, and I could recall the scene as if—no jest intended—I'd seen it a half-dozen times before. I recalled the overturned basket of figs, the ass crying as its master took turns beating it, and swatting at the urchins stuffing figs into their pockets. More than anything, I smiled because I knew the hour was near. Soon I would meet Lisandre again for the first time. Then, I would kill three men.

I was preparing to leave when a man approached my table and sat across from me. This was cause for alarm. I had spent the better part of a decade coming to that exact café at that exact time, and never in all those years had a man sat down across from me.

He was older with a refined, scholarly bearing. He saw the distress on my face and threw up his hands as if I had a crossbow trained on him.

"No need to be alarmed," he said. "I come in peace."

"You are—"

"Not from around here?" he laughed. "Indeed. Neither, my friend, are you. I saw you here last year, and a few before that. I must know, what brings a man like you to this haunted place?"

"I would ask the same of you."

He laughed again and lifted his cloak, eliciting some strange looks from passing citizens. Underneath his fine Karkil silks he wore a faded blue robe.

"An Archivist," I said. "Ah. It comes together. Why, you must be the hero of your order."

"I suppose so. My order grew out of the destruction of Karkil, after all. There was so much fear, so much rumor, so much grandeur and wisdom lost to history. It is an honor to have been chosen—"

"Grandeur and wisdom," I scoffed. "This place was a blight on history. The Gods were right in what they did." I looked towards the people thronging the streets with singular hatred.

"Oh? You believe the rumors, then?"

"Not believe—*know* to be true."

"I think I should very much like to interview you, then."

The priest's request didn't come as a surprise. Archivists were the self-appointed keepers of the histories. Their pallid blue robes could be found at every significant event in every corner of the world. The ignorant and superstitious viewed them as ill-omens, as their presence usually coincided with battles, plagues, and disasters. My own experience told otherwise, for I had seen them on happier occasions common folk rarely frequented—the coronation of Contrell the Victor, for one. There as anywhere in the past two centuries, the Archivists had been a largely ignored fixture of some far corner as they scratched away in their journals.

I heard the temple procession moving through the streets and knew that time was short.

"I would entertain your request," I said, rising from my seat, "but I'm afraid I'm late."

"A pity. I would have liked to know what brings you here. My reasons, of course, are clear. But yours—what can a man like you gain from this visiting this accursed place? By now, you surely know that any treasure won in Karkil will not last the day."

"That," I said, "is my business."

I hailed the server and pressed a gold Crown into her hands. She nearly swooned in astonishment. The gold piece was no great loss. I would pick it out of the desert sands the next morning. Time, however, was precious. I nearly sprinted towards the alleyway.

I assumed my position in the alley as I always had, and not moment too soon. A slim, darting shape rounded the corner and collided with me, sprawling me into the puddle I had placed myself in front of.

"Sir, my apologies!" Lisandre cried. I globbed some muck from my hair and gazed up at her imploringly.

Her soft, ribbon-like fingers closed around my wrists. My skin remembered the touch of those fingers and for a moment I flushed with a rising ecstasy.

I kept to the script, saying, "Now, do not be embarrassed. No harm done, after all."

"But sir, your clothes—"

"Traveling-clothes, made for hard wear. Do not trouble yourself."

"Sir is very kind," she said. I longed to fling myself on her then and there, the rapturous warmth of her touch spreading from my wrists to other, more sensitive places.

"Why were you sprinting through the alley?" I asked.

"I thought someone might be following me."

"In the middle of town, in broad daylight? That causes you such great terror?"

"You wouldn't understand."

"No?"

"I can tell from your accent that you are a foreigner. My situation, it is particular to Karkil."

Right on cue, the armed trio swaggered into the alleyway, Snot-face barking, "Get away from him, you harlot!"

They wore long, tawny coats over steel breastplates. The only one I ever bothered naming was Snot-face, him being memorable on account of once skewering my leg with the halberd in his hands.

Lisandre cowered behind me.

"I was right, they did follow!"

"Who are they?"

"Shut up, foreign dog," Snot-face answered. "We're supposed to keep her out of trouble, and that means no contact with foreign agents."

I swelled my chest and took a few long, regal steps forward.

"Agent? I am no agent, sir, but a humble merchant from Rhal. You have insulted this poor girl, and now have insulted me. I demand an explanation."

"Careful," Lisandre cringed. "These men are Mud-coats, servants of the Queen."

"I don't care who they are! Where I'm from, people have manners!"

Snot-face was as arrogant as always, saying, "Get out of here, you. This is none of your business."

"I shall not!"

"I'm warning you!"

I drew my blade. Snot-face readied his halberd. Lisandre cried out and clung to my back.

Once, I was sloppy and overconfident, a mistake I would not repeat. It had worked out, in the end. Because of the wound I sustained for her, Lisandre loved me more passionately than usual later that night. I was lucky, however, to only get a poke in the leg. Unless she was going to make love to my corpse, I knew I must go about the routine with hawkish focus.

Still, the fight got easier every year, less of an alleyway brawl and more of a dance that, for all its elegance, required only the memorization of the steps. I recalled that Snot-face would lead with a thrust. I replied with a parry that forced him to twist away from my probing blade. I remembered his weakness against feigns, aiming the point of my sword at his groin. He dropped the shaft of his halberd to deflect the blow; I circled my blade mid-thrust and slid it into his neck.

He put his hands to his throat. Blood boiled out between his fingers.

Up to then, things had played out perfectly. The plan was for the other Mud-coats to turn tail once they saw the ease with which I dispatched their comrade. But, this time, something was different. Perhaps my riposte had been too late, or my thrust too forceful, but my blade did not slide out of Snot-face's neck as expected. It stuck, lodged between two vertebrae.

I was presented with the choice of following Snot-face to the ground, or letting the weight of his body pull the sword from my hand. I chose the former. The other Mud-coats, only moments before retreating, saw me on my knees trying to free my blade. They sallied towards me with weapons raised.

So, our intricate little dance became an alleyway brawl. I freed my sword in time to block the first attack. The force of the blow sent me reeling, and before I could raise my guard another came slicing towards my brow. What followed was a spectacle. No one was willing to put himself in harm's way, so we turned our bodies and swung wildly at each other as children might when they stick-fight. More than once we slipped in the filth of the alleyway. We brought ourselves up by the haft of our weapons, only to fall when raising them to strike. That day, the Mud-coats truly lived up to their name.

My victory was hardly glorious. My adversaries were not formidable, sharing no more than five teeth and three good eyes between them. They quickly succumbed to fatigue and, with it, my advantage returned. I managed to gain solid footing long enough for a series of slashes that slew one and disarmed the other. When he stooped to retrieve his weapon, I ended the contest with one, final thrust. He died poorly, I am sad to say, crying for his mother as his life drained into the mud.

I sheathed my blade and gasped for breath. Without the advantage of foresight, I would have been killed in that alley. But, I put my doubts away, recalling my adversaries' reek of wine and frail, stooped postures. After all, the city would not dispatch her ablest warriors to guard a frightened young girl.

To that girl I offered my hand.

"Ugly business, that. I'm sorry you had to see it, dear lady."

"You— Do you know what you've done?" Lisandre said.

"My apologies. I couldn't idle while you were being hounded and abused."

"You stupid, stupid man. Come, we must leave."

"Yes, I think that would be wise. Where shall we go?"

"There is an inn near here. It is frequented by thieves and criminals, they will not talk to the authorities. We need to get you out of sight."

"What about you?"

She laughed cynically and led me away by the arm. "They will not harm a hair on my head. I am already doomed, you see."

"I'm afraid I don't."

"Hush. Come."

Lisandre pulled me through the streets and into the door of a hostelry. The innkeeper saw us arriving together and leered. I'd seen wolves eye a fattened calf with less enthusiasm than the innkeeper did Lisandre. Few women could aspire to her beauty, her features somehow combining the best aspects of girlish purity with the poise of a confident, well-travelled woman.

"You gonna stay the night, or you renting by the hour?" the innkeeper said through a toothless grin. Lisandre laid a hand on my arm as if to say *don't kill this one, too.*

"The night," she answered.

"All I got is room six upstairs, and that'll run you two Guilds."

I put a Rhalian Crown on the countertop.

"Wassit?"

"Gold," I said, leading Lisandre up the stairs.

Overall, it was a well-appointed room, speaking much to the wealth of Karkil that even a rogues' den would have such pleasant amenities.

Lisandre sat on the bed, and me on a chair across from her.

"Thank you again, Sir..?"

"Samwrit, and no 'sir' necessary. I am no knight."

"Could have fooled me, with the way you go swinging swords at the smallest provocation."

"Don't be mistaken, this isn't something I do often, Lady..?"

"Lisandre. And I'm no lady."

We shared a laugh. The laughter trailed off, the heaving of her shoulders turning into sobs. I reached over to console her.

"My lady, please, accept my apologies. You were right, I shouldn't have gotten involved."

"No, it isn't that."

"Then what?"

"I am doomed."

"You keep saying that—"

She put a hand over my mouth.

"Will you listen? Oh, Gods, how I am using you right now. No, never mind, it isn't right to burden you."

"Go ahead, Lisandre. If you promise to tell, I promise to listen."

She looked at me, the conflict playing on her face. Unlike most people, she wasn't simply extending a social courtesy. She truly didn't want to burden me with her troubles, the sweet, selfless creature. Of course, I already had every word of her story committed to memory.

"Here in Karkil," she began, "we have a queen."

"Yes, Melsephine. I've heard of her."

"That is right. What most people outside Karkil don't know is that she is a sorceress, a worshipper of the Lords of Chaos. They say she came from the East, is over a hundred years old—oh, I don't know what to believe! But, I do know that her gods demand sacrifice."

"Sacrifice? How barbaric!"

"They say there is a formula of sorts. The Lords of Chaos prefer some sacrifices over others. An unwilling sacrifice, the legends go, is of little sustenance to them. A willing one, quite a bit more satisfying. This is how Melsephine grows her power—by sacrificing her subjects to these dreadful gods. With each victim, she grows stronger. That is where I come in. I am to be this month's martyr."

"What savagery! What injustice! When is this due to happen?"

"Tomorrow, at dawn," Lisandre moaned.

"Never. Come with me, I will remove you from the city."

"No! That was why the Mud-coats were following me, to make sure I didn't lose my nerve. You need to understand, I am a willing sacrifice. If I do not meet my obligation, then they will take three unwilling victims in my place. My mother. My father. My little brother."

Tears boiled onto her cheeks. I wept alongside her. No matter how many times I had deceived that poor girl, at least I could say my tears were genuine. Her plight rent my heart and inflamed my sense of outrage.

"How can you stand it?" I asked. "Why don't the people of this city rise up and destroy her?"

"We are wealthy, Samwrit. Our good fortune is a result of Melsephine's power. Here in Karkil, the people are happy."

"If they are not chosen for sacrifice."

"Yes."

"Then it truly is a deal with devils—by both your queen, and your countrymen."

"Yes."

"But there is time. I have money. A sturdy blade. We could contrive to rescue your family."

"No, Samwrit. Thank you, but no. It wouldn't work."

"You would go willingly to your doom?"

"Have I any choice? There is only one thing that can save me, one thing the Lords of Chaos value over a willing sacrifice: a noble sacrifice, one done for love or the betterment of mankind."

A thick silence permeated the room. Then came the part of the act I hated, the part that always sent me into a year of agonizing guilt and self-recrimination.

"I will be that sacrifice," I said.

"You? No! I cannot ask that of you."

I took her hands in mine.

"Listen, I'll be alright, I know it. Please let me do this for you."

"I don't believe you. No man is that brave."

"It isn't courage, Lisandre. Haven't you wondered why I am in Karkil? Moreover, why I intervened on your behalf?"

She shook her head. I pressed her hands to my breast, saying, "We are kindred spirits. You see, I am also destined to die."

I opened my shirt where her hands were resting, revealing a chest covered with red spots.

"*The Whispering Death?*" she said, drawing away from me.

"It isn't communicable," I assured her. "It can only be caught from drinking contaminated water."

"I know."

"That is why I came to this city. Oh, were I such a fool to heed the yarns of sailors and travelers. Everywhere there is talk of a cure, though always over yonder mountains, or across the next river, or beyond the sea. Everywhere the same stories, and nowhere a cure."

"I see."

Lisandre struggled to take it all in. In silence I rebuked myself for the lies, the stage play I had put on as thickly as the makeup covering my chest.

I leaned forward and put my lips against hers. She stiffened. I pressed my advance and she relented, turning to water in my arms.

I removed my lips from hers to nibble at her ear, working down the neckline to the globes of her breasts. She ran her fingers through my hair and moaned softly. We began disrobing.

* * *

Lisandre was dozing on the bed after our sixth round of lovemaking. Every year it got better, more passionate. I had become an expert on Lisandre's body. I knew how to bring out her pleasure, and, in turn, she brought out mine.

"Drunk," I said to myself. That was the first time I had promised take her burden, when I was stone-cold drunk. Apparently, the Lords of Chaos didn't consider the lies of a lecherous inebriate to be a noble sacrifice. In a few minutes, none of it would matter.

I looked out the window and saw dawn spilling over the horizon. I considered leaving. Lying to Lisandre was enough of a tribulation. Watching her die again—I simply didn't know if I could endure it.

No. You have used this girl too long, too often. Don't let her wake thinking that you abandoned her. Don't let her die thinking she was deceived. What can witnessing her death compare to what she is about to go through, you cruel, conceited man?

Her eyes were darting under the lids. I bent over and interrupted their roving with a kiss.

"When is it?" she said, her voice still thick with slumber.

"Dawn."

She bolted upright in the bed. The covers fell off her and, even under the circumstances, I couldn't help but marvel at the body they revealed: perfection as wrought from the imaginations of the sensualist sculptors and romantic poets. I heard the percussive rumbling from far away and knew it had begun.

"I love you," I said. I nearly meant it. Curious how wronging someone, time and time again, breeds great affection.

"I love you, too." She reached out to take my hand. Her hand passed through mine as if it were made of smoke.

"W-What's happening?" she stammered. "Why can't I touch you?"

"I love you," I repeated.

She groped wildly at me, her hands passing through my phantom body with growing alarm. Outside the window, dawn's advance had been arrested. A black pall washed over the city, choking the streets with ash. I heard the first shouts, the first sounds of crumbling masonry.

"Samwrit?"

"I love you every time."

The walls of the inn crumbled. Lisandre screamed as a cascade of bricks and dust buried her on the bed. After the masonry came the fire. Karkil burned.

I blinked my eyes and found myself in the present, standing alone in the White Waste. I walked over the sands and dug, finding the gold Crown I gave to the innkeeper. Minutes later, I was on my knees digging for the one I gave the server.

I wished the tears in my eyes were from the sand carried on the desert wind. I wiped them away, promising I would not return next year, saying I needed to stop doing this to myself, to her. I made the pledge, knowing it would not be kept.

* * *

The first time I met Lisandre, the real first time, was nine years before.

My Name is Samwrit, and I really was a merchant from Rhal, at least what was Rhal before being absorbed into Contrell's Empire. My specialty was incense, as it was for my father and his father before him.

Few men brave the White Waste. If the stinging sands and burning sun don't claim them, then the Dulgeri nomads do. That was the secret of my success: I spoke the language of the Dulgeri, Karkan, a derivative of the common tongue spoken in ancient Karkil. Of course, it didn't hurt that three generations of my family had been trading along those caravan routes. For the Dulgeri, like all nomads, relationships are their gold and platinum, the obligations to kin and kind their only law.

Nine years ago, I was searching for my Dulgeri partners at all of the oases known to me. I had with me a modest caravan: four camels loaded with supplies and goods, my assistant, and three porters.

The Dulgeri were constantly on the move, and the search was becoming frustrating. In the days of ancient Karkil, when the Dulgeri were the only obstacle between Queen Melsephine and domination of the entire Southeast, they proved an impossible quarry. Even Melsephine's most potent divinations could not find the Dulgeri once they had taken to the interior of that same desert I searched with such futility.

One of the porters cried an alarm and directed our attention to a line of riders on the far ridge. Initially I was elated, believing my Dulgeri partners were sending out their welcome party. But, the riders did not stop outside bow-range, as is the Dulgeri custom. In fact, they spurred their camels faster, bearing down on us with whooping war-cries. In moments our little caravan was surrounded. My porters and assistant were slain outright. I was forced to kneel beneath an upraised scimitar. My sword was heavy at my hip, though I dared not draw it. If anything, the riders seemed to welcome the prospect of a struggle, for the Dulgeri are a sporting race.

These men were indeed Dulgeri, though of a different tribe than my usual clients. They were doubtless overjoyed to have scored so much plunder and booty, and at the expense of their tribal enemies, no less.

As the raiders ransacked my wares I clasped my hands together and wept for mercy. The captain of the raiders, amused that I spoke Karkan, and downright delighted at my willingness to debase myself, sheathed his blade. He threw me a skin of water and pointed to the desert.

I groveled at his feet, praising his mercy. This display proved too much for him, and he raised his riding crop to strike. I stumbled to my feet and left in haste, hearing the raiders' laughter as I scrambled up the dunes.

I had thought the raider captain to be merciful, but soon I knew that my cowardice had inspired not sympathy, but disgust. My release was not an act of kindness, but an invitation to a doom far more agonizing than the quick flash of the crescent-blade.

By nightfall I had gone through the flask of water. By morning, I could scarcely walk. The White Waste is no place for a Westerner's complexion, and my skin itched terribly. My lips cracked. White spots drifted through my vision, burned there by the fierce desert sun. Sometime during the night of the second day, I collapsed onto the earth of an ancient floodplain.

What happened when I awoke was entirely unexpected, and went a long ways in explaining the delirium I suffered over the ensuing day.

The crowing cock came in the form of a foot prodding me in the ribs. I woke with a jolt, fearing that the raiders had come back to finish what they had started. Instead, I saw the gnarled face of a crone looking down on me. That face, however, was the least interesting thing that came into my perception. Around me were shops, stalls, houses, people engaged in trade and gossip and every manner of quotidian task. I was in a city, lying in the gutter like a besotted rogue.

"Drunk, eh?" the crone said. "Well, you'd better get out of the street or you'll get run over by a wagon."

She spoke in an exotic dialect of Karkan similar to the courtly language used by the Dulgeri chieftans.

"Where am I?" I croaked. The old woman cocked an eyebrow. To her ears, my Karkan must have sounded as queer and idiomatic as hers did to mine.

"What a question! You're in Karkil, of course."

"Karkil? Ma'am, Karkil was destroyed by the Gods two centuries ago, razed to the earth for the transgressions of its wicked queen."

"Watch your mouth!"

There was a moment of silence as two people regarded each other, both believing the other insane. If she had any doubts as to my madness, they must have been settled when I started tearing out the threads of my jerkin with my teeth. She turned to leave.

"No!" I cried. "Don't go!"

A handful of gold Crowns tumbled out of the seam my teeth worked free, my emergency funds. She took a few steps forward and snatched one from my hand.

"What kind of money is this?"

"That is an Imperial Crown."

"Yeah, an' who's this fella on it?"

"Him? Why, that's Contrell the Victor! He united all the kingdoms of the West. Are you telling me you've never heard of Contrell the Victor?"

"Oh, well, La-dee-da."

I shook my head, sighing, "It makes no difference. It is pure gold. I am in desperate need of water, and food, and a bath."

"Come on, then. I'll get you cleaned up."

The Crone took me to her sewing shop where I was fed, watered, and allowed to bathe. She presented me with a suit of clothes, fine robes worthy of a Dulgeri chieftan. My gold Crown could have bought much more, but desperation can turn even the most miserable skinflint into an impetuous spendthrift.

I left the sewing shop and wandered the streets in a daze. There was simply no explanation for that city being there. The people had the same racial characteristics of the Dulgeri, but with a gentler, more refined countenance. Climbing a hill, I saw the city laid out before me. There were towers in the distance, higher than those in Rhal, lofty as even those in the Capitol. And, more astonishingly, a river, nearly a mile wide and bobbing with every conceivable type of watercraft. The only known river in the area was the Vena. Two hundred years ago it went underground, buried by the same calamity that destroyed Karkil.

I sat on the ground and wept, the strain of the last few days too much to bear. What, I wondered, did all these signs and omens portend? Had I died out there in the desert? Had I become the plaything of bored and capricious gods? Many of my faculties were still blunted by my ordeal in the White Waste, and rational thought was impossible. I became convinced of the delusion that I was dead or dreaming.

I took in the sights with a kind of reckless fatalism. I still had five gold Crowns and decided I would use them. I indulged my senses with rich foods, strong wine, and several pipes of hashish believing that, since I was dreaming or dead, any action on my part would be of no consequence. I spent lavishly, attracting throngs of sycophants. By late afternoon the gold was gone, my new friends remembered they had other errands to attend to, and I was left to sulk through the streets alone.

The sight of an ass that had overturned its cargo of figs, and the amusing scene that followed, cheered me a little. I was smiling when, walking through an alleyway between the market and tenements, a slim, darting shape raced around the corner and collided with me, knocking me into a nearby puddle.

"Sir, my apologies!" Lisandre cried. She fidgeted for a moment, torn between helping me up and continuing her flight. I globbed some muck from my hair and looked up at her lecherously. I had spent the afternoon in sybaritic revelry and, as is often the case, I found myself eager for further debauches.

She helped me up and I fell into her arms, her slender shoulders sagging under my weight.

"Oh no, sir, I have scrambled your brains!"

"How about a kiss, then, pretty?"

"Sir is very flattering, but I must be going."

"Come on, it'll be fun," I said through a hiccup.

"Sir, please, I've been followed, I know it. I really—"

"Get away from him, you harlot!" Snot-face snarled as he entered the alley with his confederates.

Lisandre shuddered and lowered me to the ground.

"I'm sorry again, sir. I should go now."

I staggered to my feet, shouting, "Who are you calling a harlot, you snot-faced reprobate?"

"Shut up, foreign dog! We're supposed to keep her out of trouble, and that means no contact with foreign agents."

I swelled my chest and took a few wobbling steps forward. Lisandre pulled frantically at my arm.

"Sir! Please, stop! Those are Mud-coats, servants of the Queen!"

"I don't care who they are! Where I'm from, people have manners, and I don't appreciate people calling me an agent, or anything else for that matter!"

Snot-face laughed and said, "Get out of here, you. This is none of your business."

"Eat a dog's arse!"

"I'm warning you!"

I drew my blade. Snot-face readied his halberd. Seeing me stumble and lurch about, he smiled in anticipation of an easy fight.

The wine and hashish had affected my already fragile mental state. I was fearless, still believing myself dead or subject to a particularly vivid hallucination. I charged, sword aloft, and began hacking. Cringing against the alley wall, Lisandre took in the spectacle of what must have appeared as a blood-mad barbarian in throes of the frenzy. When it was over, Snot-face's life was spilling into the alleyway. His companions fled, wounded and panting in terror.

I replaced my blade in its scabbard and howled after them, "You'd better run, you piss-stained dogs!"

"You— Do you know what you've done?" Lisandre said.

"Good riddance!"

"You stupid, stupid man. Come, we must leave."

"Where?"

"An inn. Others of your kind frequent it, you should be safe."

"Ooo, an inn, the Gods are kind," I said, putting an arm around her waist and squeezing her rump. "Yes, by all means, let's go."

That was the first time I met Lisandre, the first time I promised to take her burden from her. It was the first time we made love, as well—a tawdry, dirty thing she gave me not out of desire, but obligation. It was an atrocity I would correct in future years.

Wine, hashish, and exhaustion sent me into a stupor long before dawn. I slept through Lisandre's death and Karkil's destruction, a trauma I would experience for the first time the following year. I only came to my senses when the blazing heat of the White Waste made sleep hopeless.

I was naked, the clothes I had acquired in Karkil having gone the way of the rest of the city. Gone, too, were the measly few copper coins that remained from exchanging my gold Crowns.

For a time, I held to the belief that I had spent the last day in a fit of madness. But, the more I thought about it, the more I entertained the dreadful notion that my experiences in the doomed city of Karkil had been real. A madman might have lost his clothes while in a state of delerium—that alone was not enough to convince me. My body is what persuaded me, for it was no longer very thirsty, nor dirty, nor hungry, and the drumming in my head was unmistakably the effects of too much merrymaking.

Survival took precedence over musings on my sanity, though. I was naked and alone in the White Waste, worse off even than before. I took a few minutes to recall conversations I'd had with the Dulgeri during previous visits. If, indeed, I was in what used to be Karkil, I reasoned there should be an oasis about fifteen miles northeast of me. The Dulgeri had a powerful taboo against the area that was formerly Karkil, and I had been warned to steer clear of it. Assuming I was standing in what was Karkil, I could find water by nightfall. From there, I could wait until my Dulgeri friends visited that particular oasis on their yearly rounds.

The march to the oasis was arduous. I crawled the last few miles before I was able to submerge my head in the muddy waters and fall onto the banks with an exalted sigh. By day, I rested in the shade of the palms that clustered around the watering hole. By night, I scaled their trunks to forage figs and dates. On the third day I was met by my Dulgeri partners, their long column of camels and horses pulling up to the oases and gawking at the red, naked man scrambling out of the foliage to greet them.

* * *

I was given a set of silk robes—anything else would have been agony on my sun-scorched skin—and taken to the Chieftan's tent. We exchanged the customary greetings. He was quite interested to know my story, and once the pleasantries were over I wasted no time recounting my tale.

I told him everything, omitting my adventure in Karkil. Like I said, the Dulgeri had a strict taboo concerning the place, and for all I knew admitting to having visited it may have put me under the scimitar once more.

"When did this happen?" the Chieftan asked.

"The raid? A week ago, I suppose."

"You survived all this time on a single flask of water? You are quite miraculous, my friend."

Advice on dealing with the Dulgeri: do not listen to the words coming out of their mouths, but the words written on their faces. The Chieftan's words were gracious; his face, suspicious, the eyes narrowing to shrewd slits.

"I wish I could remember it all," I hurried to say. "But I was delirious through most of the ordeal."

"Your path should have taken you near Karkil. Did you, by chance—?"

"My friend, am I still delirious? I was under the impression that Karkil was scourged by the Gods two centuries past."

The Chieftan nodded and took a sip of his coffee.

"Yes," he said. "That is true. But, it was not scourged completely."

"I'm afraid I don't understand."

"Every year on the anniversary of its destruction it appears in the desert.

Every year, it replays its final day, its people going about their lives ignorant to the doom that awaits them."

I feigned incredulousness and laughed, "Surely, friend, you do not believe this?"

"I have seen it with my own eyes, the tall citadels and minarets appearing in the distance."

"I saw many things during my delirium. Nightmares, hallucinations, spirits of the earth—but no city from antiquity."

"Then a warning, friend: never go near that place. Only doom and madness can come of it."

I nodded. We talked a few more hours until I began to fall asleep. I did not wake as the Dulgeri carried me to a tent and bedded me down on supple carpets. That night I dreamed of Lisandre: her lips, flushed like rose petals, brushing against my ear; her breasts gently heaving as she drowsed on the bed; her hands caressing my cheek. I slept much as I recuperated with my Dulgeri hosts. Every minute, I dreamed of Lisandre.

* * *

I visited Karkil for the tenth, and final, time.

My Dulgeri partners had been driven to the brink of extinction. The raiders from a decade ago, I realized too late, were a portent. In my father's time no enemy could have penetrated so deeply into my partners' territory. Nothing comes quickly in the White Waste. The wars are long, grinding affairs, the losing tribe forced piecemeal into increasingly marginal lands. That is the fate that befell my partners, and as their fortunes went, so did mine.

My counting-house in Rhal went under. My former partners' enemies were mine, and they now controlled the caravan routes. My competitors showered in Crowns while I sold asset after asset in the forlorn hope that my allies would be restored to their former glory. They have become jackals scavenging a living off the wastes, hunted down for sport should their roving ever bring them outside their desolate haunts.

It was the last time I would see Karkil, the last time I would see her. My finances were exhausted. The protection of my Dulgeri allies was finished, and my camel's every step treaded deeper into enemy territory. Only a madman would risk such an undertaking, but when it came to Lisandre, I was indeed mad. I had to see her one last time.

Providence sent a sandstorm over the desert to conceal my advance towards Karkil. Fate, it seemed, had ordained my return. I uttered my thanks to the Gods as my camel shook the sand from his eyes and groaned his indictments.

The beast ceased his complaints as the ground leveled. He moved at a trot, the earth the baked remains of an ancient floodplain. There, I was safe. No Dulgeri would come within ten miles of that place.

I basked on the ground and waited, sleep an impossible endeavor. As dawn spread over the White Waste, I saw phantoms milling around me, buildings fading into perception. Far-off noises gained sharpness and clarity, and within moments I could hear the wheels of wagons bouncing over rutted stones and peddlers barking their morning bargains. A familiar crone nearly ran into me, crying, "Oh, damn my eyes, I didn't see you there!"

There were several hours until I was to meet Lisandre for the last first time. I supposed it would only be appropriate to indulge in my final taste of Karkil coffee, as well.

The coffee was scarcely in front of me when I heard a voice over my shoulder saying, "A girl."

I wheeled in my seat and saw the face of the Archivist beaming at me.

"I understand now," he said. "It's a girl."

"What of it?"

"You must truly love her to risk so much, and at such expense."

I nodded. At first, my visits to Karkil were a pleasing diversion from the more important, and profitable, business at hand. Yet, as I sat there absent-mindedly stirring my coffee, I realized that over the years the incense trade had become less and less important to me. Had business been my chief concern I would have attempted to ingratiate myself with the other Dulgeri tribes, would have diversified my claims and opened new routes. Sitting at the café, I knew that the incense trade was an excuse to seek out Lisandre, not the other way around.

"My words wound you," the Archivist said. "I apologize, I spoke out of turn."

I nodded again, wondering if my inner turmoil was so evident. I had aged much in the past few years. I no longer took good care of myself. I woke every day mourning the absence of Lisandre dozing beside me, and bedded down every night with arms aching for lack of her body cradled within them.

"Do you believe it?" I asked the Archivist.

"Believe what?"

"The tales about the Queen, the Lords of Chaos. The offerings."

"A noble sacrifice is a powerful thing," he admitted. "It is coveted by gods and demons. Why, in my travels to the East—"

"And what would you know of sacrifice, *Archivist?*"

"I wasn't always an Archivist, young man. Once, I longed for wealth and comfort. But, in time, I found my true calling."

The ass was braying in the market and I knew it was time to leave. Perhaps, in Lisandre's arms, I too had found my true calling. I got up, saying, "Thank you."

"Yes? For what?"

"Perspective."

"Mm?"

"You catalogue everything that happens in this city, thousands of people failing, triumphing, living, and loving. I realize now, that for all these thousands, I have only ever seen one."

I left him on those words, marching towards the alleyway where I was to meet Lisandre.

* * *

Everything went according to plan. I was at the inn with Lisandre. Mud covered my backside and flecks of Snot-face's blood peppered my breeches.

"Thank you again, Sir..?" Lisandre said.

"You should not thank me. I am a scoundrel."

"Could have fooled me."

"A scoundrel." I repeated. I ran a hand over my face and moaned. I knew I was deviating from the script, that I was perilously close to ruining my last, best chance of the ecstasy of Lisandre's love. I did not care anymore.

The look I gave Lisandre was pitiful. To my amazement, she rushed over to console me, our roles unexpectedly reversed.

"You did what you thought was right," she said. "Please, sir, do not drown yourself in guilt. They were the Queen's butchers, nothing more."

I sniffled and wrapped my arms around her. For a moment, she seemed unsure how to proceed, but her warmth and kindness compelled her to give succor.

"You are a sensitive man," she said, stroking my head. "People too often kill without mercy, without remorse."

"Thank you, Lisandre. But, killing is not the cause of my sorrow."

"How do you know my name? Did I tell it to you without knowing?"

I longed to seize her by the shoulders and confess. Ten years of lying to her, ten years of making that inn my brothel, that woman my unwitting whore.

I saw the concern in her eyes and repressed a shudder of self-hatred. On the morn she was destined to be fed to the Lords of Chaos—as far as she knew—yet her sole, singular focus was my comfort well-being. In my foolish infatuation with her body I had been blind to the wondrous heart that beat within it.

"I love you," I muttered. "I mean it, this time."

She gave me a queer look.

"This time?"

"I'm sorry."

"You've been through a great deal. Won't you lie down?"

I did as she suggested and fell back onto the mattress. A moment later, her body was beside mine, her luscious curves pressing against me. Her hand moved up my leg.

"What are you doing!" I cried.

"I don't know. I feel like I know you."

I shook my head. She thought that day to be her last on earth. Who wouldn't want to have a little fun before venturing into the hereafter?

I took her hand away and said, "Lisandre, no."

"No?"

"I'm sorry."

"No, I'm sorry. I was wrong to presume."

"You should go."

"Is that what you want?"

"No. Stay. But—I will not make love to you if you do."

She nodded and pressed herself tighter against me. "I will stay anyway."

I turned away to conceal my tears. She wasn't simply pursuing one, final thrill. She had never gone to bed with me out of obligation. All those years perfecting my seduction of her were unnecessary. She loved me, the real me, truly and without guile.

We spent the night talking. It was better than any lovemaking, bringing my soul to heights of ecstasy unknown to the mere execution of carnal love. Towards morning she drowsed. I stole my arm from under her, letting her head slide off my chest onto the soft down. The first rays of sunshine were spilling over the horizon.

I looked at my love dozing on the bed. Fresh tears came, and in trembling staccato I said, "I will take your burden."

I heard the booming report from outside the window. She tossed under the sheets, saying, "What was that?"

"I love you."

"I love you, too." She reached for my hand. Her hand passed through mine as if it were made of smoke. She bolted upright in bed and groped wildly at me.

"What's wrong? Why can't I touch you?"

"I love you," I repeated.

I reached out to pass a phantom hand over her hair. In doing so, I bumped my knuckles against the bedframe.

I withdrew my hand and looked upon the scraped knuckles with horror. Lisandre was naked, now. The sheets that had been wrapped around her had fallen through her body and pooled on the mattress.

"Lisandre, I— I—"

She smiled venomously, her face taking on an aspect I could not recognize, let alone believe.

"Fool," she jeered.

There was a brief instant of pain as chunks of masonry rained down on my head. I heard Lisandre shrieking with laughter.

Cold, hoary hands tickled me awfully. Tentacles with razor-lined suckers entwined around my body, twisting away patches of flesh. I felt myself descending, sliding into an abyss echoing with evil cachinnations as cold and mirthless as Lisandre's. The last thing I heard before the blackness overwhelmed me was her voice.

"Fool," it laughed.

* * *

Lisandre was standing alone in the White Waste. A man approached her, his dusty blue robes appearing black against the burning midday sun.

He drew to a halt and bowed at her feet. From his travel bag, he produced a silk gown. He handed it to her with a great deal of ceremony, averting his eyes as she dressed.

"My Queen," he said. "You are restored."

Though I had no eyes, no form to speak of, I could see. Melsephine wished it so. I looked upon the face of the girl I knew as Lisandre and saw it was largely unaltered. The nose and brow had a slightly different proportion, nothing a sorcerer couldn't conceal with the simplest of glamours. The real difference was in the eyes. The warm, compassionate eyes I once knew were hard, cruel, dancing with visions of steel and fire.

"Braydyn," she responded. "You have done well."

"Pardon, My Queen, but Braydyn was my great-great-great-great-grandfather."

"Then he did as I instructed. He founded an order to prepare the world for my coming, to document the changes that happened in my exile. He did well. I shall bring him back as a reward."

"M-My Lady," the Archivist stammered. "You can bring people *back*?"

"Yes. That is within my power, now."

Melsephine turned away from the Archivist. To him, it must have appeared that she was reminiscing. He could not perceive my shade, did not know that she was looking at me with a mocking smile.

"The Lords of Chaos were greedy," she began. "No matter how much I fed them, they hungered for ever-greater sacrifices. They approached me with a bargain: If I sacrificed myself with all of Karkil, they would endow me with powers unknown to Gods and mortals alike. I was to be a willing sacrifice. If I could contrive a noble sacrifice to replace me, I would be restored, more powerful and terrible than all the devils of the underworld. To these ends, Karkil would appear every year on the anniversary-day of its sacrifice. The people would go about their lives with no knowledge of their impending ruin. On this day, and this day only, would I chance at finding my replacement.

"Who would have thought the Lords of Chaos were so pedantic? I could deceive half-wits or terrify the weak-willed to accept my burden, but my masters would not accept a sacrifice inspired by anything but virtue or true love. That is when I knew I must find a man. That is when I seized three beggars and trussed them in mud-coats, for I knew that man would need to believe he was my rescuer."

"It seems the Lords of Chaos underestimated you, My Lady," the Archivist said. "I kept my distance from the merchant Samwrit but, rest assured, he never left my sight."

"Your records were indispensable, Braydyn. Without your briefings, I never could have made the fool love me."

The Archivist bowed again. He made no attempt to correct her mistake concerning his name. He could see as clearly as I that she was struggling to adjust to her newfound omnipotence. Her eyes swam in her head, perceiving all of time, dimension, and the infinite realities that lay before her like an open book.

Melsephine stooped over and dug a shining object from the desert sand. It glinted in the light as she held it up for inspection.

"Contrell the Victor," she said. "I think I shall start with him."

"We have many records on him, My Queen."

The dread queen turned to me once more and smiled. With a wave of her hand she dispelled my shade, my ridicule having ceased to amuse her. I felt the hands pulling again at my legs, the grotesque, unspeakable forms wrapping around me. The world darkened and sank into a mire of offal and gore.

Melsephine laughed as I was sent back home, back to the bowels of the Lords of Chaos. As my shade descended into the abyss, so did my hope— the hope that, somewhere within the dark goddess Melsephine, my great love Lisandre persisted.

COLIN HEINTZE *is a Colorado native whose developing young mind was warped by the likes of Ray Harryhausen, Frank Frazetta, Neil Gaiman, and Joe Bob Briggs. After a brief post-college career in East Asia and the Middle East, he returned to Colorado to become a civil servant. His fantasy novel* Funeral Games *is available in print, ebook, and Kindle formats.*

Fortune-Teller

by E.L. Schmitt

A fold of painted cards
across a rune-scribed palm.
Inked in black and red,
she tells his future nights.

Across a pampered palm
nails skitter, slip and show.
She tells his future now
in swirls of breath and song.

Eyes skitter, slip and sting,
blind in the fire-lit tent.
Swirling in smoke and song,
fate looms black and bitter.

Blind in the fire-lit tent,
the crone reveals her hand.
Fate's end bitterly near,
he reels, he leaves the seer.

Smiling the veiled girl holds
a fold of painted cards.
The fortune-teller waits,
inked in black and red.

E.L. SCHMITT *has always considered herself a wordsmith. Her poems and short stories have appeared in print and online in such publications as* Three Line Poetry, The Rectangle, Four and Twenty, Heroic Fantasy Quarterly, The Sagebrush Review, *and* The Lit Pub. *A graduate of the Universities of Texas (B.A.) and Arizona (M.Ed.), she currently devotes her days to inspiring high school students to love the English language and its literature. When time allows, she also records the history of Fred, a small planet located at the end of the universe. Volume I is forthcoming.*

The Sword

by Cullen Groves

OSWULF:
Well, sword, how much of foemen's blood have you drunk,
And into how many breasts have you sunk,
Deeper sunk than Love's black honeyed darts?
I bare another breast before your blade,
Take it! Bite deep that I might be unmade,
To lie in sleep's surcease.

SWORD:
It matters not what hand hath drave
Me through what heart; so go on, fall on me:
In silence you will lie, while I am raised
To laugh again in clash of blade on blade;
You found me in a howe-grave, laid across
A corpse-king's breast, so ancient gone
No man could ken the wars he fought against
The gods, and I was forged before his reign;
You found me, and we slaked our thirst
For blood on Gotesfeld where Glamma fell,
At Vreitness where we feasted eagles well;
We ran with blood beneath the walls of Hror;
No battle-spear had broke your mail

But Irsa, wife of Oskuld-King, just looked
And pierced you with her eyes; your uncle's wife,
A woman, killed you when no king of war could;
Did I lay naked there upon the bed
Between your naked flesh and trembling queen?
Some nights; but I knew what came the nights
That I was sheathed and hung upon the wall;
Go on then! Throw yourself upon my edge
And feel its venom-tempered hardness cold
Inside; and I will find another hand
That scorns a woman's weakness for the clash of war!

OSWULF:
Hark now! I hear them out beyond the door,
The king's wolves howling in the night for war;
So I have lain with death; discovered I shall die,
And do you tremble, sword, your thirst to slake?
No, you were always steady; my hands shake
Will you not let me sleep?

SWORD:
I will! But drive me deep.

CULLEN GROVES *lives in northern Idaho, where he studied philosophy at the University of Idaho, and now aspires to be a court poet and polymath. He has had a handful of poems published, mostly by* Heroic Fantasy Quarterly *(including the short rhyming epic "Lethe's Cup and the White Sword"), but also in* Asimov's Sci-Fi Magazine *and online at* Apex. *Alas, his writing has been somewhat put on hold of late to free time for his quest to learn Ancient Greek.*

Mouth of the Jaguar

by Evan Dicken

Hummingbird was to be the final sacrifice of the day. The man before her struggled on a raised stone slab, chest heaving as a flock of blood-spattered priests pinned his arms and legs. Sunlight glittered on the Cazonci's obsidian dagger—curved like a jaguar's claw to better hook bone and tear flesh. The crowd around the ziggurat waited, caught in the anxious pause between lightning and thunder.

The blade fell, but Hummingbird's gaze was not on the shrieking victim. Above, the sun was white-gold in a sky clear as the eastern sea. Lake Pátzcuaro sparkled in the light, the riot of sedge and cattails along its banks flecked with motes of bright color as wading birds combed the shallows for fish. The breeze shifted, cutting the heavy pall of incense with scents of wood smoke and cooking meat from the city below. Although they had been the enemies of her people for generations, the Tarascans shared much with the Azteca. If not for the guards holding her arms, Hummingbird might have even imagined herself back in Tenochtitlan as it was before the fall.

The sacrifice gave a gurgling cough as the Cazonci cut his heart free of its bloody nest of bone. The priests began a slow, twirling dance, but Hummingbird ignored them, her gaze fixed on the sun. She didn't look away even when tears stung her eyes. There was a small pulse of light, quick as a leaf on a bonfire. The crowd roared, and Hummingbird prepared herself.

The sacrifices had been denied food and sleep for the last two days, forced to participate in strenuous exercise disguised as ritual. While the others sweated and strained, hoping to honor the gods through their actions, Hummingbird had held back. She'd presided over the same ceremonies as a guard in the court of Moctecuzoma, and was wise to the tricks the priests used to exhaust their victims.

Two guards pushed Hummingbird forward as she blinked away the sun's dark afterimage. Their grip on her arms was loose, their expressions those of men ready to retire after a long day of work. It was clear they expected Hummingbird to stumble meekly to the bloodstained alter just like the hundreds who had come before her. She wouldn't be sorry to disappoint them.

The Cazonci tossed the dead man's heart into a nearby brazier, eyes narrowing as he noticed Hummingbird's hair—shaved but for a single, long lock that hung over her left ear. He tensed, about to call a warning.

She didn't give him the chance.

The guard on Hummingbird's left toppled with a startled cry, surprised by her kick to his knee. She pivoted to hammer her fist into the throat of her other captor, but the man had already stepped away, snatching a bronze-headed axe from his belt. He bared his teeth, the boredom of moments before replaced by a look of wild fury. Hummingbird ducked his first swing, then stumbled, the weakness in her legs a bitter reminder that it had been days since she'd last eaten or slept.

The guard brought his axe up and around in a wide arc, ready to split her head. Hummingbird turned her stumble into a lunge, and rolled past him to where one of the heavy bronze braziers smoldered in the shadow of the temple. The hot metal singed her hands as she lifted the bowl from its cradle and flung the contents at the guard. He fell back, shrieking, dropping the axe to paw the burning coals from his clothes. Hummingbird folded with a quick punch to the stomach, hammered her other fist into the back of his head, then snatched the axe from the ground.

The priests reacted with surprising speed, barring her path with their bodies. They were unarmed, but Hummingbird would lose valuable time cutting through them. She could already hear the slap of sandals behind her as guards rushed from the temple proper. A desperate glance over the edge of the platform gave no reprieve. Even if she managed to make it down the ziggurat steps, the crowd would tear her to pieces.

The first of the Cazonci's warriors emerged from the darkness of the ritual chamber. Hummingbird checked her blow when she noticed the young man before her wore the jade and gold of a noble. He skidded to a halt, one hand reaching to steady his headdress of stiffened cloth and eagle feathers. He wore a short skirt, the bare skin of his chest unmarred by age or ritual scars. His eyes were the light tan of polished copal wood, and his long hair a deep, lustrous black.

He stabbed at her, awkward as a newborn deer. Hummingbird slapped the spear from his hands and drove the butt of her axe into his ribs. She caught him before he crumpled, wrenching him up even as she pressed the heavy bronze blade to his throat.

80

Hummingbird dragged her hostage back, only to see a dozen more warriors spill from the sacrificial precincts. Within moments she was surrounded by a threatening jungle of spears. The two temple guards she had dropped regained their feet, if somewhat unsteadily, daggers in their hands and murder in their eyes.

A few warriors hefted javelins, and Hummingbird jerked the young nobleman around to make a smaller target of herself. He bucked forward, then grunted as Hummingbird put more pressure on the axe. A single rivulet of blood crept down his neck to pool in the hollow of his shoulder. She could smell the bitter tang of sweat through the aromatic oils rubbed into his skin and hair.

"Stop." The Cazonci raised a hand. "Release him and you won't be harmed."

The air rang with Hummingbird's laughter.

"You have my word," he said.

She regarded him for a moment. The Cazonci was a tall man, his skin pocked as old basalt by a web of ritual scars. Dried blood crusted his ears, nose, and lips where the flesh had been pierced with maguey thorns. His long hair was matted with gore, and his arms dyed black to the elbow, but his eyes were the same faded gold as those of the man Hummingbird held.

"Swear to it," she said.

He looked to the sky. "I, Zuangua, Cazonci of Tarasc, swear before the eye of Nanahuatzin. May the knives of Mictlan scrape the flesh from my bones if I lie."

She released the youth. His face flushed a deep crimson as he stumbled into the ring of soldiers.

"Take her to my chambers." Zuangua nodded to his men.

Rough hands grabbed Hummingbird.

A guard shouldered through the crowd to glare down at her. His robes were pocked with blackened holes, the flesh beneath raw and red.

"That's my axe," he rasped as he stripped the weapon from her hand

She drove an elbow into his face, feeling a satisfying crunch before the rest of the guards swarmed her.

"You swore I wouldn't be harmed," she shouted over the press.

"Don't make a liar of me." Zuangua turned back to the crowd. They appeared to have seen nothing of the fight, and their raucous cheers drowned Hummingbird's curses as she was dragged back into darkness.

* * *

The Cazonci's chambers were large, with animal skins on the floor and walls carved with the likenesses of gods and heroes. Aromatic smoke from several braziers coiled like jungle vines through holes near the ceiling.

Despite her hunger, Hummingbird had eaten sparingly from the platter of fried corn cakes brought by Zuangua's slaves, and only sniffed at the pulque in the ceramic pitcher. The fermented maguey sap had led to her capture in the first place. She'd run afoul of Zuangua's warriors at the end of a three day binge, sold to her city's enemies for a handful of cacao beans by the doe-eyed bed boy she'd taken up with outside of Yoaltepec. Hummingbird scowled, the memory of his soft caresses soured by thoughts of revenge.

Why were the handsome ones always the most treacherous?

"I thought all the Cuachiqueh were dead." Zuangua strode into the room. He removed his skirt and stood still as slaves pulled the maguey thorns from his face and genitals.

"They are."

Zuangua made no reply, but his gaze slid to the long lock over Hummingbird's left ear. Silence stretched between them, punctuated only by the soft click of thorns in the slaves' catch bowls.

"Cuachiqueh or not, you are a skilled warrior," he said at last. "I could use you against the Sea People."

Hummingbird grimaced at the mention of the invaders, a familiar coldness rising in her gut. She steeled herself against memories of water thick with poison, of a city dragged below the waves, and of what rose in its place.

Perhaps thinking her expression a response to his offer, Zuangua frowned. "My city and yours were enemies, but we share the same gods, the same history. What of the honor of your people?"

"It lies with them at the bottom of Lake Texcoco."

"Wealth, then—gold, jade, slaves, whatever you desire."

She looked to the row of small, circular scars that wound around her arm. "Another warrior won't matter."

"It might if she were Cuachiqueh." Zuangua accepted a cloak of eagle feathers from one of his slaves. "What do you know of Tamoachan?"

"The Mouth of the Jaguar?" Hummingbird waved a hand before her face as if dispelling a bad odor. "A cursed place. No one goes there."

"Not always. Under suns long past, it was a place of great learning and culture. The sorcerer-priests of Tamoachan wielded power said to rival the gods. They crafted artifacts of great and terrible aspect, perhaps even powerful enough to drive off the Sea People."

"How do you know this?"

"Because I told him." A black-robed man stepped from the shadow of the door. Hair like wet seaweed framed a long, pallid face. His nose was little more than two slits, and his bulging, watery eyes were so large that he seemed to have no brow at all. At his approach, the air in the room grew thick with the stench of low tide.

Hummingbird snatched a knife from the platter.

Zuangua stepped between them. "Calm yourself. Sahagun is a friend."

"He's one of the Sea People." Hummingbird reversed the blade, ready to throw.

"I have as much reason to hate the Esoteric Order as you, Azteca." Sahagun spoke with a pronounced lisp, his thin lips barely covering the needlelike teeth of a deep ocean predator. "I, the most powerful of my faith, barred from eternal bliss by accident of birth."

Hummingbird's blade didn't waver.

"When Sahagun first came to me, I thought the same as you," Zuangua said. "But his knowledge has won me many battles against the invaders."

"In the ruins of Tamoachan, long forgotten by man or god, lies an artifact of great power—a jade dagger from the time of the fourth sun, a relic from a world thought destroyed," Sahagun said.

"Impossible," Hummingbird said. The fourth sun and the world it shone upon were gone, swallowed by darkness along with the three others Lord Quetzalcoatl had brought into being.

"I have seen it in my dreams." Sahagun shuffled a step closer. "Carved in a time before your gods formed the first men and women from maize dough, when the world was home to—other things."

Zuangua laid a hand on Hummingbird's arm. "The swamps spread, the sea rises. Tarasc will soon fall."

"Why don't you send your own warriors?" she asked.

"My best are in the field, and none have seen"—he glanced at her arm—"have survived what you have."

She glowered at Sahagun. Creatures like him had torn down the ziggurats and raised hideous, golden idols in their place. They brought pestilence as well. She had seen people covered in blisters, choking on their own blood. She had seen streets lined with bodies, the survivors too weak even to bear the dead away. She had been in the city when the deeps finally came for Tenochtitlan.

The invaders had much to answer for.

"I want gold," she said to Zuangua.

"Bring me the dagger and I'll give you more than you can carry."

"And food, and weapons, and clothes."

"The finest."

She pressed her lips into a tight line.

"The gods brought you to me, Cuachiqueh," Zuangua said.

"Hummingbird. My name is Hummingbird, and gods had nothing to do with it."

* * *

"We're being followed." Sahagun cocked his thumb as a flock of birds rose from the trees on a nearby ridge.

"I know," Hummingbird spat the words like a curse.

They'd left Tarasc three days ago, skirting the salt marsh that had replaced the fields and rocky plains of Anahuac. Sahagun had promised he could hide them from his fellows, but Hummingbird was loath to put her life in the hands of a sorcerer. She'd first noticed their pursuers on the dawn of the second day, clued by a fine smudge of smoke against the rising sun.

"When we crest this hill, keep walking."

"As you wish." Sahagun's smile was reassuring as a knife at her back.

Hummingbird ducked beneath a huana tree, taking care not to break or bend any of the small branches as she climbed.

She needn't have bothered.

The three men walked in a ragged line, rocks skittering from under their sandals, their eyes fixed on the trail ahead. They were attired as Tarascan warriors, with spears, short skirts, and quilted cloth vests.

Hummingbird drew the macuahuitl from the sling on her back. A row of obsidian flakes was bound with dried sinew between the halves of the flat, wooden club. Sharper even than the metal blades wielded by the Sea People, it could behead a man in one swipe, although the Azteca seldom did so. The gods favored warriors as sacrifices, and that required prisoners.

"Oaca, did you hear—?" The rear man's words were lost in a whoosh of breath as Hummingbird landed on his back. She left him gasping on the ground, and bounced up to catch a thrust from the second man on the edge of her macuahuitl, sliding the edge down the spear haft to carve a red line across its wielder's knuckles. The guard released the spear rather than lose his fingers. He stepped back, fumbling for his dagger, then grunted as one of his legs gave out. Never one to ignore opportunity, Hummingbird dropped him with a blow from the flat of her macuahuitl before turning to meet the charge of the last man.

He came on, axe raised. She stepped into the swing, both to avoid the blade and rob the blow of force. Still, the impact of the haft on her forehead was enough to snatch the strength from her knees. A wild swipe with her macuahuitl set the guard back on his heels, and bought Hummingbird time to regain her balance.

"I hoped it would come to this." The guard's broken nose lent his words buzzing drone. "You liked my axe so much back at the temple, I thought I would give you a chance to see it up close."

Hummingbird eyed the distance between them, then inched her front foot forward. He would need room to swing that axe of his, if she could just maneuver inside his reach, her macuahuitl would—

"Oaca, stop." The first man had regained his feet, and stood puffing, hands on his knees. Although he'd gotten rid of his headdress and exchanged his ceremonial robes for quilted cotton armor, Hummingbird recognized the wide, golden eyes and smooth cheeks of the young noble from the Tarascan ziggurat.

Broken-nose, Oaca, bared bloody teeth, but lowered his axe. The other guard groaned, fumbling for his discarded spear. Hummingbird tensed.

"Please." The noble held up a hand. "We haven't come to fight."

"Who are you?" Hummingbird asked.

"Hetzin." He turned his head to spit blood onto the dirt.

"Why are you following me?"

"To reclaim my honor." Hetzin frowned, a smudge of blood at the corner of his lips accentuating their redness. "You shamed me before my men."

"Twice." She nodded at the two temple guards, then winced as the move set her head throbbing. Oaca must have hit her harder than she'd thought.

"I cannot show my face in Tarasc." Hetzin swallowed. "But if I were to return with the dagger— I wish to accompany you."

"No."

"I command you."

"I don't follow your orders."

"You took my father's gold."

"To get the dagger, not play bodyguard to his fool of a son." She slipped her macuahuitl back into its sheath and set to exploring the spreading bruise on the side of her scalp. The flesh was tender, but it didn't feel as if her skull was cracked.

"You could teach me to fight."

Hummingbird let her gaze roam over his body. Sweat beaded along his arms and chest, making his skin glow like burnished bronze. Though fully into his man's growth, he was of a size with her, with none of the fat or bulky muscle she found unappealing. There might be more than one thing she could teach him.

Hetzin shifted, uncomfortable under her scrutiny.

She snorted and turned away. "Go home."

"We'll follow you, all the way to Tamoachan if need be."

"Not if I tie you to a tree."

Oaca snorted. "Go ahead and try."

Hetzin caught her arm, then snatched his hand back when she glared at him. His golden eyes were wide and pleading. "How am I to lead Tarasc if the warriors laugh at me?"

Something unwound in Hummingbird's chest–a tight wariness that had dogged her since the ziggurat. If the handsome fool wished to die, who was she to stand in his way? At least he would improve the view.

She jerked her head toward the trail. "Don't fall behind."

* * *

The jerky was dry, salty, and tough as sandal leather. Hummingbird cast a sour look at the rabbits that lay on the flat rock beside her. She'd hoped to roast them, but was reluctant to eat any food cooked on the fire. The twisted, sickly trees of the badlands surrounding Tamoachan burned with a blue-green flame that cast strange shadows around the clearing.

Oaca scowled at her from across the fire, his face made skull-like by two black eyes and smashed remnants of his nose. The other ex-temple guard squatted beside him, casting anxious looks into the darkness. Despite the battered condition of his companion, the silent guard somehow managed to appear the more miserable of the pair. He hadn't said a word during the journey, only limped along with the air of a man preparing to charge into a hail of javelins.

Prince Hetzin stared into the fire, his expression troubled. Hummingbird found her gaze drawn to his muscled calves, up his leg to where the skirt had bunched, just a bit, to reveal a smooth expanse of thigh.

"We should reach Tamoachan tomorrow." Sahagun removed a stoppered gourd from the sleeve of his robe, uncorked it, and took a sip before offering it to Hetzin.

"What's in it?" the prince asked.

"The bounty of the sea," Sahagun said, with a shark's toothy grin.

"Brine." Hummingbird grunted at Hetzin's frown. "The Sea People are unnatural creatures."

"Different perhaps, but not unnatural," Sahagun said. "We each must appease our gods."

Oaca spat into the fire. "I wouldn't call what your people worship gods."

"Yes, well, they don't require us to rip the hearts from our enemies, I suppose," the sorcerer said with a mocking tilt of his head.

"Nanahuatzin created this world through sacrifice. Without blood, the sun would never rise from Mictlan and all life would wither," Hetzin said.

The sorcerer's crocodile grin caught the firelight. "What if I told you there are beings as far above your gods as your gods are above you?"

"Impossible. The gods created the suns, the plants, the animals, all of the fifth world," Hetzin said.

"And just what do you think destroyed the first four?"

"Hold your tongue, Sahagun, or I will." Hummingbird had heard enough. The Sea People had come to Tenochtitlan with the same lies, twisting their words around her people's thoughts until the city tore itself apart. Not all had been dragged into the water—some had gone willingly.

Sahagun returned her glare, his eyes luminous in the cold, blue firelight. Hummingbird felt a measure of grudging respect for the man's defiance, until she remembered his bravado had its roots in madness rather than courage.

"It matters not. You've seen the truth of my words." He gathered his robes around him and retreated from the circle of firelight.

"What did he mean?" Hetzin asked. "What have you seen?"

Hummingbird tugged her cloak over her arms.

"Cuachiqueh," Oaca said as if that answered everything.

Hetzin watched her for several heartbeats, then poked the fire. "Is it true if a Cuachiqueh ever takes a step back in battle, her companions will cut her down?"

"Yes."

"Then why are you here?" Although asked from earnest curiosity, the question pinned her heart like a javelin.

"Sometimes the only choice is to run," she whispered, curling up in her cloak. "Go to sleep, fool."

* * *

It seemed Hummingbird barely shut her eyes before she awoke. The fire had died to guttering cinders and camp was silent, but a warning prickle along her neck roused her with weapon in hand.

She could see the outline of the silent guard. He stood facing away from the fire, back rigid, his arms at his sides. She crept toward him but was halted by a light touch on her shoulder.

Sahagun's face bobbed in the gloom like a corpse on a midnight sea. "Stay close to the fire, they come."

"Who?"

"The Eel People." He hurled a handful of powder into the fire and the flames rose up.

The creatures were human shaped, with the slick, mottled skin of river frogs. They crawled through the shadows on limbs that seemed to have no bones or joints, and where their faces should've been were only featureless expanses of flesh.

Hummingbird saw the standing guard was actually held by several of the creatures. He convulsed in their grip, his flesh darkening to the shade of wet shale as one of the Eel People slowly forced its arm down his throat.

Her macuahuitl split the thing in half, and the guard collapsed. Another creature snaked an arm around her calf. A prickly numbness spread up her leg, which almost buckled as she tried to tear away. The thing held on, limb distending as Hummingbird dragged it across the rocky ground. Without room to swing her macuahuitl she was forced to saw at the rubbery flesh. The jagged obsidian teeth parted the creature's arm from its body, and the thing retreated, hissing like a cornered snake. Cursing, Hummingbird snatched the still twitching appendage from her leg and tossed it into the darkness.

Hetzin staggered into the firelight, one of the Eel People wrapped around his chest. With a ragged cry, Oaca buried his axe in the creature's shoulder. It released the Prince only to turn on the temple guard, seeming to flow down the haft of his weapon. Its fingers burrowed into Oaca's arms, dark veins marbling his flesh. Hummingbird sprinted across the intervening distance only to see another of the creatures slip from the darkness behind Oaca to wrap its long, boneless arms around his shoulders. He shoved Hetzin toward her, then doubled over to vomit up a writhing mass of fat, black slugs.

Hummingbird jerked Hetzin toward the fire as Oaca fell back into the night. She slashed about her, but couldn't seem to stem the tide. Her macuahuitl soon became mired in the things. Glistening darkness crept down the blade, and Hummingbird released it before the flood could reach her.

Hetzin shrieked as one of the things caught his hand, threading its fingers through his casually as a lover. He slashed at it with his dagger, but the blade only rebounded from the slick flesh. Hummingbird lowered her shoulder and shoved the thing into the fire. It twisted in the blaze, screeching as the blaze hissed and crackled around it. Hummingbird caught Hetzin around the waist before the creature could drag him down, and wrenched him from its grip.

Sahagun was on his knees, clutching a gold medallion in the shape of a stylized eye as he choked out words that seemed to blister the air. He rose with a triumphant shout and flung a spray of salt into the horde. Where the grains struck, the flesh of the rubber people smoldered and sparked. Blue flames limned their twisted bodies, causing them to curl like the legs of a dying insect. The smell of burnt hair was suddenly thick in Hummingbird's nose.

"What were those things?" Hetzin asked when the last had burned to ash.

"What remained," Sahagun said. "The Black Circle brought doom to Tamoachan and its people, but not all died."

Hummingbird turned on the sorcerer. "You said you could protect us."

"I did." He brushed the dust from his robes.

"Two men are dead."

"They knew the danger."

She took a step toward him.

The sorcerer didn't flinch. "There are more than we saw here. Do you think you could defeat them without me?"

"Hummingbird, no." Hetzin stepped between them. "They were my men. If anyone is responsible for their deaths, it's me. We must retrieve the dagger, and for that we need Sahagun, now more than ever."

Hummingbird turned away with a snarl and snatched up her macuahuitl. Some of the shards had splintered in the fight, and she set to replacing them. She needed something to pass the time until dawn now that sleep was beyond consideration. As an afterthought, she retrieved Oaca's axe and thrust it into her belt. The man had been an arrogant fool, but he'd shown his mettle at the end. No one deserved to die like that. And yet, as Hummingbird watched Sahagun pick through the scorched remains of the Eel People, she couldn't help but wonder if Oaca and his silent companion hadn't been the lucky ones.

* * *

The fourth time they passed the stone head, Hummingbird lost her temper.

"He's leading us in circles." She flicked her fingers at the bust. Unlike the other statues they'd passed, its features were human, although shifted in such a way that Hummingbird felt as if her eyes were crossing every time she even glanced at it.

"You don't understand," Sahagun raised two fingers, looked between them, and took another left turn—the fourth he'd made in as many minutes.

"Why would he lie?" Hetzin favored her with a helpless shrug before following the sorcerer.

Streets meandered like rivers among the domed buildings of Tamoachan, looping back on themselves in a way that tied Hummingbird's sense of direction in knots. Fluted walls sloped toward the road, seeming to press in on all sides. What few doors she noticed were long and irregular, as if torn from the rock by a giant, palsied hand. There was not a straight line or hard angle to be seen, and the whole city had a slumped, melted look to it.

"Why did they build like this?" She closed her eyes as vertigo threatened to overwhelm her.

"For protection. The Masters of the Black Circle dealt with forces that would grind your reason to dust," Sahagun said.

Hummingbird snorted, but followed the sorcerer through a plaza of crooked pillars, and up a coiling staircase made from rounded blocks of wildly different sizes.

"This is it." Sahagun spread his arms. The conical building looked no different from the others that lined the street, smaller even. It had no entrance but for a ragged hole just above their heads.

"Go on." Sahagun gestured at the opening. "Climb up."

"You climb up," Hummingbird said.

"That's not why I'm here." The sorcerer returned her glare with a sharp-toothed smile.

"Why are you here, sorcerer? You may have Zuangua fooled, but I have heard the words of your priests. I know what you and your people desire."

"And what is that?"

"A new sun, a new world."

"Actually, we desire an old one, but that is not why I'm here." Sahagun spread his hands, holding his fingers up to the sun so Hummingbird could see the thin webbing between the digits. "This, this is my father's gift to me—the least of his blessings. Among my people, birth is everything. No matter our skill, no matter our deeds, we are forever bound by the shackles of ancestry. I am here so that my so-called betters will see my hand in their defeat and know they misjudged me, that they were wrong. None of them could have come this far, the magic of the city would have blasted them to ash, but my blood is diluted enough to slip through the wards. My weakness has become my strength. You're here for vengeance, Cuachiqueh, but I come for recognition."

"A pretty speech, but I heard far prettier from the Sea People who came to Tenochtitlan. They promised salvation, happiness, eternal bliss—all lies."

"Believe what you want." Sahagun lowered his hands. "Just so long as you climb."

Hummingbird leapt to catch the edge. The stone was warm and oily beneath her fingers, but she was able to haul herself up and lower a rope for Hetzin and Sahagun. A short, circular passage led inside, opening on the edge of a columned room larger than the building's exterior.

The floor was made of irregular tiles, cut and fitted in a way that suggested a mosaic but followed no pattern Hummingbird could discern. Bronze plates set into the walls focused light without visible source on the chamber's altar—a thick slab of rose quartz cut to resemble a stepped pyramid. Stretched across it were the desiccated remains of an enormous jungle cat, the hilt of a jade dagger drooping from one empty eye socket.

Hetzin joined her at the entrance, spear in hand.

"I cannot enter. Even a drop of ancient blood is too much for this place." Sahagun stopped halfway down the tunnel, regarding the chamber beyond with a pained frown. "You must retrieve the blade."

Hummingbird drew her macuahuitl and stepped into the room, Hetzin at her heels. Their tentative footfalls echoed back, warped by the strange acoustics of the chamber into the rumble of distant thunder. As they drew close, Hummingbird made to reach for the dagger, but Hetzin caught her hand.

"Tarasc is my city. I'll do it." He snatched the dagger from the carcass and drew back, gaze searching the shadows.

Hummingbird watched the corpse, weapon poised to remove its head should the beast show any sign of renewed vigor.

Neither noticed the yellow smoke rising from the base of the altar until it was around their knees.

"Beware the angles!" Sahagun shouted. "Quickly, bring the dagger to me. I can banish the beast!"

Hummingbird took a step back. Mist billowed around her, thick and choking as the ash that had rained from Popocatepetl after the night of fire. Shapes moved in the smoke, and Hummingbird caught a glimpse of an insectile leg covered with hairs fine as spider silk. A long, hollow tube lashed from the mist to sink into her shoulder. She tore at it, fingers slipping on the pale blue slime that covered its surface. It came away wet with her blood.

She swung her macuahuitl at the shape in the mist. Her club cracked, a shower of obsidian chips slicing across her arms and face.

The thing seemed barely to notice, and Hummingbird just avoided another of the creature's long, hollow barbs. She hurled her broken club into the fog, and drew Oaca's axe. The first chop sent a shiver up her arms like she'd struck solid stone, by the third her hands were numb.

A flailing leg struck her across the chest. It was only a glancing blow, but it still sent her tumbling across the smooth tile.

Hummingbird scrambled to her feet. A few stumbling steps and she was at the door, the formless thing in the mist scrabbling behind her with a sound like teeth on stone.

She came up in time to see Sahagun snatch the dagger from Hetzin's grasp, and slash it across the Prince's chest. He toppled back into the mist with a despairing cry.

"The Black Circle is whole once again!" The sorcerer drew the blade across his arm. Dark smoke seeped from the cut, curling up into the air. "By blood I was banished and by blood I shall return. This time none shall deny me my place among the worthy! Aie, yil la khosa!"

Hummingbird raised her weapon, but Sahagun's gaze caught her and dragged her down. The sorcerer chanted under his breath–thick, wet syllables that seemed to crawl under Hummingbird's skin. Darkness bled into her vision, the crushing pressure of the deeps squeezing the life from her even as seawater filled her lungs. She collapsed against the wall of the tunnel, knowing the mist creature was close, but unable break the sorcerer's gaze. The axe hung loose in her hands, heavy as a temple stone. It was all she could do to keep ahold of it.

"Do not fear, Cuachiqueh." Sahagun pressed the dagger into the hollow of Hummingbird's throat. "You may die, but I will never let you go. Together, we shall—"

The rest of the sorcerer's words were lost in a shriek as Hetzin reared up from the mist to drive his spear into Sahagun's thigh.

Freed of the sorcerer's terrible gaze, Hummingbird struck. Oaca's axe caught Sahagun just above the ear, carving a bloody furrow in his scalp. He clawed at her eyes. Hummingbird flinched away, and the sorcerer's ragged talons dug into her cheek. She dropped the axe to grab Sahagun's wrists before he could drive the dagger into her neck. The sorcerer shrieked and hissed, his eyes rolled back to show nothing but chalky whites. Blood and brine spattered Hummingbird's face as Sahagun's jaws snapped shut a hairsbreadth from her nose.

Somewhere in the mist, Hetzin screamed.

Hummingbird twisted to secure the dagger, gripping the sorcerer's hand with both of hers. He clawed long, bloody gashes in her chest and neck, but Hummingbird only grit her teeth and forced the blade up into Sahagun's stomach. The sorcerer's blood was cold and slick, and his convulsions almost tore the dagger from her grasp. Arms burning, Hummingbird pushed the blade in until she felt it scrape across bone.

Sahagun pawed at her, but the blows were weak. His head rebounded from the stone as Hummingbird threw him off of her, and he slumped to the ground. She stooped to snatch the dagger from his limp hand.

Hetzin lay a few paces away, his back to her. The Prince was pale, one of the creature's hollow tongues buried deep in his arm, the length behind pulsing an arterial red. Hummingbird lunged forward to slash at the tube, which withdrew with a sound part way between a baby's cry and the furious yowl of a hunting cat. She pulled Hetzin to his feet, but he made no move to flee.

"It's beautiful," The prince stood as if carved from stone, staring at the thing in the mist, an idiot's slack grin on his face.

Hummingbird cursed and shouldered him down the tunnel. The opening was only a few paces distant, but she'd never reach it dragging Hetzin. She took a stumbling step toward the circle of wan sunlight, stopped, and turned.

Sometimes the only choice was to run.

Hummingbird kept her eyes downcast as she charged, expecting any moment to feel the sharp bite of the thing's barbs. The dagger was awkward in her grip, its hilt too wide for human hands. A shadow flickered and Hummingbird leapt, the blow that would've disemboweled her slipping by in a flutter of disturbed air. She brought the dagger down two-handed, and felt a hot gush of fluid as it sank into the thing's body.

Hummingbird hung on grimly, sawing through the creature's chitinous armor as it thrashed beneath her. Mist burned her eyes and lungs, but she was thankful, for it obscured the hideous form of the thing with which she grappled. The creature slammed against one of the pillars, and Hummingbird was forced to leap free to avoid the fall of heavy stones. The thing gave an echoing shriek as the pillar toppled into another. Hummingbird lurched to her feet, barely able to keep her balance amidst the teeth-rattling boom of falling rock. For a moment, she didn't know if she was running toward the tunnel or away from it, until she heard the thing rear up, keening, from the pile of rubble behind her.

A few unsteady steps brought her to where Hetzin stood. The Prince flinched away when she stepped from the mist, a terrible revenant soaked in blood and ichor.

"Run!" She shoved him ahead of her. This time, the noble needed no prodding.

He grasped the rope, sliding through the entrance without so much as a backwards glance. Hummingbird bent to do the same, when she felt sharp talons close about her ankle.

"You're doomed without me." Sahagun pulled himself across the floor. "None can stand against the might of Father—"

Hummingbird kicked him in the face, but the sorcerer didn't release his grip. Her lungs burned with each sobbing breath, the sound of the creature struggling through the rubble loud in her ears. Although she slashed at

92

Sahagun with the dagger, her arms seemed to have lost their strength.

The sorcerer lurched, claws digging into her calf. Hummingbird saw one of the creature's barbs jutting from his back. Another hissed from the mist to thud into Sahagun's shoulder. Slowly, the two of them were dragged down the hall. Hummingbird worked the dagger beneath the sorcerer's fingers, not caring that it cut her own flesh as well.

"I curse you, Cuachiqueh." Sahagun's words came with a torrent of black bile.

"You wouldn't be the first." She wrenched on the dagger, prying the sorcerer's fingers from her leg. With a low moan, he slid back into the billowing mist.

The rope left burns on Hummingbird's palms as she slid from the entrance. Hetzin staggered to her side and threw an arm around her shoulder.

The setting sun lent urgency to their flight as they limped from Tamoachan. Arms around each other, they struggled on with no thought but to win free of the badlands. The night seethed around them, alive with the hiss of oily bodies on stone. But the Eel People didn't attack, perhaps kept at bay by the dagger clutched in Hummingbird's blood-caked hand. Only when stunted shrubs gave way to grass and trees did the two of them collapse.

When they awoke, Hetzin limped to a nearby stream and returned with cupped leaf full of water.

"We should clean your wounds before they fester." He tore a strip from his skirt.

Hummingbird let him wash the blood away and bind her wounds, grimacing when he probed the deep slashes on her calf.

Hetzin drew forth a handful of red petals from his pouch and crushed them into a paste. "This flower grows only in the black ash of Popocatepetl. It'll numb the pain."

His hands were gentle. Hummingbird relaxed as a pleasant numbness swallowed the pain in her leg. He paused, and then tentatively touched the cut on her thigh. It was no more than a scratch, but Hummingbird didn't stop him. His fingers crept up, soft as spider legs, to where there was no injury.

She caught his wrist. Stammering apologies, Hetzin made to draw away. He looked up when she didn't release him, his eyes questioning.

She pulled him to her.

Hetzin's lips were hot, his body strong and supple under her hands. He fumbled at the clasp of her belt, but she pushed him to the ground, pinning him as she straddled his hips.

"Let me." She tore off his skirt, and then her own.

* * *

Hetzin was gone when Hummingbird awoke to the morning sun. At first she thought he was getting water, but as the shadows shortened she began to suspect he wasn't coming back.

It was then she noticed he'd taken the dagger.

Hummingbird squinted at the sky, a flush creeping up her neck. Hetzin couldn't have more than a few hours lead. Prince or not, she'd thrash him until he couldn't walk.

Her leg collapsed when she tried to stand, sending her sprawling to the grass. She cursed. The whole limb felt as if it had been carved from wood.

Snarling, she tore the poultice from her wound. What a fool she'd been. Magic flower indeed. Hetzin had drugged her and was no doubt bearing the dagger to his father. She could imagine the story he would tell in court, and who he would cast as the hero, and the villain. Her word would not stand against that of Zuangua's own son.

She slammed a fist against her frozen leg. The only reward she could expect now was another trip to the Tarascan ziggurat. Already, her toes prickled with returning feeling, but she suspected it would be hours before she could walk again. A glint caught her eye. Hetzin had left her pack—food, supplies, and a few pieces of gold—far less than she'd been promised.

An expensive night indeed.

Her laughter startled a flurry of birds from a nearby thicket. This wasn't over. She'd come back for Hetzin, for the Sea People, for all of them, but for now all she wanted was to find a quiet hut, a jug of pulque, and a man with a face like a dry stream bed.

The handsome ones were more trouble than they were worth.

By day, EVAN DICKEN *studies old Japanese maps and crunches data for all manner of fascinating medical research at the Ohio State University. By night, he does neither of these things. His fiction has most recently appeared in* Analog, Beneath Ceaseless Skies, *and* Strange Horizons, *and he has stories forthcoming from publishers* The NoSleep Podcast *and* The Black Library. *Please feel free to visit him at evandicken.com.*

A Matter of Goats

by Ben Fenwick

An eerie call fell down the wind from the dark mountainsides. It was a high-pitched tone that fell slowly into a humanlike, ululating sob. Anton Le Bouveret felt the hairs on his forearms and the back of his neck prickle. The dark, rugged, Balkan shadowland surrounded them and their small wagon, chilling him with its desolation. The cry struck his heart with disquiet. He slipped his flask of vile Serbian brandy back into the wide sash on his waist, a sash that held both his pistol and the insanely expensive rapier he'd bought in Rome. Feeling emboldened at the touch of them, he braved a small blasphemy.

"Their gods, I suppose. Whining in fear at our mission on behalf of His Majesty."

"Quiet, you fool," hissed Heathwight from underneath the hood of the heavy, dark cloak he wore. "Quiet until we reach the village."

The cry again sounded, the high, almost tone-like whistle that decayed once more into sluggish sobbing. Le Bouveret had never heard anything like it. The sound was behind them now.

"What do you suppose it is?" Le Bouveret asked.

"How should I know? I expect you've flushed it out of its bed with your constant yammering." Heathwight shook the reins, slapping them to the ponies. The spooked pair hardly needed prodding. The stout creatures immediately went into a full gallop, despite the day's trek through the passes. Heathwight's hood flew back, exposing his bald head.

With his right hand Le Bouveret grasped the seat in the sudden surge of the wagon, almost falling out. With his left he pulled the black felt slouch hat down tight on his black curls. After steadying himself he reached down and loosened the rapier in its gilt scabbard. He glanced back to check the load, which included their supplies and the large brass telescope with which they were to view the eclipse. He could see the cylinder, wrapped tightly in cotton batting, bouncing in its crate as they bumped over the ancient rocky road.

Then he caught a glimpse—something blue and shining far away in the darkness behind them, bobbing up and down. Was it the eyes of the thing? Was it giving them chase? He felt a thrill—something to see, to shoot—rather than skulking through the countryside in fear of the unseen. Le Bouveret drew his pistol, training it on the bobbing blue light. There were two eyes.

"I say, slow it down a moment will you? I'm trying to get a good shot here."

"Like Hell I will!"

"Now who swears?" Le Bouveret said. He peered along the long barrel of the match pistol, gleaming faintly in the starlight, trying to train it on the lights behind. The two blue discs were now quite apparent, but the shape that bore them was lost in the inky darkness. All Le Bouveret could see was a bulky black mass—almost like a tree. Probably was a tree, come to think of it, standing in some bend back in the road in a line of sight beyond the…wolf…that pursued them now. Yes, had to be a wolf. The barrel of the pistol bobbed and weaved as the wagon jolted over the rock-strewn path, jarring his aim so greatly that any shot would have been futile. Le Bouveret placed the pistol back into his sash uncocked, then grasped the seat again as the wagon lurched over a large bump.

Le Bouveret was about to curse again as the wagon passed one of the pierced haystacks that were so prevalent in the area. The large wooden spike rose from the center of the haystack like dark witchery, its top three feet over Le Bouveret's head and sharpened to a point. Tied to it on a long lead was a goat, which keened longingly at the wagon as it hurtled past. The goat seemed uninterested in the pile of new cut hay.

"Well, that's a dead goat when that wolf gets it," observed Le Bouveret.

"Wolf!" Heathwight said with disgust. "No wolf sounds like that."

Ahead, the village sat darkly—the only light was in a tall, thin bell tower next to a domed church. A high stone wall apparently built around the town was pierced by a high wooden gate, its two doors closed on the road, shutting them off from the town.

"Damn," Heathwight cursed again. He gripped the reins in large, white-knuckled hands. His eyes were large, set in a roundish face, his cold-reddened cheeks making him appear like a fearful cherub. "Ho! Hello in the village!"

No answer. Heathwight yelled once more, this time in Serbian. Then, in German. No sign that anyone in the village heard him.

He turned to Le Bouveret. "Where is that dammed horn? We need to signal them."

Le Bouveret turned and began sorting through the jumble of luggage, looking for the tin horn used for just such an occasion. He looked back up the road and saw the eyes were much closer now. He abandoned his search for the horn and redrew the pistol, waiting for the moment when Heathwight would have to stop the carriage.

The moment came immediately. The horses stopped just short of the closed gate, nervously stomping and snorting. Heathwight yelled several times at the gate with no result.

Le Bouveret once again stared down the filigreed barrel of the match pistol, drawing another bead upon the eyes.

It was as if they sensed him, their unearthly blue light seeming to regard him with interest. They were not like those of an animal, but something that understood him, unafraid. He felt a chill when he realized they also looked at him as prey.

Then they disappeared. The strange cry sounded again, joined this time by the crying bleat of the goat. Suddenly the sound cut off with a snap, then there was a wet sound as of something being sucked. So now the wolf had brought down the goat and was feeding upon it. Very well, then, they likely had plenty of time. Still, he kept his match pistol trained in the direction where he'd last seen the eyes.

Heathwight bolted from the seat of the wagon, cloak flapping like a wing from his back. Le Bouveret glanced to see him grasping for a cord hanging from a loophole in the gate. Le Bouveret grabbed the reins of the nervous ponies with his left hand, trying to steady them even as he turned and maintained a nominal aim behind them.

Then Le Bouveret saw them again—two sets of eyes now. Red ones in front and the blue ones farther behind. He was surprised to hear the keening of the goat again.

So, he thought. Had the goat, somehow gotten away, down the road? Was the—wolf?—now bearing down again? This time I've got you, he thought to himself as he drew a bead on the latter set of eyes. He squeezed the trigger.

Behind him the gate bell clanged loudly at Heathwight's insistent tugging on the cord. Le Bouveret started as the hammer fell. The report of the pistol was met with a cry from the goat, and both sets of eyes disappeared.

"Dammit, man." Le Bouveret shouted. "Must you spoil my only shot? Now I've hit the goat instead." He threw the now-spent pistol in the back of the coach and drew his rapier. It gleamed slightly in the dark.

Heathwight only glanced back at the sound of the pistol, then pulled repeatedly more on the cord, clanging the bell loudly with each pull.

Finally, there was the sound of a bolt being thrown. The gate creaked slightly open. As Le Bouveret turned, he saw an ornate musket-barrel poke out from the parted slats into Heathwight's face.

Heathwight swore softly. He put his hands up and said something in

Serbian. Unfamiliar with the language, Le Bouveret imagined it meant "friend". It could mean anything, of course. Heathwight repeated it. Then he said it French, German, Italian, and Greek. Le Bouveret recognized it was indeed the word "friend."

The door pushed farther open. The man with the musket, an ornate Turkish one, likely more than a hundred years old, walked out from the gate, followed by a large bearded man with a felt hood, bearing a wood-axe. Then another, smaller man bearing a scythe.

The Turkish man looked behind Heathwight, as if he thought someone was standing behind him, then glanced up at Le Bouveret, pointing the bell-shaped muzzle of the gun at him.

Le Bouveret managed a smile, bowed slightly, tipped his felt hat and said "Friend" in Greek.

The man with the musket was about five years younger than Le Bouveret, which would make him about 25 years old. He had a dark cream complexion, yet with aquiline features that made him look less like a Turk and more like a dark-skinned Greek. He frowned.

"Ignoramuses," the man with the musket snapped to them in Greek. "You chowder-heads are out too late. Get yourselves and your carriage inside and pay the tax so I won't shoot you." He turned and said something Serbian to the man behind him. The doors were pushed open to reveal the cobblestone street of the village. Standing in it were at least a dozen townsmen, all carrying some kind of weapon, whether an axe, thresher or scythe. All looked like they were ready to flay Le Bouveret and Heathwight. The Turkish man took his musket from his shoulder and waved them in. Le Bouveret took up the reins and slapped them on the ponies. The ponies charged in despite the crowd, clearly eager to be in the confines of the gates.

As they stopped just inside, the townsmen on the gate slammed it shut, deftly replacing the wooden beam across the bolt-rack.

The dark-skinned man, musket at his side, held out his hand. "The tax, please sir. Ten marks," he said in Greek.

Le Bouveret climbed from the cart and strode to the gate. He stopped when he felt the eyes upon him, standing with legs apart, sword drawn. He stood down peacefully and slid the attention-getting rapier into its gilt scabbard. He slipped his hands into his sash and fished out his red leather purse, its gilt scrolling gleaming in the yellow lamplight. He handed it absentmindedly to the Turk.

"Please take from it our fees for lodging and livery as well," Le Bouveret said politely. "And what is your name?"

The Turk held the purse for a moment, as if weighing it, but then returned it to Le Bouveret unopened.

"I am Mahmud. And I am the constable. I am no stable boy," he said. "But you can pay me on the morrow for your tax." He turned and whistled to a youth, who stepped out of the dozen or so men and took the reins of their team. Le Bouveret looked at the jumbled crowd of buildings—most looked empty— and his eyes rested on one with the sign of a goat hanging from it. He pointed at it, eyeing the Turk. The man nodded in reply. So, their lodgings for the time being settled, they made their way to the inn, which overlooked a surprisingly well-ordered town square. They began walking to it, the Turk escorting them.

The domed church, which Le Bouveret guessed to be Orthodox, if his time in Greece was any guide, looked like it may have once been a mosque—but who knew, as many times as East and West traded pieces in the chessboard of the Carpathian provinces. The slender bell tower was likely once a minaret, and the ornately carved columns in front of the doorway looked as if Doric flourishes were added to them almost as an afterthought. Magyar? But the thing about the square that most intrigued Le Bouveret was the huge, ornate cannon that set in the front of the church. Verdigris lay thick upon the bronze barrel, the muzzle of which was cast like a lion's mouth.

The inn itself—Goat of the Woods—was unremarkable and the stable boy deposited their considerable bulk of luggage in the room without fanfare. The innkeeper—the large, bearded axe-wielder who'd met them at the gate—told them in halting Greek the rules and hours of breakfast and supper then bid them goodnight. He shut the door, leaving them to the light of a candle.

Le Bouveret lay unspeaking, wanting to smoke but deciding his companion would complain about it. He thought about the cannon.

"I say, what is that doing here?" he asked Heathwight, almost rhetorically. "Suleyman's siege cannon. Our Turkish friend said Suleyman left it behind in Bosovo to ensure that the village would be protected."

"Hmmm," said Heathwight, obviously wishing Le Bouveret would just go to sleep.

Le Bouveret sighed. "For the want a nail, a shoe was lost, and of that, perhaps he might have taken Vienna after all."

"You can prattle on about anything, if after what we've been through tonight you can muse over a war two-hundred years gone," he said gruffly.

"Don't you see the irony of it?" Le Bouveret insisted. "Here we are. You, an astronomer, and I, a poet. You are to catalogue the stars and I'm to write pretty little bits about this land, all for 'King and Country'—and the Greenwich Observatory. Is it lost on you that our Prince Regent has armies too? Might he not cast his eye also over this very land where so many have killed and killed? Could that be the real purpose of your readings, and my descriptions?"

"It's best not to talk such things," Heathwight said. "They are paying me to catalogue the rising and setting of the stars, and they are paying you write about it. Why speculate?"

"At least," Le Bouveret said, feeling chastened by the accuracy of the remark. "It must be so, I suppose. Until my debts are paid."

"That should ensure your employment for at least until the sun of home shines on us again."

Le Bouveret shrugged. "Perhaps."

The next morning, the stable boy awoke them with bowls of water for washing, speaking in Serbian, which Le Bouveret didn't understand. It turned out to be the call for breakfast, which was some kind of local ale soup, bread and cheese. Le Bouveret insisted on the keeper making water for tea. Then the constable came in, followed by a boy in dark coarse robes whom Le Bouveret deduced was an acolyte in the church they'd seen. They spoke to Heathwight.

"The Father wants to see us," Heathwight said

"Of course. Probably wants us to pay the tax as well."

The walk through the town square was short. Le Bouveret noticed the green cannon bore a crack down one side of the barrel. An attempt had been made to strengthen the flaw with cable, but Le Bouveret wouldn't want to be near it when the thing sounded. So, Suleyman wasn't eager to drag several tons of siege cannon that would likely blow up if used. Nevertheless, it was a lovely piece.

Upon taking the front steps of the church, Le Bouveret noticed the pillars were unusual. They were marked faintly with characters that looked indecipherable to him. Irregularly etched, they formed a spiral train around the columns all the way to the top, where they held up the colonnade roof. And though they were both massive, the left column looked ever so slightly larger round than the other. Both were out-of-round, crude if one were expecting the exactitude of Roman or Greek architecture.

"What do you make of it?" Le Bouveret asked his friend.

"The characters? I'd say they predate Cyrillic. Beyond that, who can say?"

"It was the Pagans who carved them," said a heavily accented voice in Greek, startling the two men.

They both looked up from the characters that had absorbed them. A white-haired, white-bearded man bearing the black robes and round headdress of the Orthodoxy stood with the door slightly open, beckoning them in.

Le Bouveret bowed, removed his hat, and smiled. "Tell me, Holy Father, why would Pagan handiwork grace the Lord's house?"

The old man shook his head. "Much too complicated to discuss on steps here. Please to come inside and talk me there."

Inside, they again saw more of the pillars like those of the foyer, which led up into the open-air, square-domed interior of the typical architecture of a mosque. The inner pillars also bore the same markings.

"My," mused Le Bouveret quietly in English. "I do love the east. Pagans beset by Mohammedans, usurped by the Christians, and so on."

"Try to hold your tongue, Anton."

"I'm speaking English, Jonathan."

"It's your attitude that worries me."

"You and my mother."

The priest led them to a rear door, beyond the sanctuary. Le Bouveret noticed the altar was also stone. It looked to be a flatter version of the pillars, laid on its side and converted to the same Christian use.

Through the door they paused briefly in a robe room, then into a small alcove with a desk, some chairs and a pitcher with three glasses. The Turkish constable, who had accompanied them from their room, walked first inside, then stood with his dark eyes showing hard at them as they entered.

"Please to join Mahmud and I," said the priest. "We can raise a glass—of course, not Mahmud."

They both bowed and took their chairs. The priest filled the three glasses, raised his to them and drank. Le Bouveret and Heathwight followed. Le Bouveret felt the familiar sting of Slivovitz trickle down his throat, dispelling the sour aftertaste of the morning's milk.

The priest said something in Serbian to Heathwight, who translated.

"He says he wants to speak freely, but wants to in his own language. Since I can translate, he asks if you mind?"

"Tell him if he barks like a Spaniel he may use Serbian."

"I'll explain," said Heathwight, the edge ever so slightly in his voice at Le Bouveret's remark, "that you are quite happy with his comfort."

The two men talked for a moment. Le Bouveret heard Heathwight use his name.

"He wishes to welcome us to Bosovo, and asks if we are the English on their King's errand to watch the sun. I explained yes, and he said a messenger on the way to Sarajevo had spoken of our mission while traveling through two weeks back. He also asks about you."

"Tell him something appropriate." Le Bouveret said. "Please, Anton. They can read your expression."

"Just testing them, good man. Seeing if they toy with us."

The priest spoke more.

"He says you are special, that God has sent you. He says yours is the same name as the saint who founded this church."

"There is a Saint Le Bouveret? I'd not realized—"

"Anthony. It's to Saint Anthony. Anton is a derivative of that name."

"Oh. Well, tell him I'm flattered. And to think I don't even believe in Him."

The two talked more. "He asks if you've given your life over to Christ."

"Yes, yes," Le Bouveret said impatiently. "Ask him about the wolf problem here."

The man's white, deep eyebrows went up at the mention from Heathwight. The two talked for some time.

"He says what chased us was no wolf."

"So you exclaimed to me when it was chasing us in the cart. What ate the goat?"

Heathwight asked, received an answer and frowned. He asked again and, as near as Le Bouveret could tell, got the same answer. "He claims the thing is a goat itself."

"A goat that eats goats? How interesting."

"He said the villagers tied the goat out there to placate the thing. It is an old creature who lived here long ago, and was defeated by the Turks and Suleyman."

"Defeated he says?"

"Defeated and imprisoned in a cave next to the old pagan temple."

"If it was defeated and imprisoned in a cave, why did it chase us into town?"

"He says that's a problem. It must have had something to do with the earthquake."

"There was an earthquake? When?"

Heathwight talked more with the old man. Le Bouveret noticed the Turk seemed uninterested in the story, but kept his eyes steady into his own. Le Bouveret met his gaze.

"He said it was four months ago. The disappearances started after that."

"Disappearances?"

"First sheep went missing. Then a hunter who went to look for what was eating the sheep. He says the hunter has been seen by one of the children next to the old temple and that the cave has reopened."

"If the hunter has been seen, why is he missing?"

More discussions in Serbian.

"He has not come home. The Great Goat takes those who are chosen. Only those who are to die see those who are lost. If they live, they do only with the blessings of God Almighty."

"Amen," Anton said. The priest smiled in recognition at the blessing. Le Bouveret smiled back at him and cheerfully continued talking to Heathwight. "Tell him we are sorry we can't stay and we wish him luck."

Heathwight glared at him incredulously. "What say you? How are we to make our observations for Greenwich? The orders are to make specific observations for this location."

"I just remembered that there are other ways to pay debts. Go on, tell him."

"You'll not do this to me." Heathwight grabbed his forearm, even as Le Bourveret began to stand. He stopped and glared into the astronomer's eyes.

The old man suddenly spoke up excitedly. Heathwight talked with him for a moment, then turned back to Le Bouveret.

"He said you are to bring him your sword so he might bless it. He said you, I, and Mahmud will then go to the pagan temple up the hill. Mahmud can show you the cave."

"I said tell him we will be moving on by noon. Think we can leave by noon? Sjelek is the next stop. I think we can make Sjelek in a fortnight if we leave by noon. Best to be about it."

Mahmud, without taking his eyes off Anton, said something quietly to the attending acolyte who'd led them in. The boy was off in a flash.

"Where's the boy going?"

"He sent him for your sword."

"Dammit. This isn't our fight."

"It is now. Besides, you seemed eager enough last night after you took that shot at it."

Le Bouveret opened his mouth to speak—but found he had no retort. He sat with the others uneasily in silence. Eventually the youth showed back up, carrying the rapier in its finely gilt scabbard. He gingerly handed it to Le Bouveret.

Glancing sidelong at Heathwight with an angry stare, Le Bouveret stood up, bowed, partially unsheathed the sword and handed it to the priest.

The priest pulled the blade from the scabbard, examining the scrollwork. He pointed excitedly at the writing on it.

"What's he saying now?"

"He says the sword bears your name. That it's some Anthony fellow owned it." Heathwight strained to follow something. "He said that it belonged to the táltosok of Vienna."

"Taltosok? What is a taltosok?"

They talked for some time. Finally Heathwight nodded in some kind of recognition.

"It means wizard," Heathwight said finally.

Le Bouveret stared at the characters on the long, light, thin blade, tapering to a razor point. He'd long looked at the characters, told they meant "Maestro" by the broker who'd arranged the buy. The woman who sold it said her family had owned it for two centuries but that being Basques found their fortunes failing in recent years. Her eyes had stared into his and she mumbled something to him as he'd taken it from her hands. He'd never understood what she'd said. The broker refused to translate.

The priest cleared his throat, bringing Le Bouveret back from his brief reverie.

"We should find such a wizard right away," he said to Heathwight. "This must go into his hands."

Heathwight gave him a sardonic stare, then spoke to the priest. He turned back.

"I told him that you were doubly humbled, both by your responsibility with me to chart the eclipse here for his majesty, but now as well by your newfound status. I expressed your hope that we might get to the bottom of the disappearances before we have to leave."

"Ask him what the constable sitting there is for. Why is he not the avenger of the lost?"

A moment's discussion.

"He said that of course Mahmud will accompany us to the temple area or anywhere else we are needed. After all, he is the civil authority of the Pasha for this region."

Le Bouveret sighed in resignation. "Why, pray tell, are you going along with all this, volunteering me and getting our arses in some kind of neck-or-nothing battle with imaginary giant man-eating goats?"

"Because there is no such thing as a man-eating goat. It's probably just a wolf—"

"But you said it wasn't!"

"—that we can kill or shoo off. Then make our observations. Then move on to Sjelik without losing our pensions or our heads. We are in this together, so be a good chap and let him bless your sword like he just asked."

Le Bouveret looked into the eyes of the priest, who smiled warmly at him, nodding approvingly. To the priest's left, Mahmud's stony stare. Le Bouveret sighed, stood up and bowed deeply, then picked up the sword and, keeping his head down, offered it to the Holy Father.

The priest bowed slightly and took the sword, then rose and led them into the sanctuary.

As if on cue, the normally overcast midday sky had gathered enough sun to illuminate the domed sanctuary through the stained-glass oculus in the center of the dome, a shaft of colored light beaming to one side—no doubt by the intention of the builders—to a stone chair inset into the wall. Le Bouveret saw the figure of a bearded man in the center of the oculus, holding a cross. Must be the good Saint Anthony himself.

They gathered before the altar. Le Bouveret, Heathwight and Mahmud on one side of the altar, the old priest on the other. The priest drew the sword and laid it on the altar stone, which was draped with a purple velvet cloth. He bent down beneath the stone, and remained down for some time, moving as if rummaging through something. He hefted up a large, ornate, bronze cylinder, about a foot high and less than a foot across. It had figures worked on it in a Byzantine—no—Persian fashion. Warring men, with curved swords fighting demons of the air and ground. Their swords were devised as if they had flames rising up from them.

Mahmud looked surprised. He then launched into an animated discussion in Serbian with the priest, and the priest moved his hands in a way that seemed placating.

"It's some kind of relic from Suleyman," Heathwight told him off-handedly. "Mahmud questions whether it should be used now, by us."

"And the father thinks yes?"

"It appears. He says if it is the goat, then the only thing that may work would be either your sword or the relic, or maybe both."

"What is the thing?"

"Holy fire, or some such."

Le Bouveret looked intently at the object, trying to find something to understand, something that made sense. The fine-filigreed writing on it remained indecipherable. It had fanciful figures on it. A fish that spit flame. A lion belching fire on enemies. Birds that appeared to be on fire, flying at hapless swordsmen that appeared not unlike old Crusading knights. Le Bouveret plainly could see a shield with a cross, the man bearing it bathed in flames from the lion. Something about the lion stirred in Le Bouveret's mind. Le Bouveret reached for it, hesitated until the priest motioned his acceptance, then picked up and examined the object. It was middling heavy, several pounds, and appeared to be sealed with lead. It was cylindrical, tapered on one end like a missile, but flat on the bottom. He sat it back down on the stone altar.

The constable erupted in protests again, but they diminished and died with stony silence from the priest. The priest then incanted in a sort of church Greek that Le Bouveret could follow. The priest gestured, pleaded, engendering the help of the Almighty, his Son, Mother Mary, the Archangel Michael, and St. Anthony to use their fire against the scourge, as well as aid the wizard (Le Bouveret gathered it must be him) in defeating the dark minion.

Afterward, they left the church and stood on the front steps, Le Bouveret gazing out onto the town square with its verdigris, cracked siege engine, the small shops crowding the streets on all sides. They left the artifact with the priest until they could determine some kind of use for it. Le Bouveret buckled the sword about his waist.

"I wish us to have understanding," said the constable. He had an edge in his voice.

"Oh," Le Bouveret said, not knowing quite what to say next. He cast a gaze in the direction of Heathwight, who seemed to be studying the inscriptions on the pillars, obviously trying to ignore the conversation.

"Let us be direct with one another. I am a follower of God, and Muhammad is his Prophet. I do not follow the beliefs of Father Kolack, but I swear by my faith I will stand by him and I will die for him and this village. He is my friend. Don't insult him or these people."

"Well—my apologies," Le Bouveret stammered. "My own feelings are that I am hardly a wizard. I am a poet. A broke one."

"We all have debts. Some not as obvious," the constable answered. "As the book says, you must render unto Caesar, but also unto God."

"Ah. Well, then you heard my thoughts on God."

"Your blasphemy does not release you THAT debt, either. You carry the sword of Anthony, whatever that may be. Shall we go?" He walked down the steps.

Le Bouveret turned to Heathwight. The astronomer looked up from the inscriptions. "I think this is some kind of Sanskrit. What a pity I can't read it. But this"—he indicated a curled symbol—"is an Arabic notation for Aldebaran."

Le Bouveret nodded. At least that much he'd learned working for nearly a year cataloging stars. "What does it say about Aldebaran?"

"That's the part I can't read."

"Wonderful. Well, perhaps we can take some charcoal rubbings when this whole thing is over."

"I can't help but imagine that this might have something to do with our plight," Heathwight ventured.

"Why?"

"Didn't they say these pillars were taken from the old pagan temple?"

They agreed the speculation might prove itself when they viewed the ruins. They left the steps and repaired to the inn. In a short time Mahmud had a wagon waiting for them. As they drove out the town gates, Le Bouveret noticed a goat being tied to the stake outside the town's walls. The two men were tying the goat at the same stake where the last one had been killed, which Le Bouveret had seen.

"Why do they do that?" he said as the rumbled by on the cart.

"It's an old custom, a legend," Mahmud answered. "Having a goat tied outside the walls would keep the thing from taking a person instead."

"Don't they go through a lot of goats that way?"

"Did you hear me? I said it was a legend. At least it used to be until now. They'll try it until they have no goats."

"What else do the 'legends' say?" Le Bouveret asked, emphasizing the word as had Mahmud.

Mahmud glowered. "Just that it attacks at night. And, if you see someone whom the creature has taken, then you will be taken too. Or one hopes."

"What if the person was just gone a while to the next village?"

"You are to look behind them," Mahmud said, his voice flat, as if to signal he was tired of Le Bouveret's manner. "If they have no backside, then they are souls captured by the darkness."

"Hmm. Again, showing one's backside is the prudent measure," Le Bouveret quipped.

Mahmud rolled his eyes, turned from him, and began talking with

Heathwight about stars. Le Bouveret watched the horses plodding the old Roman road, weighing his thoughts, daydreaming about lions spewing forth fire. Hadn't Suleyman been a "lion" in battle? But so had Richard. And on.

The cobbled road branched off from the main one to a smaller, older one that went up the side of the foothill in a series of switchbacks. The forest grew taller and darker, the undergrowth thicker. Soon a line of crags became visible, jutting out of the thick forest. When the road ended at a flattened area of the hillside, Mahmud stopped the cart and they climbed out, the Turk tying the skittish team to a tree. Interestingly, Le Bouveret noticed he took up a lantern in his left hand, lit. He laid his musket across his shoulders and they walked a short trek through the forest until it opened into a sunny vale. Covering the clearing were large, flat stones, greenery growing between cracks, forming a circle that appeared as large as the town square. Beyond, a gray bluff showed through the gnarled trees bordering the clearing to the east.

"Here is the place," Mahmud said simply.

"You say the pagans worshipped here?"

"One might call it that," Mahmud said. "Look close. See the stains?" He indicated the stones.

Le Bouveret and Heathwight strode slowly onto the slabs, noting the elaborate carvings that covered them. Visible in the center were irregular swaths of brownish discoloration. He might not have noticed it, or thought it just something in the rock, had he not seen the bloodstained steps of Damascus dating to the Crusades, or even the overgrown steps of the ruined Pergamom in the war-torn regions to the south.

"Sacrifices?"

"Or something worse," said Mahmud. "We have heard stories of children born as their mothers died bloody deaths. Of course, these might be just tales."

"Except for that thing."

"Silence," Mahmud cautioned. "Speak not of it here."

Le Bouveret shrugged. He walked across the expanse. Shards of broken columns jutted up from the slab in an intricate pattern, one that looked familiar, but he couldn't place it.

"That," Heathwight pointed at a character engraved in the floor, "is the same character as one on the columns at the village church."

"Oh yes," Mahmud said. "Those columns once stood here."

"Ah, thus I have seen them before. They stand in the same pattern at the church, do they not?"

Mahmud nodded. "Oddly, they stand in the same manner as Moses' tabernacle to God."

"Yet that character is Arabic," Heathwight continued. "It's very similar, in any case, to the notation for the star Alioth."

"Yes, I've noticed that the characters appear to be Arabic. But it's different. Something else about it. I can't read it, just recognize it."

"It would be archaic, then?"

"Perhaps."

Le Bouveret left them in their discussion, and walked over to the edge of the clearing. Something dark beyond. It was a cave opening in the bluff. Le Bouveret thought something flashed within it. He walked quiet through the underbrush, into the trees, toward the opening. It flashed again. A sparkle, like gold. Then he saw her.

The glimpse was quick. Le Bouveret saw her tanned, smiling face, framed with dark hair that blended into the darkness of the cave itself. Something sparked on her forehead and a diamond stud glittered from her nostril. Her strange, brown eyes, flecked with gold, met his and her sanguine lips parted with words that seemed to sound in Le Bouveret's head. She spoke softly, soothingly, and a slender, braceleted hand beckoned to him gracefully. Her voice lilted with a soft, soothing tremor, whispering like water through rushes.

"Never," she said. "Never have I seen one like you."

Where had he seen this woman?

He slowly parted the bushes and walked on toward the cave, never taking his eyes from the elegant, rippling figure.

"My kiss is your dream," she said. "Maker of words can have far more than words can make."

He stood just before her now. She looked dolefully at his hand resting on the sword, and he instinctively removed his hand from it. Her smile brightened once again. She opened her mouth and leaned forward to say something more. Le Bouveret felt himself tremble in anticipation.

Thunder sounded loudly behind him and the passing musket ball cracked the air next to Le Bouveret's ear, causing him to involuntarily cover it with his left hand. He doubled over at the pain and ringing sensation. A shot! His hand went to his sword.

When he rose back up, the woman's face had changed.

A new hole appeared next to the caste mark on her forehead, a brownish liquid spurting from it. Her forehead bulged outward, eyes bugging in opposite directions. A greenish tendril shot from her open mouth.

The sword sang from its scabbard, Le Bouveret whipping it into a parry, as if the tendril were a blade. The upward slice of the light, stiff, filigreed point met resistance Le Bouveret could feel in the pommel. He stepped back into a proper defensive stand.

The woman melted like a wax statue, her face a twisted mass. More tendrils shot out from her shoulders, her waist, and her arms. Her long, ochre sarong parted indelicately as another shot out from her knees.

Le Bouveret parried each whip like tip. He heard the voices of Mahmud and Heathwight far away, shouting as if from a high hilltop behind him. He dared not turn. Instead, he parried, stepped back, parried again, stepped back. But he knew he couldn't keep it up for long.

"None like you," came the voice again. But the face was a ruin of strange flesh. Suddenly another voice sounded behind him.

"I said aside, you fool!"

Someone shoved hard on his shoulder, knocking him sideways. Something flew past, shining, and smashed against the writhing thing that had been the strange woman. Le Bouveret saw it had been their lantern. A burst of fire caused Le Bouveret to hold his left hand up, shielding his face as he fell back from the conflagration.

"Up now, and run for your soul!" said Mahmud's voice next to him.

Le Bouveret got up, turned and ran up the trail, aware that Mahmud followed close behind. Through the trees he saw Heathwight standing, pale, mouth open.

"On the cart. For our lives!" yelled Mahmud again. They dashed up the stony path to the road. As they piled onto the cart, Heathwight grabbed the reins and slapped them against the ponies. But they were still tied. Le Bouveret jumped down, slashed the tie-outs with his rapier, then heaved back into the cart.

The ponies leapt into a dangerous gallop down the unkempt road. From the back of the cart Le Bouveret saw other figures coming out of the forest, dark, murky, unable to quite make them out. And one that shined with flame. A host of screams followed them from the glen as reached the main road.

"God in Heaven!" Le Bouveret exclaimed as they sped along the main road.

"Finally, he swears with something that might help," Mahmud said angrily. He loaded the musket in the back of the lurching wagon, holding the powder keg to the bell barrel, tamping the powder in desperately with the musket's long wooden rod. "Not that even God will help us now."

"What was it?"

"You have seen the woman of Rama. They say those who built the temple sacrificed her centuries ago to the thing. She only shows herself to those about to die. We have all seen her, so we will all die."

"Devil you say. That was no woman!"

"It was the Devil, as you say," Mahmud shot back, angry at Le Bouveret's renewed cursing.

"What was it? What happened?"

"It is the goat of the woods. When one sees those now dead, and they beckon, the goat has chosen they who are called. It will come for you, for us."

"What stops it?"

"Stopped? Nothing has ever stopped it."

"But my sword stopped it."

"Child's play."

"But the fire!"

"The fire slowed it. And angered it."

"Something stops it. Surely something."

"Only Suleyman ever stopped it."

The cart rattled over a particularly rocky section of the road, drowning out their conversation. Eventually the road smoothed again. Le Bouveret continued.

"With what did Suleyman stop it?"

"With fire from God, fool. I doubt he will favor you with it."

Fire from God. Le Bouveret smiled. He told Mahmud his plan.

* * *

The wagon clattered to a stop inside the gates. Le Bouveret bounded out of the back, standing as Mahmud and Heathwight stepped down from the wagon.

"We have no choice, you see?" Le Bouveret said.

Mahmud glared at him, at the peasants gathered around the in the square, at the sky darkened with approaching evening. Then they walked briskly across the square, Mahmud glancing only slightly at the moldering, verdigris-covered siege cannon on the village green. He shook his head.

"The Holy Father must agree to this."

"This is what Suleyman meant!" insisted Le Bouveret.

"So you say."

In the sanctuary, the bearded priest stood with the fading light behind him facing the two men with a wizened look. Mahmud spoke to him in quiet, earnest conversation, broken only by occasional questions from the priest. Once, the priest frowned and asked Heathwight something, Heathwight responded. Mahmud seemed to contradict him. All the speaking was Serbian, completely unintelligible to Le Bouveret.

Finally, the priest, with tears in his eyes, picked up the holy relic held it close, put his forehead on it, letting his tears fall onto the raised bronze battle scenes on it, then kissed it. He handed it to Le Bouveret, the weight of it heavier than he'd remembered.

He looked down at the artifact, at the lion breathing fire onto the Crusader. Le Bouveret hoped the canister was what he thought it was. He turned to Mahmud.

"Would you fetch that powder keg? And do you have something we can use for a tamping rod?"

* * *

It was as Le Bouveret expected; the conical canister, wrapped in a cotton cloth, fit closely down the barrel. But getting the huge siege engine to where it pointed toward the gate was an excruciating exercise. It took two oxen and ten of the village men to drag the heavy sledge bearing the cannon. They were unable to get the cannon very close to the point of aim. A ledge from which the village square was raised proved to be unworkable to drag the huge gun across. Instead they pushed and hauled until it had clear aim at the portals—but farther than anyone would have liked.

"Now we tie the goat out to the stake just within the doors," Le Bouveret said. "And we wait."

Mahmud shrugged. "The goat will tempt it but little."

"Why do you say that?" Heathwight asked.

Mahmud looked Le Bouveret in the eyes. "It will come again with the darkness," he said. "It will appear as the woman again—because it has chosen you."

"Very well. We'll touch off the bombard before it gets far through the gates."

"And risk losing our one shot?"

"What you would have us do?" shouted Le Bouveret in exasperation.

"I wish we had better bait than a goat," Mahmud said. "Our one chance may be not enough."

Darkness fell with disquiet by the time the priest finished blessing them. Neither Le Bouveret nor Mahmud took the offered communion.

"It's not proper, refusing the wine and wafer," Heathwight told him. "A man of noble birth such as yourself."

"My conscience is clear," Le Bouveret said.

"Because you don't have one?" Heathwight asked.

"We're saving this village, are we not?"

Before the other could answer, the call came down again on the wind.

Again, it was a high-pitched cry that fell into a sob like that of a woman crying for her child.

It's her, Le Bouveret thought. He felt it deep inside. She cries for me. He loosed his sword in its scabbard and cocked the pistol where it hung in his belt.

Le Bouveret saw the hapless goat suddenly disappear. Something dark enfolded it in the growing twilight. In the flicker of a moment, the bleating goat silenced, even as something dark slid around its midsection and pulled it out of torchlight. So quick was its disappearance that the leash upon which the poor creature was tied shot back out toward the square.

Le Bouveret took one stepped toward the gate.

"Hold ground," barked Mahmud. "This is not yet the time."

"Do you hear her?" Le Bouveret asked. "She's out there."

"It is the creature," Mahmud barked back. "Hold, I say."

They stood. The strange cry, rising and falling, its warble echoing through the village.

Suddenly, two goats hobbled into the circle of light just inside the gate. A man, wearing the rough felt jacket of the peasant goatherd, staggered strangely behind them, shooing them on, his staff in hand.

His eyes were red-rimmed as if from drinking or crying. They searched the town like those of a man looking for a lost love. He croaked something, like a name, shuffling with the two goats in front of him. But something dark and large shadowed him behind. The creature?

"Josef!" screamed a voice from behind them. An outcry of unintelligible grief followed it. Le Bouveret turned to see an old peasant woman run hobbling past them, her arms outstretched to the man.

The man looked up and smiled. He seemed to recognize her. He spoke something in Serbian Le Bouveret could not understand. It sounded soothing and loving. And yet, Le Bouveret saw the dark, treelike shape seethe and boil behind him.

Mahmud shouted for her to stop. She ran on, unheeding, calling for her Josef.

Le Bouveret shook himself from the trance that seemed to grip him. He drew his pistol and ran after her.

"No, Hansa!" Shouted Mahmud.

Le Bouveret grabbed for the old woman's back, but came back with her homespun shawl in his hand. He stopped a dozen feet from her as she fell into the man's waiting arms. Tenderly, lovingly, the old man embraced her, his arms circling her back and pulling her to him. She wept as she repeated his name again and again, "Josef, Josef."

Then from behind the man, boiling darkness uncoiled. Dark tendrils licked out and swiftly surrounded the couple, then lashed down. The woman shrieked as the man before her turned into a spongy dark mass, and her cry was cut off.

Le Bouveret fired his pistol into the mass, only vaguely aware of the shouts of Mahmud and Heathwight behind him. The shot seemed to have no effect— like shooting into a muddy river. He threw the spent match-pistol aside and drew the shining blade he'd purchased in Spain. He stretched it before him and stood en guard, waiting for what he knew would be next.

And he saw her. She of the gold-flecked eyes and dark, flowing hair. Her saffron dress flowed and shimmered as if her body glowed with a light of its own. Her eyes locked on his and her sanguine lips parted with the all-encompassing, all-promising whisper.

None like you. Come to me, maker of words.

Le Bouveret saw the tip of his sword quiver, the point dancing with little starts. He wanted to go to her. Wanted to have her as his. Her voice soothed him.

She stepped closer, swaying so sweetly, as if some beat from her native lands moved her, drawing slightly closer. Le Bouveret shook the desire from his resolve, like rain from a branch.

She slipped closer.

Le Bouveret stamped his foot forward and fell into a lunge. He drove the blade deep into her throat, at least a foot, and drew it quickly out.

No sooner had he when a dark, whip like tendril shot out from the wound and grazed his cheek. He started back, touching his face and drawing back blood. Then it seemed like hundreds were slashing for him, humming in the air with the intensity of their movement.

Le Bouveret fell back, dodging and parrying, even as they lashed him with burning kisses. The woman seemed oblivious of his attack, appearing unaware of the brownish fluid spurting from her neck.

He fell back farther. Bits of fabric ripped from his right sleeve as the dark whips bit and tore at his sword hand.

Suddenly he heard a cry from behind.

"FIRE!"

They were touching off the cannon! He threw himself to his right, rolling across the hard cobblestones as the dark whips thrashed at him like brambles, tearing away streaks of his clothing and leaving red furrows in his skin.

With a roar the world erupted into smoke and flame. The flash of light dazzled Le Bouveret's sight and heat washed over his upturned face. He put his left hand up to shield himself and something hot touched his left cheek. He rolled away farther, trying desperately to wipe the burning substance from his face.

A terrifying, warbling cry suddenly split the air. The death shriek of the thing burst forth so loudly that Le Bouveret's hearing fell numb with shock.

Then it was gone, replaced by a great rushing sound. Le Bouveret drew himself up from the pavement, sword still in hand. A great, burning, writhing tree of flame, as tall as ten men, assaulted his vision. It weaved and danced, as had the woman, liquid flame dripping from it like molten gold. A stench of burning offal wrenched his sense of smell. Le Bouveret staggered back from the scene like a holy man before the face of God. His mind swam. He fell back, even as the arms of his comrades caught him before he hit the pavement again. A dark comfort enfolded him.

* * *

Le Bouveret awoke with the smell of tea. Something warm gripped his hand. He saw the smiling, white-bearded face of the priest staring into his. His eyes were wrinkled with kindness and warmth. He said something then stood up, made a sign and stepped away from the bed. Le Bouveret saw Heathwight and Mahmud standing behind him, smiling. Heathwight held a steaming cup of tea. He stepped forward.

"They said you were coming to, so I had them make this."

Le Bouveret sat up shakily in bed, and took the cup of tea. He saw his sword hanging from the foot piece of the bed, his oversize black boots on the floor next to it.

He stared hard at Mahmud as he sipped the tea. He felt a burning sensation on his cheek, reached up and touched it. He started with a sudden lance of pain from it. His fingertip came away oily.

"Don't," said Mahmud. "You were touched by the fire."

Le Bouveret nodded, glancing past Mahmud at the open window from which streamed sunlight.

"The creature?" he asked.

"Ashes." Mahmud answered. "You were right. The holy vessel was filled with fire. It consumed the monster." His gaze cast down for a moment. "How did you know?" he asked.

"Obvious, once you consider the context," Le Bouveret said. "Your Turkish ancestors learned a bitter lesson at the hands of the Byzantines in the battles for Constantinople. Then, it appears Suleyman himself must have gotten the formula, at least for a bit. Did you see the devices on the object? The Crusaders bathed in flames?"

"Greek Fire," Heathwight said in realization.

"Yes," Le Bouveret answered. "Great fellows those Greeks." He tipped his teacup to Mahmud. "To them. And to Suleyman, peace be upon his name," he said, adding the proper honorific for Mahmud's sake.

Mahmud said nothing but managed a smile.

BEN FENWICK *is a reporter and editor who has written for* Reuters, The New York Times, Reason Magazine, *and* Playboy. *In 2017, he appeared in "Oklahoma City" , an American Experience documentary for PBS about the Oklahoma City bombing, a Sundance Film Festival selection. However, his passion is fantasy fiction. He has written three fantasy novels under a pseudonym. This story was his first appearance in* Heroic Fantasy Quarterly.

The Tomb Robber's Tale
by Sean P. Robson

T he funeral procession wound like a wailing snake through Mourner's Row, out the Death Gate, and around the sepulchral neighborhoods of the necropolis to the grand mausoleum of House Torenescu. As the priests—one each to represent the gods Thanatos, Mithra, and Heka—began the rites of lamentation, two mourners detached themselves from the snake's tail and slithered out of sight behind neighboring tombs.

Tariq pulled off his robe of bereavement and tossed it aside, unslung the satchel of tools that was hidden beneath, then pulled out a flask and took a long swallow before handing it to his nephew. "We've got a long wait ahead of us, lad." He sat down on his discarded robe, leaned back against the tomb wall and stretched his legs out. "Might as well get comfortable, eh?"

Faysal raised the flask to his lips, eyes bright with excitement, and took a long swallow. This was his first foray into the necropolis and he was eager to begin his apprenticeship in earnest. He surveyed the avenues of tombs, which sprawled over the hills and through the mist-shrouded valleys, punctuated by towering moss-covered cenotaphs.

"Quite a view, isn't it," said Tariq. "Nearly as big as Catapesh, itself, but with a hundred times more residents. You want to keep your head about you in here; it's easy to get turned around. You get lost, either the barrow wardens will get you or a gastlich will."

"What's a gast lick?" Faysal asked. He sneered, but his bravado was betrayed by the tremor in his voice.

"It's gastlich, you ignorant little trouser-stain; a spirit of the dead. Six-toed

Tirsh reckoned he saw one once. Got himself all turned around after a job and saw something rise up right out of the mist, all pale and gaunt and grasping. He ran shrieking and gibbering straight to the wardens with his swag-sack still in hand, the silly bugger. They sent him up for grave-robbing and he was glad to go, even though they hanged him in the end. Anyway, they say this here's their city we're intruding in, and anyone not under the protection of the priests, like that lot," he gestured in the direction of the funeral party, "is fair prey for the gastlichs."

Faysal looked around nervously and then took another long swallow from the flask. "Here now!" said Tariq, grabbing it away from him, "That's got to last us all afternoon, you greedy little nose rag."

"Have you ever seen one? A gastlich, I mean."

"Not even a wisp," said Tariq with a twinkle in his eye, "and I've been cracking tombs for going on ten years."

When the day began to wither with age and tenebrous shadows reached from the tombs like cold, beckoning fingers, Tariq peeked around the corner of the shelter and checked that the mourners were all gone and the neighborhood was deserted. He pocketed the nearly empty flask, shouldered his satchel then rolled up the robe and stuffed it down the front of his shirt. "We'd best be about our business."

Faysal hurried after Tariq and tried to imitate the sense of purpose in his uncle's stride as they wove their way along the avenues lined with the houses of the dead. Every now and again, Tariq would pause and examine a brass plaque above an entrance, and then quickly move on. He was obviously looking for a specific tomb.

"We should just hit that Toronescu place," said Faysal. "Everyone's gone now. Rich family like them's bound to have left a fortune in grave-goods."

Tariq shot a scornful glance over his shoulder. "Rich family like them's also bound to have the barrow wardens keeping a close eye on the place, is bound to have trapped the tomb to do for the likes of us, and is bound to find out if anyone tries fencing their family jewels so soon after the funeral. You some kind of idiot? This is no business for idiots. They hang idiots."

Faysal's face reddened. "It was just a suggestion," he muttered. "I was only trying to help."

"You reckon I brought you along for advice? You're here to learn the trade, not teach it so keep your mouth shut and your eyes open; this is serious business not an evening stroll along the fucking quay."

Faysal muttered something under his breath that Tariq didn't catch, but he let it pass. He'd never much cared for Faysal, but he had loved the boy's mother dearly. Tariq had been only ten years old when their parents died; Farah, just three years older than he, supported them both by selling herself on street corners to anyone with a few coins or some food to trade. By the time Tariq was old enough to make his own way Farah was worn-out and vacant-eyed. When Faysal came along, the by-blow of some back-alley paramour, she supported him the same way she had Tariq, and when she died of the pox Tariq swore to look after her boy, half-wit bastard or no.

"You see that mark scratched on the tomb over yonder?" said Tariq in a gentler tone. "Looks like a pair of horns? That means the tomb's cleaned out. It's professional courtesy to make the mark after you've done a job and let others know not to waste their time."

They wound their way deeper into the necropolis, and Faysal gaped at statues of strange alien gods, abandoned and long forgotten. "What's that," he asked, pointing at the likeness in granite of a three-eyed, elephant-headed man.

Tariq shrugged. Catapesh had been conquered more times over the centuries than he could count: ten, at least; probably more. Each invasion washed over the city like a surging tide and then receded, leaving murky puddles of culture in its wake. Bloodlines had become so mingled that it was no longer possible to tell who came from where. Even the noble houses had become so polluted that only their names hinted at their origin.

"Don't know," he said. "Maybe nobody does anymore. Everyone who ever conquered the city brought their gods with them. Some stuck, but most of them fell by the wayside, like this fellow here. Don't reckon a god that's so easily tossed aside is much of a god. Course, the priests say our gods are the true ones, but I reckon someday, some tomb-cracker will look at a statue of Heka and ask the same question you did. What do you think?"

Faysal shrugged and scratched the scraggly hairs on his chin. He turned to the elephant-headed effigy and asked it to watch over them in their endeavors.

"Here, now!" said Tariq. "Don't go praying to strange gods; they might be long dead, but then again they might only be sleeping."

"I thought we ought to show respect to the elephant god if this is its ground, and to call upon its blessing; my mother said to always take your blessings where you could," said Faysal.

"Your mother died raving mad of syphilis; you might not want take her every word to heart. Best not risk waking things better left aslumber; not here in the necropolis. Save your prayers for your own gods and let the forgotten ones lie."

Twilight was encroaching upon the city of the dead when Tariq finally led them to his goal: a long-neglected tomb concealed by overgrown brambles in a mist-shrouded gully. Its weathered granite walls were encrusted with lichen and overgrown with moss. A heavy bronze door stained with verdigris hung ajar on twisted hinges and was held fast by rusted iron chains. The plaque above the door bore the sigil of the noble house of Younes, whose last scion was laid to rest decades ago after the Overlord's conquest of Catapesh, leaving none to maintain the vault or to safeguard its contents.

"Pick your targets carefully, lad. This is a big place and there's plenty of choice to be had. The charnel pits near the gates ain't worth the effort; that's where they toss the convicts, slaves, and the indigent—anyone too poor to pay the priests for a proper interment—with neither grave-goods to bribe their way into Thanatos's realm, nor prayers to guide them there. Fresh-laid nobles are tempting, but risky. No, it's best to go deep—into the older avenues of the necropolis; there's hundreds, probably thousands of years worth of noblemen resting in these grounds, from lines gone extinct with no one left who'll recognize family heirlooms turning up in the bazaar. These are the ones to go for if you don't want to wind up doing a noose-dance in the plaza like old Tirsh."

Tariq unrolled an oilcloth satchel containing a dozen curiously shaped iron picks, of which he broke three while attempting to open the weathered padlock. "Bloody rust," he muttered, half to himself. "Someone should keep these tombs in better repair. No respect. No respect at all."

The lock finally yielded to his deft touch and sprang open with a loud click. "Aha!" Tariq exclaimed in triumph. He removed the chains and pulled open the door, which squealed in protest. "Now open wide, my darling, and surrender your treasure to us." He turned to Faysal and winked: "Tombs, like women, demand a soft touch; if you're clumsy and impatient you'll never get in."

Tariq lit a torch and handed it to Faysal, then led him down a short flight of stone steps into the cellar-like crypt. The stale air was thick with the sickly-sweet stench of spice and decay. Faysal gagged, then clapped a hand over his mouth and bolted back up the stairs; he returned shortly, pale and with a handkerchief covering his nose and mouth.

Tariq rolled his eyes and made an exaggerated bow. "Did you forget your pomander, your Grace?"

"It stinks," said Faysal. Tariq laughed.

"This is nothing, lad. The youngest of these corpses was laid decades ago and the embalming spices mask the worst of the stink. Wait till you smell a corpse-fart: when a belly, swollen with gasses of putrescence, bursts in your face. Happened to me once, and splattered me with rotting foulness I don't even want to think about."

Faysal paled even more. "How do you stand it?"

"By keeping my mind on the job and thinking about how I'll spend the swag. Speaking of which," Tariq gestured with a sweep of his hand to the burial alcoves that lined the walls.

They lit a few more torches and placed them in wall sconces and then set to their work, liberating the noble house of Younes of its assorted charnel goods. From the occupant of each coffin, whose name was engraved upon a brass plaque, they took their bounty: from Lord Omar's withered finger, a gold signet ring; from Lady Danira's shroud, a silver brooch; from young master

Kaelan's stiff-clutched grasp, an intricately carved ivory soldier; from mistress Sibilia's withered brow a gilded coronet. Then, from between the legs of Lady Shahira, Tariq plucked a jade phallus with silver filigree and emeralds set around its base.

"Now we know where they kept the family jewels," he said with a wink, thrusting the phallus back and forth between a circle formed by his thumb and forefinger. Faysal blushed.

"Never had a woman before?" Tariq said. Faysal shook his head, his face reddening even further.

"Well, we'll have to remedy that. With a bath and some new clothes they might even let us into Orchid's Blossoms, and with what we get from this haul we could even afford it. Orchid's prices are dear, but so are her girls. She buys them from all over the world: dusky-skinned beauties from the Jungles of Zahar, sultry and well-versed in the arts of love; alabaster-skinned wenches from the northern marches who know every way ever devised to keep a man warm at night; tribeswomen from the Kurgani Steppes, as wild and passionate as the four winds. What do you say lad, how'd you like to be savaged by a she-panther? It's like I said, keep your mind on the job and what awaits you at the end of it, and pay no heed to the unsavory aspects of the work."

Faysal returned to his work with renewed alacrity, jasmine-scented slave-girls dancing in his mind. He ventured deeper into the crypt and espied the family altar, laden with canopic jars and a golden effigy of Thanatos as its centerpiece. Entranced by the golden idol, Faysal reached out his hand to take it.

"Don't touch that!" Tariq yelled; such obvious treasures were often trapped. Too late: Faysal had already picked it up. A sound of stone grinding against stone was the only warning Tariq had. He hurled himself across the crypt and into Faysal, knocking him arse over tit. Faysal's furious protest was cut short as a massive stone block fell from the ceiling and landed where he had been standing half a second earlier.

Tariq threw himself to the ground and covered his head against debris raining down from the ceiling. When it finally stopped, he looked around, coughing in the cloud of dust, and saw that the block had crashed through the floor of the crypt leaving a ragged hole like a gaping maw. He crawled to its edge and peered over the side; cold stale air wafted up from the darkness.

Tariq took one of the torches from the wall, tossed it into the pit and reached a slow count of two before it hit the ground below; a large chamber was briefly illuminated before the torch extinguished on impact.

"Sixty feet, more or less," said Tariq. He looked at Faysal who was climbing to his feet, still shaken by his brush with death, and continued: "For as long as I've worked the necropolis I've heard tales of the ruins of Golgotha—the place of suffering—buried deep beneath; older, much older, than even Catapesh and said to contain a trove of Atlantean wealth. I've never paid the stories any heed—old tomb-robber legends were what I took them for. But now—" He broke off and licked his lips.

"An Atlantean city?" whispered Faysal, his eyes wide. "I heard that Atlanteans were sorcerers, dark and terrible; that they bound the spirits of the dead and even demons to their will."

"Aye, they were terrible, and at the height of their power they ruled the world; all nations paid tribute to them—incalculable wealth, and when they were driven from our shores they left it all behind." Tariq ran his fingers though his hair. "There is a time for caution," he glanced again at the pit in the floor, "and there is a time for boldness."

"Let's just go now," whispered Faysal. "Let's take what we have and visit Orchid's Blossoms, like you said."

"Forget Orchid's," said Tariq. "If what lies below is, indeed, the storied Atlantean ruins we'll score enough swag for you to buy your own harem. We'll, neither of us, need to work ever again; we'll spend the rest of our days at ease, sipping fine wine and eating fresh dates from the hands of naked slave girls."

Faysal hesitated a moment, savoring the vision, then nodded and joined his uncle at the edge of the pit. They tied together their two coils of fine silk rope then secured one end around the Younes family altar, and the other around a burning torch, which they lowered carefully to the ground far below. Then, Tariq leading, they descended the rope, hand over hand into the ruins of a dead city that lay beneath the city of the dead.

* * *

Tariq retrieved the burning torch that was tied to the rope and used it to relight the one he had earlier dropped, and then handed one to Faysal. The dim torchlight barely illuminated the full expanse of a huge karst cavern shaped by uncanny artifice into a large courtyard. The perimeter of the courtyard was surrounded by a series of seven-foot-tall alabaster statues depicting a human-like race with broad high foreheads, long pendulous ear lobes, and slack flaccid lips that drooped from their wide mouths.

Faysal gaped at the statues, inadvertently mimicking their vacant expressions. "Are these Atlanteans?" he whispered. Tariq shrugged. He'd never seen one. The sinister black barges of Atlantis would sometimes make berth in the harbor of Catapesh, but all commerce was conducted by their human slaves; Atlanteans, if any were aboard, never came ashore. So far as he knew, none had set foot on Lemurian soil since mankind rose up against them centuries ago and threw off the yoke of servitude.

From the courtyard, numerous passageways extended like spokes from a hub into the depths of Golgotha. Tariq chose one at random and they proceeded slowly, exploring its avenues and branches, searching for some chamber—a temple, perhaps—in which treasures of the ancient race might repose. The pair marveled at the ancient architecture, for the buildings that lined the subterranean avenues were not merely built from shaped rock, they were carved into the limestone, blending seamlessly into the walls. The skill and effort required to build such a city was beyond Tariq's imagining.

In a dining hall they found a long table set for banquet. Silver cutlery, golden goblets and crystal decanters lay lonely and abandoned, awaiting a dinner millennia overdue. The stone walls of the hall were adorned only by empty gilt frames; the paintings they contained had long since crumbled to dust. Faysal rushed eagerly to the table and began sweeping cutlery into his bag.

"Ease up, lad," said Tariq. "Don't overload your bag with tableware; remember, we can only carry so much, and I've a feeling there are more valuable troves than this to be found."

As they penetrated deeper into Golgotha, Faysal became increasingly nervous, jumping at shadows and at the echoes of every dislodged stone that tumbled from ruined walls and ceilings. The boy was high-strung and foolish and, Tariq suspected, unsuited to a career in tomb-robbing, but even he, himself, was feeling ill at ease. Tariq was as comfortable in abandoned crypts and sepulchers as he was sitting by the fire drinking cold ale at The Slippery Vixen. He was not prone to flights of fancy or excesses of imagination, but he thought he caught glimpses of movement in the shadows, and heard sibilant whispers in the tomb-dark alleyways and buildings. He knew they must be his imagination, or else stirrings of the long stagnant air from some opening to the surface. Nonetheless, he had the distinct feeling that they were being watched; and followed.

They entered a vast, colonnaded plaza fronting a jade ziggurat with a gold-domed chamber at its apex. It towered high above all the other buildings and monuments in the city, dominating them with its eminence and grandeur.

"This is it, lad," said Tariq. "I can feel it in my gut; here's where we make our score!" They paused a moment to gaze in awe at the structure looming over them. Unlike the ruins crumbling in the rest of the city, the ziggurat was undiminished by the ages; its cyclopean blocks of jade were unworn and untouched by moss and lichen and it stood sovereign as it had for time immemorial, its magnificence uncontested.

"What is this place," asked Faysal, softly.

"Don't know. Looks like a temple, or maybe a throne room. Just look at it though; if there's swag to be had anywhere in these ruins, it'll be in there. Mark my words."

A long flight of steep steps ushered them to the gilded chamber at the ziggurat's apex. Tariq paused, hands on knees, to catch his breath while Faysal fingered the golden filigree that ornamented the chamber's arched doorway.

"After you," he panted, gesturing for the boy to proceed. Faysal hesitated and scrutinized the entrance. "Shouldn't we, you know, look for traps like you said before?" he said.

"I think we'll be fine; tombs draw thieves like flies to a dung heap so they're bound to be trapped. Wouldn't make sense to lay traps in a place like this, whether a temple or a throne room—too many people coming and going. More likely they would've had guards to discourage anyone with light fingers back when the city still lived. But it's good to know you were paying attention for once." Tariq smiled and clapped his nephew on the back.

They entered and were confronted by a riot of decadent opulence: jade walls carved in bas-relief depicting human figures engaged in activities sadistic and perverse, their faces contorted in agony and ecstasy, were adorned with golden censers and silver-chased sconces, and decorated with murals inlaid with lapis lazuli and ivory. Gem-encrusted golden candelabrums lay scattered on the floor, and nude statuettes carved from ebony and ivory were entwined in contorted positions of coital embrace. At the center of the chamber loomed an idol of jet and bronze: a four-armed, pot-bellied monstrosity squatting naked before an enormous bronze brazier. Its lower two arms gripped the edges of the brazier; its upper two held a massive, barb-edged sword above its head. Its demoniacal, leering face sported a wide toothy maw and two enormous rubies for eyes—each nearly as big in diameter as a man's head. It was this last feature that drew Tariq's particular attention.

As Faysal hastily emptied his bag of assorted cutlery and began refilling it with the treasures from around the room, Tariq climbed the idol, perched on its head and pried out its eyes with a chisel he withdrew from his tool bag. After wrapping the gems carefully in sack-cloth and stowing them safely down the front of his vest he climbed down and beamed at Faysal.

"What did I tell you, lad? We're set for life, you and me. Sometimes the reward is worth the risk."

"Can we go now, Tariq? Please? I don't like this place—I feel like it's watching us."

"That's just nerves, boy," said Tariq, chuckling at his own earlier apprehension. "Nothing ever lived here that is now aught but dust with nary even a memory to give it life. But, yes, it's time to go home. Let's get you a woman. Hells, let's get you a dozen!"

They started back down the ziggurat steps, hauling their heavy treasure-laden sacks behind them.

"How are we going to climb back out with these?" said Faysal.

"That part's easy: we tie the sacks together at the end of the rope and haul them up after us. The hard part will be smuggling it all back into Catapesh. We'll have to cache most of it, then bring it in a little bit at a time. But I've got a few stashes hidden around the necropolis where no one will—"

Tariq stopped short, put his finger to his lips, and looked around the plaza. The sense of being watched was even stronger now than it had been earlier. He thought he heard whispering in the darkness beyond, first to his left, then to his right. Ahead, he heard the soft clatter of stone: litter falling from the crumbling columns?

Quietly, step by step, Tariq advanced towards the edge of the plaza, alert for any sound. A shadow shifted at the edge of his vision: a trick of the torch light? The shadow detached from the darkness ahead, then another, then two more from each side. Whatever was out there had them surrounded.

The dark figures advanced into view, slowly closing the circle around Tariq and Faysal. They were gaunt and long-limbed; their faces, framed by wisps of lank hair, were pallid, with parchment-thin skin stretched taut over their skulls. Their mouths were a rotting ruin of stained, broken teeth, and their milky-white eyes, sunk deep in the sockets, gleamed balefully in the torchlight. They had no noses, just gaping holes in the middle of their faces, and their black, slug-like tongues writhed over thin, withered lips, tasting the air instead. Their dry, sibilant whispering gave way to chuckling that sounded like the crumbling of dead leaves.

When they reached out towards the pair with emaciated long-nailed hands, Faysal's paralysis gave way to a paroxysm of fear. "Gastlichs!" he cried, then dropped his sack and bolted, bursting through the ring of creatures. He fled screaming into the dark—directly away from their path of exit.

Idiot! But the gastlichs—as Tariq guessed they must certainly be—were surprised by Faysal's sudden flight and lunged belatedly after him, opening a gap through which Tariq could escape and flee back the way they had come.

I'm sorry, Farah. Tariq made for the gap in the circle, then stopped, cursed silently, and turned back toward the creatures massing behind him. He swung his loot bag and hurled it into the chest of the nearest gastlich, knocking the gaunt creature off its feet; Tariq leapt over the prone figure, batting aside the grasping hands that clutched at his tunic, and sprinted after his nephew.

The gastlichs were close on his heels; their crumple-rasp laughter crawled down his spine and sent icy tendrils of fear trickling from his gut down into his legs, sapping their strength. He closed tight his mind's eye, which saw only ragged talons clutching at his shirt tails. He focused instead on Faysal's torch, which bobbed, jigged, and weaved in the darkness ahead and, in a feat borne of desperate terror he pulled ahead of the shadows skittering at his flanks and left them behind.

Faysal's bobbing torch suddenly winked out. Tariq strained to catch any glimpse of movement in the darkness ahead. Unbidden, his mind's eye sprang open again: this time it saw Faysal, ambushed and dragged to the ground then torn open by grasping, dirty, sharp-nailed hands, writhing in agony amidst his spilled entrails. Next, it showed a gastlich leaping onto Faysal's back and ripping out his throat with its jagged, broken teeth as the boy silently screamed out his last breath. These, and similar grisly vignettes, played out in Tariq's mind in a matter of seconds, overwhelming the more rational but less compelling explanation that the boy's panicked flight merely took him out of Tariq's line of sight.

Tariq's lungs burned, and his legs were becoming leaden, and although he had left the gastlichs behind he could still hear them following. Soon his pace would flag and fatigue would cause him to stumble, and they'd be on him in seconds. This was a race he could not win. Worse, his torch was beginning to gutter, its flame dying. He thought he might be able to face his end bravely as long as he had light for company, but the prospect of stumbling around lost in the dark, awaiting the grasp of unseen dead-cold hands, nearly unmanned him.

The ruins ahead were more dilapidated than elsewhere, as if he was entering a neighborhood that was long neglected even while Golgotha still lived. Crumbling remains of walls jutted up from the ground like jagged teeth and the ground was littered with debris. The rocky ceiling hung low, and long dangling roots brushed Tariq's head as he ran. Tariq stumbled over a stone block and fell, and as he scrambled to his feet he saw Faysal, cowering in a corner, his torch extinguished. Tariq ran to him, grabbed the boy by his collar and hauled him to his feet.

"Run, you fool," he rasped. "They're right behind us."

Tariq ran, half dragging Faysal sobbing, gibbering, and stumbling behind him towards a narrow gap in a nearby rock fall. He pushed Faysal through the crevice and into an unworked cave beyond then crawled through, himself. It was a tight squeeze; they'd be able to hold off the gastlichs here unless there were other ways in. There'd be time enough to worry about that later, though; in the meantime Tariq crouched at the entrance and watched. In the dim light of his dying torch, he saw the pursuing gastlichs slow and then halt, almost warily, in front of the shelter. They tasted the air with their blackened tongues and then melted back into the shadows.

Damned odd, Tariq thought, why give up now? Unless—

"Faysal! Scout around, look for any other ways in."

"Faysal!" Dammit, where was that idiot boy? Tariq was torn with indecision; he didn't want to leave the crevice unguarded, but if there was one way in there might be more, and the bloody things could be sneaking in to flank them. He peered through the crevice again; still no sign of the gastlichs. Tariq sighed, took one last lingering look through the crevice then went in search of Faysal.

He clambered over fallen debris and through a narrow passage that opened into an even larger cavern. Its niter-encrusted walls and the stalagmites that grew up from the floor scintillated from the faint bioluminescence given off by a fungal efflorescence that carpeted the cavern floor, casting the chamber in an eerie glow.

"Mithra's blessed bosom," said Tariq, blinking hard and trying to adjust his eyes to the dim light. For as far as he could see, fungi of every shape, size, and color sprouted from the ground like some unwholesome subterranean forest overgrown with tendrils and hyphae and gigantic mushrooms with pale white stalks as thick as tree trunks.

Tariq stepped into the cavern and grimaced at the sickening squelch of molds and slimes bursting under his feet as he picked his way between massive stalks of hyphae that sprouted like rushes in a marsh. They swayed toward him as he passed, as if aware that the juice of life was near at hand, and Tariq used his now-dead torch to push them aside so that he wouldn't have to touch them with his hands. He also took care to avoid the crops of huge mushrooms with their lurid red and purple caps, and the abundant clusters of puff-balls that were pregnant with spores and waiting to burst. In the midst of this putrescent bloom was an ancient stone altar, moldy and crumbling. Faysal knelt before it, beseeching its unnamed god for salvation, while a nearby brain fungus twice the height of a grown man pulsed and coruscated red and pink and blue. Filamentous tendrils extended from the enormous rugose mass and entwined about Faysal like a jealous lover.

"Faysal, no!" Tariq dashed forward, slipping and sliding across the slimy floor, heedless of the risk. He grabbed Faysal by the shoulders and hauled him to his feet and away from the altar. There was slight resistance and a soft sucking noise as the fungal filaments parted reluctantly from the boy's flesh. Tariq spun Faysal around and shook him roughly.

"What were you thinking, boy? Gods only know what those Thanatos-damned tendrils would have done to you let alone what you might have awakened with your prayers. What did I tell you about letting sleeping gods lie?"

Faysal smiled beatifically. "Don't worry," he said. "Sapros will watch over us."

Tariq paled slightly. "Faysal," he said, in slow, measured tones, "who is Sapros?"

"You'll soon find out," he said. "Everyone will soon find out." He picked his way through the morass of mushrooms that sprouted up from the mold-carpeted floor towards the far wall of the cavern opposite the entrance, stooping every now and then to pluck a swollen puff-ball from its stalk.

"Don't touch those, they could be dangerous," said Tariq.

"We came down here for treasure, didn't we?" Faysal looked over his shoulder at his uncle and grinned. "We mustn't go home empty-handed."

"Treasure? What are you talking about? What in the seven hells do you want with those things, Faysal?" The boy didn't reply; he just stood fondling the spore-laden balls with a rapturous expression on his face. Tariq wondered if terror had unhinged the boy completely, sapping away what little sense he'd had to start.

Near the back of the cavern a huge, fleshy stalk grew out of a mass of pustulose sacs on the floor and up through the crumbling ceiling far above. Without a word of explanation, Faysal began to climb, using the numerous shelf fungi growing along the length of the trunk for hand and foot holds.

Tariq paused a moment, mouth agape, and watched Faysal ascend the stalk. The fungal growths bent slightly under his weight, but they held. He sighed, then shrugged and followed the boy; at least he was heading in the right direction. He placed his hand upon the stalk and shuddered; it was smooth and soft like a fish's belly, and it pulsed like some huge pallid artery. He repressed his revulsion and started to climb towards the ceiling high above, cringing each time one of the fungal shelves bent as he put his weight on it. He was high enough now that a fall would surely kill or cripple him, and he didn't fancy the idea of lying, dying and helpless upon the fungal carpet below, feeding the greedy, grasping tendrils with his life blood.

Finally, he reached the cavern ceiling and climbed into the darkness above. Though he could see nothing, his nostrils were immediately assailed by an all-too-familiar scent: the stench of decay.

"Faysal?"

"I'm right here," the boy replied calmly.

"Hold up while I get us some light." Tariq fished a candle out of his satchel. He always carried some to test the air quality of old tombs, a habit he was doubly glad of now. Lighting the wick in complete darkness was harder than he expected, and the scrape of steel on flint echoed loud in Tariq's ears, but after a few minutes a spark caught. The small candle was a poor ward against the oppressive darkness, but even the tiniest flame helped to hold panic at bay, and by its light he was able to assess his surroundings.

Dead bodies, clad not in rich funereal finery, but in tattered rags, were heaped, one atop another, in huge mounds. Tariq knew that he and Faysal must be in a charnel pit, a long trough quarried deep into the ground, located far from the mausoleums of the wealthy. Each day the human detritus from such neighborhoods as Hope's End was swept up, dumped into the pit, and covered over with rock and soil, creating a long line of partitioned chambers. It was into one such chamber that Tariq and Faysal intruded, but they were not the first to do so; feeder tendrils extended from the main stalk and permeated the corpses. Most of the bodies were now just withered husks, and Tariq saw that the tendrils had penetrated the walls into neighboring chambers, too. The charnel pit, he realized, was a huge feeding trough.

"Come on, lad," said Tariq. "Let's try to find a way out."

They made their way slowly through the narrow confines between the mounds of desiccated bodies as Tariq searched for an exit to the surface. The flutter of his candle flame alerted Tariq to a wisp of breeze from some nearby opening. Yes, there! Soil had eroded away revealing a small gap between stone blocks; it wasn't much—only the size of his fist—but if he could shift the rock slightly and widen it they might be able to squeeze through.

Tariq withdrew a hammer and chisel from his satchel and set to work with single-minded determination. He chipped, and hammered, and pried, and little by little the opening grew until it was nearly wide enough to fit head and shoulders. He looked over his shoulder to share his progress with Faysal and saw pale, milky-eyed revenants crawling amid the corpses towards them.

"Mithra, fuck me," he whispered. "Not now." He looked desperately at the opening then turned and flung his hammer at the nearest gastlich. The creature skittered aside, and the hammer vanished into the darkness. Tariq half slid down the pile of bodies he was perched upon, to the floor where Faysal sat, unperturbed.

"Time to go," he said. He grabbed the boy by the back of his vest, dragged him to his feet and shoved him up the pile of bodies toward the gap and freedom. The boy's languid indifference to their peril was confounding and inexplicable. Was he so caught fear's grasp that he'd completely given up hope or care of escape?

"Move your body, you fermenting sack of pig piss! I'll not die in this stinking pit, nor shall you. I promised your mother I'd look after you, and by the gods I mean to do it; now move—your—arse!" With a feat of strength born of desperation and fear, Tariq pushed Faysal all the way up the shifting corpse heap. His exhortation appeared to have jolted Faysal out of his languor, for he began to wriggle through the narrow opening of his own volition. Tariq shoved hard on the boy's backside, trying to hurry him through. He was absolutely certain that at any moment clawed hands would clutch his leg and pull him back down into the pit to join the nameless corpses in the pile; a juicy morsel to feed that which dwelt below.

With one final hard push, Faysal was through the opening, and then Tariq frantically squirmed through, heedless of the cuts and scrapes he suffered in his haste to be free. The kiss of the cold night air on his face as he emerged from the stifling, fetid confines of the charnel pit was just about the best thing he had ever felt; better than his first time with a woman; better, even, than a good long piss after a night's hard drinking. But there was no time to relax and enjoy its cool caress. He scrambled out of the breach and away from it as quickly as possible, fearing the gastlichs that might follow him out.

Moments passed and there was no pursuit. Why? They'd been keen enough to chase Faysal and himself through the ruins of Golgotha; why not now? It was damned odd, but Tariq reckoned it was better to accept the rare boons that Mithra handed you without putting them to the question. He sighed deeply and felt the tension of the past few hours drain from him.

"We did it, lad. We're out, safe and clear." He put a fatherly hand on Faysal's shoulder. "Come on, let's go home." They moved quickly away from the charnel pit and back into the necropolis proper, aiming for Death Gate. Faysal remained uncharacteristically silent.

"I know you're thinking about all the loot we had to leave behind, but we aren't going home completely empty-handed," Tariq said with a smile. "This'll put some spring back into your step." He reached into his tunic and withdrew one of the enormous rubies he'd chiseled out of the idol. "This gem alone will set us up for the rest of our days. We should thank Mithra for her blessings—by all rights them gastlichs should've had us in the charnel pits. We got lucky, lad."

"Luck had nothing to do with it, uncle, nor did Mithra. You said it yourself: those not under the protection of priests are fair prey for the gastlichs."

Tariq stopped short and stared at Faysal. Suddenly everything started to make sense. "What did you do, Faysal," he whispered. "What promise did you make before that altar in the cavern?" Faysal's reply was cut off as four barrow wardens stepped out of the shadow of a nearby tomb and leveled their crossbows at the pair.

"Look what we've got here, lads; it's either two lovers out for a moonlight stroll in the necropolis or we've bagged ourselves a pair of thieves for the Overlord's dungeon." Tariq spun around, surprised, and cursed himself for his inattention and for this sudden bad turn of luck. It seemed that what Mithra gave with one hand, she took away with the other. The sergeant stepped forward and plucked the ruby from Tariq's hand.

"Looks like we won't be going home empty-handed, either, eh, boys? A couple of fine ornaments for the gallows, and a nice tip to boot." The sergeant chuckled and held up the ruby for the men behind him to see.

"Here, now, what's that you got," the sergeant asked, seeing a curious-looking sphere in Faysal's outstretched hands. "Give that here," he said grabbing it and holding up to examine it more closely in the moonlight. "What do you lads make of this," he asked his men. The puff ball suddenly burst, filling the air with a cloud of spores. The sergeant and his men dropped their crossbows, blinded and choking, and began to claw at their eyes.

Faysal reached out and grasped the sergeant's head with both of his hands and pulled him in close as if for a kiss. The warden's mouth was penetrated by something that Tariq was certain wasn't Faysal's tongue; he fought desperately to escape Faysal's grasp for a few moments, then his struggles began to weaken. The man's cheeks became sunken and his eyes bulged from their sockets; his face started collapsing in on itself, as if was being sucked dry from the inside. After what felt like an eternity, Faysal broke his embrace and let the withered husk fall lifeless to the ground. He stared hard at the three other wardens who stumbled frantically away from him, their crossbows forgotten on the ground.

There was an uncharacteristic sense of focus and fierceness in his gaze.

"You are the first," he told them. "Now go forth, and multiply." The three men, still coughing and wheezing, turned and fled without a backwards glance.

Tariq stared in horror at what his nephew had become, and wondered what it portended for himself, for Catapesh, for the world.

Faysal looked over his shoulder at Tariq with a feral gleam in his eye. "Now, uncle, let's get me a woman. Hells, let's get me a dozen."

SEAN P. ROBSON *is a palaeontologist specializing in invertebrates. He holds a Ph.D. in Geological Sciences from the University of Saskatchewan. When not studying the chitinous, squamous, fanged, tentacled, and multi-appendaged monstrosities that haunted Earth's ancient seas, he writes dark fantasy fiction, and draws wildlife and fantasy art, while drinking more coffee than is probably healthy.*

LADY CARDULA AND THE GRYPHON

BY SHAWN SCARBER

D uncan hated human-sized books. Sadly, they were the only tomes created, and though he wrote long letters to the monks who lived in the Sambata monastery imploring them to copy larger editions, his letters often went unanswered.

"If I were a dragon, they wouldn't ignore my letters," Duncan mused aloud to no one in particular, because he rarely received guests. He tried once more to squint at the etchings, but it was no use. He tossed the book over his right wing onto a pile of other unread volumes.

"If you were a dragon," answered a small voice with a cockney accent, "you wouldn't read. I've seen them and they always have someone else read their messages. Usually a human slave or a tiny elf."

He hadn't noticed the crow perched at the edge of Duncan's nest. The small bird bowed and cocked his head sideways, a friendly gesture among the birdfolk. Duncan returned the bird's courtesy with a nod despite the fact a large, plump crow made for a tasty snack. Duncan was always willing to set aside his base nature for civility.

"Message for you, Governor," the crow said offering a bit of rolled parchment to Duncan. "It's from her Ladyship Elizabeth Erin Cardula of the Castle Carpatia."

"I've never heard of such a Lady," Duncan replied. "Why would the Castle send me a message when all they've ever sent before were knights attempting to make a name for themselves?"

"Would be rude of me to read the contents, Governor," said the crow with another nod and a step back from the gryphon nest. "I just deliver the messages."

And with that, the crow was aflight and not but a dark dot on the evening sun's horizon.

Duncan uncurled the rolled letter. He noticed immediately the oversized paper and the larger text size. For once he didn't have to strain his eyes to read.

> *To Our Closest Neighbor, The Gryphon,*
>
> *Please excuse my ignorance. I do not know your formal name. However, I didn't want this barrier to remain between us and spoil an opportunity to make introductions and acquaintance.*
>
> *It's my understanding the previous occupant of Castle Carpatia, the Honorable Duke Carlos Hallowell, failed to formally welcome you when you nested in the region.*
>
> *I hope to remedy that failure and cordially invite you to our home for dining and conversation. It will be no elaborate affair, just a simple gathering between two neighbors.*
>
> *Please meet me at the castle gates at sundown.*
>
> *Yours,*
> *Lady Elizabeth Erin Cardula of the Castle Carpatia*

"Hmm," he said scratching the underside of his beak. "This is a new ploy! I guess they've finally had enough of me and plan to lead me to the castle where I will be trapped and caged and sent off to some traveling carnival as a spectacle. Well, Lady Cardula, I will not be so easily fooled."

Duncan stretched his back and flapped his wings. The nest creaked under his claws and with a single leap he took to the air.

* * *

His timing worked well and he arrived at the Castle just as twilight settled gently over the gray hills leaving a warm glow to the otherwise frigid landscape. He remained alert, waiting for any moment to be met with a ball fired from a harquebus or a ballista's dart from behind the castle's walls.

As circled the castle twice upon approach. He noticed the banners and flags flying the dark green and black colors of the new occupants. Fewer guards manned the castle walls and those that did appeared to be of Romani ancestry.

The only other human Duncan saw was a little pixie of a girl standing outside the castle's open gate wrapped in a coat of wolf fur. Duncan lowered himself slowly, and deliberately created a small dust storm around the child with the ferocious flaps of his great wings.

To her credit, she didn't cover her eyes or cough, but kept her smiling face fixed on Duncan's eyes.

When his claws finally dug deep into the cool, rich earth he announced, "I am Duncan, the gryphon who nests north of the Castle Carpatia. To whom do I have the pleasure of addressing?"

The girl bowed, but kept her gaze fixed on Duncan.

"I am Lady Elizabeth Erin Cardula, daughter of Duke Vlad Draco Calisto Cardula and the late Duchess Aurora Elizabeth Cardula and I am pleased to finally know your name, Master Duncan of the northern hills."

"Lady Cardula," Duncan said. "Please don't take offense to this observation, but I cannot help but notice you are a young child. Perhaps not much more than ten winters."

"That is very perceptive, Master Duncan," she said. "I feel my knowledge of your race is woefully lacking. I don't believe I could possibly know your age. In fact, I was unaware a gryphon with your coat colorings even existed. All I've seen of your kind have been in pictures and the artists always depicted your brothers and sisters as having the white head of an eagle and the tan body of a lion. You look more to me like a raven and the blue and black sheen of your feathers is beautiful, much like my late mother's hair."

"I have always thought a lion had a gryphon's body and an eagle a gryphon's head, but that is not as important as the obvious."

"My apologies, Master Duncan, but 'the obvious'?"

"Yes," he said. "The obvious."

The girl continued to stand and stare with a look of complete confusion. Duncan considered just devouring her then and there. It would be a favor to her race. Was it possible that a human could be so ignorant of her kind that she didn't even understand the basic food chain?

"I am a gryphon, Lady Cardula," Duncan said. "You are a little girl. Gryphons eat little girls."

"Have you?"

"Have I what?"

"Eaten a little girl?"

Duncan had to think about it. He'd of course eaten humans. They weren't the tastiest creatures. Not like lamb or goat. No, they were more like pigs, but crunchier. And unless you lucked upon a fat one there wasn't much there to really savor. Thinking back on all his meals, he couldn't remember once eating a child.

He shook his head.

"You know, I don't believe I have."

"Do you feel that you desperately need to eat a child? I did state in the invitation that I would provide food and beverage, didn't I? If I failed to mention it was a dinner invitation I must apologize, you see I've only recently taken this role of castle host for my father and I am afraid of failing at it miserably."

"No," Duncan said. "I believe you were clear in your letter that it was an invitation to dinner. I guess I don't feel a desperate need to eat a child. I doubt you taste much better than your adult counterparts. What I fail to understand is how you can stand there, braver than any knight I've ever faced, and simply expect to continue living with a hungry gryphon not but two claw lengths from your persons."

The young girl's head cocked a little, not unlike the little messenger crow's, and stated, "But you've answered my invitation."

Duncan nodded and still couldn't believe the look of astonishment on the young girls face. The sadness and the hurt in her gaze was so penetrating to his two hearts that he couldn't possibly eat the little girl now, but then he realized the error of his ways.

The invitation was genuine.

Not only was the invitation genuine, but also he now found himself on the side of being a terrible and deplorable guest. The shock and horror of such a thing struck him to the core harder than any knight's lance or huntsman's musket blast. In that moment he wanted to fly away, back to his nest, where he would hide his beak in shame for his remaining years.

"Lady Cardula," he begged and pleaded, "please forgive me. I was under the impression your invitation was anything but genuine, a ruse meant to lead me here to my demise, but now I see that I was greatly mistaken. I have lived these many years in solidarity, hunted and hated by the Castle Carpatia's previous holders. I should have realized when such care was put into the invitation to fit easily into my gryphon claws and read easily to my gryphon eyes that it had to be legitimate. However, I am still at a loss as to why you would want to befriend an old bird like me."

The little Lady Cardula smiled and Duncan wondered why he hadn't noticed her teeth before.

"It's my father's way," she said. "We are like you. Hunted and hated. Creatures existing on the outside of humanity. Despite these setbacks, it doesn't mean we creatures of the night can't behave toward each other with warm civility."

Duncan bowed in agreement.

"Well then," the gryphon said. "What's on the menu?"

As Elizabeth guided him through the castle gates, she asked, "Have you ever tried an old fat duke before? I hear they're delicious."

SHAWN SCARBER *creates web applications for a major telecom company by day, but in his off hours he writes about strange worlds and characters at http://www.shawnscarber.com/. He lives in North Texas with his daughter and a cat. His work has appeared in* The Best of Abyss & Apex, M-Brane SF, *and his teenage zombie novella* Restless *is available on Amazon. He is a Clarion West 2006 graduate, and a member of the Future Classics DFW Speculative Fiction Writing Group.*

At the Sign of the Midpoint Tavern

Three volumes covering six years of *Heroic Fantasy Quarterly*. Incredible!

Once again, we were amazingly lucky that our fans backed our Kickstarter campaign to fund the creation of this book and surpassed the goals we had hoped for. Once again, our writers spun imagination into words, and our artists turned words into images. We cut Robert Zoltan free to do the cover art, and were wowed by what he made; and, for the third time running, Keanan Brand played the role of Samwise Gamgee, carrying our exhausted carcasses those final steps in the production process.

Choosing the best works from issues 17 through 24 was no easy task for us, but we dove in and made the hard calls, exuberating in the effort. Going through those issues reminded us how lucky we were able to get such great stories and poems in the first place.

We know that you will enjoy this volume, and after this short interlude we will get out of the way so you can get back to the adventure that you came for!

—*The Editors*

CHIRON

BY GARY EVERY

A horse has the heart of a hurricane
and while running the tail and mane
flutter furiously as if in a flurry of wind.
Horses often run fast just because they can
but horses run different from you and me.
Horses leap into the air
while the earth spins beneath them
before landing with a thud
and then leaping airborne again,
the earth spinning and spinning beneath them.
Their voices rise in song comprised of whinny, neigh
and maniacal laughter.
There was no need for these noble steeds
to ever bow to the yoke of domestication
but some horses with huge chests holding giant hearts
still the wild winds of freedom beating inside
and offer their broad shoulders to humans
in moral support.

Such a centaur was Chiron
who abandoned wild afternoons of lust
frolicking among the wood nymphs
to spend his days in study,

learning the ways of flower power,
studying the plants and herbs
until he became a master of healing,
teaching the first doctors.
Beast of the forest, dweller of caves
he taught heroes their ways
until one fateful day
Hercules accidentally shot Chiron
in the leg with a poisoned arrow.
Immortal and unable to die
Chiron was forced to roam forever
with horse legs which were unable to gallop.

Chiron was always an admirer of Prometheus
stealer of fire
whom Zeus had punished in horrible ways.
Chiron offered his own life as a substitute
and Zeus accepted
freeing Prometheus from eternal prison.
Zeus allowed Chiron the centaur to die in sacrifice,
surrendering his beast-like chrysalis,
half man, half horse,
so that man might metamorphosis with technology
beginning with fire and knowledge of the stars
gifts of Chiron, wisest of the centaurs.

GARY EVERY *is a well-published author, writing history, science fiction, nature essays, and journalism. He has won consecutive best lifestyle of the year features from the Arizona Newspaper Association for "Losing Geronimo's Language" and "The Apache Naichee Ceremony". These stories are included in his anthology,* Shadow of the OshaD. *He also has two science fiction novellas available:* Inca Butterflies *and* The Saint and the Robot

Shadows and Foxfire

by R. Michael Burns

"Everything in this world is but a marionette show."
–Yamamoto Tsunemoto
Hagakure, ca. 1700

That night, the gods raged.

Fūjin's winds lashed the towering pines, bowing them before him. Raijin slammed the narrow valley with fists of rain, his thunder-bellows shaking the earth. Caught in the heart of their fury, the young samurai bent under his straw rain cloak, his flesh sodden, dull with cold. Such ferocity in this storm—he could almost believe that the kami had sent it to mock him, to ridicule his failed pilgrimage, leaving him lost and soaked and frozen in this deep valley. He knew as well as any man the gods' capacity for cruelty.

Blinking away the icy freshets that streamed down his face even beneath his wide sedge hat, Hokagé searched the darkness before him.

There—light, winking through the trees.

Hokagé quickened his pace, his waraji sandals squelching in the mud.

Such lights couldn't be trusted, of course—not at any time, and less still on a wild autumn evening like this. Even a samurai might be lured to danger by ghost-lights and flickers of foxfire on such a storm-cloaked night, but the thin hope of shelter spurred Hokagé onward. All around, the wind howled like a chorus of demons, driving frigid squalls.

Hokagé cursed the carelessness that had led him here. Just when he had lost his way, he couldn't say. Now, though, he could only seek shelter and hope daylight would restore his senses.

Lightning strode the mountaintops, livid brilliance outlining a shape not far ahead—a thatch-roofed building crouched at the foot of a steep hill. Four forlorn oilpaper lanterns shimmered under the shelter of the eaves, ghostly behind veils of rain. He stumbled onto the veranda and shrugged off his straw raincoat. Such a lonely and forsaken spot for an inn, he thought, but dared not bless his luck. The gods were fickle, after all, and baited their traps with false hopes.

His half-numb fingers went to the hilt of the long sword at his side. Prayer and magic trinkets had never protected him from the terrors of the world, but folded steel served well enough. If indeed danger awaited him here, he would trust his blade to ensure his safety.

He removed his dripping hat and ran a hand over his fresh-shaven pate, tugging his topknot back into its proper shape. It still felt out of place, that bound and oiled queue of hair, mark of the warrior class to which he had so recently ascended. Proof, if any were needed, that the boy called Toshihiro had gone from the world, the last vestiges of him cast away somewhere far behind.

Shivering, Hokagé tugged the sliding door open.

The girl across the threshold stared at him for a moment, an unreadable expression on her face. More than surprise—shock, almost, or fear? Or perhaps a flicker of hope? Then she noticed the swords at his side and her eyes went wide and she bowed deeply. "Welcome, noble sir, welcome! Please, come inside!"

She moved aside in a flutter of kimono silks. Hokagé stepped out of his soaked waraji and into the dim vestibule. As he did, another figure emerged from the shadows of some inner chamber, a bent and spindle-thin fellow with a withered face and a hooked nose. He bowed and rose, offering a smile filled with straggling yellow teeth.

"Welcome, honored guest," he said, voice all rattles and creaks. "So kind of you to grace my humble inn. It is a poor place for such a fine gentleman, but please allow me to offer you a room where you may dry yourself and rest until this dreadful storm passes."

Behind the old innkeeper, other faces peered from the dark, then vanished again with a clamor of mumbles and muttered laughter. At the sound, the girl seemed to tremble oh-so-slightly.

Hokagé bowed, but not too low, restrained by his new station. "Your accommodations are—most suitable, master."

The master of the inn gave another broken-porcelain smile. "You honor me," he said, bowing. "Moriko-chan, see our guest to his room!"

He cast a dark look at the girl. Moriko bowed and quickly ushered Hokagé up a steep flight of stairs, down a dingy corridor and into a tiny room. The walls were mottled, the straw tatami mats ragged, but Hokagé hardly cared—a warrior had little need of creature comforts. He was fortunate to have a roof above him and a floor beneath.

He thanked the girl with a nod. Then, with due reverence, he unbound his swords and placed them on the floor. The room had no ceremonial alcove in which to store them properly. For an instant he paused, admiring the long sword—a Toshinaga blade, from Ômi province, a gift from his master in recognition of his promotion. Not priceless, but still of greater value than anything he had ever before possessed. Testimony to what the new man, the warrior called Shadows-from-Firelight, had accomplished. And a reminder of all he had lost.

Hokagé turned his eyes away and began to peel off his soggy clothing, mud-spattered haori coat and undershirt—then stopped, all at once starkly aware of Moriko still standing just inside the door. Something about her, something in the shine of her eyes or the set of her lips, made him hesitate, uncharacteristically self-conscious. Certainly she was beautiful—hair like silken midnight, face pale as cherry blossoms, eyes dark and round. Her beauty, though, didn't explain the sudden doubt clouding his mind.

He regarded her with narrowed eyes. She returned his gaze, face wholly innocent.

"Eh, excuse me," he murmured.

"Oh!" Moriko said, like someone shaken from a dream. "So sorry. You must be cold! Please, wear this." So saying, she placed a folded yukata just inside the doorway. "I will bring saké to warm you up." She backed away with a bow, sliding the door closed after her.

Hokagé stripped to his breechcloth and donned the robe—a moth-eaten thing with a lingering odor of mildew to it, but dry. He had just settled fatigue-heavy and still shivering onto one of the limp floor pillows when the door rattled open and Moriko reappeared. Kneeling, she placed on the table before him a tray laden with lacquered bowls and a porcelain bottle attended by a single mismatched cup. From somewhere behind her came voices, gruff, muffled—the men Hokagé had spotted earlier, perhaps. How many travelers might find this place? Without some better sense of where he was, he could venture no guess.

"Please, eat," she said, nodding at the tray.

Hokagé picked up the chopsticks and prodded the food— ragged cuts of sashimi, clumps of sticky rice, bitter pickled vegetables. He had scarcely eaten in two days, but this food merely set his gut churning.

"Please," Moriko said again, pouring the steaming rice wine and pushing the little cup toward him.

He took it and drank. Warmth spread through him at once, ticklish and vaguely numbing. Smiling, the girl refilled the cup and he drank again. With each swallow of wine, the food grew a bit more palatable, and little by little he found his appetite again.

Moriko really was quite lovely, Hokagé thought, so delicate and refined. Even her gowns were elegant, beautifully draped layers of embroidered silk that fit her small frame perfectly. It all made her seem quite out of place in this shabby inn on this lost mountain byway. She sat across from him, silent and watchful, eyes full of thoughts he could only guess at.

"Why do you stare at me?" he asked, again feeling that prickle of suspicion. "You wonder about these?" He ran his fingers over the straggling scars marring the left side of his face—scars which marked the night the novice priest had died and this shadow-warrior had risen.

The girl blushed and bowed her head. "Please forgive me! I only wondered why a strong, handsome young samurai looks so very weary."

"I've had a long journey."

Moriko filled his cup again, and he drank, almost reflexively, listening again to those other half-glimpsed guests. Something odd about the sounds, muddy and guttural... Yet the more he strained to hear, the less he could make out above the storm's fury.

"It is not my business, of course," Moriko went on. "But I will listen if it suits you to talk of it."

Perhaps the *saké* had loosened something inside him, or perhaps the earnest light in the girl's eyes warmed the dead cinder of his turned-to-coal heart, because he heard himself saying, "I come from Aomizu-machi. Do you know it?"

Moriko shook her head.

"It is my family's village. I have not visited in many years." He took another swallow of wine.

The girl smiled. "Your family must have been pleased to see you."

Hokagé said nothing for a moment, the silence disturbed now only by the constant drumbeat of rain on the thatched roof. Then he sighed, acutely aware of misery and loss he'd thought properly interred at last.

"I went to visit their graves."

Moriko lowered her head.

"So sorry. I did not mean to cause you pain."

"I was only a boy when they died," Hokagé went on, letting himself tell it as he had only once before. "Brigands from the Akkihito clan. They attacked us, without provocation. Without mercy. They slaughtered us and set the village ablaze. My father, my mother, my elder brother, my two sisters—all murdered. Everyone. Only I survived. Why the *kami* chose me, I know not."

"Such a terrible story," Moriko said. She let her fingertips brush the back of his hand, then withdrew them quickly to refill his cup.

"I was to be a priest," he went on, the words coming slowly, but each a tiny relief, like barbs plucked from a wound. "To spend my life in the service of the *kami*. But they abandoned me." He bit back his rising anger, chased it with another swallow of *saké*.

"So unreliable, the gods," Moriko said, a strange light in her eyes.

"Lord Kumamuné of Yamagumo allowed me to join his forces," Hokagé continued. "I devoted myself to the *bushido* in the hope that I would someday be given the chance to put an end to the Akkihito—to all such barbarians and murderers."

Across from him, Moriko nodded, waited for him to continue. The expression with which she'd greeted him had resurfaced, expectant, or apprehensive, or even frightened. Untranslatable. In the warm haze of the rice wine, it scarcely seemed to matter.

"As a peasant soldier, I carried the banner of my Lord's clan in many skirmishes, and brought honor upon his house. Last month, we marched on the Akkihito bastion at Yukai-jo. The siege lasted less than a week. When we broke their defenses, they did not fight, nor commit *seppuku* like honorable men. They fled in cowardice. We hunted them through the mountains and struck down all that we could find. I myself claimed thirteen enemy heads. Perhaps I killed the men who slew my family. I shall never know."

"Then you have had your revenge," Moriko said, a sort of bleak smile on her pink lips. "Well done, honored sir."

Hokagé stared into his empty cup and said nothing. Any satisfaction he had earned in spilling Akkihito blood had guttered out of him before that blood had grown cool.

"After the battle, Kumamuné-sama made me samurai. I returned to my village to tell my kinsmen of all that had happened. I hoped their spirits might rest more easily if they knew that their murders were properly avenged."

"I have no doubt of it," the girl said with a dark smile—something almost fierce, even a bit cruel, like moonlight flashing from a dagger's blade.

Hokagé nodded, letting his head hang heavy with drink. He had felt nothing there, in the wreckage of Aomizu village, the charred remains overgrown with autumn foliage, only his own makeshift *sotoba* posts to mark the graves of his family. The rest had been left to the animals and the elements, rendered untouchable by death, their picked-clean bones gleaming among the weeds and ruins. As for spirits, though, he had seen, had sensed nothing. Perhaps the ghosts of the dead had moved on after all, or simply scattered to the winds, or faded with the passage of time. Wherever they might be, they had not been there.

Still, he had visited the graves and said what he'd gone to say, whether anyone might hear or not. But whatever peace he'd naïvely hoped to find there had eluded him, and he had departed feeling emptier still than when he arrived, solitary as a mountain priest on an endless pilgrimage.

A profound quiet settled over the tiny room. The storm had ebbed some, and the strangers' voices from below had fallen still.

Lovely Moriko studied him, eyes intent. Then, noticing the quiet, she glanced over her shoulder and rose abruptly. "Excuse me," she said, turning the empty saké cup over on the tray. "I should leave you in peace. Rest now, and think no more of your troubles."

She backed away, gave a hasty bow, and departed without another word.

Hokagé blinked at the closed door as if unsure what he had just seen. Then, with a yawn, he pushed aside the low table, slouched to the floor, and let his eyes droop closed.

* * *

In the darkness, movement, subtle as a cat on the prowl.

Hokagé's eyes snapped open. His left hand lashed out at the shadow hovering over him, latching around a narrow wrist. His right hand drew his *tanto* dagger from its scabbard and brought it straight up, its blade kissing the flesh of an exposed throat. The intruder, a phantom in the gloom, gave a muted cry.

The samurai glared into Moriko's ghostly face. The girl stared back, eyes round as twin moons shining down on him.

"Wait!" she sputtered. "Please, I came to warn you—"

"Indeed," Hokagé whispered, sitting up, keeping his blade at the girl's throat. "Your wine may have loosened my tongue some, but I am not fool enough to surrender my senses in such a place as this. What is your game, girl?"

"No!" Moriko said, frantic, "Not *my* game! My master, he insisted. He wanted me to be sure you drank yourself into a stupor. Then he and his associates would kill you as you slept and steal your belongings—my master especially covets your swords. But I couldn't allow them to do it, not after the tragic tale you told."

"You associate with thieves, yet I am to believe that you are not one yourself?" Hokagé asked, the blade unwavering.

Moriko's face shattered with grief. "I am their prisoner here," she said, tears shining on her cheeks. "They keep me like a cur. If I ever tried to flee, they would surely kill me. I've had no choice but to serve them. Until now."

"Eh?"

"You are samurai," Moriko said, breathless. "You can help me. Protect me. Together, we can escape this place!"

Hokagé said nothing, only studied the girl's face, naked with fear.

"We must hurry!" she said in her tiny, fragile tones. "They will come at the hour of the tiger! I dared not warn you sooner, and now time is so short—"

Even as she spoke, there came from the hall beyond the chamber the low moan of ancient floorboards shifting under some prowler's weight.

Hokagé gave Moriko a last look, trying as best his instincts could manage to read her eyes in the dark. Something in them denied trust, but her fear seemed genuine enough, and he could see no option now but to accept her strange tale and prepare himself for whatever might come next.

Still clutching her fine wrist, Hokagé traded the dagger for the long Toshinaga blade, then rose and stood beside the doorway, dragging Moriko along with him. He released her and placed his hand over her mouth. With a glare, he demanded her silence. She nodded and pinched her rose-petal lips tight. In the deep gloom, she looked as pale and insubstantial as a specter, a wraith there beside him.

Scarcely breathing, Hokagé stood, waiting.

The shoji door slid open a hand's span, then further. A rawboned figure in ragged garb the color of thunder clouds slipped into the room, feeble light winking from the knife in his hand. Noiseless, he crouched beside the neglected table and tossed aside the tangled blankets.

"Where—?" the intruder demanded, voice a strangled croak.

Hokagé struck even as the bewildered man rose to look for his missing prey. The Toshinaga blade plunged through the dark, deep into the fellow's chest. The man gave a snarling cry, something more fury than pain, as if outraged at the samurai's audacity, his knife slashing the air blindly. He raised his head and for the first time Hokagé saw his face—an oblong, misshapen thing, corpse-pale and green with mold and decay, sunken eyes as red as blood-blisters, mouth filled with teeth that jutted and leaned like splintered chopsticks.

From somewhere behind Hokagé, Moriko gave a most unladylike cry of shocked disgust.

The impaled creature screeched at its attacker, then staggered forward, driving Hokagé's sword deeper into its chest, heedless of pain. It lashed out again with its knife, and Hokagé saw the hand that gripped the blade was emaciated, the nails yellow and jagged as claws. He ducked away, just avoiding the weapon's path, and gave his sword a twist, snapping balsa-brittle ribs under moldering gray skin.

Moriko gave another yelp as a second sickly figure lurched into the chamber, a rusted short sword in its corpselike grip.

Hokagé sidestepped, slamming the run-through intruder into its companion. Wrenching his sword free, he feinted left, fell back and struck again. The Toshinaga blade flicked and stabbed, biting into rotten flesh, brackish black water splashing from the wounds. The monster gave a horrible sort of cackle, then came on again, its knife darting about like a wasp, swift and stinging. The second creature followed, gnashing its gruesome fangs, waving its sword.

Hokagé took another pace away, backing Moriko into the corner of the room, keeping himself between her and the mewling creatures. The second beast, an almost-perfect twin of its companion, took a sudden swipe from behind the first. Hokagé parried the blow; a severed claw flopped to the floor, still holding its rust-stained sword. The creature spluttered with wrath, then came again in a flash of teeth. Pain blazed up the samurai's arm as fangs tore into his naked flesh, but his sword responded quick as a serpent's tongue. The creature's jaw dropped open like a sprung hinge . . . and then its head fell free of its spindly neck. The body crumpled to the floor—but still its claws lashed and clutched, still its legs kicked and flailed, its every impulse bent on attack. The severed head worked its rotten lips and wagged its wormlike tongue and gnawed chunks from the rotten *tatami.*

Hokagé forgot the fallen thing at once, and the pain sizzling through his arm, his whole attention focused on his remaining opponent. The ghastly creature swung its knife wild but fast, slashing and stabbing mindlessly, so random in its attacks that Hokagé could scarcely anticipate a single action. He turned aside each strike as much by luck as skill.

"Swords," the thing hissed, "*mine.*"

The creature took a stumbling step forward, thrusting straight ahead with its knife, burying the blade in the rotten plaster wall inches from Hokagé's scarred face.

Hokagé saw his chance and seized it. His sword whickered through the air with the precision of a calligrapher's brush dancing over parchment. The creature, all rage and hunger, gave up its trapped weapon and came on unarmed, teeth questing for Hokagé's unguarded throat. It managed one last step before the samurai sliced its legs out from under it, and had scarcely hit the floor when the Toshinaga blade fell again, cleaving its head from its shoulders.

On the mildewed *tatami,* the broken bodies and severed limbs went on twitching, writhing.

Hokagé prodded the ghastly things with the tip of his sword, eyes narrowed.

"*Jikininki,*" he muttered, and the dismembered things seemed to flinch from the word. No mere thieves, these, but ghoulish monstrosities, their karma poisoned by their avarice, their wretched souls doomed to be reborn into these debased forms through countless lifetimes, forever failing to satisfy their insatiable greed.

Deep within him, the ghost of the priest he had never fully become mourned for these pitiful beings, and for his own inability to help them. But he had long ago abandoned the way of the *kami* in favor of the way of the warrior, just as these creatures had abandoned their humanity for covetousness. He could do nothing for them now.

Instead, he tore several long strips from their tattered robes and bound his wounds as best he could.

"Horrible," Moriko said from behind him—too overwhelmed, it seemed, to offer any assistance.

His injuries dressed for now, Hokagé took in the rest of the room, seeing it fully for the first time since he'd awakened—the water-stained ceiling, the crumbling wattle-and-daub walls, the mats sunken and insect-eaten. It all had the look of long abandonment to it, as if no living soul had set foot within for many years. Only some now-broken magic, Hokagé guessed, had given the shunned place any hint of civility at all—enough, just, to lure in the occasional wayward traveler, to tempt lost men to their doom, like cicadas snagged in a spider's web.

"Come," Hokagé said, quickly tugging on his still-damp clothes, "I should get you to safety before their master comes for us both."

But Moriko only shook her head.

"Forgive me, but I cannot leave—not yet."

"There is no time to –"

"I cannot!" the girl said, weeping now. "The master, he took something from me, something precious, and I cannot leave without it, I dare not –"

"This is no time to concern yourself with trinkets," Hokagé growled, stealing a peek into the darkened hall then scowling at Moriko. But again she shook her head, adamant.

"Please, I *must* have it!" she said, fighting back a sob. "It is an heirloom of my family—I would disgrace myself and all my kin were I to lose it. Leave me if you must, but I cannot retrieve it by myself, and I dare not go without it."

Hokagé stared at the girl. She looked so tiny, so helpless in her corner, flinching with each quiet thump and scrape of the cut-apart things scattered over the straw mats. Again instinct warned him not to trust her, and again some voice in his heart begged for compassion.

The samurai let out a slow sigh.

"Where is your master's chamber?" he asked.

* * *

They paused outside the door of the inn's topmost room, listening. At first, Hokagé could hear nothing over the sounds of the tempest outside, water dribbling through the rotten roof, pattering to the floor. Then he perceived a sort of guttering snort, as of some feral thing sleeping fitfully. It was all the help he was apt to get.

Hokagé gave his companion a warning look, then wrenched the door open and stepped into the room, sword ready.

In an instant, he took in the whole scene—the ghoul's den, the thieves' cache. Heaped clothes and scattered coins, lacquered boxes and porcelain ware, worthless farmers' tools and countless other trivial things, all the plunder from previous victims. And scattered throughout, human bones, too many to count, gnawed and broken and discarded, black with long-dried blood and scraps of crusted meat.

For a heartbeat's time, nothing stirred.

Then the master of the inn sprang from its bed of rags, robes hanging in filthy tatters, all pretense of humanity abandoned now, in the deep of night. Its jaw gaped in a sort of madman's grin, revealing row after row of thorny teeth, maw as wide and deep as a stone well.

"I will have those swords," it rasped, snatching up a long, elegant blade, one of the finer things in its stash, and brandishing it. The master, Hokagé saw, moved with greater control, greater deliberation than its companions had managed.

Hokagé stood motionless, reading his enemy and waiting, letting instinct guide his response to whatever it might do.

The creature lunged, its pilfered sword held straight out before it—but even as he batted it aside, Hokagé realized the thrust had been a ruse, leaving him open to the jikininki's following claw. He turned the Toshinaga sword just in time to intercept the attack with the flat of the blade. Unfaltering, the ghoul pressed forward, holding its place between the samurai and its treasures, using its steel to keep Hokagé's sword occupied as it snatched his shoulder in its free claw. Hissing, it tilted its head, jaws angling for his throat, deadly-quick. Hokagé gave a mighty heave, forcing the creature back a precious few inches, fangs snapping shut just shy of their target.

With a warrior yell, Hokagé sank the Toshinaga blade into the spongy hollow at the base of the ghoul's throat, then twisted and tore the sword free, shredding rotten flesh and brittle bone. The *katana* turned and fell, cleft the creature's forearm from its elbow—and still the claw kept its crushing purchase on his shoulder, blood pulsing from five deepening wounds there.

Hokagé put out one foot and kicked the master away, the creature's sword narrowly missing his leg as he toppled to the floor. He yanked the disembodied claw from his shoulder and flung it aside, then rose into a crouch, forcing himself to wait. Let his every action answer his enemy's.

"There!" Moriko cried, shattering the moment. "It's there!"

At the edge of his vision, he saw her waving frantically from the doorway—pointing at a small silk bag slumped up against a pile of other stolen belongings, no more than a hand's span from where the hideous master stood. Something about the bag—its delicate stitching, its simple elegance—seemed to mark it as hers and hers alone.

The *jikininki's* eyes flickered, following the girl's gesture.

Hokagé struck.

The Toshinaga blade clove the dark, a wink of polished metal in the black. The ghoul flopped backward, diving just under the sword's deadly arc, scrambling across the rotten straw mat to its treasure. It cast its sword aside and snatched up the bag with its remaining hand, clutching the thing like a crazed woman cradling an infant.

Then Hokagé saw that he hadn't missed the creature after all. As it crouched, clinging to its prize, brackish, watery blood spilled down its face, and a lopsided bowl of skull, garnished with ragged flesh and wiry hair, dropped to the floor at its feet. The ghoul glanced down at its severed skull cap, then up again at Hokagé.

And grinned that lunatic's grin.

"You waste your strength, boy!" it bellowed, its voice a ragged snarl. "You cannot take what's *mine*—and now *you* are mine, too! Even the gods won't protect you here, foolish child. They have forsaken this valley and all who enter it!"

Despite the press of his sword in his hand, the *jikininki's* words sent a chill through Hokagé, a sensation of ice and darkness he hadn't experienced since the night of the Akkihito, the slaughter. *Fear.* The vast, suffocating horror of utter abandonment. How easy to accept that this haunted vale was shunned by the gods—that he, too, was shunned, cut off from them for this lifetime and countless others to come. For all the times he had said and thought it, he had never fully believed it. But here, in this hellish place, faced with an undying foe, it had the sting of absolute truth to it.

"Drop your sword and try to run, boy!" the ghoul screeched. "You will get nothing of mine! All you'll find here is death!"

With that fatal word, it lurched again. Acting purely on instinct, Hokagé ducked and whirled, striking out for the embroidered bag. The ghoul master yanked back with his remaining talon, screeching with fury. "*Mine!*" it cried, like a petulant child. "*It's mine! It's all mine!*"

Framed in the doorway, Moriko watched like a spectator at some mad sport, eyes wide with fear.

Hokagé swung the Toshinaga sword, one-handed.

The ghoul gave a last desperate tug.

The bag's seams split, spilling its contents to the floor at the samurai's feet—just beside the ghoul's still-grasping claw. Moriko yelped again, a pitiful, plaintive sound.

For a single thunderstruck moment, both Hokagé and the *jikininki* gaped down at the thing that had fallen from the bag—a pearl-bright orb about the size of a man's clenched fist, starlight-vivid in the darkness.

The ghoul master made a low noise in its throat: *aaaaaahhh.*

Hokagé glowered at Moriko, his gaze piercing. Knowing.

The girl, still barred from her strange treasure by the ghoul and its enemy, stared back with a hopeless, naked expression on her round white face.

Hokagé bit down on the rage that flashed through him, extinguishing it by force of will. For a rare moment, he found himself at a loss, unable to choose his next action, unsure what path wisdom suggested.

The ghoul master had no such qualms. It seized the opportunity, snapping at the samurai like a rabid dog, snatching a ragged divot of flesh from his upper arm. Hokagé spun and dropped to the floor, snatching up the orb in fingers that sizzled with pain.

For the barest of instants, he felt it in his grasp, warm and curiously *alive*, measured its weight and worth—and its owner's worth as well. So much to be gained by keeping it, so much to be lost by returning it, and yet— He cast doubt aside, and cast the ball away with it. He and the ghoul master watched together as the sphere arced through the air, a pale moon scudding across a winter sky.

Moriko caught it, gazed down at it with an expression of wondering relief, perhaps even a twinge of regret. Then she lifted the fold of her gown and cradled the shining sphere to her chest. The light blazed—and winked out. Gone, along with the sphere itself. And yet, Hokagé thought, the glow shone still in her dark eyes.

Ever a slave to its greed, the ghoul master spun to chase its lost plunder. Hokagé leapt to his feet and struck one last time, the Toshinaga blade splitting the dark like lightning.

The ghoul master took a single wobbling step, then twisted to the floor in a hideous heap, its body split from crown to groin. Even as Hokagé sheathed his sword, the *jikininki* went on thrashing, mindless as a beached fish, maggots and tiger beetle larvae squirming in its fetid black viscera.

In the doorway, Moriko gave Hokagé a final glance—then turned and fled into the night.

Acting on some incomprehensible instinct, Hokagé followed.

* * *

He chased her through thickets and streams swollen with rainwater, followed flashes of movement between the trees, splashing through the mire of mud and dead leaves, until it seemed he was only a shadow following a shadow.

Then he burst into a clearing, and stopped.

Not ten paces away, a single lonesome *torii* gate rose among the trees, weathered yet graceful, austere. Beyond, a miniature shrine hunkered beneath a green copper roof, its little altar empty but for a few tenacious cobwebs. It stood flanked by two carved-stone foxes, their ears upright and alert, their tails rising in elegant curls behind them.

Moriko knelt at the foot of the altar, her silken kimono pooled around her. Though the rain still fell in driving veils, the gown, he saw, was perfectly dry.

Lightning flashed behind the hills, painting the foreground an unspoiled black. In its aftermath, Hokagé saw a new shape perched atop the steep-pitched roof—a great fox, as white as fresh-fallen snow, nine broad tails fanned out behind its lean form.

"Great-grandfather," Moriko said, her voice reverent but no longer even mildly feminine. Indeed, it wasn't the girl at all, Hokagé saw, because the girl had vanished just as the great spirit had appeared. In her place sat a small red fox, fur matted with rain and mud.

"Sasa-kun," the great white fox said, in a voice as resonant as the thunder, "again you disappoint me!"

The fox—Little One, as the other had called it—bowed its head meekly, ears folded.

"I only meant to have some fun. Isn't that what we *kitsuné* do? Is that not your legacy, oh venerated Inari-sama?"

Hokagé caught his breath. *Inari-sama.* So—he was in the presence of the Fox God himself, and one of his countless pups.

"You were careless!" boomed Inari, with an angry flick of his tail. "Didn't recognize those *jikininki* for what they were, did you? And so you let them steal your fox-orb." Inari cocked his head, made a deep, disapproving sound in his throat. "Had it not been for the kindness of that samurai, you would have been trapped in that human shape until old age claimed you just as it claims them!"

"But—but I *did* fool him," the fox said in its boyish voice, cocking its head. "Obviously he fell in love with me, just as I'd planned—poor helpless maid, pressed to horrible crimes by murderous thugs. Surely only a man mad with love would risk his life to return a poor girl's bauble!"

"Oh?" Inari boomed. "Shall we ask him? Samurai-sama, come forth!"

Even one who had abandoned the way of the gods could not deny that summons. Hokagé strode forward, legs half numb, and bowed deeply before the alabaster figure.

"Tell me, samurai-sama," Inari said, an edge of amusement in his resonant voice, "did you return my fifteenth great-grandson's orb because your lust for his maiden's disguise had blinded you? Or did some other motive move your hand?"

Eyes downcast, Hokagé said, "I—felt pity for your great-grandchild. It seemed the correct action."

"Is that so?" said Inari, with something like a smile on his long white muzzle. "We shall see just *how* correct. Sasa-kun, you were careless, and very nearly lost the heart of your power. I suppose I might have warned you about the *jikininki*—but where would the fun have been in that—and what might you have learned?" Now the Fox God turned his gaze down on the young warrior, still bowed before him. "Samurai-sama, your kindness was brave indeed—but even great kindness may have unintended consequences. My great-grandson owes his life to you, and this makes you responsible for that life. Well, better you than me!" The Fox God smiled then, a gleam of fierce glee in his eyes. "You imagined yourself forsaken by the gods, eh? Then from this day forth you shall have one for your constant companion—whether you would wish it or not! Forever hereafter your destinies shall be intertwined, joined as are the strands of a spider's web—separate, yet crossing frequently, and always dependent each upon the other. Break one and all are weakened. Sever but a few, and all fail."

Hokagé felt objections rising in his throat, but again Inari spoke before he might give voice to them.

"Do not curse me, samurai," he said, and there was a gentleness in his tone now. "You passed this way because you sought to be free of the loss of your family, and of the man you might have become. But you cannot retrace your steps and bring the dead back from the past with you. That path leads only to sorrow. Even among your comrades, you are a solitary man, Hokagé-san—yes, I have seen it. You have walked alone for far too long. It is time you had a companion."

Hokagé could only answer with a low bow, knowing that no words would alter this decree. This was karma, and karma could not be undone.

Sasa had no such sense.

"Wait!" he barked, looking straight up into his great-grandfather's eyes. "Don't I have any say in—"

"It is done, Sasa-kun, so I hope that you shall make the best of it. I suggest you begin by learning something of humility!"

As the Fox God finished, lightning flared and thunder droned. By the time it fell silent, the rain had stopped and the shrine's patinated rooftop stood empty, illuminated now by the faintest glow of daybreak.

The little red fox looked up at the samurai. The samurai gazed down at the fox.

"So," Sasa said at last, the word perfectly clear despite the vulpine snout that shaped it, "what now?"

Hokagé thought a moment, but the future seemed more uncertain to him than it had since the day he'd first raised a katana—a road cloaked in fog, keeping its secrets.

"I shall return to Yamagumo," he said at last, "to the service of Lord Kumamuné. I cannot say what may happen beyond that, or along the way."

"Well," Sasa said, "I suppose we'll find out, won't we?"

Hokagé felt the slightest of smiles rise to his lips. "Yes, Sasa-kun," he said. "I suppose we will."

R. MICHAEL BURNS *is an October child with a background in theater, philosophy, and other dark arts. He is the author of the novel* Windwalkers *(originally published by Evil Jester Press) and more than two dozen horror, science fiction, fantasy, and other harder-to-classify short stories. His essays on the craft of fiction have received accolades from* Predators *and* Editors *and have been used in college creative writing courses. A Colorado native, he taught English in Japan for nearly half a decade before returning to the United States in 2005. He currently resides in the deep dark swamps of Gainesville, Florida, with his feline familiar, Hermia, and the relentless voices in his head. More of his work, both fiction and non, can be found at www.rmichaelburns.com.*

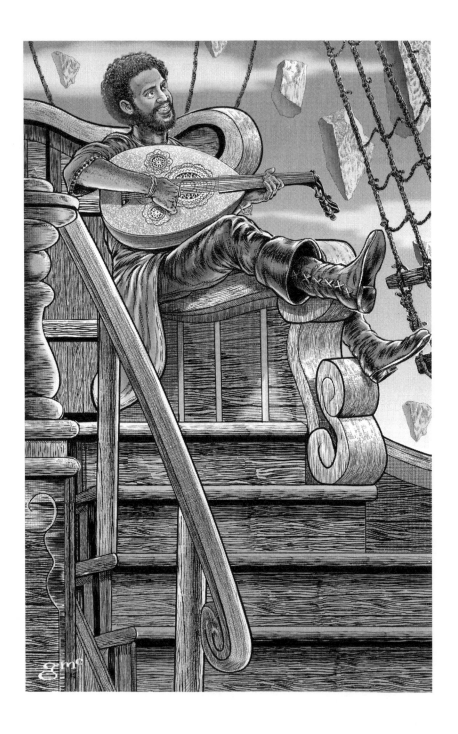

With a Golden Risha

by P. Djéli Clark

The Hanging Stones of Ispa had been aptly (if also quite boringly) named. Twenty or more boulders floating high above the Jade Sea, as if unaware their weight should have made such a thing impossible. Some held a sorcerer had convinced the fool things they were feathers rather than stone; others said it was the practical joke of a mischievous Efrit, though the humor had been lost to time. The erudite scholars of the college at Alm dismissed such tales, claiming the stones were filled with ore that repelled the earth much as a magnet—or some such thing. The lone figure that sat perched on one of the hovering rocks weighed these many arguments, deciding in the end they were irrelevant. All that mattered now was that he was trapped here, with little chance of rescue.

Saleh plucked the strings of his pear-shaped oud with a worn tortoise-shell risha, sending music into the air that turned and danced in time to his song: an ode to a fat-bottomed girl named Neshi, who liked to watch him dance with silver bells in his hair. He once had the fortune of meeting the celebrated oud player Mahir the Magnificent, who between a haze of hashi smoke dispensed sage advice: *Sing what you know, tell tales that you have lived.*

Mahir the Magnificent shared other secrets to his success: keep a salted fish tied to your beard for luck; gargle with bitter black leaf tea for the voice; use only one name; and earn a sobriquet, which every musician of note carried. Saleh passed on the first two bits of counsel, but followed the third, to the mortification of his family. They hoped his pursuit of music a passing phase, until he dropped out of the college at Alm. Lectures on law, mathematics and alchemy moved him little. He wanted to travel the world, see wondrous things, compose songs that would be sung forever—and earn a sobriquet.

None of that included ending up here.

Saleh lay down his oud, eyeing the azure expanse that stretched in every direction. Who ever knew there could be so much sky? Peering over the edge of the airborne boulder, he stared down at the Jade Sea. He could almost make out its glittering surface between patches of clouds, where birds soared on the drafts. A few came up at times to regard him—curious of this flightless interloper.

Not for the first time, he cursed the spineless captain who deposited him on this rock. *Don't have a choice boy,* the man told him—*not when you've made enemies of a high caste noblewoman threatening to have my airship impounded at the next port!* He muttered apologies, for all they were worth, leaving food and a cask of water. But that was two days past! Saleh finished most of the food that first night—how else was he expected to ease his troubles? His water was near gone, and he could already feel his belly touching his back. A few more days, and the next passing ship might find nothing but his bones. The thought wilted his spirit. If that happened, who would ever complete his songs?

He ran a hand through his bushy hair in frustration. His mother had warned that his smile and pretty face would one day land him in trouble. He'd only taken the job as Neshi's music teacher to gain passage out of the port city of Bukra. Who could have guessed the tongue in that pampered noble mouth was so skilled? Her large eyes were tearful when her mother had him put off ship. He wondered if she cried for him now?

Saleh scowled, pushing Neshi, her eyes, and especially her fat bottom, from his head. Fishing through the pockets of his trousers, he retrieved a set of wooden beads. Despite his naming, he was not the most pious of men. But this seemed as good a time for prayer as any. He had been raised to revere the One God, though his mother still kept a small chapel to honor the Many. Sitting cross-legged, he began to recite the ninety-nine names of the One passed down from his father, hoping for miracles, mercy and favors. It was as he was on the thirty-second, that he spied the ship.

It was a speck in the distance, so far away that he first mistook it for a bird. Only birds didn't leave trails of smoke in their wake. Scrambling to his feet, Saleh shouted, his voice echoing through the expanse as he jumped, waving his arms in desperation. When the ship turned towards him his heart soared, sending his legs into a frenzied dance. The One truly was Beneficent! But as the craft drew closer and he spied it for true, his elation and shouts died away.

The sky above the Jade Sea was a shipping way for cargo vessels and barges. This ship was neither of those. Black and sleek, it cut through the empty sky like a steel shark, its engines and propellers unnaturally silent. The flag it flew was plain enough: white with crimson calligraphy worked into a serpent with clawed feet. Not the standard of any kingdom or federation, not even a merchant's guild. That was the flag of a pirate.

Saleh cursed anew. Of all the misfortunes! Not some spice drug smuggler or sky squid hunters, but pirates! He must have been a brain-addled fool. He was above the Jade Sea! How could he forget that nearby was Adaal? Or what had once been Adaal: a sultanate splintered by wars of succession and now ruled by scores of clans, each their own fiefdom. Other kingdoms had taken advantage, fishing Adaal's waters openly, roaming its skies, and plundering its goods. Adaali fisherman and farmers had turned to piracy, exacting what they called "the local tax" upon any vessel they captured.

Frantic, he wondered at his next course. Hide? Eyeing the barren rock he laughed aloud at the impossible. Should he perhaps wave them away? And do what then, he mused, remain here? Resume his title as the lone Lord of Ispa? But pirates! The stories said they flayed captives alive, killed for sport and ravished women. Come to think of it, those tales said they ravished pretty-faced men too!

Kissing his prayer beads, Saleh stuffed them back into his pocket. There was no way out of this, and he needed more than prayer now. Strapping on his oud, he placed the risha to its strings and began plucking out a tune. Mahir the Magnificent claimed the truly skilled could soothe men or beasts with their music—though Saleh was not sure where pirates fit along that line. So it was, when the sleek black airship finally reached him, it found a lone figure in a garish green kaftan, tan trousers and the worn tan boots of a city dweller, playing an oud and humming an idle song.

Adaali faces stared down at him from the railing of the airship's hull, bewildered. A few pointed and laughed, exchanging words and incredulous looks—as if they'd happened upon a talking mule. Saleh continued to play. If they were laughing, they weren't skewering him. Finishing a final chorus, he bowed. There was no applause.

"A wonderful serenade to the clouds," someone remarked.

Saleh looked up to find a man leaning over the side of the ship, weighing him like a fisherman eyeing a strange catch. He was unmistakably Adaali, lean with dark taut skin. His voice was so high-pitched and melodious Saleh almost mistook him for a woman—but for the beard. A ransom of gold circled his neck, matching the stitching worked into his ivory kaftan.

"Peace be with you," Saleh greeted amiably. "I'm Saleh, a musician by trade, born in the city of Koms, recently departed from Bukra. It's my fortune—my very life—to come upon you."

The man arched an eyebrow. "And how is it, Saleh, music maker of Koms, recently of Bukra, that you find yourself—" He gestured to the length of sky and hovering rock. "Here?"

Saleh put on a half grin. "I owe a necromancer in Bukra a bit of money. Well more than a bit actually. But this latest setback, was a noblewoman's idea of a joke."

At that the man wrinkled his lips, as if tasting something sour. Before Saleh could discern what he might have said wrong, another voice called out from the ship. This one was deep, and not at all melodious.

"You're often in the company of noblewoman?" it rumbled.

"If I was," Saleh called back loudly to the unseen voice, "I'd probably know to keep away from their daughters."

"So you're no rich man."

Saleh laughed. "Rich men don't borrow money from necromancers to pay gambling debts."

"A rich man's pet then?"

Saleh's smile faded. His family were petty artisans, hardly wealthy. And while he wouldn't mind riches, he'd gladly take fame first. As for someone's pet… "I am rich in talent," he said pointedly. "What I earn is honest, created by my own hands. And I am no one's pet."

There was quiet. Chagrin momentarily heated Saleh's face. Not very smart if he had just insulted his would-be rescuers. But instead of anger, there was laughter—a booming thing that rose up from that unseen voice.

"Now that is a proper answer!" it bellowed. "Bring him on then!"

There were new shouts, and in short order a plank was lowered. Saleh breathed in relief as he walked up its length. His anxiety returned however when he stepped on board.

There were Adaali everywhere, more than he had imagined. Most wore the long colorful sarongs common to Adaal, alongside an outlandish clash of embroidered kaftans, silk shawls and other garments. The ivory hilts of pistols and knives showed from where they were tucked into folds and sashes. Not just Adaali either now that he looked close. Bronze and even pale hues dotted the bunch. At least three were Yuangari, their faces bearing the tattoos and curved eyes of the Dragon Kingdoms. One of the pirates was actually a woman—with long raven black hair and coppery skin, though she dressed little different than her companions. Saleh's gawking at the strange crew was broken as a tall figure strode from their midst.

This man was decidedly not Adaali—with broad shoulders and muscled arms that looked better fitted on an ironworker. His black skin was darker than even the Adaali, clashing with his blue gold-trimmed coat and crimson trousers. And were those papers stuffed into his pockets? He towered over Saleh, a wide grin flashing from inside a rich black beard.

"So this is the oud player," he rumbled cordially. "Fell into debt with a sorcerer? Plucked the wrong noblewoman's daughter with your risha?" The crew cackled at this, some grinning to show dark stained teeth. The raven-haired woman cackled loudest of all.

"She was my patron," Saleh explained. "I taught her daughter—"

"Oh I'm sure you were a master teacher," the big man cut in. This set off a new round of mirth. Saleh tried to smile along, though he felt ill at ease among the raucous lot. They had it all wrong anyway; it was Neshi who chased him, like a hawk after a mouse! He was the one they should feel sorry for!

"Still," the big man said, his tone turning serious. "Your honest work was worth more than whatever this wretched noblewoman paid you. She robbed you of your true worth."

The crew murmured solemn assent at this and Saleh nodded feebly along. He supposed that was the case, though he'd never thought of it that way.

"I owe you thanks," he said graciously. "I would have starved out here. You must have been sent by the One." He paused and then hastily added, "Or the Many." People could be touchy about religion. Best to cast a wide net.

The big man smiled wryly. "Don't thank us yet. We're not putting to port for another month. You'll be here a while." Saleh felt his stomach fall away. A month? Among pirates? The One preserve him!

"And there's the matter of what to do with you," the big man continued, fingering his beard. "Labor is cherished here; everyone earns their keep. You have any skill working an airship?" Saleh shook his head. Airship work? He couldn't even change a carriage wheel.

The big man grunted. "Well, looks like it's the bowels for you then."

"The bowels?" Saleh asked. That didn't sound pleasant.

"The engine room," the big man explained casually, "where we keep most of our 'guests' helping feed the fires. Hard work, dirty work, but honest." He turned to the melodious voiced Adaali, whose sour face now wore a satisfied grin. "Qooleey, see that he's shown his proper place."

Saleh started in alarm as Qooleey took hold of his arm. The engine room? He'd heard of such places, so hot you had to strip to the waist, spending days shoveling coal into furnaces. He looked down to this brown delicate hands. They were his life! He couldn't ruin them between gears and soot!

"Wait!" he cried, trying to pull away. "I can do other work! I've been to school! I speak three of the old tongues!"

"I speak five," the big man shrugged, already turning away.

Saleh tried again. "I'm a musician remember? I could entertain you!"

The big man seemed offended. "Do I look like some pampered noble, oud player?"

"Your crew then!" Saleh urged, desperate. "I could sing for your crew!"

This earned a dismissive wave. "My crew is busied with their labors. There's no time for song."

"There's always time for song!" Saleh retorted. "All you do here is labor? Your crew has no enjoyment?"

That seemed to catch the big man's interest, as if Saleh had offered some challenge. He walked back, bending close to speak. "Everyone you see here were fishermen once, or toiled on merchant vessels. They were treated like beasts. On this ship, they work for themselves. And they are treated like men. There's contentment in that."

There was such surety in his proclamation, Saleh almost faltered. But remembering his predicament, he held his ground. "Didn't ask if they were content. Asked if they had enjoyment. What's the purpose of work if you can't enjoy yourself now and then?" He swung the oud from his back, patting its wooden frame. "What I do is work. Not just for the wealthy, but those who labor. It gets them through the day, and soothes them after. Reminds them there's life, beyond their tasks. I wager if you asked your crew, they'd tell you the same."

The big man listened earnestly, then turned an inquisitive eye to his crew. There was silence for a moment and Saleh looked into those Adaali faces, pleading. *Place your faith in the music,* Mahir the Magnificent had told him. *It will always bring you through.*

"I could use some music," someone finally voiced.

Saleh saw it was the raven-haired woman and smiled appreciatively. She shrugged in response. "Let him play. If he's no good, we'll throw him and his silly oud over the side." The crew cheered in agreement and Saleh lost his smile.

The big man appeared to mull this over, then nodded. "You're quite the philosopher oud player," he remarked. Saleh almost laughed aloud. Philosophy? That was boredom itself! "Seems you've convinced Dali. And with her the crew. Keep them satisfied and you might just avoid the bowels yet." He chortled at this. "Good luck. Qooleey, let's get under way. And give him what he needs."

Qooleey snapped at the command, barking out orders that were picked up and carried. The crew scattered, going about their varied duties with precision. In moments the sails of the airship billowed as the propellers spun, sailing them away from Ispa. Saleh watched the hovering rocks recede in the distance, hoping he'd made a fair trade.

"Suppose you need food?" sour faced Qooleey asked finally.

Saleh clutched his stomach, which growled in answer. The man rolled his eyes, but beckoned him along.

"Your captain—" Saleh began as they walked. He motioned to the big man, who now stood upon the deck with arms clasped behind his back like an immovable statute.

"He's not a captain," Qooleey cut in. "No captains on this ship."

"Your leader then," Saleh tried. "He doesn't look Adaali."

"Not Adaali," Qooleey responded dryly. "He's from farther south, though he's traveled much the world, more than most men. A great amount of wisdom in him." The man's melodious voice seemed to sing now. "In his homeland, his given name was Aganda. In the kingdoms however, he goes by Usman."

Saleh stumbled to a stop and gaped. Qooleey turned back with a toothy grin, his dark eyes mischievous. "So you've heard the name," he purred.

It wasn't a question. Everyone had heard of Usman, the most notorious pirate in memory. He attacked merchant and imperial vessels alike, and spoke treason against the Emir—calling for the end to rulers. A madman certainly. The bounty he carried was rumored enough to buy a small kingdom, though none who tried to collect it returned alive. Many named him, the Pirate Prince.

When Saleh finally got his legs working again, he trudged along in silence, whispering to the One—and the Many—that he managed to leave this strange affair alive.

His work on the airship—which went by the peculiar name *The Beggar*—began that very day. After gorging on a meal of rice, caramelized onions and lentils with spiced lamb, he found a place with shade on the deck and set about his task. The crew however proved less than receptive. His best melodies of skillful heptatonic scales produced barely a glance—certainly no applause.

He went to sleep frustrated that first night; sharing a cramped space with an Adaali who snored like a boar had not helped. Still, it was better than the alternative. He learned that the "guests" assigned to the engine room were nobles and merchants, captured from vessels and held for ransom. While they remained, they were put to work feeding the furnaces. Usman was determined that for at least that time, they would know honest work.

With that threat hanging over his head (the bit about throwing him over the side had to be perverse pirate humor), Saleh took another course. The next day he did not sit. Instead he roamed the airship, walking among the crew as they labored. He also remembered one of Mahir the Magnificent's bits of wisdom—*give the people the music they want, not what you believe is best for them*. That morning he struck up a popular Adaali song, playing it in the manner of their kaban—a type of oud. He'd listened to a few Adaali play, and remembered well their tempo and lilting voices.

The crew reacted with surprise, at first suspicious but eventually granting grudging approval. A few soon asked to hear songs from their home, as if putting him to a test. At first he was uncertain. But if he was sung a verse, he often realized he did know it—though by different names. The fast-paced *The Dancing Dervish* turned out to be one in the same with the Adaali *The Whirling Star*. And the well-known folk tale *The Pearl and the Fisherman* was, for the Adaali, *The Fisher's Fortune*.

In short order, it seemed the whole crew had requests. Some tried to teach him more obscure Adaali songs, and bits of Adaali to go with it. At night, the tunes called for turned bawdy. The exploits of a dashing Adaali seaman with private parts of iron; the fisherman's daughter who was always easily talked out of her dress; the eel with a curious shape that startled all who caught it. Saleh sang them shame-faced, to boisterous laughter. The odd women of the ship—four in all—seemed to enjoy the bawdy songs most, taunting him for even coarser lyrics.

Most especially however, the crew enjoyed songs of the less fortunate: the tale of the nobleman's daughter, who became a pauper to live with her poor lover; the story of the boilermaker cheated from his pay who died for lack of medicine; the girl thief who duped a foolish king from his wealth.

His music brought him acceptance among the pirate crew. They showed him around the airship, teaching a bit of rigging and knot work—at which he was terrible. They also displayed other talents. Some Adaali were remarkable dancers, clapping their hands and moving their hips as Saleh played. A thick mustached Yuangari dazzled everyone with the ability to make coins and even knives disappear from his fast-working hands. He offered to teach Saleh the trick, if he could learn the oud in turn; but thus far neither had picked up the other's skill.

Even Usman engaged him, during evenings on the windswept deck sipping mint tea with sweet milk and cardamom. Unfortunately, all the man talked about were the many ways the wealthy robbed those who labored for them, and how the poor would soon overthrow their masters. Saleh listened politely, though he thought it all boring to the point of numbness. He had known more than a few poor men. All they hoped for at the end of a day was to drown their sorrows with hashi or with a wide hipped woman—and they would expend their meager earnings for both.

But Usman was not dissuaded. The man fashioned himself one of the philosopher-kings of old who had ushered in "divine faith"—reconciling the worship of the One and the Many. Usman claimed to be writing a treatise of labor and rebellion that would be just as inspiring—which explained the papers he kept stuffed in his pockets. When it was complete, he planned to spread his book far across the lands to begin his "revolution." What grand delusions!

Still, these pirates were not what Saleh expected. They spent their days at storytelling, trading jokes or assigning biting nicknames. There was One Leg, Six-toes, Scarface, Big Teeth, Knock-Knees, and so on. Qooleey it turned out was itself a nickname—a chirping bird particular to Adaal. Usman was the only one it seemed above such taunting. Though claiming no one land or ruler, the pirates held a zealous faith in their leader's vision. Saleh might have simply called them naïve wanderers—if not for the raiding.

The day of his first raid had started out like any other. He spent the morning flirting with the cook for an extra bit of the honeyed flatbread Adaali preferred (the woman was old enough to be his mother, but tittered like a girl at every joke) and took to strolling the deck with his oud, strumming a light song. It was a traditional Adaali folktale about a giant whose heroism had healed their broken lands long ago. It was said when he returned, Adaal would be united once more in peace. The sailors hummed along, starting out their day's work.

Stopping to rest, he leaned against a railing beside a hawk-nosed sailor nicknamed Bidar, on account of his balding pate. Hailing from one of the Pasha kingdoms, the veteran sailor had once been an officer on an imperial vessel—an amazing feat considering he started as a lowly Zanja working the gas flats. His reasons for turning pirate were a mystery. But he found favor among Usman's crew, where rank counted for little but age was valued. At the moment he was busied spying through a brass telescope, eyeing the distance.

"Peace be with you uncle," Saleh greeted. "Catch sight of something?" He nibbled at the bread and a few sweet dumplings he kept in a trouser pocket.

"Could be," Bidar drawled beneath curving white whiskers that looked much like tusks. "There's something big out there, moving behind some clouds."

Saleh turned to look, unable to make out anything beneath the sun's glare. "What do you think it is?" He paused his eating, eyes going wide before whispering. "Is it a sky krayken?" In his two weeks aboard *The Beggar*, the pirates had regaled him with tales of fantastic sights in their journeys—herds of green horses that galloped upon the waves, great rainbow-hued serpents that lived in snowcapped mountains, and monstrous sky kraykens with tentacles that could crush an airship within their armored bulk.

Bidar barked a laugh. "Sky kraykens don't hide behind clouds boy." His voice lowered to a mutter, and he frowned as if recalling some memory. "Unless it's a female nesting with her young. Brood swarm like that can pick a ship clean. By the One and the Many, that's not something I want to see again."

With a shake the old veteran brought himself back, unaware of Saleh's ashen expression. "But don't you worry boy!" he assured. "That's no krayken. That's a ship. A big, lumbering beauty of a ship." He offered a crooked grin at that. Then shouted. "SHIP!"

Saleh jumped as his cry was picked up across *The Beggar*. As one, the pirate crew raced to the railing, jostling one another for a good look. Usman soon appeared, reaching them in long strides. "Found us some good hunting uncle?" he asked.

Bidar cackled, making his whiskers dance. "Fat and ready for the plucking." He handed the telescope to Usman who peered out into the distance. Saleh still could see nothing, but the big man smiled broadly. "The One and the Many bless your marvelous eyes uncle."

He turned back to the crew. "We go as three! Select your parties! And be quick!" His eyes fixed on Saleh and something in them flickered. "Oud player. Grab your instrument and come along. Your skills might prove helpful in this raid."

Saleh almost choked on a sweet dumpling. "Raid?" he croaked. But Usman was already moving, and he ran to catch up. The crew scurried all about them, like an ant's nest that had been kicked over. Clearing his throat he tried again.

"I think there's a mistake."

"Oh?" Usman asked, never stopping his hurried paces.

"I play an oud. I have no skills with…raiding." He stopped, gawping as an Adaali ran forward and handed Usman the largest rifle he had ever seen. The weapon began with a mahogany frame etched with gold designs, and ended in two long silver barrels that flared open at the front like trumpets. Catching his stare, Usman grinned and patted the weapon with affection.

"I unburdened this from a Jawgan noble. The man used it to hunt giant thrice-tusked Maroodiyaal. Majestic beasts. And he slew them for no more than sport. I let him spend extra time in the bowels, denying his family's ransom five times. I've never hunted Maroodiyaal, but I've put this rifle to good use." He leaned closer. "You may have never raided a ship, but you are going to put that oud to good use as well."

Saleh barely recalled how he came to be on the small dhow, what the Adaali called a beden. It was one of three, with long iron hulls sporting wing flaps and small engines along with a lateen sail. It had all been a flurry of activity. What he mistook for disorder was in fact the well-honed precision of a crew of brigands. He was bundled into the vessel with Usman and several others. Qooleey of course. The melodious voiced man leaned casually in the stern, eyeing Saleh's nervousness with barely suppressed glee. A grey-eyed woman named Barisha, whose amber skin showed more muscles than most men, sat beside him. The two openly made bets on if the oud player might empty his last meal or his bladder in the raid to come. Truth be told, he felt he might do both.

A chip-toothed Adaali nicknamed Genay prodded him, offering a small bit of jaad. The green leaf that stained the teeth and made your mouth dry as dust; but chewing it brought a bit of euphoria—and maybe bravery. Saleh accepted, stuffing a bit between his jaws and biting to release the nutty taste.

"Ready yourselves," Usman declared. The big man stood at the dhow's front, his head wrapped in bright yellow turban in the Adaali fashion, and that giant rifle slung over one shoulder. "We're right on top of her." And they were. Saleh gasped as he set eyes on the massive airship. It was slate grey and bulbous, with at least eight spinning propellers that carried it slowly through the sky like a lazy whale. It dwarfed *The Beggar* several times over. And in these dhows they were gnats in comparison.

"We're going to raid that?" he sputtered, almost swallowing the jaad.

"Looks can be deceiving," Usman replied. "This is a merchant freighter. Too big, too slow to outrun us. With a small crew and a small guard. They'll run before putting up much of a fight. When we board, stay close to Qooleey and Barisha." He turned to them. "Watch after him."

Saleh looked to the two, who grinned toothily now like wolves. And they were to protect him? "Shouldn't I have a sword?" he asked. "Or a pistol?"

Usman glanced down to him. "Do you know how to use either?"

"No," he admitted. He was a musician, not a fighter.

"Then no. Don't fret oud player. You'll be looked after. What I want you to do now however is play a song. Play it loud. And play it clear."

Saleh brought his oud around, uncertain. "What kind of song?"

Usman thought for a moment. "The one about the rich man and death."

"Oh I like that one!" Barisha perked up, earning a reproachful glare from Qooleey. "What? It's good!"

Saleh looked to the oud that sat heavy in his lap. An odd request. But what about this day hadn't been odd? *Place your faith in the music*, he heard Mahir lecture again. With a held breath, he put a tortoise shell risha to the strings and plucked out the tune.

The song told of a rich man who lived in a mansion atop a hundred stairs. Learning that Death would come for him, he sought to cheat his end through trickery. He dressed a servant in his place and took up the garb of a poor gardener. Masked, the rich man watched as Death began the long ascent up the hundred stairs, knowing the servant would be taken in his stead. But after reaching halfway, Death let out a weary breath and turned to the rich man saying, "I came for your master, but I'm too tired to walk these stairs further. I will have to take you instead." And the gardener, who was the rich man, dropped dead. The servant, now rich beyond measure, treated his workers well, paid them fair, and spent a lifetime giving away his wealth. When in the end Death came for him as an old man, he went willingly, and at peace.

Saleh finished to find that he had gained an audience. The dhow was now close to the freighter and several figures peered at them over the railing. They stared in confusion, trying to make sense of the approaching craft that made music as it came. For a moment there was silence, as the two groups merely watched the other. A sudden cry shattered the quiet, succeeded by the sound of pistols. Saleh cowered, thinking they had been shot at. But no, the sounds came from elsewhere on the freighter. It was followed by a second set of cries from yet another part of the airship. The two remaining dhows of the raiding party Saleh fast realized. He hadn't noticed their disappearance. They had broken away, no doubt boarding the freighter elsewhere. His music had been a diversion, to distract the airship guards. The gathered figures on the freighter seemed to grasp as much, many of them running off to meet these new threats.

Usman beamed at his plan's success. Lifting his rifle high, he fired it once into the air. The boom that followed was like thunder, enough to scatter the remaining figures on the railing. With a lurch the dhow picked up speed, racing now to the freighter. When they reached, Usman jumped out even before the grappling hooks moored them, his booted feet landing easily on the deck. Qooleey, Barisha and the others followed. Someone was sent back to fetch Saleh, who was lifted and all but dragged aboard.

"Play us something lively oud-player!" Usman bellowed. "Something to move the spirit!"

Saleh willed his trembling fingers still and began plucking out a song—a fast-paced tune usually accompanied by Adaali clapping. This time it matched the sounds of battle.

Saleh barely understood what was happening. He seemed to be running to and fro with his small group. Barisha brandished two leaf-bladed short swords and fought while screaming curses. Qooleey's movements were as melodious as his voice, smiling as he whirled a slender sword. And Usman lived up to his fearsome tale. The pirate leader had left his great rifle in the dhow, and now wielded a long pistol and a heavy wide-blade saber. He led their charge, the sight of him alone sending challengers scurrying from their path.

Saleh scrambled to keep up, plucking his oud as swords rang out and the scent of gunpowder filled the air. The airship's guards often stopped to stare at him, dumbfounded. He offered them awkward shrugs as Usman and the others took advantage of their confusion to press the attack.

It was in the middle of this tumult that the man appeared. Saleh watched as he peeked a long face about a corner, sending furtive eyes darting about. He didn't look to be a guard, dressed as he was in a long violet kaftan and golden slippers. Glancing about, he sprinted across the deck, his arms laden with items. He appeared to be trying to reach a dhow anchored to the freighter, carefully avoiding any skirmishes.

Saleh wondered if he should say something. He was no brigand. Did he care if someone on this hapless airship fled? The decision was taken from him, as a handful of frantic guards appeared. They shoved the man aside, ignoring his protests and clambering onto the dhow. It seemed Usman was right. These hired sentries weren't willing to further risk their lives. They broke and ran everywhere now, making their escape.

A nearby melee sent the man scurrying heedless for safety—directly towards them. Saleh tried to shout a warning to the man, whose long face looked in every direction but the one he was running. Trying to move out of the way, he somehow tripped on his own feet. The collision was not graceful.

Saleh went down in a heap with the man, careful not to fall on the oud—which was more precious to him than his own bones. The man bawled pitifully, trying to pull away. But his long kaftan prevented any extraction and the two lay tangled in a mass of twisted cloth and limbs. It seemed to Saleh they rolled about on the deck in an undignified manner for a long moment. Then hands were upon him, separating them and lifting him up.

"Well caught oud-player!" Usman complimented.

Saleh nodded shakily, dusting his clothes and checking his oud. No broken strings.

"Thieves! Bandits!" the man howled. His long face was flustered, as he wagged a finger adorned with rings menacingly in their direction. "Do you have any idea who I am? I work for the Imperial Ministry! In the Golden Archives! My family is noble born! Have you any idea—!"

"Be quiet!" Barisha growled. She slapped his backside with the flat of her sword, causing him to yelp. Usman bent to inspect him, plucking away the items he attempted to clutch onto. Some were books of all things, and rolled parchments.

"Perhaps you know who I am," Usman greeted with a smile. "I hear I am called the Pirate Prince—though I've never cared for the name."

At that, the man's long face quailed.

It was some evenings later that Saleh received a summons to Usman's quarters. He groaned. It had been two days since the raid on the freighter, during which Usman had sequestered himself to his hold. Two blessed days of not having to listen to the man's philosophical lectures, now come to an end.

With flirting praise to the blushing cook, he finished off a bowl of stewed chicken and beans cooked in buttery sugar, then made for the upper deck. Along the way he tried again to complete the Yuangari's sleight-of-hand trick with a rice cake, but to no avail. Raven-haired Dali passed him, laughing at his fumbling, her pearl-black eyes smoking with possibilities. He turned to admire her swaying hips, but no more. Dali shared her bed with Barisha and a whip lean, adept, knife-wielding Adaali called Xiito. Saleh had no intention of intruding upon their tryst; that was trouble he could do without.

Downing the rice cake, he made his way to Usman's cabin, where he knocked before being admitted entrance. The room was larger than most quarters of the ship and Usman used it as a general meeting place, sleeping in a simple woven hammock. Flickering tallow candles lit the space amid stacked books and manuscripts, which Usman claimed to consult for his grand work.

This evening the Pirate Prince stood in the center of the room. Qooleey, stood beside him. Saleh looked past the man's sour stare to find more persons of general importance among the crew—including Barisha, who idly twirled a dagger while staring down at a lacquered table. They were all staring at the table, where a broad parchment lay stretched across its length.

"Peace be with you oud player!" Usman greeted, looking up to acknowledge him.

"Lucky fool," Barisha teased, tossing a lone greying forelock from her eyes.

Saleh returned the evening's peace with a grimace. The raid had been celebrated for its haul—mostly trade goods and some new workers for ransom and the bowels. It was the One's own mercy that no one on either ship had died. Barisha attributed it to the oud player's fool luck, and the crew eagerly affixed him with the nickname.

"Fortune smiles on the just," Usman said by rote, never losing his grin. "But I didn't call to have you pluck your risha today." He beckoned Saleh closer, pointing to the table. "Recognize it?"

Saleh looked down and nodded. As was custom on *The Beggar*, one twelfth of the looted goods had been split among the raiding party; all else was divided evenly under Usman's watchful eye. Saleh never fashioned himself a thief, but what else to do among bandits? This particular item had been one of the rolled parchments bundled in the arms of the fleeing imperial archivist.

"I speak five languages in the old tongues," Usman said. "And devils take me if this isn't written in one I cannot. What do you say oud player?"

Saleh looked to the faded brown parchment, where a mishmash of shapes sat imposed on a blue background. Lines of unbroken script surrounded the crumbling edges, with more writing on the inside.

"I can read it," he answered. Perhaps his time at Alm wasn't a full waste.

Usman clapped his large hands. "Praise the One and the Many! You are good luck!"

Saleh smiled sheepishly and scrutinized the parchment. "Some of these are names. And others look like directions. I'd say it' a map."

A murmur rose up in the room and Saleh looked about. Usman met his questioning gaze. "Just the confirmation we needed oud player. The man you liberated this from was indeed an archivist. And quite corrupt. He pilfers rare writings from the imperial libraries and sells them to wealthy collectors. He was on this way to deliver this parchment and other items to a buyer. He tried to use it as his ransom, claiming it was a map. To a place called Arakhee."

"That's here," Saleh nodded, pointing to a shape on the map emblazoned in calligraphy. "Where is that? Arakhee? I've never heard of it."

Usman paused, his dark face lit by shadows and candle flame. "Because it hasn't been called that in a thousand years," he murmured. "Most today remember it as Jabel's Doom."

Saleh's eyes rounded. "King Jabel? Arakhee is where King Jabel ruled?"

Usman arched an eyebrow to him. "So the stories say."

"The stories say many of things," Qooleey chirped.

That they did, Saleh thought. Jabel was a king dead now at least a thousand years, long before the founding of the kingdoms. He ruled a city of vast riches that travellers spoke of in wonder. His power, and that of his kingdom, had been gained through dark sorcery. By some means Jabel summoned and bound terrible Efrit, which plundered other lands, bringing him their riches. Fearful rulers bowed and offered tribute, lest the Efrit be loosed upon them. But Jabel grew careless. The Efrit broke from his control, and laid waste to his city.

"They say a dark cloud covered Arakhee," Barisha recalled, "even the ships at port. And from that blackness all that could be heard were screams. Passing sailors went mad, leaping into the sea to their deaths. Then the island and all its inhabitants vanished. Jabel's Doom."

Saleh shivered. He had heard those tales as a child. How could an entire island vanish?

"They also say," Usman countered, "that King Jabel's wealth remains there, ripe for the taking. No one's known where to find the island-city, until now."

Saleh goggled, parsing his meaning. "You mean to try and go there?"

Usman grinned wider. "Oh I mean to do more than try." He turned to the others. "And I ask all of you to come with me. Keep quiet for now. The crew may be put off by this venture. I'm sure they'll come around in the end. But best we're in the thick of it by then."

A stillness descended about the table as a yowling gale sounded outside. Everyone exchanged glances. Raiding merchant vessels was one thing; plundering some cursed island was another. Usman patiently waited them out, as if knowing that was all he had to do.

"Devils take me," Qooleey sighed finally. "I'll go. Too rich a chance to pass up." He swung his gaze to Saleh. "But only if the Lucky Fool comes along. He found the wretched map. Seems only fair."

Saleh took a step back. "What?"

"Yes!" Barisha echoed, her grey eyes aglow. "The Lucky Fool found the map! I'd feel better with a bit of his dumb fortune. Wager the rest of the crew says the same when they find out he's going."

"I'll go if the Lucky Fool does," a scarred Adaali called Canjeh agreed. Saleh listened in stunned silence as others joined, each nodding approval at the brilliant plan.

"Wait!" he shouted above their conversation. All eyes turned to him. "No one's asked Lucky Fool—I mean me, if I want to go!"

Usman frowned, genuinely perplexed. "Why wouldn't you?"

Saleh gaped at the man. "Perhaps because it's a haunted island? With a mad king and the One knows what else!"

Usman laughed. "Do you really believe those fanciful tales oud player?"

"Something happened to that city," Saleh countered. "It's in the histories!"

"I've read the histories these past two days," Usman remarked, gesturing to a stack of books. "They say only that Arakhee fell. There's nothing about a curse. The wealthy rely on fear and superstitions to keep the masses oppressed."

Saleh was in no mood for philosophy. "Why not take the archivist? It's his map!"

Usman laid a hand on his shoulder. "Because he's not a member of this crew, and sits where he belongs—tending the furnace in the bowels. Fortune brought you to us oud player, and you brought us this map."

Saleh shook his head. "I'm just an oud player. Nothing more. I'm sorry."

Usman stared at him for a while then sighed. "Very well. You won't be forced. Only as you found the map, it's a shame you will not claim your share of the twelfth. That amount could be substantial. Enough to pay off your necromancer."

Saleh eyed the man dubiously. "You expect to find that much?"

Usman shrugged. "You know the histories as I. The wealth of Arakhee is legendary."

"Mountains of gold I have heard," Barisha put in. She elbowed Qooleey.

"Yes, mountains," the sour man sang. "Jewels too I expect."

Saleh licked his lips. That would indeed be enough to settle his debts—enough to whisk Neshi away from her mother. Maybe even buy up her estates. The thought of putting the noblewoman in the streets actually made him giddy.

But there was still that matter of a dead king. And a curse.

"Think of the songs you could tell of Arakhee," Barisha added. "What other oud player will be able to make such boasts?"

Saleh paused. Now that was tempting. The words of Mahir the Magnificent played in his ears: sing what you know, tell tales that you have lived. He looked about at the expectant faces. Usman grinned at his silence, like a man who knew he'd just tossed a winning hand at dice.

"Are we decided then oud player?" he asked.

Saleh slowly nodded, wondering if he'd lost all sense since being around these brigands. But how could he say no to riches and songs? The One keep him alive long enough to tell of both.

The trip to Arakhee took them far out onto the open sea. The crew was curious but dutiful. Keeping a secret on *The Beggar* however, turned out to be futile. As expected, when news of the plan broke, there was uproar. Saleh feared a mutiny. But Usman stood inside the melee like a rock in a storm. He instructed Saleh to play something soothing, and then the big man's booming voice broke through the din. Mouths fell silent and he seemed to reach every ear, promising each treasure for their troubles and stoking their courage. By the end, they were cheering.

But as they neared their destination, apprehension grew. Seasoned sailors like Bidar complained that the winds flowed oddly. Others claimed the seas were strange too, as were the clouds. Saleh himself knew nothing of either, but he could feel a difference in the air: a cold that prickled the skin. The crew took to completing their tasks in silence, and he plucked his oud with somber tunes to match the mood.

Arakhee appeared one morning out of nothingness, shrouded by a mass of black clouds that sat upon the waters, extending high like a mountain. There were no screams like the stories told. Only silence. And stillness. Saleh watched that dark veil churn as if boiling, and his spine turned to ice.

"Jabel's Doom," Usman proclaimed, appearing at his side.

Saleh turned to regard him. "I thought you didn't believe in that."

"The One or the Many cast down Arakhee for its greed," Usman replied. "Destruction wrought by folly. That I believe in."

Saleh looked into the blackness and shivered. "But what we do now, isn't that greed?"

A slight smile creased Usman's face. "We liberate stolen wealth. That is justice, not greed."

Saleh didn't bother to argue. "How has nobody ever seen it?" he wondered aloud. "It's so—obvious."

"I have thought on that myself," Usman responded. "Perhaps Arakhee remains hidden unless it is sought. Sorcery can be strange."

Saleh frowned, looking up at the man. "You make it sound like the island's…alive, like it's expecting us." Usman said nothing more, walking away and leaving the disquieting notion unanswered.

A short while later, the small party was on a lone dhow that skimmed low across the waters. Saleh clutched his oud tight as they approached. They were twelve altogether now, each with large sacks and a few burly Yuangari with wooden chests strapped to their backs. All had weapons. Usman carried his great rifle and saber. Saleh was this time given a small pistol, which he tucked into his waist. The thing felt like a snake coiled there, but it gave some comfort.

"We're going in!" Qooleey cried. It was the only warning before the cloud enveloped them.

Saleh looked around, blind. He could see nothing. Not even his hand. Everywhere was darkness, a black thick as a wall. The coldness grew here, like thousands of tiny unseen teeth biting into his skin, threatening to freeze his blood. There was suffocation and a moment of panic as he fought to breathe. Then they were through.

He drew a long breath, clutching at his pounding heart. Most of the others seemed similarly shaken—except for Usman who stood resolute. He sometimes wondered if the man was human. In the newly revealed sky the sun shone dully as if filtered through a veil, rendering midday as twilight. The waters here barely moved, and the sail of their dhow turned limp in the lifeless breeze. There were no birds either, not a single gull that winged or cried. It was as if everything was gone, or worse, Saleh feared, dead.

The dhow arrived at a white painted pier. Ancient seaborne vessels with pristine sails and dozens of oars bobbed upon the waters—their decks empty. Disembarking, the small party walked along a stone pier and stood gaping. The lost city of Arakhee lay sprawled out before them, an array of bulbous spires with colonnaded buildings that competed in opulence. They seemed built one upon the other, with walls that gleamed beneath that unnatural sun.

"It's very—clean," Saleh murmured. Not a single building looked to have fallen into disrepair. Trees and gardens sat tended, as if recently pruned. Even fountains spewed water that flowed uninterrupted onto colorful mosaic tiles. A thousand years gone, and the vanished city Akharee remained untouched by time.

"So where do we go now?" Barisha asked as they reached the pier's end. Her blades were sheathed, but she kept hands on the pommels.

Where indeed, Saleh wondered. The city was a labyrinth. Searching it would take days.

"If I was a greedy king," Usman pronounced with an air of certainty. "I would make my palace large and magnificent, and surround myself with my wealth." He pointed and every eye followed. In the distance, a golden dome rose high above all else like a second sun, in what must have been the heart of the city. Its surface glittered even in the dull light, while a twisting spire reached from its top towards the heavens.

"Jabel's palace," Saleh marveled. He could already imagine the songs this sight would inspire. "The stories say under the midday sun, the sight of it blinded those who stared too long."

"Then we should stop staring and get about our business," Usman proposed. Motioning them forward with his rifle, he began walking.

Saleh took a place in the middle of the small party that moved through Arakhee's lonely streets. They passed shops and markets, where goods hung ready as if expecting buyers. Food remained piled atop stalls unspoiled, as if awaiting the return of those who made them. Saleh wondered to himself what this city would have looked like filled with people. More to the point, where might all of them have gone? When one of the Adaali reached for some fruit that lay in a basket, his companion stopped him with a hiss. Saleh agreed. He would starve before taking a morsel from this unnatural place.

As they moved closer to the palace, the grandeur of the city grew. Saleh stared up at vast halls and towering statues of winged beings cut from cobalt blue stone, monuments he speculated to rulers or gods. It was then that he first felt the odd tingling at the nape of his neck, as if he were being watched. His gaze darted to cut out windows and arched doorways. All were empty. Still, he could not rid himself of the feeling. Voicing his concern, he found he was not alone.

"Eyes," Barisha said looking about. "Endless eyes, following us. I feel it too oud player."

The others murmured in agreement, peering into alleys at still shadows.

"Keep your mind on the task," Usman ordered, never breaking his stride. "Or it will wander down dark paths. The palace is near now. Come!"

They quickened their pace. But try as he might, Saleh could not push away the uneasiness. Neither could his companions, whose fingers strummed along weapons as if expecting an ambush. When they reached the steps of the palace, the small party took them hurriedly, eager to leave the open streets. They stopped before two towering doors of dark wood worked with gold. Usman and the burley Yuangari took hold of bronze handles fashioned in the shape of lions and pulled, until the muscles on their arms strained in exertion. The wooden doors groaned and creaked stubbornly, but slowly parted, revealing their hidden secrets.

Saleh gawked as they stepped through the open doors. Jabel's palace was even more opulent on the inside, filled with statuary and pottery that could have come from a hundred different lands. Rich tapestries decorated the walls, covered with designs of sunbursts and bright flowers, competing with intricately woven rugs that extended the length of the halls. Walking the corridors in silence, he marveled at craftsmanship made by hands over a thousand years dead.

When they stopped again, it was before a set of black doors adorned with interlocking stars. This time Usman ordered two other men to pull them open, standing with his rifle at the ready. Saleh stood ready as well, a hand on the small pistol at his waist and his heart pounding. He was not certain what to expect, as fanciful tales of angry spirits and other fears danced in his head. When the men finally pulled the doors open his breath caught, and he thought he might faint away.

It was a chamber. Gold sat piled within, making dunes a man could climb—coins and bars, plates big as platters. Fist-sized jewels sparkled among them, alongside ivory carvings and silver chalices ornamented with sky blue sapphires or blood-red rubies. Saleh swooned at the sight. Enough to pay off a sorcerer? Buy Neshi's mother's estates? There was wealth enough here to make him perhaps the richest man in the kingdoms.

Usman began a low laugh that fast built into a booming rumble. The others joined in, cheering like wanderers who had completed some quest.

And then the looting began.

The small party ran amidst the heaps of wealth, filling sacks, chests and pockets. There was little need to squabble; the room contained more than enough to go around. Qooleey lauded over a curved sword, its hilt adorned with orange gems. Barisha lifted a necklace of ruby fire drops, each large as a hen's egg, which she claimed as a gift for Dali. Saleh followed suit, picking through the valleys of riches, at times wishing he had brought a larger bag. And that was how he came across the man. Or what had once been a man.

Saleh shrieked at sight of the shriveled corpse wrapped in bright saffron robes. It sat against a golden mound, its once living skin stretched like parchment across bony limbs withered to bone. A bulbous hat layered in gems was fitted onto the corpse's head, though it seemed overly large for the shrunken frame. No, Saleh corrected, looking closer. Not a hat, a crown. He jumped as the others found him.

Barisha frowned, glancing around with her swords drawn. "We heard a scream."

"Like a woman's," Qooleey purred.

"It did not sound like a woman!" Saleh snapped, indignant.

Qooleey only snickered.

Saleh began another retort, but took a breath. "I was startled by this." He pointed to the corpse.

Usman stepped forward, bending down to lift the rigid body upright, so that its empty sockets stared out from a contorted visage fixed eternal in death. "King Jabel," he murmured. "So this was your fate, wealthy man."

Saleh's eyes rounded. The mighty and fabled King Jabel! "He must have locked himself in here, with his riches," he surmised.

"As his city died about him," Usman derided. "He came to be with his gold."

"He looks frightened," Barisha noted with unease. Saleh agreed. On that dead man's face was fear that reached through the ages.

"Maybe he knew what his greed reaped for him in the next life," Usman jeered. Standing, he shifted his big rifle to one shoulder. "Let's finish here and leave the king to his realm."

The others turned away, returning to their looting. But Saleh found himself still staring at the Jabel's unhappy corpse. Here was the man of stories and legends, who had unleashed a terrible evil that consumed his people. He wondered if wherever Jabel's spirit lay in torment, it now howled in rage at their pilfering.

It was by chance that his eyes fell to the man's lap. Clutched in those desiccated hands was a thing of wood and strings. Saleh bent to look closer. Did his eyes deceive him? An oud! Or something similar—more square than pear-shaped, but in many ways an oud. Sure enough, in the other hand, the dead king held a small glittering item between his thumb and forefinger. Saleh reached down, grimacing as he pried withered fingers apart to pluck out the small treasure.

It was a risha! A golden risha!

He stared at it in wonder. The thing was perfectly shaped, smoother and lighter than gold should have been. Yet who had ever heard of a golden risha? Hardy tortoise shell, eagle quill or cow horn made for a good risha. And why would a king surrounded by all this wealth, clutch so hard to this? Had he spent his final moments amusing himself with song while his city fell? Was Jabel truly such a monster? He would have thought on these things further, had he not heard the voices.

Saleh jumped up, whirling to look about. No one was there. But the voices remained, a buzzing that grew louder by the moment. They were many voices, like people talking all at once. No, not talking. They were singing. A clash of discordant melodies. Yet strain as he might, he couldn't make out its content or source. It was as if there were people looming right over his shoulder, whispering into his ears. Seeking his companions he found they had gone still. So they heard it too.

"What is that?" Qooleey asked, shaking his head as if to rid it of a fly.

"It's coming from all around us," Barisha said. Her swords were back out, and she spun about searching.

Saleh looked back to the dead king, an uneasiness gnawing inside him. Stuffing the golden risha into a pocket, he backed away. "I think we should go. I think we've been here long enough."

Usman frowned deep, his eyes roaming. For the first time, uncertainty marred his face. "Take what you have," he said at last. "We leave now."

No one needed to be told twice. They packed their plunder, rushing from the chamber and staggering beneath the weight. It was Barisha who noticed what little light that existed disappearing from the hall, consumed by creeping shadows. Their walk soon became a run, the unseen voices now blaring like trumpets. Saleh almost cried out in relief as the palace doors came into sight. He passed through them in a sprint, eager even for the open discomfort of Arakhee's streets. What he found however was horror.

Beneath a sky roiling with black clouds, the once empty city was filled with people—men, women and children. They ran through the streets, screaming, wailing, crying and clutching their ears. And the things they did…

Men hacked one another with swords. Women plunged knives into their own throats, all the while weeping in terror. Children tore at each other with teeth and nails like animals. And the dead did not remain so. Saleh watched in horror as a man was ripped apart, only to have those same pieces knit back into some grotesque semblance, now walking on hands with his head nestled into his belly's glistening entrails. He shrieked his terrible song, lashing out with misshapen limbs.

"The song!" Barisha stammered through clenched teeth. "It is the song!"

And then, Saleh heard the words that poured in his ears for true. The song spoke of death. It called to him, crooning, besieging him to rip out his own tongue, to rip out the tongues of his companions, to break their bones and suck their marrow, to make their bodies dance anew. It not only sang, it compelled, pushed, urged and enticed him to join in the murderous revelry, to become part of this carnival of chaos. This was Jabel's Doom, what had destroyed the fabled city and claimed its inhabitants.

There was a shout, and Saleh turned to see one of the burly Yuangari clawing at his face. The chest on his back slipped away, crashing to the ground and spilling its contents. He looked up at them, screaming with laughter as he offered up his plucked out eyes between bloodied fingers. With a bloodcurdling howl he ran off to join the mayhem, dancing to his death song. Saleh tried to hold the contents of his stomach down, and found he was unsuccessful.

"Get to the pier!" Umsan shouted, pointing with his rifle. "Move you fools!"

The big man's words were like the crack of a whip. They ran, stepping into the maelstrom, going around the damned when they could, or through them. Make shift staves pummeled flesh. Swords cut down reaching limbs. Usman's great rifle thundered, tearing through bodies.

Saleh learned fast these were no apparitions. One took hold of him, a woman, her neck oddly twisted about as she ran on all fours like a beast. He floundered for his pistol, only to have it tumble from his shaking hand. The woman bore him down beneath her, teeth snapping viciously—until a sword swipe from Barisha severed her head, sending it spinning. She pried the still groping body from atop him, kicking it away. Together they stumbled to what remained of their party, which now took shelter beneath the broad wings of a statue.

"We won't make it!" Qooleey wheezed, doubled over in exhaustion.

"We go on!" Usman growled. He bent to reload his rifle, where smoke poured from the flared muzzle.

"But they are too many!" Barisha panted. "And they don't die!"

She was right. The press of bodies had grown. And those cut down rose anew, more grotesque. They had lost two more of their number to the song, one ripping out another's throat. Saleh wondered which of them would be the next to surrender.

He clutched at the prayer beads in his pocket, fervently begging that the One carry them from this nightmare! But the song competed with his pleas. He tried not to listen, but it was insistent, seductive—burrowing into his mind. If he could just shut the voices out, do away with the damned song!

There is only one cure for bad music—better music.

Mahir the Magnificent's words reached him through time and a haze of hashi smoke. Swinging his oud around, Saleh fumbled in his pocket for a risha and plucked the oud's strings.

There was a resonance, a terrific roar that surged outward, so strong it seemed to Saleh he could see it—a wave of golden light that flowed as it went. He turned to find every eye staring at him.

"By the One and the Many!" Qooleey's melodic voice was a whisper. "What was that?"

Saleh had no answer. He looked down, confounded, to find something unexpected between his fingers—the golden risha. He had distinctly reached for his own. Yet this one found its way into his hands.

"Look upon this," Barisha breathed.

Saleh followed her gaze to the streets. Wherever the golden wave had touched, the chaos vanished, leaving clear paths empty of people and murder. Even the horrid song seemed to have lessened.

Usman reached to grip Saleh hard by the shoulders. His face was a grim mask splattered in gore. "I don't know what you've done oud player. But by the gods do it again! The rest of you, we run! Drop the cursed gold if you must. Riches aren't worth our lives!"

Saleh required no further urging. Putting the risha to the strings he played. Once more the beautiful melody of golden light flowed from him—pure and cleansing. He was singing now, words to a song he didn't know, as the risha guided his lips and fingers. It told of Arakhee and King Jabel, who through a magic risha played music so sweet, it enslaved Efrit to do his bidding. They were his to control, until one day the Efrit learned the secrets to his song. Freed from their bondage, they sang their vengeance on the doomed city. Jabel tried to stop them. But he found the risha would no longer work for him. In fear and horror, he locked himself away, desperately trying to retrieve its lost magic.

Saleh played on, the music of his oud and the golden risha drowning out the deathly voices. Paths opened up for them, and wherever the golden wave struck the damned vanished into motes of dissipating light. They were almost upon the stone pier, the survivors laughing giddily at the rescue of their lives, when the great roar crashed around them.

It sounded to Saleh like a hundred beasts, all screaming in a mangle of tongues. He turned in time to see a monstrous shape descending from the sky in a swirling torrent of black clouds. They parted to reveal a terror tall as a mountain, with fiery wings wreathed in flames. It stood in the midst of the doomed city, its horned head shrouded in shadows, its gaze and a gaping maw burning with the light of ten suns.

"By the One and the Many!" Qooleey cried in dread. "It is a devil!"

Saleh shook his head. "No," he replied through clenched teeth. "An Efrit. Goragan, the Keeper of Songs."

He stepped forward, his feet as guided by the risha as the words on his lips. The thing seemed alive, speaking to him, telling him all he needed to know. Plucking the oud once he released a wave of light towards the fiery giant, who clove it in two with a forked sword, all the while screaming its rage. The rage of its enslavement. Its humiliation. Its insatiable vengeance.

The Efrit began to chant, weaving a cacophonous song that Saleh could now see—tendrils of blood that snaked in every direction, seeking out ears to listen. He struck back, plucking the oud this time in a continuous rhythm, creating a scale of such complexity he could not conceive it in his mind. His fingers danced across the strings. And with each stroke, waves of light crashed into the Efrit like a sea, severing the bloody tendrils. The two settled into battle, the mortal with a golden risha against a being that had seen worlds born and spun to ash.

Saleh faintly heard the voices of his companions, calling out to him. But they seemed far off. All that he knew now was the music, the beautiful celestial song of the oud made by the golden risha. It swept him up in a whirlwind, wrapping him in armor against the Efrit's onslaught. His fingers tore and bled, and yet he played, the power of the song building in him like untainted light. By the One God, by the Many, he was light! He was the song! And the song was everything! There was a scream, his own, competing with the roar of the Efrit. And then there was nothing.

* * *

Saleh sat on the bow of *The Beggar*, watching clouds fly above the airship, feeling the sun and air on his face. The ship's healer—a tall Yuangari who claimed to have studied medicine—said it was good for him. Then again, the man had also forced him to drink that wretched bitter black tea. And then had wanted to stick him full of needles!

He managed to escape by claiming he was better. After all, their ordeal in Arakhee had been days past. He awakened to find himself weak as a child, in a bed Usman assigned to him specially. The man had personally carried Saleh back to the dhow to make their escape. But Barisha, and even a grudging Qooleey, had told the entire ship of his deed—his battle of songs against the Efrit. Now they fashioned for him a new nickname: "Saleh the Great." He had long wanted to earn a fitting sobriquet, but he never imagined it would be among pirates.

"Rested now?" a voice asked.

Saleh turned from staring at this bandaged fingers to find Usman striding towards him.

"Much rested," he replied. "I haven't had a chance to thank you, for rescuing me."

Usman barked one of his big unnerving bouts of mirth. "Way I remember it oud player, you're the one who did the rescuing. Make sure you get that part right hero, when you tell your song."

Saleh felt a heated blush beneath his skin. Him? A hero? He wondered what Neshi would think?

"Your share of the gold from Arakhee is in my hold," the man went on. "Much smaller than you probably hoped."

Saleh sighed. Most of the riches they pilfered had been lost in the escape. What they managed to bring back, once divided among the crew, was not even enough to settle a quarter of his debts. There had been half-hearted talk about making a second trip. But the island had vanished again. And Usman and his inner circle had the map burned. Saleh didn't blame them.

"We'll make port by week's end," Usman said. "I can drop you off in Amsra. But if you're looking for refuge, at least while still in this sorcerer's debt, you're welcome here." He paused, a frown darkening his face. "And what of the risha?"

Saleh had known that was coming. No one forgot something like that. Reaching into his pocket, he withdrew what he had tucked away so carefully. The risha glinted gold in the morning sun, deceptive in its smallness. The thing had rarely been from his thoughts.

"Where do you think it comes from?" he asked.

"Who can say?" Usman murmured, his eyes hardening on the risha "The world is full of wonders. It's undoubtedly a thing of magic. Powerful enough to ensnare even an Efrit."

Saleh thought momentarily of the fiery being. "It had so much anger. If you could have felt—" He shivered. There was no way to describe it.

"The hatred of a slave," Usman asserted. "Anger was its right. As was its vengeance."

Saleh regarded him in shock. "You sound like you're on its side! It would have killed us if it could, done to us what it did to Arakhee. All those people…" He shivered again.

Usman nodded solemnly. "Who is to blame when the slave rises up and set's its master's house on fire? No being deserves to be shackled."

Saleh let the matter drop. He would never understand this strange man. His eyes went back to the golden risha. "I could probably become the greatest oud player in the lands. Create music that would be remembered for ages."

"But would it be your music oud player?" Usman probed. "Would such music truly be guided by your hands?" He paused. "I tried to take it from you."

Saleh looked up in alarm.

"While you slept," Usman confessed, his voice low. "I thought on the good to which I could put a thing of such power. I am after all, a man of vision. With that risha I could lift the veils from the minds of so many, make them see how they are exploited, fill them with the fire to overthrow this corrupt order that oppresses us."

Saleh stared at the big man. There was a hunger in those eyes. And it unsettled him. "What stopped you?" he asked.

Usman's gaze hardened on the risha. "Jabel," he said tightly. "The doomed king achieved much with this magic, but became a slave to it himself. That is the secret of power oud player. It corrupts the just as well as the wicked."

Saleh looked down to the risha, tracing a finger along its length. Its promises whispered across his thoughts. But catching sight of Usman face, he saw a man waging an inner struggle. He might try to take the risha again if given a chance. The Pirate Prince was indeed a man of vision, and he would yearn the risha's power much perhaps as it yearned for him.

"Probably for the best," he sighed. Placing the risha on top of his thumb he held it aloft, then in one motion flicked it over the bow—sending it to the sea far below.

Usman released a held breath. "For the best oud player," he agreed. Clapping Saleh's shoulder, the Pirate Prince prince turned and walked back to overseeing his crew.

Saleh watched him go—and then with satisfaction pulled the golden risha from inside his sleeve. He smiled at the sleight-of-hand. He had finally mastered that Yuangari trick. And just in the nick of time at that.

Perhaps he would rid himself of the thing one day. But not just yet. His visions after all, were much smaller. With a chuckle, he placed the treasure deep into his pockets and pulled out his worn bit of tortoise shell. Leaning back upon the bow, he returned to plucking out an unfinished tune—an ode to a fat-bottomed girl named Neshi, who liked to watch him dance with silver bells in his hair.

PHENDERSON DJELI CLARK *is the Nebula and Locus award-winning and Hugo-nominated author of the novellas* The Black God's Drums *and* The Haunting of Tram Car 015. *His short stories have appeared in venues such as* Tor.com, Daily Science Fiction, Apex, Lightspeed, *Beneath Ceaseless Skies, and* Heroic Fantasy Quarterly. *Find him on his official author site pdjeliclark.com or rambling on about issues of speculative fiction, politics, and diversity at his aptly named blog* The Disgruntled Haradrim *(https:// pdjeliclark.wordpress.com/).*

BRONZE-ARD, THE FERRET MASTER, AND
AUSPICIOUS EVENTS AT SWIFT CREEK FARM
BY ADRIAN SIMMONS

T he remarkable occurrence of both Bronze-Ard and the Ferret Master
arriving on the same day at Swift Creek Farm presented Bellaw and her
siblings with a rare opportunity to slip out of a day's work. And, since the
farm was blessed with plenty by the Goddess in the pool, Her sister spirit in
Swift Creek itself, and Her brothers in the hills, all the chores ground to a halt.

Bellaw watched, rapt, as the traders and their helpers went about unpacking
and securing their animals and goods. They would all stay, for the night at
least, for that was the law and the farm was blessed with prosperity. If it was
prosperous enough to pay for either of the services that the two travelers
brought, that was a decision beyond Bellaw's age and station.

Bellaw was uninterested in such matters anyway, such grown-up concerns
like deciding if it would be better to have the team of barely-tamed polecats
rid the farm of the rats and mice, if only for one spring, or if it would be
better to have four fields plowed by the gleaming metal ard and thus save the
wooden ones they had carved during the winter. To Bellaw, Bronze-Ard and
the Ferret Master had brought something far more interesting with them—
boys her own age.

Sons, surely, and bondsmen, traded for their services. Boys who had walked
hundreds of miles and seen many things, and were just exotic enough to be
interesting without being so foreign as to be frightening. They hadn't even
stowed their gear when Bellaw had narrowed her preference down to two: the
reedy-tall boy in bondsmanship to Bronze-Ard and the easy-moving son of
the Ferret Master.

She had to be careful about such things; broken noses and blood-feuds had started for less. So, as another cold and fitful rain began and everyone moved inside, Bellaw slipped up to the Goddess pool to ask Her advice.

It was improper, but she couldn't help but find the Ferret Master's offering of a polished and carved shell at the bottom of the pool, and not far from it what looked to be a wolf's tooth from Bronze-Ard. She herself made the common offering of a pebble and whispered for the Goddess to give her a sign of some kind.

* * *

The Goddess, or as the people of the farm knew her, Helikkeel, wasn't listening to Bellaw on that day, although she certainly did hear. No, this was the night to honor the First Agreement, and she coiled in a low slow spot in Swift Creek, listening.

"Destroy them, destroy them all," urged Rabbit. He sat on the great flat stone that leaned into water, asking what he relentlessly asked. "Flood the valley as you have before. Wash them away and return the valley to us."

Rabbit's hatred of the men was unslaking. But he always asked the wrong questions, asked for things he could not possibly understand, so Helikkeel always said no.

Weasel came next, touching noses with Rabbit's vessel as they passed on Truce Rock.

The polecat stood on the rock, scratched behind his ears then licked himself. Just a weasel, then, not Weasel Himself.

"Ask," she prodded.

He popped up, made to bolt, stood very still.

"Men have my kind. Female. Female in sweet-season. Want to mate. Must get past was-wolves."

She knew a hundred ways, and prepared to offer one that he could maybe understand, when he surprised her by asking:

"Make clever. Clever enough to get around was-wolves to female in sweet season."

And, because it was within the bounds of the First Agreement, Helikkeel did so.

* * *

Run! Run! Run!

The weasel, Ate-Tadpoles, bounded from the safety of the trees and into the grass. *Stop! Duck!*

He waited low, sniffing. He popped up quick and sniffed the air. Smells of the old was-wolf were nearby, and of the man-stink and fire-smell and the musk of the strange weasels. It wafted on the night air from the house. Horses, too, and oxen, and other things. The female in sweet-season was there, too. Strong and sharp in his nose.

Hafta mate! Gotta get past was-wolves! His tiny brain reeled with the smells and the desires. Then he remembered it. *The woodpile!*

He popped again. The house was a massive blurry blob in his weak vision, and firelight glowed from its windows, and another blob in front of it was the woodpile.

Woodpile! Run!

Ate-Tadpoles shot through the grass, low and swift, keeping the strong scent of the was-wolf in front of him.

Gotta run! Gotta get to woodpile! Could die here!

The woodpile grew distinct in his nose and vision. He skidded to a halt there. Was-wolf was not far on the other side. Now he could make out the smell of pine-tar and horsehair that made up the was-wolf's rope.

Hafta get past! Up to the big burrow! Hungry!

He was suddenly keenly aware of his hunger. His thoughts, his small scheme, all scattered, leaving only: *Hungry! Could die!*

He sniffed around the base of the woodpile. Wood and mold and dirt and old bark and—grubs!

Dig! Fast! Quiet—could die! He found a grub after making only a few scratches in the cold wet earth. Yanking it out of the ground he devoured it messily.

Why am I so close to man-burrow?

The wind brought him the answer. Sweet-season! Gotta mate! Run!

He ran from the woodpile to a smaller stack of wood and sticks and slithered in among them. It worked! The was-wolf was close, but didn't smell him! Didn't hear him! Other weasels covered him up! Man-sounds covered him up!

Next part hardest! Have to wait for exact moment! Have to wait! Wait—

Zzzzzzzzzz.

Whoa! What? Gonna die?

He was in a woodpile. Near the man-burrow. The smell of sweet-season brought him back to his plan.

Run!

He ran up to the house itself. He'd never been this close. The men were making noises, lots of noises, like a stream over rocks but with their mouths. And the smell of weasels and fire was strong.

He slipped along the base of the house, sniffing for a way in. Rats found it, he could find it—

Freeze! Something moving around the curve of the wall ahead! Rooster!

The bird puffed up and lashed out its wings. Terrifying! *Bite neck! Bite neck!*

The was-wolf let out a deep bark.

Gonna die! Was-Wolf'll get me! Run!

* * *

The icy rains started again the next day and kept both the Ferret Master and Bronze-Ard from working. And the day after it was still too wet, and Bellaw feared that the musk of ferret would never get out of the house. People slipped outside doing what tasks they could, just to get away from the crowding and the smell.

The musk made Bellaw's feelings for the Ferret Master's son, Walol, complicated. He was handsome enough, and clear-eyed and smart. But that smell— And he was lazy. Bellaw brought it up as she and her sister prepared one of the muddy fields for plowing.

"Lazy or ignorant?" Vanwan asked.

Bellaw's foot caught on a stone under dirt that was trying its best to be mud. She'd have to pick that one up later. "What do you mean?"

"Not a farmer, is he?" Vanwan said. "Heard him tell that his great-grandfather went on the road with the weasels. Never plowed a thing since."

"Not farmers? That makes no sense." Bellaw pulled her ox and it trudged through the not-quite-dry ground. "Everybody is a farmer."

"Kings aren't." Vanwan, for being her younger sister, was quick to point out Bellaw's mistakes.

"He's not a king."

"He has a house by Leog's citadel. Lives close to a king."

"Not the same thing."

Vanwan and the ox she was leading had a momentary disagreement about the direction and after a few hard pulls on the rope Vanwan won. "Rootless aren't farmers."

"They are so. They grow things up in the hills."

"No, they come down here in harvest season, work, then they take some of the food back."

Bellaw had feelings for some of the rootless boys, too. Delicious and forbidden feelings, steeped in taboo and simmered in mystery. But they were a poor folk, who may have farmed, but not the rich fat life she and her kind enjoyed.

"They don't grow enough for a whole year," she said to her younger sister, while quietly thanking the Goddess that those exotic boys did drift in to help with the harvest.

They prepared the ground with a few more passes of the oxen, then hobbled the animals and began to go through the field and gather rocks.

One field away, Bronze-Ard's bondsman worked much like they did. At least he knew how to prepare a field for plowing, whether it was for a bronze-ard or a wooden one. The metal ard wasn't going to get splintered and chewed up on the smaller stones, so Bellaw and her family could avoid digging those out of the dirt for a change. Of course, the smaller stones would wait for them, and bring their cousins up from below, next year.

"Either way," Bellaw said, watching the bondsman guide the oxen, "Walol would make a poor match. Once he was out of the business of killing rats I'd have to teach him things about proper living that even a child knows."

"Yes," Vanwan said. "But that could be fun, too."

They tied their baskets to the ox's back and led him back into the field, picking up rocks, fist-sized or larger, piling them in the baskets, then emptying them on the field's other side. Later they'd add them to the wall.

While her hands were busy with stones, Bellaw thought about the Ferret Master's boy and watched Bronze-Ard's bondsman. The young bondsman was tall, not quite Rootless tall, but close. The field he worked was just in front of Wild Hill, a little rise covered with brambles and great flat stones that her family never bothered to clear.

"Instead of making Walol into a proper farmer, you could go with him and travel with the Ferret Master," Vanwan volunteered as they unloaded the third pass of rocks.

"Ugh. The smell—"

"Maybe you'd get used to it."

"I don't even think the Ferret Master gets used to it."

Bellaw passed over a rock that was borderline size. "Now, the bondsman. He'd make a good match. Strong. Smart. Already knows how to keep a farm running."

"Battle captive," Vanwan said simply.

"He was very young, and he's worked off his debt with honor."

"He'll have something to prove. They always do."

"Maybe I could go with them? I wonder if Bronze-Ard would offer to take him on as a foster-son after his bondsmanship ends? Been known to happen."

Vanwan didn't say anything, which Bellaw knew meant she didn't agree.

They worked in silence, clearing that field and then the next. Sometime in the late afternoon the bondsman hopped over the wall and pointed to the sky. "Do you think another rain is coming?"

They looked at the sky for a while. Clouds were coming in, again, and it looked like it could go either way.

Bellaw could see that Tolnal, Bronze-Ard's bondsman, spent a lot of time looking at the sky, he had those kind of brown clear eyes—which reminded her of the rootless, which was nice. And he was growing chin-hair, unlike the rootless. Not a real beard yet, but something in between. It made her feel funny inside.

Rain or not, they had a lot to do, and spent another few hours prepping the fields before they all went down to the icy creek to wash off the day's mud and dust.

Tolnal had nice legs, too.

* * *

Helikkeel was both in the creek, and the creek itself. She was in the Goddess pool, too, but only in a small part. And she was keenly aware that Ate-Tadpoles was back at the sacred rock. The sun wasn't even down yet, and it certainly wasn't time to honor the First Agreement again, and she was tempted to ignore him.

But he was close to the offerings, and that made her nervous. His tiny fuzzy mind might have the idea to steal something shiny from under the rock. Plus, just as water flowed downhill, Hilekkeel's curiosity drew her back.

"I've granted your favor," she said from the creek itself, "go back to your business."

"Can't get to weasel in sweet-season," he chittered. "Get close. Not enough! Another favor!"

She knew where there were other in-season weasels, and it would have been the easiest thing in the world to tell him to just follow the creek for a day. But that wasn't how things were done.

"GO!" she boomed. He jumped in fear, then slipped away into the high weeds.

She was about to go away when he came back and did it.

It hit the surface of the water like thunder, and as it slid down the few inches to the bottom her entire being shivered. It hit the pebbles along the bottom with a crunch like her cousins the boulders splitting from the mountains.

Her boneless toes dug deep into the tiny gravel and her claws pulled her forward to look.

A bronze arrowhead lay in the water. Ancient, still sharp. She could feel its two-hundred flights, see each nick and scratch and blemish—all adding to its majesty.

"Want a favor!" Ate-Tadpole said. "Want to figure out trick to get to weasel in sweet-season."

And, since he had made the Offering, Helikkeel granted it.

* * *

Ate-Tadpoles was on his fourth attempt to get into the house when it struck him—this was his fourth attempt. Four. One less than the claws on one paw. It was an odd feeling. Like a smell he had never noticed but had been there all along.

The feeling left his mind almost as soon as it had entered, but it left a kind of track, a smell even, that lingered after. It cluttered his head with all the other things that had left thought-smells in his mind lately.

He slunk out of hidey-hole, where the metal bits that the Goddess valued so much where hidden, and then crawled through the brambles.

The offering had been a kind of thought-smell, too. Worrying and nagging at him as he slept. He had known about the metal almost all his life, he had known that men gave metal to the Goddess, but the idea that he could make the same offering was new. And, since he was now *counting*, and getting ever wilder schemes, he supposed the offering had worked.

Threading through the brambles, Tadpoles scurried onto one of the big square stones. His vision was poor, but from here he made the most of it. He spied on the farm for a while. Many of the humans had left, and this time they had taken the dogs with them. He popped, took a long slow sniff of the air blowing from the farm. Dogs, yes, but not near.

He jumped down, ran across the field to the rock wall, slid half over it, then looked and smelled. Turned earth and ox still lingered. He had no idea why the humans did it, but he had a thought-smell-trail that led his brain back to memories of watching them, the humans, leading oxen back and forth across the— *Grubs!*

He could smell them. So they were looking for grubs, perhaps? But they never ate any. *Grubs for me!*

Beneath the patchy snow the earth was wet and soft and no match for his claws. In moments he had dug up and devoured more-than-the-claws-of-one-paw worth of grubs and worms.

Birds had gathered on the wall, attracted by his success, and he left them to try their luck. He ran around the inside perimeter of the rock wall until the smell of oxen grew overpowering.

He checked the sky, to make sure there were no hawks with ideas, and then he scaled up the rocks, dropped down the other side and ran in among the oxen. He slipped around among their hooves, letting their powerful pungent smell cover him as he got closer and closer to the house.

He caught the muddy, matted tail of one ox and slithered up onto its back before it could swat him away. The big bull let out a moaning call of alarm that Ate-Tadpoles could feel vibrating through his paws. He broke into a run as the ox lifted his head to look back, ramped up the thick neck and jumped.

Beneath the melting snow covering it, Ate-Tadpoles discovered the grass that made the roof of the humans' burrow was not just piled, but tightly woven—a complete surprise! For a few long moments he struggled, all his wet claws scrabbling among the thatch until he found one of the lateral-weaves and hauled himself up to it. He sprang up to the next one, then the next, and finally got to the very top of the thing, where the smoke-hole opened.

Thick dried mud and was packed around the thatch of the opening, and a couple of layers of old ox hide were tied on top of that.

Inside was a great drop that led to a barely glowing fire. The house was dim and smoky and Ate-Tadpoles could see the tin cages that the other weasels were in, against a far wall under the window.

There were furs and skins hung on a frame by the small fire. Tadpoles walked around the opening, looked, sniffed and built up his courage. He caught the smell of the female weasel in sweet-season and jumped with all his might.

Falling through the thin smoke, he spread his legs and flexed his claws then thumped onto the furs. They were damp and hot and not as soft as they looked and he slid down a bit before getting a grip.

He let himself down, nosed the furs aside, and slipped underneath them.

From his hiding place, he tried to get the smell of the room. There was too much! The dirt floors and the thatch roof and everything in between overwhelmed him.

He darted out from the furs and crossed over to the cages. They were all asleep, wheezing and snoring. *Not these! She wasn't here, she was—there!* A smaller cage off to the side. He rushed up.

Sweet-season-smell washed over him, made all his senses swim and swoon. The thought-smell-trails in his head scattered like scents in a strong wind.

Bars! Cage! How to get in? He bit into the metal and pulled. Nothing. He shook it and she popped up out of her clay shelter.

She chittered at him for a moment: alarm and curiosity.

How did the humans get in?

Some of the other weasels were awake—they popped and ran to the edge of their cages and began pulling at the bars. The noise! Sweet-Season was alarmed and forgot about him for a moment and looked at the others. She looked back at him and started.

"Cat!" she chirped.

Tadpoles folded in half to look just as the big tabby charged. "Gotcha!" the cat yelped.

Tadpoles, thwarted so close to his goal, lost all the thought-smell-trails and jumped full into the tabby.

* * *

Cold and drizzly rain kept conditions wrong for either Bronze-Ard or the Ferret-Master to ply their trade. On the fourth day the men, those who lived at the farm and those who were visiting, went out to hunt the wild thigh-high ponies that lived in the glowering hills around the eastern end of Elskdale.

Bellaw's day was spent in the dozens of tasks that kept the farm running, cumulating in four hours of separating good grain from moldy grain. How she hated separating grain. The idea of slipping away from Swift Creek with either group of traders grew more attractive with each hour she spent at the job.

The dogs set up a loud barking when the men finally returned. They had three ponies they had killed and Bellaw was eager to help butcher them—anything to get away from moldy grain.

She, her two sisters and her mother, were all elbows-deep in the job when Tolnol, Bronze-Ard's bondsman, slid up to her. "Can I ask you a favor?"

"What?"

"I speared one of the ponies, and your father cut me a piece of its mane and said I should make an armband out of it. He seemed to think it was important."

"It is. You have to honor the pony's spirit."

"So I braided it and then I asked your brother to tie it around my arm and he told me that the other tradition was to have a girl do that part."

Because she was trying to cut the liver out with her stone knife, Bellaw's arms were hot with blood and the heat of the pony's lingering spirit. But her insides were tingly and cold as she looked at Tolnol. "'First the braid, then the tongue.' It is an old tradition."

"I'd like you to do it. When you get a chance."

Vanwan snickered beside her and Bellaw gave her a shove with her hip.

"I've got to get the liver out and-" Bellaw started.

"We can finish up here," her mother said, waving her bronze-knife in a dismissive motion. "You go and clean up."

"Awww!" Vanwan began before a sharp look from her mother silenced her.

Bellaw walked to the small wooden bucket by the outbuilding and dunked her arms in and hurriedly rinsed them, then her hands, and dug out the bits beneath her fingernails. She could see Tolnol's eyes had their far-away look, but a small smile touched his lips. He almost, almost, had a moustache.

"We always do the first rinse here," she said nodding toward the bucket, "and then another at the goddess pool."

They walked out back of the house and its buildings. The sun was nearing the western horizon and it lit Charred-Stones Hill with a light that drew out every branch and root and leaf-bud.

She dipped her arms into the cold waters of the pool, rinsing them a second time. Tolnol handed her the braid; he must have killed the little spotted pony. Not really something to be all that proud of, but she kept that bit to herself.

"So what is it like to travel far and wide?" she asked instead, tying the braid around his right arm.

And as the sun went down he told her, and he listened to her like she was the greatest of storytellers as she talked about what life at Swift Creek in the midst of Elskdale valley was like.

* * *

Helikkeel was fascinated by the goings-on at Swift Creek Farm. Most of the family and several of the visitors had made offerings and requests. They had hung three pony-hides over her pool. Then there was Fights-Cats. There had been, in her long existence, other animals that had captivated her, had asked the right questions, but he was remarkable. He had brought her two bronze arrowheads and a bronze spear-point. Untold wealth to a family like the farmers at Swift Creek who often chipped flint.

The older women at the farm had whispered to her that there was something wrong, some spirit or something, causing trouble at the farm. That was a supreme joke that Helikkeel couldn't stop laughing at.

* * *

Fights-Cats watched the man-burrow. It seethed with activity like a stirred ant bed. Many of the men were busy in the fields, using the ox and some contraption of wood to dig for grubs. Birds feasted in their wake. Others, men and birds, were out in the woods, checking traps and picking berries. There were a few more inside the burrow, where Sweet-Season was.

He had been watching for a long time. So long that he could almost see the thought-smell-trails that the men followed. And, more importantly, he noticed that sometimes one of them would bring a weasel out and carry it to the wagon by the smaller workshop. The wagon had a bunch of wooden cages that held chickens, and a great clay jug—almost as tall as one of the wagon wheels. The weasels, although they strained for the chickens, were always put into the jug for a while, then carried back inside. That intrigued him.

It intrigued him that the men did things in a fairly routine way. Now, with the Goddess' gifts, he could see that their chaotic behavior was generally ordered. And they brought the weasels to the clay jugs in the same order every day. And Sweet-Season always came last.

It was easy enough to slip past the dogs, and the rooster, and the cats had learned not to cross his path, and in full daylight Fights-Cats made his way to the Ferret Master's cart. He jumped up to the wheel-hub and climbed up a spoke and into the cart itself.

"Polecat!" screamed the chickens, as they always did. "Gonna die!"

He ignored them and prowled around the great clay jug. The smell of pine and horsehair was strong around it from where it had been wrapped in ropes. But through it he could smell damp earth and—worms!

Yes. It made perfect sense. Worms made more worms faster than chickens made more chickens, so feed the weasels worms. And knowing that… knowing that…

He clucked to himself as the idea hit him—an idea so clever that it almost ran out of his head like it was alive. All he had to do was wait until it was Sweet-Season's turn, climb into the jug and then mate! He began climbing the ropes to get to the jug's lid when a flaw in his plan entered his mind.

She might be too hungry to mate. That might lead to fighting, not mating. Which would not be how he'd want his plans to end.

Ah! He'd dig up worms for her, so she'd have plenty when she was put into the jug. Yes! Perfection! Just like he did with Goddess. He had seen men offer shiny things to her, and that had worked well for him. Now he would repeat the trick with Sweet-Season and the worms. Yes! An idea so sharp it had its own teeth.

But the ropes did something unexpected at the top–they twisted and folded around themselves in a weirdly tangled organized fashion.

No match for his teeth! He had already began to chew through the rope when it occurred to him that the men would notice—and, now that he thought of it, they always did something with the rope first before they opened the jar.

One more question, then. He'd go to the hidey-hole and get another metal-thing and take it to the Goddess and ask her to teach him how to untie knots.

* * *

Bellaw spent her day knapping flint with her grandfather. The old man was making hammer-axes. They had a pile of two-fist-sized stones and he would chip one end into a blade, chip the other into a flat striking surface, and then do the complex operation of carving grooves along the sides. Now, in early spring, was the time to drive the new hammer-axes through the fast growing limbs of the trees so that by summer the wood would have grown and tightened around the grooves and they could harvest them.

She was in charge of making the rough blade straight and sharp. And she was embarrassed by the number of chips and misses she had marred them with.

While he didn't appear to notice, her grandfather finally said: "Where is your mind, Bellaw? Not on the hammer-ax, that's for sure. The stone will remember and resent this treatment."

He wasn't angry; his tone was soft and matter-of-fact. And he was right, the tools had to be shown their proper respect, as did the tree they would drive it through.

She stole a glance out to the field. Bronze-Ard and his team were cutting furrows with ease. Tolnol was out front, leading one of the ox teams.

"Bronze-Ard and his folk will be leaving tomorrow," she said.

"We need the room. They need to go to the next farm." Her grandfather was gnarled as an old root, and fierce, and proud, and he spoke blunt and short. But he favored her with a long look as his hands clipped and chipped the stone in his lap. "And why are you so concerned with when they leave?"

"I—" she started, then finally confessed. "I like his bondsman. We never got any time together."

"The bondsman?" He snorted. "Can't be too smart to be a bondsman."

"He was young," she said, then chipped a big notch into the blade she was working on. "And he did fine during the pony-hunt."

"I had heard," he said. "Ah, I miss the pony hunt!"

"I don't even know where he is going next!"

He finished another groove. Still watching the work in his lap he said, "Perhaps, tonight you can find some time."

"He'll be tired from plowing all day."

"Why when I was his age, and you're grandmother had just moved in, the plowing was just the start!" He sighed. "I miss that, too."

* * *

For the first time in a long while Helikkeel realized that she might not have been asking the right question. Men fought each other often and bits of bronze littered the earth. But these points that Fights-Cats had brought her had not been buried. They were too clean, no dirt was in their grooves and nicks. Just where was Fights getting them?

* * *

The gorging-dream slipped from Kaalvaas' mind. The taste of red flesh leaving his tongue, taking the smell of burning fat and the sound of shrieks with it.

The sound of metal grating on stone replaced it. And then laughter—a self-congratulatory clucking. And a smell, acrid musk and arrogance and the lust of furred creatures.

Eyes snapping open, Kaalvaas looked out into his den. The thief was a long-bodied creature, small like a rat, struggling to drag a spearhead toward the jumble of massive stones that used to be the North Gate.

Hatred, strong and familiar, burst into Kaalvaas' mind. Muscles unused for centuries flexed and he surged through the bones of his kin and stretched his jaws wide to destroy the intruder.

The beast yelped, jumped, dropped the spear-head and ran. Kaalvaas closed his maw around empty air as the creature ran into the rocks. Hatred sparked the tinder of his belly and the flames blasted forth, bathing the rocks, the thief, the wall, Kaalvaas, the broken and gnawed bones, in a searing heat.

Thrusting his muzzle into the blocky stones, Kaalvaas took a great long sniff of the air. The fear-stink of the creature was strong, but there was no smell of burning hair, no cries of pain.

None yet.

He spun, a mass of coils and claws and wings. The treasure of kings that had been his bed seemed to be intact. But no, no it wasn't. No! There were bits missing. The creature had snuck in and stole from him, from beneath his very nose as he had slept. This had the stink of meddlesome men who dared to match their greed and spite against his own.

The east gate was destroyed, but his nest-mates had been careful to pile the stones such that there was a small twisting path to the surface. Kaalvaas shoved through the rocks and tore through the earth and finally broke through the tangled roots of tree that had grown over the long years of his torpor.

Heavy night air bathed his scales as he slithered out. A bellow of rage formed in his throat, but he held it back. No. Best to get a feel for the land, for the men who had replaced the Great People.

His wings spread, greedy for the air and he sprang into the sky. No sooner was he over the trees when he noticed a house a very short way off. He coursed up toward the cloudy sky. A fat moon glowed fitfully behind the clouds, and in a few moments he had climbed high enough to see the full length of the Valley of The Seven Bravest, and into those valleys neighboring it.

The land was dark and dreaming. None of the lights of towers or great citadels glowed there now. Kaalvaas grinned, feeling the cold air whistle through his teeth. He and his brothers and sister had destroyed them all, as they had destroyed the great city. Destroyed it, killed and devoured all who lived there, burned it and the lands around, and then pushed down every wall and building to utterly erase the memory of the men from the land. Then he had devoured his kin, utterly erasing them from the world. He was the most cunning. He was the cruelest. All he saw was his.

But men had come back. He counted the hovels, none any bigger than the wretched huts so near his lair. Three here in the Seven Bravest valley, a scattering of others nearby. More than he could destroy in just one night. He hovered in the sky, draping his coils over and against one another as he looked and planned.

Then he letting the love of murder flood from his heart, he let out the war-shriek and dove at the miserable shack that marred his lawn.

* * *

At the western end of Elskdale, a good day's walk from Swift Creek Farm, Bellaw's closest neighbor, Lonlan, heard the sound. The indescribable sound carried to him on the wind. The whole family and their guests jumped at it. A noise like that had to mean something, something horrible and woeful.

His eldest boy looked over his shoulder at the great bronze-rimmed horn that hung on the south wall. They could blow the meeting call that could summon the different farms to the leaning stone at Mag Rufel. Lonlan's hand shot out and he pressed his son firmly down. Any sound to answer that…even a roster, would only draw its attention. His old mother, silent as a cat, began scooping ash up in a cow-shoulder scoop and smothered the fire.

* * *

The Rootless, high in their hills and ridges, shuddered and wrapped their hides and skins tighter around themselves. Their shamans cringed and clutched their fetishes and waited, praying they would not hear the wolves.

The wolves heard, and the elders of their race started a high lonely howl. And those shamans among the rootless who could still understand such talk recognized it as the dread words. "It is time."

Rabbit cackled in his den.

* * *

Bellaw was in the outhouse when the sound struck her. She cringed, raising her hands to protect her head. A silence as deep as the sea followed the noise and then it, too, was rent by a whooshing of air and then a splintering crash.

Her family, their guests, their pets and stock, screamed and bleated and yelped before being blotted out by another roar. Around the hide-door of the latrine a fierce orange light grew, matching the intensity of the screaming and crashing.

Her first thought, when she could think again, was to hide, to do anything but face the horror outside. Digging her fingernails into the wood of the bench, she had almost pulled the lid off and was prepared to follow her own dung.

Her brother was screaming long ragged yowls, nothing like words, nothing close. His meaning was clear: run. Run until your legs won't support you anymore. Run until you drop. Run and don't even turn to look.

The hide door was the only way in or out of the outhouse and Bellaw summoned what courage she could to pull it back.

The house, the house her grandfather and his brothers had built, was gone. The walls of wattle and daub were cracked and split and the roof was folded in. It was on fire. The very ground burned. A beast roiled and seethed in the flames like a monstrous bird in a great nest. The creature's loops entwined the ruins, the bodies; claws dug into the flesh of her mother, wings fluttered and folded, fanning the flames. The creature's head lifted high—as big as one of the great forest boars—lifting what was once her brother's head and arm before throwing it back into the burning ruins.

Bellaw's body, every bit of animal that she was, only wanted to run screaming into the night, but she couldn't turn away from the grotesque sight. The poor dogs on their leads gnawed and strained at their ropes, trapped and waiting their turn. Somewhere out of the wreckage a man stood. Bronze-Ard, balancing on his one good leg, hefted his crutch and swung a mad blow at the beast, batting one of the great wings. Then…then… the thing simply engulfed him; coils and claws wrapped and swallowed him like a deadly wave. Bits of the burning house broke away and tumbled toward her.

One of those pieces was her sister Vanwan, running, burning, screaming.

Bellaw sprang from her hiding place and swept her sister up to her. Vanwan seemed weirdly light, like the infant she carried following her mother's skirts. Bellaw's legs pumped, her feet pounded sinking into the damp earth and she flew to the Goddess pool. Crashing into one of the fresh pony-skins, she bore Vanwan into the shallow water and mud of the sacred pool.

She flattened herself and held her sputtering sister close; they had to hide, if it wasn't already too—

The blow struck her through Vanwan. She could feel the great paw against her arm, hard and sharp and hot. It pressed them both into the soft mud, then it pulled at Vanwan. For a moment Bellaw held, but she might as well have tried to hold up a falling tree. Her sister was gone.

Hands that were not truly hands gripped her ankles and pulled her deep into the mud until she was sure the weight would crush her. She reached up into the burning light of the water's surface, still grabbing for her sister. Something huge and horrible blocked the flickering orange light and then she was pulled down and away. She gripped, numbly, one of the pony skins.

There was a path, then a gate, and the mud became tiny gravel and Bellaw was borne into and born into Swift Creek.

The flat stone of the sacred rock was at her back and Bellaw vomited up mud and water and the last mouthfuls of pony. The slick flowed, illuminated by the light of her burning house not terribly far away, and spread slowly toward the edge of the stone where it dipped into the creek.

Bellaw's mind moved slow as well, wrapping itself around the concept that this was a sacred place, sacred to Helikkeel, and that she shouldn't foul it. She wrapped her arm around her vomit, the same arm that had held her sister, and scooped it back toward her. Her arm was cut open, a gash ran from her elbow almost to her wrist and blood flowed freely from it, mixing with the mud and water and meat–becoming the leading edge of the flow and clouding the lapping edge of the water.

She heard something move on the other side of the stone. She looked and saw a polecat ease itself through the high grass. Lifting its head it sniffed at her, and then lowered its head to look at her. Then it spoke.

"Did you bring Sweet-Season with you?"

The idea that a speaking polecat should surprise her didn't occur to Bellaw after the night's events. Instead she simply shook her head. Her mouth made words independent of her mind. "I think they all died." After a moment she added: "They died with my family."

The burning ruin of the house was perhaps five spear throws away. Somewhere beyond that she could hear the monster killing oxen.

The polecat sighed heavily and lay against the rock, looking like it was lost in thought. Then it scratched and turned to lick itself.

The trickle and rush of the creek changed its tone slightly and the hairs on Bellaw's scalp pricked. Helikkeel was behind her.

Turning, she took a look at the Goddess, the first time she had ever seen her. It was said the spirits of the rivers and hills most often appeared in dreams, and that perhaps once in a lifetime one might see them in the waking world. Helikkeel's head was human–human enough–but the arms and body were something else. It was hard to focus on her, like looking through water, or smoke, or smoke in the water.

Helikkeel eased toward her, rattling the stones along the bottom of Swift Creek. Her appearance settled to that of a woman of indeterminate age, with long hair and breasts that had never felt the lips of a baby.

"A great and woeful thing has happened," Helikkeel whispered. She whispered; even the Goddess was afraid. "I've fueled it," she continued, then nodded toward the polecat, "and he sparked it."

Bellaw was still shaking her head, short hard twitches back and forth. She could never rebuild the house by herself. Her mother had never showed her the fast way to carve pegs, and there would be hundreds of pegs. And the rope, and…and…

One of the oxen lowed as it was killed. And that was another problem. "I really need those," Bellaw managed to say.

The Goddess was right next to her, close enough that she could feel that her body wasn't warm like a person's should be. Bellaw forced her neck to stay still and forced her mouth to form words. "Help us!"

"I've done too much already," Helikkeel answered. "He'll probably come after me, now."

Bellaw needed the oxen, and the hounds, and the chickens, and the walls and roof. She needed her family, she needed her brothers and sisters and her father and…and…

Helikkeel stated the situation firmly. "No family," she whispered. "No help. No way to call the neighbors. They wouldn't come if you did. They are too afraid."

Helikkeel reached out and her chill hands wrapped the sopping pony skin around her shoulders. "An Agreement. Not friendless. Not without allies. Are you too afraid to whistle?"

To make such a noise- suicide! But the goddess of the pool, their goddess, would not have rescued her only to have her die here at the creek's edge. Air sucked over her trembling lips the first time she tried, and the second. A squeaking note finally sounded and Bellaw cringed as she made it, fearing that it would hear.

"Just a bit louder," Helikkeel urged.

Bellaw put her fingers to her mouth and blew out the long high note. The note that, before the first snows of the year fall, sometimes the cat-faced-owls answered. No owls called back; nothing stirred save the creek and the cries of oxen being murdered.

Three dogs, one hers and two that had followed the Ferret Master, slunk out of the night. They nosed at her, making sure she was alive. Helikkeel they acknowledged with lowered-heads and raised-eyes.

"And you," Helikkeel said, lifting up the polecat. "Wakes-Terror, have any idea how to solve this?"

Bellaw watched the animal as it hung between Helikkeel's fin and claw. His beady eyes glittered in the distant firelight and he might have been looking anywhere.

"In exchange for telling me where another sweet-season is?" he asked.

Helikkeel's frog-mouth tilted in a lopsided grin. "Yes."

The polecat looked at Bellaw, then the dogs, then the pony-skin, licking his lips.

"Yes."

* * *

After killing all the men and most of the dogs and all the cattle, and after eating his fill after his long fast, Kaalvaas turned his attention to the one little man that had gotten away.

The smells of fire and burning flesh and hair overpowered any smell from the escapee. The fact remained: two had gone into the water here, he had pulled one out, but the other was gone. There was a tiny walkway that led toward the center of the pool, and propped against its end was a wooden plank covered with carvings.

This would have to be dealt with. The men still venerated those wretches?

Once he wouldn't have trusted himself to be strong enough to beat one of their ilk, or clever enough to find it. Not tonight, not now.

He found the trail, the faintest one that led toward the creek, and followed it. Some of the hounds had escaped this way. Man-smell and rank pony-smell grew as he came upon the creek itself, but where they might have gone after that was a mystery. The scents died—or were covered—at the creek's edge.

Dipping his head into the flowing water he could see the glint of metals gleaming at the base of the flat stone. Some of it was his metal. He scooped up a great mouthful and the water's sound changed, like it wasn't sure where to flow anymore.

His mouth full of metal, Kaalvaas slithered back from the edge, but she leapt—tail and all—out of the creek at him.

He lashed at her, his coils springing to catch her, his claws reaching to tear her. She was spiny and toothy and furious writhing. He tried to pull her further from the water, but she was too clever and turned soft and slippery and squelched out between his claws. With a snap of his neck he threw the spear-head and bits of bronze far into the field, but by the time he turned his fire back toward her, she was well under the water.

He burned at her anyway, at the water, at the stones, at the trees. Lips peeled back from his teeth as he waited for the steam to clear.

She pushed up to the surface. "Don't touch my offerings again!"

"Such a small horde after so long?" he said back. "Did you think I would come and deal? That we could reach an Arrangement?"

She said nothing, just watched him with her great cat-eyes.

"There is double your poor pile in the ruins of the house," he taunted, "further away than you'll ever have the courage to venture. And no men will dwell here for a long age. Again." He licked at the night air, tasting her fear and frustration. He could beat her. Kill her and devour her. Mate with her and sire beings to finally throw himself down!

She hissed, a low hateful sound. "A hundred trickles, a hundred pools full of riches. You have a long night ahead of you if you want to rob me." And then she slunk down beneath the rippling waters to guard her meager horde.

Kaalvaas was no egg-toothed hatchling to let his small hatreds distract him from his greater. The one man was missing. The spirit had moved it here from the pool, but after that, where? Surely she didn't have the power to move her out to another pool at one of the surrounding steadings?

For all her pettiness and weakness, she was right. His own great treasure was left unguarded, and he was eager to return his stolen goods, add to the horde, then hunt down the last of the miserable men and destroy the other houses in the Valley of the Seven Bravest.

* * *

Wakes-Terror made one last circuit around the ruins. The ruins were hidden, of course, he could see that now. Should have noticed that the rocks that kept the men from plowing here were too uniform to be natural. Of course, at the time, he didn't quite grasp that the hidey-hole full of metals was bigger than the man-burrow he had been so intent on getting into.

"Courage, was-wolves!" he chittered to the three trembling dogs. They whined for the girl and begged for her to come back.

"No whining!" he snapped. "Remember to keep upwind until it is time. When it is time, remember the wings!"

He looped back through the thin passageway that the monster had left in its flight from its lair. It led down through the rubble, and he followed it until the cold wet-earth smell turned to char, then further until he popped out into the great chamber.

He bounded across the room to check on the weakest link in his idea.

No, not an idea. Something more. A plan. No. That wasn't quite right, either. A strategy.

He chuckled to himself at the novelty of it. Not just reacting to the actions of others, not even anticipating them, but creating them. A wonder!

The girl waited where he had told her. She shivered under the dripping pony-skin. Did the Goddess have any idea how young she was? Still a kit! Should be eating tadpoles.

"Ready?" he asked her.

She jumped. "Is it here?"

"Soon!" he clucked.

Wakes-Terror would have to be more clever than she was weak, and more cunning than the monster was strong. The fur on his tail stood on end and he couldn't help but dance about at the thought of what was to come.

He settled himself, then scratched behind his ear and licked himself. One more look at the girl and he ran to his hiding place.

Yes, he wanted to see what happened. Mating would be nice, too, but first this. Now all that was to be done was to wait and see, to keep on his toes and be ready to pop at the slightest—

Zzzzzzz.

* * *

Kaalvaas, high in the air, worried as he spiraled down to his lair. There was no sign of the missing man. None. And the spirit's threat worried him. Surely if she had the power to send the man to another of the farms then she would have done a better job tangling with him at the water's edge. Or was this just part of a greater scheme? But their kind didn't really have schemes, they liked to make deals, set up arrangements and agreements. Perhaps he could take that big lump of bronze in the ashes of the farm and make a deal with her. No. That was his. He would bring it here to add to the rest, and look at it when he felt like sleeping to spur himself into hunting.

He also worried at the alarming conspicuousness of his lair. The dry brambles and dead leaves must have caught on fire when he tried to kill the thief. Fires still burned here and there. Maybe, his heart grinned, maybe the thief had been burning and left a trail of flame. That would be nice. That he would have liked to see. The youngling had run while her hair was on fire. That was good, but then the other had pulled her into the water and ruined it.

Hitting the ground with a thud, he settled his bulk and sniffed. Ash and fire, and the stink of dead dogs and burned men rose off of his scales like a perfume.

Holding the spearhead and arrowheads in his mouth, Kaalvaas nosed the stones aside, and pushed his way back under the earth. Before he came into the great hall he realized something was wrong.

He was halfway back out when the thief, the odd little rat-thing, scuttled across the flagstone floor, dragging a gold—a gold!—armband behind it and cackling like it didn't have a care in the world.

Spitting out the bronze, Kaalvaas shrieked and surged forward, stretching his mouth open to unleash the fire.

The creature jumped then danced backward, cackling.

Something flashed just on the edge of Kaalvaas' vision and the pathetic yelp of a man echoed again in the Emperor-To-The-Sea's hall.

Pain, foreign and strong, blossomed in the corners of his jaws, the back of his throat and the base of his tongue.

He yanked back, crashing his head into the tilted lintel stone of the gate. A female, a youngling, swung a sword at his face, splattering him with his own blood.

Fire exploded out of him and the bleeding edges of the cuts in his mouth seared in pain. The youngling disappeared in the flames. Kaalvaas flowed out of the east gate and spread his wings, and the curs leapt out of the smoldering brush at him, leaping and tearing at the thin membranes.

He caught one in a bite, crushing its ribs. But his bite was weak and wrong, as if he bit too hard his jaw would break. The taste, the taste was wrong, too.

He threw the cur's corpse aside, the other two dropping off of his wings as they turned to run. The joy of hunting and killing, of pursuing something smaller and weaker and terrified, overcame Kaalvaas and he turned to pursue them. Then the clucking chuckle of the polecat drew him back to the east gate. The creature came out, pulling something long and pink and bloody-tipped behind it.

It leapt among the rocks, capering and shouting. "Got your tongue!"

For the first time in his long fierce life a new feeling blossomed in Kaalvaas' brain. Not fear—he had experienced that as a hatchling—but blind panic. The youngling, still alive, was climbing out behind its horrid pet, a steaming pony-skin tied loosely around her shoulders and that same bright-edged and bloody blade in her hand.

"Gonna die!" the polecat chattered. "Gonna die!"

Kaalvaas' wings gobbled the air, pulling him and his writhing coils into the sky and to safety. The bites taken out of his wings tore a bit with each desperate flap; Kaalvaas didn't care, didn't care about wings or his tongue, or his treasure and the glory of his dead siblings; Kaalvaas cared only about what remained of his skin and what life remained him.

* * *

As long as she held the sword Bellaw felt better. It spoke to her, kind of. Assured her that fame and fury were hers as long as she kept its edges ground mirror-sharp. All the greatest heroes had swords that dreamed with them. Her grandfather had a leaf-shaped blade as long as her forearm, but it was a trophy from long ago, from when Loeg's great-uncle fought the neighboring tribes.

This sword was as long as her leg, and made with an abundance of bronze. The cross-hilt could have easily been used to make a spear, or four arrowheads. She held it all night, in the cavernous hall that was under Wild Hill, and wore the reeking burned pony skin. It wasn't a trophy, though, this sword. It was a tool, like the bronze-ard. The trophy was the tongue.

Although she had a choice of fine bronze daggers and axes within the old hall, Bellaw carried the tongue back to the farm as the first weak glow of sunrise grew in the east. She dug through the ashes until she found her mother's simple straight knife.

She didn't look at her mother's body, or that of her brothers, sisters, and guests. Try as she might she couldn't help but see, out of the corner of her eye. That was one of Tolnal's nice legs thrown out by the woodpile. It hurt her far worse than the oozing gash on her arm.

She cut off the forked tongue's tips and fed one each to her remaining hounds. Another bit, from the ragged root where it had run down the creature's throat, she sliced off and threw to Herder-of-Horror. The next cut, a hand's breadth of it from right behind the fork, she forced down herself. It was gamey and chewy, with a buttery finish.

"Would you like some?" she asked the Goddess. The sun was up, rain threatened as it had all these last few accursed days.

"A few drops. Yes."

Helikkeel stood a dozen steps from her pool, looking as human as she probably ever could.

The girl nodded and got on with the task of slicing the tongue lengthwise, then butterflying it. The blood, thick and black, that oozed out of the spongy flesh she rubbed on the arrowheads and daggers that she was going to give to Helkeleel. She pounded the tongue flat, and then began rubbing it with powdered lime. She had no idea what to do with it once it dried. Normally you hung such a trophy from your belt, but this was long and would hang like a scabbard and be in the way. There was probably a way to make it into a scabbard, but that sort of knowledge had died with her father.

She couldn't help but see their bodies, pieces of their bodies. Split from the heat, or torn in spite. Vultures waited in a lopsided ring around the house, watching her and her hounds.

She finished her work on the tongue and then walked to the edge of Swift Creek. Helikeel was waiting there, standing in the water, eerily beautiful.

"All along the edges of Swift Creek and its sister flows," the Goddess said, "men have made offerings, men have asked questions. And the animals. They all heard the war-shriek. Some have long memories, some have good instincts.

Many ask questions."

Bellaw was not surprised. She dropped one of the bloody arrowheads into the water. "Where is it now?"

"I don't know. Not in the water, or any of the water of mine."

Bellaw tossed in another arrowhead. "Why did you never tell us?"

"I didn't know. I was higher in the mountains in those days, and far to the east. Kaalvaas and his brood-mates were cunning."

The water splashed around another arrowhead. "Will he come back?"

"If he survives, which he most assuredly will. His hate will keep him alive if nothing else."

"The people who built the hall beneath the ground, who were they?"

"You call them the Rootless. They had roots here and in many other places."

The Rootless. The strange tribes of the lonely hills.

"And do they know what's happened?"

"Oh yes. Some of them."

"And what will they do?"

"Those that are wise will seek out the one who had the courage to give Kaalvaas such a horrible wound. They will look for their—" and Helikkeel used a word that Bellaw didn't recognize.

"It was luck," Bellaw said, of her wild swing into the open kiln of the creature's mouth. "Just like bridling a wild pony. Bronze-Ard's last stand, that was brave."

For the first time the Goddess took her eyes off the growing pile of bronze and looked at her and spoke the strange word again, slowly. "Empress. It means the queen from the west crags to the sea. I suppose that it means you."

Bellaw had a hundred other questions, and the wealth to ask them. She ran her hands over the edge of the bronze-ard, watching the Goddess' eyes caress it as well.

"The world has changed, hasn't it? Beyond Elskdale. I feel it, like a great limb has cracked away and the tree leans a new direction."

"Yes. Many things have heard the war-shriek."

"This is not an offering," Bellaw said, hefting up the ard, "this is a task. Protect it until a peaceable age comes back."

If the Goddess was angered at being ordered around, she made no sign.

The ard splashed and sank and the Goddess disappeared with it.

Bellaw walked back to the ruins, to find the dogs still snarling and snapping; vultures had come down from the high hills. Herds-Horror popped up and ran to her.

"The birds want to know why you keep them from their due," he said.

"Tell them to go away."

He chattered and they croaked in answer.

"They say their philosophers tell that the world was built as a gift to their race. They say all history supports this assertion. They have knowledge of the fate of dead flesh and say that by the time you bury them your family will be food for maggots anyway."

"I'm going to burn them."

"The vultures want to know why you hate them so, your family, to condemn them to be meat to be wasted."

She looked at the vultures. Their black eyes glinted in the light, watching her. Vultures were dreamers, it was said, gifted by the gods with enviable time free of hunting and farming and the other necessities that cursed so many other creatures of the world.

She had been a good daughter, had done what her family had asked. She had followed the Goddess' instructions, she had followed Herds-Horrors plan. Helikkeel had given her no further instructions, the polecat and the dogs and the vultures, and the spirits of her family all watched her, waiting for some kind of decision.

"Do their philosophers know where Kaalvaas has fled?"

After a round of chattering and croaking: "Of course."

"Let me at least turn my family's faces to their final sunset."

She steeled herself, reached for the cold flesh of the people she loved, many she couldn't even recognize anymore. One after another. She took a long breath and nodded toward one of the vultures. Another offering then. And an agreement. And a plan.

"Feast and be welcome."

ADRIAN SIMMONS *is a founding editor of* Heroic Fantasy Quarterly, *and a writer of fantasy and science fiction. His work has appeared at* Lackington's, Giganotosaurus, Cirsova, *and* Weirdbook.

Witch and Palidin
by Reilly S. Blackwell

Let me pull you into blackberry blood and tangled thorns.
Let me teach you of skin and bone and meat that you saw,
breathing,
moments before it died.

Let me teach you that your faith
and your willpower,
your selfless conviction,
are nothing against a bear's claws.

Take off your golden armor.
Lay down with me in the grass that scratches and cuts.
I can tell you stories of how we used to be, before morality took over.

I can tell you stories of how we could be together,
if you leave that armor in the stream.

Let the water wash it away,
wash away purpose and selfless devotion.
The steel is beautiful, rippling there in the sunlight.

Let me take you back to thorns,
to earth and light through trees.
Find your epiphanies in my skin and
the smell of my hair.

Find your protection in the land
and what it asks.
Leave your armor behind.

REILLY S. BLACKWELL *lives and works in Southern Appalachia. These days Reilly writes mostly about her experiences in the world of caving, as well as regularly writing poetry. She has been previously published in* Exercise Bowler, Inwood Indiana (Tracks edition), *and many anthologies of works centered around pagan and nature-based religions. She has published a chapbook entitled* For Artemis, *and is currently working on another, devoted to the roads and hills of Southern Appalachia and their season cycle, and keeps a blog at migratorycaving.wordpress.com.*

CRAZY SNAKE AND THE CIGUANABA

BY ERIC ATKISSON

I

elp me.

The horseman froze. He could not be certain if he had heard a voice at all—little more than a gentle whisper above the murmur of the falls, the branches rustling overhead in the night breeze, and the soft crunch of his pony's hooves as it grazed in the thick undergrowth nearby. At length he shrugged it off. After several weeks of weary travel in these densely wooded mountains, he was in need of a long rest. And a cold bath.

His bare chest and arms, freshly scoured in the swift current, bore the myriad scars of war and wilderness, man and beast. Such was the lot of his people, the Nermernuh, or Comanche, whose enemies named with awe and trembling the Lords of the Southern Plains. But in truth those plains were far to the north now, and Crazy Snake, who was only half Comanche, was further south than any of his tribe had ever ventured before, or ever would.

He sank beneath the stream's surface and rose again, throwing his head back and running his hands through his thick mane of wild, black hair.

Help me.

This time there was no denying the voice, though where it came from he could not tell. *Aahtaqui* would surely have nickered at the approach of a stranger, so Crazy Snake turned his attention to the thick woods on the opposite shore. At first he saw nothing and was about to turn away, but then his eyes caught something there in the darkening gloom: the faint shape of a head and slender shoulder peeking from behind a tree.

"Hello?" he called out.

The shape withdrew with a single, soft sob.

Crazy Snake looked to the near shore, where his buckskin breeches and moccasins were drying on a boulder, alongside his few other earthly belongings—among them his weapons and medicine pouch. The wisest course would be to grab his things and leave, swiftly, for he was a stranger in this land and an unwelcome one at that. And even were the reputation of the Comanche not known this far south, his appearance alone was enough to invite unwanted attention, which is why he traveled so cautiously, avoiding people and settlements in favor of remote trails and wild game.

Better to err on the side of caution once more, he decided, and turned to go, but a forlorn wail stopped him fast. Where before he had seen a head and shoulder stood the source of sorrow in her full form now—a stunningly beautiful form, in a thin white shift that accentuated the contours of a shapely body. Her face was concealed behind a veil of long, dark hair that seemed not to have been touched by hand or comb in weeks.

"Are you lost, woman?" he called in Spanish.

At first there was no answer. Then, like a whisper of wind, he heard her voice: *No. I— I have lost someone.*

"Who?"

The woman retreated a step.

Please. I need your help.

Her voice, like the sight of her body, pulled at the horseman, and he discovered that he was already striding toward her, fighting the stream's current. The woman stayed where she was, watching, her face still obscured by the veil of hair.

Crazy Snake emerged from the water like a creature freshly born unto the world, wet and naked as the day he was pulled from his mother's womb. The stranger took a tentative step toward him, hesitated, took another. Just as he thought she might turn and flee back into the forest whence she had come, she reached for one of his hands and seized it gently, her touch sending a pulse of desire through the horseman's body. He drew her gently against his chest and felt her body softly shaking.

"*Shhhh*," he whispered. "You are safe now."

The woman's presence was intoxicating. They might have stood there for the span of a few heartbeats or an hour for all that he could tell, and only gradually did he sense an unwelcome interruption of his bliss, a sound that years of familiarity had conditioned him to hear even through the din of battle and chaos. It was the sound of a horse, he remembered—*his* horse—urgent, even frantic, as it had sounded in desperate situations before. As in a dream he lifted his gaze slowly toward the far shore, and there, prancing along the edge of the stream, was Aahtaqui.

At that moment whatever bewitchment had fallen upon the horseman lifted, and he thrust the woman away. From the mass of wild hair protruded not the face of a woman at all but the nightmare visage of a horse's skull, random patches of dead skin still clinging to bleached white bone, and twin orbs of hellish light for eyes. Across the river Aahtaqui stamped and screamed impotently along the shore.

Crazy Snake stepped back and tripped, scrambled away as the creature approached him. He could see now that her nails were long and sharp, her hands flexing in anticipation.

You cannot help me. You are unfaithful—like all the rest.

He felt the world spinning, his mind teetering on the brink of insanity. But still he was moving backward, and as soon as his hands felt water he twisted and plunged into the stream like a wild animal in blind flight.

Half running, half swimming he fled, the creature's words pursuing him like shrieking birds of prey. Whether it was her sharp nails that slashed his skin or branches and rocks he could not tell, but still he pressed on, letting the swelling current take him as far and as fast as it could. What had been the distant murmur of falls now seemed a dull roar, and the current quickened, sweeping him forth with little effort.

And then he fell.

One moment he was soaring through open air, the next he was plunged into a tumult of foaming water and shaken violently, like a bauble in the hands of an idiot child, before being tossed out, gasping for air and thrashing wildly toward the nearest shore.

Soon he felt rocks beneath his bare feet again, and he stumbled to the shore. There he collapsed and lay for many long minutes, panting, attempting to quell the raw terror clawing its way back. When he felt that he could move again, he rolled onto his back and stared up at a swath of moonless night above the stream. His eyes drifted toward the falls and the rapids below it, and then to the water at his feet.

And there, amid the swirl and foam, something stirred. First emerged the long hair, followed by the horse's skull on a woman's half-naked body, her arms spread wide as if to greet a long lost lover.

Unfaithful. Like all the rest! Unfaithful!

Crazy Snake screamed, and he did not stop screaming as he fled through the forest, night and day, hounded by the hellish voice.

II

"Well I'll be damned. He ain't got no tomahawk, no clothes, and no horse, but this'n here's Comanche all right. Or at least half Comanche. I'd recognize one a these brown devils a mile away."

221

Crazy Snake opened his eyes. He lay in a small cell enclosed on three sides by old stone walls and on the fourth by iron bars. Before him knelt a sullen-eyed white man with a thick, reddish beard sporting dark stains and a wide-brimmed sombrero tilted back from a balding forehead. A holstered pistol and long Bowie knife hung from the leather belt around his ample, bulging waist. Beside him stood an older man in a black wool robe, holding a key and gazing impassively at the horseman beneath sharp eyebrows and a thin mane of silver hair. Beyond the two visitors and the cell door, flickering torchlight illumined a narrow stone passage.

"Where am I?" Crazy Snake croaked. His lips and tongue were parched, and his naked body felt like it had been dragged through miles of prickly pear by a pride of quarreling mountain lions.

The squatting man chuckled and spat a stream of tobacco at the floor, drawing a reproachful scowl from his companion.

"See. He even speaks Comanche."

"Where am I?" said Crazy Snake again, this time in English.

"You ain't in Texas no more, chief, that's for sure. I can't for the life a me figure how you made it so far south, but you're in Nicaragua, and this here is *El Castillo*. Your prison for now, until President Walker gets wind of you. I reckon he'll be mighty pleased we bagged ourselves a Comanche. Yessir, mighty pleased."

Crazy Snake could make little sense of the man's words, nor could he reconcile his Texan drawl and talk of a president named Walker with the fact that he was as far from such white men as he had ever believed possible.

How had he come to this place? He had no clear recollection, though memories of his encounter with the creature in the forest were slowly clawing their way back, unbidden. He had a dim impression that he had fled for days and nights through forests and fields, as if in a nightmare, but nothing more.

"Course, I had my way," said the man, standing with a grunt and resting a hand on his knife's hilt, "we'd just take your scalp and send it to Walker instead. I reckon it's no less than what you done to plenty of decent white folk before, ain't that right, chief? Huh?"

Crazy Snake didn't answer, and the Texan kicked him.

"Well, least you're not babbling like a madman no more. Drink some of that water and get your strength back. I have my way, you're gonna need it."

He spat again and withdrew, and the older man—whose opaque, expressionless eyes lingered on the horseman a moment longer—closed the door, locked it, and retired as well.

Crazy Snake took stock of the room. He saw a rusted bucket of water next to him and gratefully scooped handfuls of fresh water to his lips, though his wrists were bound to the wall by chains and he could not move far. He could see now the scratches covering his body from his mad flight through the wilderness.

His thirst at last slaked he stood slowly, wincing at the pain.

"You'll want to put these on," said a voice in Spanish, and a pair of clothes landed at Crazy Snake's feet. "It can get cold in here at night."

When Crazy Snake turned, he found not another white man, but a short, heavy, cherubic-faced Mestizo boy, or perhaps a young man—his age difficult to discern in the dim light—wearing a striped poncho over plain pants and shirt and standing on crooked legs. He raised a half-eaten banana to his mouth.

"Who are you?"

"Cipitio," the boy mumbled, chewing. "At your service."

"You're a guard?" asked Crazy Snake skeptically, as he put on the clothes, hissing at the sting of the coarse fabric on his raw cuts and scratches.

Cipitio swallowed the last of the banana. "No, nothing like that. I work for the old sourpuss who was just in here. The castellan."

"The what?"

"The castellan. *Lord of the castle.*" He made a theatrical bow whose meaning was as lost on the horseman as the word castle, and seeing this, Cipitio shrugged and added, "The guy who runs this place."

"He lets you talk to prisoners?"

Cipitio tossed the banana peel over his shoulder. "I can do whatever I want as long as I don't leave the keep or lift a hand against him. Besides, you're the only prisoner here. Except for the slaves."

"Slaves?"

"You haven't heard? Slavery is legal again, courtesy of General—excuse me, *President* Walker."

"Walker is a white man's name."

"White as the man himself," Cipitio agreed.

"And the other who was just here, the one with the red beard and foul stench?"

"Also white."

Crazy Snake grunted, eying the strange boy curiously.

Cipitio held his hands up with an apologetic smile. "His name is Vance. Jeremiah Vance. A hired gun in Walker's army. When some villagers found you and brought you in, Vance said he recognized your kind from his days as a Texas Ranger." He grabbed the bars and leaned closer. "Is it true?"

"Is what true?"

"Are you really *Komantcia*?"

Crazy Snake grunted, and Cipitio's eyes widened. "Fascinating. And what happened to you out there, to drive you to such madness?"

The horseman said nothing.

"I don't blame you for being suspicious, my friend, but believe me when I say that you can trust me. I'm the only one you can trust here, in fact." Cipitio pressed his face between the bars and lowered his voice to a conspiratorial whisper. "It was the *Ciguanaba*, wasn't it? A creature with the body of a beautiful woman, but a horse's head and long nails? Ah, it *was* her," he said, noting the reaction on Crazy Snake's normally impassive face.

"How do you know this?"

Cipitio shrugged. "Everyone has heard of her in these parts. Some believe she is real, some think she is just a myth. Every once in a while a man is found, crazed out of his mind and babbling about her. As far as I know, you are the only one who ever recovered your wits. The others just stayed crazy."

"You seem to know a lot for a boy."

Cipito chuckled. "I'm older than I look. Besides, I have nothing else to do in this dirty old keep but run menial errands for the castellan and watch the world go by." His smile faded slightly. "What did she say to you, the Ciguanaba?"

Crazy Snake closed his eyes. He had no desire to remember that night, but this boy, or young man, or whatever he was, seemed harmless enough, and it was a waste not to learn what he could from him. "She was looking for someone. When I tried to comfort her, she said I was *unfaithful*. What does that mean?"

Cipitio was silent himself for a time. "It means you betrayed or abandoned someone close to you. A spouse, a friend, a country—that kind of thing. I suppose you are in good company, then. Aside from the slaves and the castellan, there are nothing but mercenaries and womanizers in El Castillo."

Crazy Snake nodded and opened his eyes, but the boy was gone. The horseman frowned, wondering if he had dozed off while Cipitio was talking.

He pondered Cipitio's final words. By now, his fellow braves would have long since returned from Mexico with news that Crazy Snake was gone, swallowed by the jungles of the Yucatán, presumably dead. His quarrelsome wives Weakeah and Chonie had no doubt cut their hair in grief, divided his share of the raid's spoils, and quickly found new husbands. Such was his hope, in any case. Marriage had never suited him. To lay with a woman was one thing, he had often reflected, to live with her quite another. And to live with *two* in the same tipi, well— If he had to court death, better to do it on the open trail and the warpath.

Nor had he ever felt completely at home among his tribe, any more than with his own wives. "You are more than Nermernuh. Never forget that," his mother had told him more than once. Her blood flowed in his veins as well, but where it came from or what it meant he knew not. She had been captured in Mexico and traded to his father as a girl, but had always told Crazy Snake her ancestors came from further south—from a land of great medicine and

225

power, high among the mountains. She herself was a powerful *bruja* who could speak with spirits and sometimes see the future. Before she died she gave her son and only child the talisman she wore around her neck, and he had sworn to himself that he would one day find the land where it came from. Perhaps even the people who had fashioned it.

But now it was gone, along with the medicine pouch he had carried it in, left by the banks of a stream he could not possibly find again on his own. He had failed his wives, failed his people, and now it seemed he had even failed his mother. Perhaps he *had* been unfaithful, to everyone in his life, and the Ciguanaba had seen fit to punish him for it.

For the first time in as long as he could remember, imprisoned and cut off from the things that gave him his *puha* and his sense of purpose, Crazy Snake felt truly naked. Vulnerable.

Alone.

* * *

From the darkness of his cell he could hear the muted work of picks and shovels by day, punctuated by the occasional crack of a whip and cries of a slave. At night the sounds gave way to drunken revelry as the American mercenaries consumed whiskey, danced to fiddles, and fired their pistols and rifles. On one such night Vance returned with two other men like him—one tall and moon faced, the other shorter and thicker than Vance himself, with an ugly crooked nose—to gawk at their prisoner and taunt him with useless insults, but aside from a few clumsy kicks and blows there was no great violence; even drunk, Vance seemed to appreciate Crazy Snake's value as a gift to Walker, something that might earn him a promotion in their makeshift army.

On the next night, Crazy Snake awoke to the sound of a woman's voice in the corridor. Though she spoke in a language he had never heard, her words sounded unmistakably frantic and pleading, fraught with terror.

"There, there, my child," said the voice of an older man, in Spanish. "Look into my eyes. Look deeply. That's it. Calm yourself. Focus on my eyes, only the eyes." His voice trailed off into a strange chant. Although the horseman did not recognize the words, they sounded similar to Spanish. Older perhaps. It went on for about a minute, until the voice spoke again in Spanish. "Now, step inside of this cell, where the candles are. You see the star drawn on the ground? Lay down in the middle, with your arms and legs spread into the points of the star. There, very good, lass. Very good."

Crazy Snake heard more quiet chanting and then a sound he recognized all too well, of a knife striking flesh, hard and fast, followed by a short cry and a long silence during which he could hear very little but the occasional swish of a robe and the soft pad of feet on stone.

"Cipitio!" the voice snarled, minutes later. "Cipitio!"

"Here, *master*." There was an edge of weary sarcasm in the voice.

"About time. Now clean up this mess while I take these to my chamber. Then dispose of the remains in the usual manner."

"As you wish. *Master*."

Crazy Snake did not sleep well the rest of that night.

Cipitio returned the following afternoon, limping on his crooked legs and carrying a plate of food for the horseman. Although Crazy Snake had even less reason to trust the boy now and picked at the food suspiciously, he listened without comment as Cipitio chatted idly about the fort, the mercenaries, and the slaves, chewing on bananas as he did, as if nothing strange had happened the night before.

"Tell me more about this Walker," Crazy Snake interrupted, tired of everything to do with El Castillo.

"What would you like to know?"

"To start with, how did white men come to rule this land?"

"Which white men? The Spanish or the *gringos*?"

"You know what I mean."

Cipitio smiled. "Of course." Walker had come a year ago, hired by the previous president to help defeat a rebellion against his government. The American *filibustero* quickly became a powerful chief, capturing the capital and fighting several battles against neighboring countries. Now he had declared himself president, reintroduced slavery, and was appealing to white men in the United States to join his cause. It was all very confusing to Crazy Snake, but he understood enough. It was much the same as he had seen since childhood. Always the white man wanted more land, and would drive out or enslave those who resisted.

Finally, on the fifth night, Cipitio brought Crazy Snake news that he and several slaves were to be transported by river to the capital on the morrow, now that Vance's men had commandeered a suitable means for the journey.

"I will be sorry to see you leave," he added, with what sounded like genuine regret.

The horseman studied him. "Will you?"

"Of course."

"So I won't be murdered in my cell like the girl?"

Now Cipitio studied the horseman. "You heard that, did you? Good. Don't forget it. The castellan is a dangerous and wicked old man, and the sooner you are gone from this place the better, my friend."

"Then why not free me now? The two of us can escape, together. Surely you have a mother or father who would like to see you again?"

Cipitio smiled sadly. "I have no idea who my father was, and my mother—

Well, she was never cut out for the role. And I would free you if I could, but the castellan has the keys and I cannot disobey him, much as I would like to. I have often wished he would slip on one of my banana peels and break his neck, but alas my prayers have gone unanswered."

Again the boy seemed sincere, but Crazy Snake felt he was hearing less than the full truth. The news of his delivery to Walker was not entirely unwelcome, though. He had no desire to remain in this accursed cell a day longer, and an escape might be easier outside than it would be here, with so many armed men around. After bidding Cipitio a grudging farewell, he cleaned himself as best he could from the bucket of water, sat in a cross-legged position, and began to chant to the spirits for their blessing and good fortune. They had answered his prayers before, and might yet again if he proved himself worthy.

III

The next morning, Vance returned with the castellan and the same two surly companions who had taunted Crazy Snake before, this time sneering down the barrels of muskets. The castellan unlocked his manacles while Vance placed new chains around his wrists and ankles. As the three mercenaries led the horseman shuffling out into the light of day, the castellan remained behind with the hint of a sardonic smile.

The sky was mercifully overcast, but after days in the darkness of his cell Crazy Snake still blinked and squinted at the harsh glare. The door from which they emerged was at the base of a small keep in a larger rectangular fort with diamond-shaped bastions at each corner, situated on a high bluff above a bend in the river with a commanding view of a wide valley. Mountains loomed behind them to the east, while to the west lush fields and forests stretched for many miles toward a more distant mountain range. In the central courtyard before them and along the surrounding ramparts about twenty slaves toiled, improving the fort's defenses under the watchful eyes of a nearly equal number of white men armed with pistols, muskets, and knives. The slaves themselves were dark-skinned, of mixed African and Indian ancestry; Cipitio had called them *Garifunas*, a people normally given to singing and dancing and colorful works of art. Nearby, one of them—a man no older than Crazy Snake himself— was tied to a post, shirtless, the skin of his back welted and bleeding, while one of Vance's men whipped him for some offense.

His captors led Crazy Snake down a long stone ramp over which people, animals, and wagons passed in and out of the fort's main entrance, while bored mercenaries ambled upon the ramparts, watching the river and the countryside with muskets propped lackadaisically over their shoulders. As he glanced at the fort one last time, Crazy Snake saw Cipitio watching him from a balcony in the keep, a banana in one hand and the other waving at him in farewell. Though it may have been a trick of the horseman's imagination, the boy seemed to vanish from sight as quickly as he had appeared.

A dirt road led downhill from the fort to a cluster of wooden buildings by the riverside and a strange sight that drew a sharp breath from Crazy Snake. It was a boat—that much he could tell, since it floated on water and carried people within it—but it was no simple canoe of wood and pitch, as he had sometimes seen on the shallow rivers of *Comancheria*. This was a great white behemoth, two decks high, with a room and two giant pipes protruding from the upper deck and a strange wooden wheel at the ship's rear, as wide as the ship itself. Large English letters were painted on its side, though Crazy Snake had no idea what they said, for he had never learned to read or write in any language. Men were at work loading a variety of goods and supplies on to the boat, including three shackled Garifunas, while Vance strode upon the deck cursing lustily for greater haste. When he saw Crazy Snake and his armed escorts, he spat into the river and joined them.

"Never seen a steamboat before, huh, chief? Be careful. They're known to bite, and they're awful fond of Injun flesh."

Moonface and Crooked Nose bellowed with laughter, and Vance permitted himself a smile, though his eyes remained fixed on Crazy Snake with a hint of cruelty that no amount of mirth could seem to extinguish. When the others had stopped laughing, he gave curt orders to ensure their prisoner was secured with the three slaves, and to keep a watchful eye on him at all times.

"Comanches're devious little devils," he said. "And they ain't afraid to die. Remember that. You get this'n and them three Garifunas to Walker, I promise you can have any one of the women slaves you want when you're back."

This seemed to have the desired effect, the two men slapping each other on the backs and promising they wouldn't fail Vance. He simply nodded with a final glance at all of them, Crazy Snake included, before returning to his duties supervising the loading of the boat. The men followed him on board, and Crazy Snake was lined up with the Garifunas—two men and a woman who were similarly chained, wearing tattered clothes and looking mistreated and ill-fed, but otherwise in their prime—and told to sit silently with their backs against the low bulwark near the ship's bow, on the bottom deck, while Moonface and Crooked Nose leveled their muskets on the prisoners and made idle bets about which one would fetch the best price on the auction blocks "back home."

Crazy Snake closed his eyes and attempted to relax, conscious of the Garifunas' curious stares. Thus he remained for the better part of an hour, savoring the fresh air and the warmth of the sun as it began to emerge from the clouds. In spite of the unfamiliar smells and the sounds of activity around him, the horseman let his thoughts drift back to the dry plains, hidden canyons, and cool river valleys of his youth. He could almost hear the beating of the drums and the whooping of braves around the campfires, could almost smell the sizzling fat of buffalo meat and taste it on his lips.

And yet, he had to admit, part of him did not miss it. It was as if the further he traveled from the land he once called home, the more some other part of him stirred, always looking to the south. Even now, when he had no reason to expect that he would live to see them, he could only imagine what strange new lands lurked just beyond the horizon, awaiting his passage.

The laborers had almost finished loading the boat when a commotion interrupted their work and the horseman's reveries.

Two Mestizos under the supervision of a haughty, finely dressed merchant with an impeccable, straight mustache were cautiously leading a hooded brown horse with white spots over the ramp to the boat's deck, and it was not making their work easy, jerking at its reins and snorting and squealing irritably.

"Whoa, where the hell you taking that thing?" demanded Vance, blocking their way.

"Please, *Señor*," said the merchant, reaching into the folds of his coat and deftly producing a colorful bill. "I cannot afford to wait for the next steamboat, since your army has disrupted travel from here to the coast."

"Not my problem."

"But *Presidente* Walker said he needed as many good horses as he could get, no?"

Vance nodded.

"Then please, have your men present this horse to him as a gift, compliments of Juan Rodriguez. He will recognize its worth as the best he can find anywhere within hundreds of miles. Tell him my sympathies and my fellow merchants are with his cause, and the sooner full commerce is restored, the better."

Vance spat and took the bill in his grubby hands, then slapped the horse's rump to get it moving again. It kicked a hind hoof at him, which he just barely evaded.

"Ornery bastard, aintcha?"

The horse snorted beneath its hood and jerked a little, but let the handlers pull it forward.

"All right," Vance called, stepping off the boat and pulling the ramp after him, with the help of another mercenary. "You heard the man. Make sure Walker gets the horse and the message. That's it. Boat's full and ready to take off. Bon voyage, amigos. Don't nobody let me down, or there'll be hell to pay."

The two Mestizos led the horse between crates and bags of goods to the open-aired deck near the bow, with the prisoners. From their cursing conversation, Crazy Snake learned to his joy that Aahtaqui—loyal as always—

230

had been found not far from the fort and captured unharmed by employees of the merchant, but not before biting one man's arm to the bone and staving in the knee of another.

"That horse is bad luck," one of the Mestizos grumbled.

"No. That horse is the devil himself," replied the other.

But to Crazy Snake it was nothing less than a sign from the Great Spirit, and it made his heart soar like a hawk.

Somewhere within the steamboat an infernal racket commenced, and the great wheel in the rear began to turn. Smoke churned from the tall pipes, and the ship began to move, slowly at first. Soon enough they were in the middle of the wide San Juan River, gently cleaving against the current. From what Cipitio had told him, the river meandered many miles west before connecting with a great water, Lake Nicaragua, beyond whose far banks the capital sat. It would be a journey of several hours upriver—time that he would have to use profitably, before they reached the open water of the lake. True to their word, Moonface and Crooked Nose kept a vigilant watch on their prisoners, and there was no opportunity to move or speak without being sharply rebuked by a pointed musket.

Close to an hour passed. There was little Crazy Snake could see but the tops of trees and crests of distant mountains, for Aahtaqui and the other bulwark blocked much of his view. Some of the mountains were strangely shaped, as if their peaks had been sheared off. These he guessed must be the *volcánes,* or mountains of fire, his mother had once spoken of, and which Cipitio had mentioned during his rambling descriptions of the land.

Crazy Snake's eyes wandered to the upper deck, which started about fifteen feet back from the ship's bow. Another mercenary stood sentry up there, a black-haired man with sharp cheekbones and close-set eyes, gazing at the surrounding countryside. As he had since they first left El Castillo, Close Eyes would stand in that location for about a minute, disappear, and reappear around five minutes later. By now the horseman was certain he must be the only one of Vance's men up there, making a continuous, slow circuit of the upper deck. In addition to the two guards here, that made three armed men, plus about a half dozen Mestizo workers who did not appear to be armed with more than machetes, and who may or may not feel any loyalty to Walker's army.

Crazy Snake casually stretched his head right, toward the rear of the boat, and then to his left, where the first Garifuna sat next to him. He was not as tall as the other, but more thickly muscled, and with a wilder head of curly hair. His eyes stared ahead over pockmarked cheeks. "If you speak Spanish, nod," the horseman said, too softly to be heard by the guards over the engine and the lapping of the waves against the hull. "Slowly."

The Garifuna tensed. And nodded.

"Good. If you want your freedom, move when I do."

When Close Eyes left to continue his circuit of the upper deck, Crazy Snake closed his eyes and began a silent count. As two and a half minutes approached, he opened his eyes slowly and took in the scene one last time. Nothing had changed that would alter his plan. He cleared his throat and looked at Moonface.

"Aahtaqui!" Crazy Snake spoke sharply, in the tongue of the Nermernuh. "Come!"

A moment of questioning anger on the mercenary's face quickly vanished as the horse behind him squealed into motion, ripping the reins from the Mestizos' hands, veering toward the unexpected sound of its master's voice, and plowing obliviously into Moonface, slamming him backward against the bulwark and knocking his musket from his hands. Crazy Snake leapt to his feet and smashed the man with his chained hands, sending him over the edge and into the water. Crooked Nose, blocked from sight by the horse, shouted but was silenced as the male Garifuna on the far side of the three tackled him to the deck and attempted to wrest the musket from his hands. Crazy Snake grabbed Moonface's musket and stepped out of the horse's way, aiming toward the upper deck, where Close Eyes quickly appeared, drawn by the commotion. The horseman pulled the trigger, flinched at the blast and the recoil, and Close Eyes disappeared with a scream, clutching his throat.

No other gunmen appeared, and the Mestizos who had been handling Aahtaqui fled toward the rear of the boat. For a moment, the only souls on the forward section of the lower deck were Crazy Snake, the three Garifunas, the horse, and Crooked Nose, who was being bashed senseless with the stock of his own musket. Crazy Snake grabbed a hold of the hood covering Aahtaqui's head and gently pulled it off. The horse bobbed and shook its head, nickering excitedly, and nuzzled its master's face.

"Good boy," said Crazy Snake, stroking its side, and then to the Garifunas: "That guard! Does he have any keys?"

"No," cursed the female, who had quickly searched the now motionless Crooked Nose. "Maybe the one you knocked overboard had them?"

Crazy Snake grunted. "Or maybe Close Eyes has them."

"Who?"

"The one up there." He nodded to the upper deck.

With the chains binding their ankles, it would be a long shuffle to the rear of the boat to get to the stairs, and then up and across the upper deck, and there was no telling who else might be up there, armed and ready to shoot.

As he considered those difficulties the boat began to turn, ponderously, in a long arc.

Downriver. Back toward El Castillo.

"Lift me up!" he shouted, and the two Garifuna men quickly came forward, stooping and offering cupped hands for footholds. Once Crazy Snake had his feet planted firmly in each, they boosted him high enough to grab the upper deck's railing. With his ankles bound, there was no easy way to swing a leg up for purchase, so the Garifunas continued to lift until their arms were high above their heads, and Crazy Snake was able to heave himself over. Close Eyes lay dying next to him, blood pumping steadily from his throat, and the horseman quickly searched his pockets, finally locating a single key. He fumbled it into the keyhole on the manacle around his left wrist and was relieved to hear a promising click. He took the manacle off and then the other, followed by the ones around his ankles. Then he tossed the key down to the waiting Garifunas, who, at his beckoning, tossed one of the muskets up to him. He turned toward the pilothouse, aiming the musket at the window. Within was an older man with flecks of grey in his dark hair and beard. He took his hands off the wheel and raised them in the air. Crazy Snake nodded, keeping the musket pointed at him as he circled around the pilothouse to its rear. He grabbed its handle and was about to pull it open when the door burst open, slamming into his hands and knocking the musket to the deck. A younger man jumped out with a pistol aimed at Crazy Snake and pulled the trigger.

The shot went wide, blasting a small hole in the deck. The horseman seized the fallen musket by the barrel and swung it like a club, smacking the man's head with the stock. He stumbled toward the railing, dazed, and Crazy Snake gave him a shove as he passed by, sending him over the railing and into the water, where like Moonface he was heard and seen no more.

"Turn this thing back or I kill you now," said Crazy Snake in Spanish, reversing the musket so it was pointed at the pilot.

The old man nodded vigorously and turned the ship back upriver.

Crazy Snake called out to the Garifunas, and the one who had been beside him earlier came up with a musket of his own.

"What is your name?" said the horseman.

"Madal."

"Watch him, Madal."

"Gladly," said Madal, cocking the musket's hammer.

Crazy Snake took the stairs to the lower deck. Below were a few terrified Mestizos, cowering in the rear of the boat with their hands up and the other two Garifunas guarding them. Several others had jumped overboard and were swimming toward the nearest shore.

"Is there a place upriver to let us off? Somewhere far from any people?" Crazy Snake asked the Mestizos, who all nodded. "Good."

"You have a plan?" asked the male Garifuna, who introduced himself as Nakili and the woman as Hayá.

"Yes," said Crazy Snake. "Land this boat somewhere safe and take to the woods where no soldiers will be able to find us."

"And then what?"

The horseman shrugged. "Go wherever each of us will."

"There is another way," offered Hayá. "Friends and family of ours are still held prisoner at the fort. We could gather others and attempt to free them."

Crazy Snake shook his head. "It is strong and well-guarded, and they may expect an attack after they learn of our escape."

"Aye," said Nakili. "And they will most likely take revenge for our escape on the ones still held there. We must do something to help them, and fast."

"Do what you must. Aside from the boy Cipitio, I have no friends or family there."

Hayá began an angry response, but caught herself, only now realizing what Crazy Snake had just said. "Boy? What boy?"

"Cipitio. About this high and this wide. Walks with a limp. Eats bananas. Works for the castellan."

Nakili and Hayá looked at each other. "I never saw any boy there, and no one by that description," said Nakili. "Perhaps you were still… delirious from whatever madness afflicted you in the forest."

Before he could reply, Crazy Snake noticed the Mestizos talking quietly among themselves. Cipitio's name had been mentioned.

"You there," he said. "What know you of the boy?"

The one he had addressed swallowed. "Forgive me, Señor. There is a local legend about a boy named Cipitio. Someone who looks as you described."

Crazy Snake frowned. "*Legend?*"

"A story we tell our children, passed down by our elders before us."

"I know what a legend is," the horseman snapped. "Tell me the story."

Nodding eagerly, the Mestizo continued: "They say he was born of a queen named *Ziquet*, who was unfaithful to her husband. When the king found out, he prayed to the god *Zeotl* to curse his wife and her bastard child. So Cipitio was born with crooked legs and doomed to live as a child forever, while Ziquet was cursed to wander the forest in search of him, never to succeed. They say Cipitio only appears to children, or sometimes to holy men or the mad."

Crazy Snake felt a growing sense of disquiet. "And what stories do your people tell about El Castillo?"

The Mestizo shrugged. "The locals have feared the place since the Spanish abandoned it many years ago. There is a legend that a Spaniard remained behind, a man who worshipped the Devil and could bind spirits to his will. People sometimes disappear, never to be seen again. Some believe the man is still there, or that the place is haunted by the ghosts he commanded."

The disquiet had grown and begun to take full form as Crazy Snake considered the Mestizo's words. A question formed in his mind, one that he was afraid to ask for he believed he already knew the answer.

"Cipitio's mother. This—Ziquet. You said she too was cursed. What became of her?"

The Mestizo touched his forehead, chest, and two shoulders in the same reflexive motion Crazy Snake had seen from Catholic priests in their missions along the edge of Comancheria. As the Mestizo answered, the horseman's skin tingled and the hairs on the nape of his neck stood straight. Indeed he *had* guessed the answer, and it was not at all to his liking. But all the same, a new plan began to form in his mind.

"Perhaps I can help you after all," he said to Nakili. "But first I need your help. There is somewhere I need to go. A place I cannot find on my own."

IV

It took the better part of three days, but at last they found the waterfall. It was not yet dusk, and leaving Nakili and Aahtaqui behind Crazy Snake took the trail that led uphill and back to the same part of the stream where he and Aahtaqui had first come, almost two weeks past, oblivious to the terror that awaited them.

His weapons and gear were still where he had left them near the bank, damp but otherwise no worse for the wear. Discarding the musket and machete he had taken from the boat, he gently lifted the Mayan necklace and Nermernuh medicine pouch from the rock where he had set them and—finding his mother's amulet still within the pouch—tied them back around his neck where they belonged, along with a breastplate of white bones bound by rawhide straps and decorated with brass beads. He then settled himself into a comfortable cross-legged position on the boulder with the buffalo hide war shield strapped to his forearm and the tomahawk in his lap. Ignoring the fear of the place that still lingered, like a bad taste, Crazy Snake breathed deeply and exhaled, eying the far bank. At length he began to chant, a song he had often heard from his mother's lips when communing with the Spirit World on lonely, barren hilltops.

An hour after night had smothered the dying embers of the western sky she appeared, her hair again hiding her face. This time there was no sobbing, no pleas for help; only the soft, strangely melodic cadence of Crazy Snake's song, which finally trailed off and was swallowed by the sound of the gently rushing stream.

You.

Crazy Snake nodded.

Why have you returned? Did I not say you were unfaithful?

"You did. And I was."

She vanished, and for a moment the horseman feared he had failed. But then he felt a presence beside him. A horse's skull leaned into view, and a long nail pointed at him, while the other hand settled on his shoulder with a tight, piercing grip. *Then why have you returned?*

Crazy Snake looked the Ciguanaba in her blazing red eyes.

"Because I know where you can find your son."

* * *

Jeremiah Vance stalked the ramparts of El Castillo, checking his men and their muskets for the third time in an hour. Gone were the nights of fiddling and heavy drinking. Since the Comanche and the three Garifunas had killed his men on the steamboat and fled into the countryside, rumors were rife of an imminent attack on the fort. The castellan had berated him for a careless fool, and though Vance held no loyalty to the old man he needed his knowledge of the fort's defenses and the surrounding area now more than ever. Something about the Spaniard unnerved the hardened mercenary, who had seen his share of cruelty and bloodshed—much of it at his own hands. He knew of the slaves the castellan had taken into the dungeon in the darkest watches of the night, never to return, and there were the odd times, too, when the castellan thought he was alone, that Vance had seen him talking to himself, or to imaginary companions. It was unnatural.

The Texan had almost completed his circuit when one of his men—Cadwallader, a lanky Mississippian with a fondness for lashing errant slaves—called from the gate that a stranger was standing without. That was unusual enough, but something about the man's tone piqued Vance's interest, and he descended the stairs to the inner courtyard, then crossed toward the gate to see for himself.

"Would you look at that?" said Cad, nodding toward the gate with a dumbfounded grin. Standing just beyond was a shapely young woman clad only in a white shift, her face concealed beneath a thick tangle of long, dark hair.

"What does she want?" Vance looked past her to see if she had brought company. But the ramp was otherwise empty and the guards had seen no others—in fact, had not even seen her approach, Cad admitted sheepishly.

I want to come in. The woman's soft voice seemed to carry on the night breeze. *There is someone here I wish to see.*

"Which lucky devil is that, I wonder?" said Cad, winking and nudging Vance with his elbow. But Vance only looked at him with a cold stare, and Cad swallowed nervously. "Sorry, boss. What say? Should I let her in?"

Vance didn't like it. Having a half-naked woman in the fort would only undermine the fragile state of order he'd drilled into his men, even if she was crazy. On the other hand, the creepy old castellan might have some use for her.

One that could buy Vance some good will with the man.

The Texan nodded. "Let her in."

Cad gave the order, and the gate slowly creaked opened on its rusty hinges. The woman made no move, standing eerily still with her hands hanging at her sides, face still hidden. Cad looked at Vance, and the Texan just shrugged. "We ain't got all night. If she's done forgot how to walk, just grab her by the hair and drag her in." He turned to go, thinking to let the castellan know about their new visitor—only to find the woman blocking his path to the keep. The men behind him gasped and cursed in disbelief.

Where is my son? Where is Cipitio?

Vance staggered backward, speechless, and began to fumble for the pistol at his side.

Where is he? she demanded, a horse's skull now protruding from her hair and long nails extending from her fingertips.

The fort erupted into chaos. Vance and Cad fled toward the open gate, screaming madly. One of the guards upon the ramparts fired in terror at the creature, and in the blink of an eye she appeared before him, wrenching the musket from his arms and tossing it into the night. *Where is he?* Other mercenaries poured out of the barracks, drawn by the screams and the gunshots, and at first no one had any clear idea what was happening until they caught a glimpse of the Ciguanaba, appearing before some hapless soldier, who would drop his weapon, scream, and flee in terror. *Where is he? Where is my son?* Within five minutes, every one of Vance's men had either disappeared through the gate or leapt from the ramparts, breaking legs and crawling in the dirt as if the hounds of Hell were howling in pursuit.

But a more earthly menace waited for them that night: small bands of dark-skinned Garifunas armed with machetes and waiting to finish the job the Ciguanaba had started.

Among them was a Comanche brave with a grim smile.

He, Nakili, and Madal had hidden from sight not far beyond the rear of the fort, where the keep was closest to the ramparts. When the screams of Vance's men began to pierce the night and the guards disappeared from their stations, the three men picked up their burden—a long siege ladder, lashed together from local timber—and carried it toward the wall, where they planted one end in the ground and slowly raised the rest of the ladder until the far end was leaning against the stone wall just below the top of a rampart.

Crazy Snake went first, climbing fast. His face was smeared with stripes of black war paint, his hair neatly braided and festooned with the brilliant feathers of eagle and macaw. His bow and a quiver of arrows were strapped to his back, and his tomahawk bounced at his side. His black companions bore muskets and machetes and followed swiftly behind.

237

* * *

The castellan had been deep in study among the old, yellowed tomes and jars of human organs within his inner sanctum when the first sounds of commotion interrupted his concentration.

"Cipitio! What is happening outside?"

The boy appeared at his side. "It seems we have an unwelcome guest, *master*. Would you like to have a look?"

The castellan frowned and rose from his desk. "Stay here." He opened a door, crossed a torchlit hallway to his austere bedchambers, and strode through to another door that led to the keep's balcony. There his eyes raked the scene below; the last of the American mercenaries were fleeing through the gateway and leaping from the ramparts, and standing in the center of it all, staring up at him with hellfire eyes in a horse's skull, was the Ciguanaba.

Where is my son?

"Cipitio?" said the castellan, stepping back. He smoothed his robe and stood straighter. "He is here, with me, where you cannot touch him."

Release him.

"I think not." The castellan began chanting, and when his voice at last fell silent, the Ciguanaba disappeared without a sound. Leaning against the wall, the old warlock rested a moment before turning back toward his inner sanctum.

To find an unwelcome intruder blocking his path.

"You," he snarled.

Crazy Snake nodded. "And others."

Outside, Garifuna men were beginning to enter the courtyard, laughing and cheering. Nakili was among them, and when he saw the castellan glaring down at him from the balcony, he threw a mock salute and bowed deeply before gathering several others to break into the shack that housed the remaining slaves. Another group of Garifunas began to tear down the whipping post with zeal.

"Savages! You are all savages!" cried the castellan, turning to Crazy Snake. "You think you can defeat me? You have no idea who I am. What I can do."

"I know enough."

"And what is it you *think* you know, *Comanche*?"

"That you are as old as these stones and have some control over spirits. What I don't understand is why Cipitio, and why you murder slaves."

"No, you wouldn't," said the castellan with a sneer. "The dark arts of my people are as far beyond the primitive magicks of yours as the stars from the earth. They require experimentation. Sacrifices. Victims. Mortal subjects like those worthless slaves"—he gestured at the grisly contents of the jars—"but they will only get you so far. Creatures like Cipitio, on the other hand, hold within them the key to true immortality. In time I will find it and free myself of his place."

"No," said Crazy Snake. "You won't." He lunged at the castellan with his tomahawk, but it passed through empty air. The Spaniard had vanished.

"You see?" He stood behind the horseman now. "I may not have learned all their secrets, but I've picked up some of their parlor tricks."

Crazy Snake circled the castellan warily, flexing his grip on the tomahawk.

"Would you care to try again?" said the old man.

The horseman lunged again, and again the castellan vanished, but this time Crazy Snake felt the sting of a blade across the back of his arm. The Spaniard stood behind him, a long stiletto in hand, smiling. Crazy Snake touched the spot he had cut. His fingers came away with blood.

"It's poisoned, in case you were wondering," said the castellan, tapping the blade with his other hand. "Within a minute or less you won't have enough strength left to swing that crude axe of yours. Want to try your luck once more? No? Then let's make it more interesting." Four more of the castellan appeared, all five surrounding Crazy Snake. Each of them held an identical knife and moved in unison with the rest, circling closer toward the horseman. He swung at the one he thought had spoken last, but it too proved to be just an illusion. Again the knife slashed him, this time across his back. He turned with a snarl, stumbled a little, and the five castellans laughed.

"Getting tired, are we?" they said. "Come on, one more try. And then it will be all over." They raised their blades and stepped closer, the circle tightening around Crazy Snake like a noose. He pivoted, facing each one in turn, the poison weakening him. He didn't know how much longer he could stand, much less swing the tomahawk. Only one more shot.

"Farewell, savage," said the castellans.

Crazy Snake dodged the blade and swung.

The castellan dropped to his knees, eyes crossing in disbelief at the tomahawk protruding from his forehead.

Crazy Snake planted a foot on the old man's chest and pushed him backward. The Spaniard crumpled to the floor, the last breath of his unnaturally long life rattling like a snake in his throat. The horseman slumped against the wall and slid to the floor himself. His eyes were heavy, and he wanted only to sleep. Yes, sleep...

But he felt a vial pressed to his lips, and a liquid trickling into his mouth.

"Drink," said Cipitio's voice. "Drink, my friend."

Crazy Snake did as he was told. Gradually, he began to feel his strength return. Cipitio helped him up, and the horseman steadied himself against the wall.

"Thank you," he said.

"It's the least I could do." Cipitio fished another banana from somewhere beneath his poncho, peeled it, and was about to take his first bite when he paused to admire it, as if it were the last he would ever see.

"Does the old man's medicine still bind you to this place?"

"His magic? No," Cipitio mumbled, his mouth full. "It's dead now, with him."

"Then there is someone waiting outside to see you."

"So there is." He wiped his mouth with the back of his hand. "I am greatly in your debt, my friend, one that I fear I can never repay. But tell me, how did you know which one of the five was him? A lucky guess?"

"Their knives," said Crazy Snake. "Only one had blood on it."

Cipitio snorted. "Parlor trick indeed. The old warlock never was half as smart as he thought. Burn his body and scatter his ashes in the river as soon as you can. His books, too. And tell your friends that the remains of those he murdered are buried in the keep's old cellar. The key is hanging there on the wall, and I have marked their graves with their names."

"You are going?"

"Yes. My time in this world is at an end, thanks to you, and at last I can know peace. Goodbye, Crazy Snake, and good luck to you. One day you will find what it is you seek." He tossed the half-eaten banana onto the castellan's body and disappeared.

Crazy Snake grunted, looking about the place with disdain. The castellan's sanctum reeked of bad medicine. He had seen enough of its macabre jars and strange sigils and was ready to be rid of the fort, though first he would help Nakili and the others loot what they could, then do as Cipitio had said with the castellan's body.

As he joined a cluster of hugging and dancing Garifunas in the gateway, a movement on the road beneath the fort caught the horseman's eye. There he saw Cipitio, held tight in the arms of a kneeling woman. Gone was the monstrous visage that had driven Crazy Snake and so many other men mad. In its place was a beautiful, slender face that gazed upon her long lost son with love and regret. Tucking her long hair behind her ears, Ziquet stood at last, and taking Cipitio's hand in hers, they turned toward the river, walking as any mother and child might have walked through ages past, until finally they were swallowed by the night.

"What do you see?" asked Nakili, following Crazy Snake's gaze.

Crazy Snake turned and withdrew his hand from the medicine pouch around his neck, where it had strayed. "Nothing. Now let us leave this place. I have a horse that needs riding and a score of arrows for as many white men as I can find—maybe even this President Walker himself—before I turn south once more."

ERIC ATKISSON *was born in Texas, grew up in Wisconsin, and now lives in Northern Virginia. A retired National Guard officer and veteran of three wartime deployments in the Middle East, he is the author of articles, short stories, and essays in a variety of publications, including, most recently, an essay in* Entropy Magazine. *This was the second of four Crazy Snake stories he has written for* Heroic Fantasy Quarterly, *including the two-part "Crazy Snake and the Tribute for Pachacamac", and he swears there are more to come. In addition to writing, he enjoys history, photography, hiking, and kayaking.*

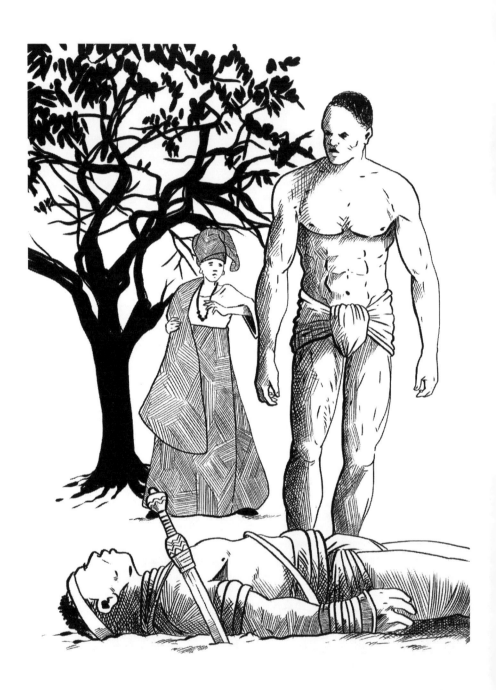

The Madness of the Mansa

by Cullen Groves

One summer night, a great storm arose over the western ocean, and many citizens and sailors in the port of Asongai told how they had seen the demons of madness walking the black winds in the darkness. The gales made wrack of the galleys in the harbor, and many a ship-owner suffered the storm's wrath, and yet it had howled itself out by morning.

When the royal servants entered the Mansa's apartments that dawn, they found him already awake and deep in the tides of an evil mood. They entered to dress him in silence, wary of his anger.

The chief servant drew the Mansa up to stand naked and blackly gleaming in the morning light before a great window. Then his servants bathed him with water poured from silver ewers and with sponges harvested from the nearby coasts. After that, they wrapped the Mansa's body in robes, and one of the younger servants began to hum under his breath as he drew a belt about the Mansa's waist. The youth even sang quietly to himself as he helped to drape the royal leopard-skin mantle over the Mansa's shoulders. It was an old song, a traditional song, sung by the men of the river tribes as they plied oars on the streams.

The Mansa's scowl broke, and a smile creased the corners of his mouth as he listened.

Emboldened, the young man ceased his song and said, "How magnificent you are today, great Mansa!"

At that, the Mansa's glower returned, darker than before. He thrust the youth from his side with a stiff arm, and sent the young man sprawling. Then the Mansa spoke, with a voice like breaking thunder, and said, "This man offends me with his clapping tongue, like ill-tuned bells that clatter out their din; so get him gone, in fetters clap his wrists, and let him sing for freedom in the mines."

"Please lord!" the youth cried, crawling toward the Mansa on his knees. "Forgive my chattering, I beg you!"

But before he could reach out to grasp the Mansa's knees in supplication, the other servants hauled him up and bore him away in silence, leaving only their chief in the Mansa's presence.

The Mansa's frown deepened. He gathered the leopard pelt around his shoulders. Without a word, he beckoned for his chief servant to follow him to court.

The broad courtyard lay open to the sky, its walls covered in gold lattices like the intertwining boughs of locust trees from the savannah, while pairs of trees flanked each of the three doorways. The courtiers of Asongai had already gathered there, along with crowds of supplicants from the city, and others from the neighboring tribes of fishermen and herdsmen. The courtiers and the city-men stood together gossiping, while the tribesmen crouched in silence; but as the Mansa entered through a wide archway, every voice was hushed.

The Mansa took his seat in the only chair, situated on a wide, stepped dais against the northern wall. His chief servant sat at his feet. To the Mansa's right hand stepped his executioner, with a broad ceremonial sword, while his herald came to stand at his left, with a leopard-headed staff.

Then the herald stepped forward to address the court, but the Mansa forestalled him with his own voice, which rolled forth like a pealing storm.

"Ye subjects I command, now hear my will, that each shall henceforth speak in metered verse, in measured phrases marking out his words, to lend some beauty to this ugly place. Too long I've listened to the flatterers and courtiers with crooked tongues crab truth as if the bones of meaning are the form of language, though they lack the living flesh of sinews and the muscles that give strength, and by expressing less than living truth they lie. No more! I would but truth-songs hear."

The tribesmen applauded, while the courtiers and the citizens stood in shocked silence.

"But who can be bothered to learn the old meters?" one of the courtiers cried out.

The Mansa gestured to his chief servant, who directed others of the household to drag the offending courtier out through the gates of the court. When others complained, the chief servant had them hauled away as well.

Then the tribesmen came forward. They couched their supplications in the meters of the old heroic songs, and they got their hearings, and the boon of justice, too.

And the Mansa smiled.

244

II

More than half the ivory of the world changed hands in Asongai, carried there by camel caravans across the deserts and savannahs to the south and east. There was also much gold there, and slaves, salt, and diamonds. All these things were shipped east from Asongai, through the Pillars of Malqar, to the Aulorad and the cities beyond.

The native men of Asongai and the local tribes were black skinned, but merchants and ship-owners from every nation flocked to their rich harbor. It was not unusual, therefore, to see such a pair as ebony-skinned Draba and sun-burned Mendax walking together in seek of a wine-tavern. Draba stood huge, half again as tall as his companion, and he moved with a restrained power that Mendax lacked. He wore the open shirt and simple trews of a seaman, with a long knife thrust through his belt, while Mendax wore the sword and black cloak of a mercenary soldier.

Draba's face contorted into a dark scowl as he and Mendax conversed in the Koine, a tongue from far to the east, and foreign to Asongai.

"I tell you, I don't trust the man," Draba said. "I've walked into enough ambushes, and I know that Aska thinks I stole my goods from others on the sea."

"Didn't you?" Mendax asked.

Draba crossed his arms over his breast as he towered over Mendax. "What does it matter how I get my gold, if it gleams the same?"

"Because stolen goods can be seized by force, and only a third given to the Mansa—and acquisition by the sword is cheaper than by gold."

"That's why I need you," Draba said. "You and I together could sell ourselves dearer than is worth any hoard."

"I know I'm worth a talent or two in silver," Mendax said. "But you?"

Draba laughed, his white teeth flashing in sudden contrast with his skin. "You were always full of jokes," he said, and clapped Mendax on the shoulder. "I've never lost a fight."

Mendax halted and pointed to the low entrance of a tavern, flanked by a pair of lion statues. "There it is, the Lion's Den. They have good wine there—not just that local swill." Even Mendax would have to stoop through the low archway.

"But how shall we deal with the faithlessness of Aska?" Draba asked.

Mendax threw up his hands. "Enough!" he cried. "Turn your mind to wine, for now. Wine is never unfaithful."

Draba's smile widened. "Lead on," he said, and Mendax led him to the low door. They had to duck through, Draba bending almost double, and passed through an antechamber with benches along either wall, on which lodgers could sleep. After that, they stepped into a courtyard open to the sky where tables had been set out on one side for foreigners and merchants. Four trees spread their boughs over the court from the corners, while other archways around the courtyard led into chambers where local wine fermented alongside imported amphorae.

A number of Asongai locals crouched together in the open dirt on one side, dressed in simple robes and sharing wine that they drank directly from a goatskin. Another group sat at one of the tables, and they were dressed in finery of silks and wore gold on their fingers and around their necks. They had a bowl of wine in the middle of their table, and dipped cups into it when they wanted more. Silence fell over the tavern as Draba and Mendax entered.

"That's what we want," Mendax said, pointing to the bowl of wine. He and Draba took the table closest to the door, and chatter resumed in the local tongue as they settled themselves.

Draba smirked as he heard the talk. "It seems the Mansa—the king here— has gone mad," he reported to Mendax.

But the smaller man beckoned to a servant of the wine-tavern, a man dressed in a simple loincloth. He approached and bowed low to Mendax, but then stood with his face contorted in confusion as he listened to Mendax mangle the local language.

"Damn this tongue!" Mendax said in the Koine as he saw the servant smirk. "Ask the man for a bowl of wine, Draba—the stuff from the Aulorad."

Draba laughed and slapped his palm down on the table. "I'd almost rather watch you flounder," he said. "But I am thirsty." He turned to the servant and ordered a bowl of wine in Asongan.

The servant bowed again and turned to fetch the wine, while a smirk flashed across his face. Moments later, he returned with a companion, bearing between them a deep bowl of bronze, two silver cups, a clay ewer of water, and a krater of wine. "You pay—I ordered it," Draba said. "They want a bracelet of cowries. I think two silver pennies should cover it."

Mendax laid the coins on the table; the servants didn't leave until he'd placed a third with the others. Then they bowed, took the silver, and left the two to their wine.

Mendax poured the wine out into the bowl, but neither he nor Draba moved to mix in the water. "The Bull-God be thanked!" Mendax said as he dipped his cup into the wine and then poured its contents out to the dust behind him. "Now let's drink." He refilled his cup, but scowled as he sipped it. "This isn't worth three pennies. Those bastards cheated us."

"You sounded a fool with your chattering," Draba said with a grin.

He dipped his own cup into the wine with an invocation to the goddess of the vines. Then he and Mendax drank for a while in silence, content to listen to the low babble of the Asongans speaking, and to look around the courtyard. The red clay walls had been painted with white figures in a stylized dance, while birds hopped through the leaves and branches above, adding their songs to the babble of voices.

"So," Draba began as he dipped his cup for more wine. "Come now, Mendax. Why don't you fight for me? You're good with a sword—almost as good as I am. And your strategy is better. I'll give you a captain's share, if you join with me. Help me against Aska!"

Mendax shook his head. "I'm contracted with the Hunter's Girdle. I never renege on a contract."

"Aren't you sick of slavery?" Draba asked. "Slave of Anaxes, slave of the wars, of contracts, and in the gladiator pits? But a life at sea is freedom—autarcheia." He whispered the word, as if it were a sacred taboo, and fixed his eyes past Mendax as if looking over the grey horizons of the sea. He breathed deeply. "I tell you, the salt sea air tastes better on your own ship, steering where you wish. With your hand on the tiller—"

"I'm not a slave!" Mendax interrupted. He hid his right hand from view in the black folds of his cloak, where Anaxes' name was tattooed from of old. "I have freedom as a mercenary, to go where I wish."

Draba shook his head and leaned back. "You are strange to me, Mendax. On the day we escaped from the fighting-pits together, I swore that I would never fight or kill for another man again—only for myself! Yet you go off and sell your sword for other men's wars."

A smile quirked Mendax's lips. "But you are a pirate and a criminal, while I am a respectable fighting-man," he said.

"I am a respectable merchant!" Draba roared back. "I may have some unorthodox means—but you are a weasel." And then in verse, he said, "You sneaking weasel, supple like a snake—you spineless vermin, creeping through the halls, and birthing lies by gaping wide your mouth!"

Mendax meditated a moment before responding, "And you, a jackal, prowling through the night—you dog-heart, sniffing bitches out, why howl? If you want faith, just flash your coin at whores."

A smirk crossed Draba's lips. "This weasel makes his home in others' walls, and in his mouth he carries far and wide the offspring of his evil tongue, false words conceived by falsehoods uttered in his ears."

"I'd rather be a polecat in the house, half-tolerated, than a jackal cur who in the garbage finds his foetid feasts, ere driven off by shouts and arrows sharp," Mendax returned. He drained his wine and dipped his cup for more, and Draba followed suit.

But when Draba opened his mouth to reply, one of the Asongans at the table distracted him. The man stood up and thrust a gold-ringed finger at Draba, speaking suddenly in the Koine. "You are man of verse and poetry!"

"Me?" Draba replied, raising his brows. He exchanged a glance with Mendax.

"You!" the Asongan said. "Not that pale-faced weasel. Will you share words with me?"

Draba laughed as Mendax flushed. He stood up and stepped over to the Asongan and his fellows, leaving the mercenary to his wine and chagrin.

"Do you speak Asongan?" the man asked in the local tongue when Draba stood beside him.

"I know it," Draba replied in the same tongue.

"Good!" the man said, and his fellows nodded among themselves. "Sit, drink. I am Bukra, a great man of this city. Drink, I say! I wish to talk business with you."

Draba drank the last of his wine. "I am Draba," he said. "Draba of Hilakkia."

"Good!" Bukra said. "A foreigner. It is better that way." He nodded, and his entourage did the same, and sipped silently at their wine.

"What business would you have with me?" Draba asked.

"The Mansa of Asongai is mad," Bukra said. "He has decreed that only verse may be spoken in his court. There can be no justice, because only poets can speak, and poets know nothing of law."

"I know many cities where poets keep the laws," Draba said. "That is not madness, unless half the world is mad."

Bukra scowled. "But Asongai is a city where books keep the laws," he said. "Now listen. I am a great man in this city—a wise man!—I have increased my fortunes, from a mere half-share in a galley to owning a whole fleet of ships. I have done this on my own wit!" He paused and looked around at his companions, and they nodded agreement.

"I wished to bring suit to the Mansa that I should be made governor of the salt mines at Azagouc," Bukra continued. "The old governor is dead, and I could increase its output tenfold times, as I have increased my own wealth. The profits would redound on the Mansa. But I am a simple man. I know no verse. If I were to bring suit before him, I would be cast out in shame."

Draba smiled. "And you need a man who knows verse," he observed.

"Such a man could speak for me," Bukra said, nodding. "My profits would be his profits."

"It is tempting," Draba said. "But I have no say in the courts of Asongai. I am a foreigner."

"Indeed," Bukra said. "But an unrecognized man might be claimed as a nephew, and the Mansa would be no wiser to it."

"A mountain heaped of silver, hills of gold, might any man make tremble in his knees—but if he's prudent, takes a small cut first, and after that returns for promised wealth."

The Asongans applauded and raised their cups of wine to Draba. Bukra's smile was the broadest, brightly white, while from his wrists he removed seven golden bracelets. "Here is your first cut, Draba of Hilakkia," Bukra said. "Spend it on wine, or women, or whatever you wish. But come to my household tomorrow, and I will dress you in silks and gold. Then you will be called Camba of Gaoa."

Draba laughed and raised his cup to the Asongans, and drank it down. Then he stood, and collected the bracelets from Bukra. With a bow, he returned to Mendax's side.

"What did they want?" Mendax asked. He had begun to glower, for he had finished half the bowl of wine to himself.

"A poet," Draba said, and laughed. "Cheer up! Let's drink, and I will tell you." He called for another krater of wine and a roasted goat, and he paid with a half of a golden bracelet, hacked in two by his knife.

III

Unlike many of the merchant princes of Asongai, who preferred to live far from the noise of the wharves and ware-hawkers, Bukra maintained his household near the harbor, not far from his warehouses or from the market square itself.

The house had been built along lines similar to the Lion's Den, but on a grander scale. When Draba arrived, Bukra had him dressed in the finest silks, and in the pelt of a lion killed on the southern savannah, all of which Bukra bought with his vast wealth. From his own hoards, he arrayed Draba's strong neck and arms in torcs of gold, and Draba's fingers with glittering jewels. Bukra even bought the Hilakkian a fine heavy kopis with gilded hilts, because such a clean-limbed man looked naked without a sword.

Bukra called it an investment, and stinted nothing on Draba's appearance. "I will make back tenfold times what I spend on you, if you will only win me the rights to the mines at Azagouc," he said as he surveyed the effect of the lion skins on Draba's broad shoulders.

Draba noted the appraisal, and rolled his shoulders so that the lion skin cloak rippled around his muscles. Bukra clapped his hands in delight. With his black form draped in silks and pelts, Draba could easily pass as an Asongan.

Bukra continued, "While I farm the Mansa's quotas, I will pocket everything else for myself—and cut you in as well. I will break rods of iron on the backs of my slaves, if I must, to ensure endless caravans of salt!"

With a grim smile, Draba intoned, "Their backs made raw, and hands worked down to bone; from blood flows silver, life transformed to wealth."

"Good!" Bukra cried. "It is good that I found you—good for both of us, as we shall both be richer for it. Camba, my nephew, how great you have grown! What does Udrash, my dearest half-brother, feed you in Gaoa?"

"The marrow of elephants, uncle," Draba replied with a sly smile.

They clasped each other in a mock-familial hug. Then, as they stepped back, each burst forth in laughter, Draba's deep and rolling, while Bukra crowed his delight.

But when Bukra fell silent, he looked again on Draba-cum-Camba, and tapped his own lips with his ringed fingers. "How very handsome," he said. "And yet, something is missing. Ah!" He snapped his fingers. "A prince needs an entourage of slaves. We will go now to buy and outfit such an entourage. Tomorrow we will attend the Mansa at his court."

Then Bukra led Draba into the city, toward the market, and Draba went as Camba, arrayed in the magnificence of his new robes. An escort of slaves walked around them, carrying parasols to keep off the heat of the late afternoon sun. With Bukra and his entourage at his side, Draba seemed indeed like a prince of the land.

They walked west, and passed through a crowd of women returning from the river Ambla with bundles of laundry on their heads. The river bounded the city to the west, and the women came from its banks, singing in a babble that rose like the song of the mountain streams. They bowed to Draba as they passed, as if he were a lord of the city.

In the market, they saw the stalls of merchants from a hundred nations, hawking wares in the Koine, in Asongan, and other tongues. In the midst, over the Executioner's Stone, the bodies of the worst criminals—sorcerers and witches of black magic, and pirates, and traitors against the Mansa—were hanged, pecked at by the black beaks of buzzards.

They continued on, and Bukra led Draba to a great estate that Bukra identified as Tanthamas' house. The plan of its structure resembled others in Asongai, with chambers arrayed around interconnected courtyards, but inside lay much that had come across the seas from foreign shores. In the first antechamber stood a pool of still water, with a bearded sea-god and his daughter-nymphs depicted together in mosaic at its bottom.

Tanthamas himself had come from distant lands to partake in the universal trade far from his native city. As dark as the men of Asongai, he had nevertheless come out of the mountains of Kash in the east, and he greatly admired the men of Lavus, Nera, and the other great trading cities across the seas.

He and Bukra embraced as cousins, and then Bukra introduced him to Draba, using the Koine. "Here is my nephew, Camba, come up from Gaoa and wealthy with salt-money," Bukra said, sweeping his arms to indicate Draba. "But he comes without slaves, for his household was delayed by a siroc in the desert crossing."

"How unfortunate," Tanthamas declared, turning to Draba. "Shall a man live without slaves to carry a parasol over him? Must he lead his own camels?

But it is fortunate that Bukra is your uncle, for he has brought you to me, and I have many slaves."

"We want strong men," Bukra said. "Men with strong backs, who can bear my nephew's baggage across the deserts without collapsing."

Tanthamas nodded, and showed them a number of slaves whom he was willing to sell, men from the black kingdoms of southern Binan, and others from the Aulic tribes across the northern seas. But Bukra pointed out six young men from Makesh who had been captured by the Mansa's warriors in a recent battle at Ashawa. He bought them all for the price of three bolts of silk and two camels.

"These will serve as your entourage at the Mansa's court," Bukra explained to Draba when they had come forth from Tanthamas' household. "And then, when you have won me the rights to the salt mines, they will dig salt from the desert, turning their strength into profits."

Surveying the six young men, Draba nodded, smiling grimly. They had long and powerful frames, like younger visions of his own herculean stature. They could last many years laboring in the mines before they'd spent their strength. But they would also make fine warriors—if they were free.

IV

When Bukra led Draba to the Mansa's court, the watchmen at the gate demanded that Draba leave his new gilded kopis in the antechamber.

"Shall I walk about, naked of arms?" Draba growled.

"All walk unarmed in the Mansa's palace, save his own sworn men," Bukra whispered in Draba's ear. Then, to the guards, he said, "Camba, my nephew, comes from Gaoa, where the law is less strict." He smiled ingratiatingly. But the watchmen did not let them pass until Draba had unbuckled the sword from his belt and surrendered it to them.

"It was a fine blade," he lamented as Bukra led him to the Mansa's court, while touching his hips to reassure himself that the pair of knives hidden under his robes there remained hidden.

They went, then, with their entourages and stood on the right-hand side of the courtyard with the other courtiers, merchants, and citizens of the city, who also wore silks and golden rings. On the other side of the court, tribesmen from the fishing villages mingled with nomadic goatherds, each dressed in his tribe's traditional costume of loincloths or simple cloaks. Many crouched on their haunches rather than stand.

The Mansa sat above them all, on his great dais, with his chief servant, executioner, and herald around him. Leopard skins draped over the Mansa's shoulders, and the head of a were-leopard, slain by his great-grandfather, lay over his right shoulder. The Mansa leaned forward with his chin resting on one hand, and his eyes stared around without blinking. They had grown dark, and many said that he could not sleep at night because of the troublous dreams that descended on him.

Nevertheless, The Mansa kept court, attending to the business of the land before the midsummer sacrifices, though it seemed that calls for justice had increased tenfold. The city-men clamored against the tribesmen of the hinterlands, claiming that they robbed and abused them because the tribesmen alone could sing the old meters to the Mansa, while the city-men fumbled at the formulae and were cast out.

The herald called supplicants forth in metered words, tapping his leopard-headed staff, and the supplicants knelt before the Mansa's dais, and kissed the earth before him. They chanted their metered cases, as well as they could, and the Mansa listened, offering judgment only to those who spoke correctly. Meanwhile, the herald's servants went among the crowd, asking men what business they had there, and always speaking in verse.

Draba had just spoken to one of these servants when the herald stepped forth and tapped his staff again. He cried, "Let bold Ganesa of the Iba tribe step forth, and to the Mansa sing his case!"

A courtier stepped forth, a wide man dressed in orange robes and finely carved ivory trinkets. Before the Mansa's dais, he and his dozen slaves fell to their knees as one, and bent to kiss the earth. Then Ganesa looked up to the Mansa and began haltingly, and in a trembling voice, "The Mansa sprawls like the sun seated on the sky, and justice from his rich mouth should be light for all. Like the lamps that even poor people keep lighted in their pitiful hovels—at night; even last week the Mansa made good rulings with his mouth—but now a man gets only darkness from the sun while mean-hearted others—with knife-eyes take things and money—fishmongers from the Onga-tribe came through the open doors of my house—"

Here he paused, his lips moving as he murmured to himself to remember his poetry. Finally, he continued, "And they were rude and boasting that they could sing away any charges—they took away my ivory my gold, my silk, drank my wine—insulted my wives and daughters, and also broke many of my beautiful things—great, sprawling Mansa, will you not curse the Onga to be hanged at the Executioner's Stone?"

A shout arose from the gathered tribesmen. They sprang to their feet. From their midst stepped a knot of men with thick beards and potbellies. They wore loincloths and goatskin cloaks, while bone bracelets rattled on their forearms as they shook their fists at Ganesa. They came forward and made obeisance before the Mansa, kissing the ground before his dais.

Only one from among them spoke, crying, "What slander's this, against the Onga-tribe? The monkey chatters in his tree—he likes to hear himself insulting passersby, but when the leopard comes, he wisely stops, or else the panther kills his ceaseless tongue; shall humble fishermen invade and wrack a well-respected house like hungry dogs? Ganesa's grievance is mere jealousy from one so long accustomed to receive false justice as a boon of flattery."

"But they did!" Ganesa cried. And his face fell as he saw the Mansa glower. "They invaded my house, and tore everything apart like dog-faced monkeys. Will you let them lie to you, because they speak the old meters?"

But the Mansa had turned his face from Ganesa, and the chief servant arose with a stern gaze. Rather than suffer indignity, Ganesa kissed the ground before the Mansa, and then fled back through the crowd of courtiers for the door, followed by his household men.

As the Mansa's eyes turned away, his gaze fell on a man of magnificent figure, who stood beside Bukra, and overtopped the merchant-prince by head and shoulders. Before his herald could call the next supplicant, the Mansa leaned forward and beckoned to him. In a low voice, the Mansa said, "Who is it, stands at wealthy Bukra's side? Go to, and learn his name and business here, for he is strange to me, and fain would I discover what has brought him to my court."

The herald replied quietly, "Already I have learned his purpose here; great Mansa, Camba is his name, and he from Gaoa-town has come to test his tongue by bringing Bukra's suit for salt-mine rights."

"So let him speak, and let us judge his tongue," the Mansa said.

With a bow, the herald turned back to the gathered courtiers and tribesmen. "Let Camba, Bukra's nephew, state his case!" he cried.

The huge man at Bukra's side flashed his teeth in a grin. With his six servants in tow, he approached the Mansa's dais, and together they sank to their knees and kissed the ground there. Even in kneeling the man's size was evident, like a dark lion crouched in the courtyard.

He did not speak with the accent of Asongai, but his mastery of its measures rolled from his lips: "O! Mansa, sun of justice, shed your light on all Asongai's avenues of gold, and every man who walks the gilded streets. Some say the leopard's pelt is beautiful, while in his heart is ugliness and night, but they are those who cannot see, he stalks in realms his own, unknown to mortal ken. Hear now, I beg, nor judge on mortal whim, good Bukra's suit to oversee the salt of Azagouc; remember how the man was born in humbler days, possessed of sand, and yet, through skill, the grains within his hand transformed from grains of dust to hoards of gold. So too, the salt that in the desert lies will increase tenfold times and multiply your boundless wealth if placed in Bukra's hold."

The Mansa leaned forward as he listened, appraising the man and his words as one. He smiled as Draba came to a close.

But before the Mansa could speak, the same man who had spoken for the Onga-men gave a wordless shout. He and his companions came forward, and fell on their knees before the Mansa at Draba's left. The speaker was younger than his fellows, and had a long, lean build with only the beginnings of a patriarchal paunch. The patterns of ritual scars on his right upper arm recorded his wrestling victories, while no defeats marred his left arm.

He looked up to the Mansa for a long moment of silence, and then cried, "This ape of Gaoa comes with honeyed words, pretends the truth is fair while fair's the form. But do not be deceived! He is an ape, a beast in human form, who on behalf of dog-faced Bukra clouds your mind with lies—that Bukra who our wealth sends overseas! Much better, Mansa, if the Idrash tribe regain their ancient holdings of the mines."

Draba laughed and almost immediately canted back, "If Bukra overseas sends desert salts, then too, he brings back distant wealth and wares, as if the desert sand itself were gold." He turned to gesture at the Onga-man. "This snake upon his belly crawls and speaks in subtle verses with his two-forked tongue. Will tribesmen of the desert share their wealth, or hoard it with their herds and goats?"

The rest of the court fell silent. Even the Mansa raised his brows.

"Though laden with the wealth of foreign lands, the ships of Bukra share it not with us," the Onga-man declared. "To trust him with your gold is like to trust hyenas with the antelopes you've shot while hunting on the plains with arrows sharp."

Draba frowned as he replied, "Do serpents mandate what the Mansa wills, or does the man himself determine deeds? That snake winds sideways through the desert sands, and sidles up as if to meet a friend, but from his fangs the viper's venom stings. Great Mansa, if you would the salt's white gold made multiplied, to Bukra give this charge."

The Onga-man leaped to his feet and turned on Draba with fists balled, but Draba only laughed.

"I'll suffer no hyena's laughter shrill!" the man cried.

Draba flexed, and his powerful muscles rippled under his lion skin cloak.

"Be silent, and return ye to your posts!" the Mansa declared, rising from his seat.

The Onga-man sank to his knees and again kissed the earth, before returning with his fellows to the other tribesmen. Draba and his servants withdrew more slowly, to stand again at Bukra's side.

When things quieted, the Mansa continued, "My mind is yet divided on this thing; though justice seems to lie with Bukra's claims, Idwara's fears are more than meritless. So therefore, stay this argument, and hold your tongues until the morrow brings new light; but Camba, will ye not remain the night and test the Mansa's hospitality? But rarely have I heard such sure exchange, and fain would I have further words with thee."

Draba bowed low to this request, while the eyes of all the tribesmen burned as they looked on him.

Bukra clapped Draba's shoulder. "I knew you were a good investment," he whispered, while the other courtiers and city-men murmured congratulations.

"This is the first case that Idwara has not won outright," one of them whispered to Draba.

Meanwhile, the herald called another supplicant forward, and the court of the Mansa continued. But none could forget the presence of Draba, standing silently at Bukra's side with a wide and close-lipped smile.

V

The Mansa ended the business of his court shortly after noon, and devoted the rest of the day to his own pleasures, as was his habit. He repaired to his own chambers, where he would take a lunch of cold meat and chilled fruits. Then he would nap through the heat of the afternoon, or listen to his jalis sing, until in the fading light of the evening, he would bathe again, and prepare for the evening's feast.

For there was invariably a feast every evening in the Mansa's palace, except on certain sacred days when eating was taboo, or when the Mansa was away at war. If the royal hunters had caught and killed an elephant, the feast of its body could go on into the next dawn; but other nights, the fare was merely of antelope or water buffalo, and boiled yams and fried bread.

The royal household ate together, with the Mansa on his stepped dais, attended by his chief servant. On his right sat his sons, a dozen young men and boys, while on his left sat his wives—only five, though his court jalis remembered songs from the days when Mansa Zuwai feasted all fifty of his wives every night, and caused a famine in the land.

The rest of the household—the warriors of the Mansa's personal troop, his captains, and his hunters—all sat on the open ground before the dais, and ate only after the Mansa had taken the first bite. The Mansa's guests also ate on the open ground, in a place of honor just below the youngest of the Mansa's sons, while jalis sat around the edges, each bent over the long neck of his harp-like kora.

Draba took the place of penultimate honor, and had Bukra sit on his left, as the most honored guest. The youngest of the Mansa's sons, a child of seven years, looked away from Bukra with haughty indignance but Draba paid him no mind. His and Bukra's servants knelt behind them in two rows.

"What if we are rebuked?" Bukra protested quietly to Draba in the Koine. "The tribesmen are well-honored in the court, now. They will send us down the line."

Draba saw the Mansa's dark glance their way as Bukra spoke without verse, even in the Koine. To Bukra, he said, "Stop braying like an ass and seat yourself;

with this, our honor is assured, so hush!" He brandished a papyrus scroll filled with clumsy writing, on which he and Bukra had worked all afternoon, and Bukra said no more.

Presently, the other guests and the Onga tribesmen arrived. The Onga-men glowered at Draba and Bukra, and Idwara's dark eyes gleamed like sharp sword-points as they sought out Draba's. But they relinquished their accustomed place and sat in silence. Idwara sat on Draba's left; the two men found each other to be of like size.

When all were seated cross-legged on the ground before low tables, the jalis began to play and to sing together the old songs of the history of Asongai. Servants entered with platters bearing yams, bread, and roasted buffalo. These they placed on the low tables in reach of six men at a time, so that all might eat communally.

All awaited the Mansa to take the first bites. He sampled each of the dishes once, with an approving nod for each. Then the feast began in earnest. Everyone ate from the common platters, by tearing off strips of bread and grasping yams or steaming meat in the fold. Bukra, Draba, and the great men of the Onga-tribe all shared a platter; while Draba ate lustily, Idwara barely picked at the meal before them.

The Mansa ate well, but quickly. When he had finished, he sat back in silence and listened to the songs of the jalis. His eyes drifted especially over Draba, Idwara, and Bukra.

As Draba finished eating and sat back in satisfaction, the Mansa caught his eye, and gestured to him. He said, "Now come, great Camba of the silver tongue, will you not lift your voice in song for us, the Mansa of Asongai and his host?"

Draba bowed deeply and kissed the earth before him, while Idwara bristled at his side. The jalis ceased playing on their koras, looking on in curiosity at this man from whom the Mansa deigned request a song.

And when he straightened to look again at the Mansa, Draba said, "Give me a moment to compose myself, and I shall sing a foreign lay that comes from far across the frothing eastern seas, though canted to me on the desert sands."

The Mansa nodded his head, and Draba produced the papyrus scroll from his robes. He unrolled its first section, revealing a jumble of clumsily drawn characters from the Koine, but which spelled out Asongan words.

Then Draba began to sing in a rolling voice, and the jalis accompanyied him with chords plucked out on the strings of their koras. He sang from the Aristiad, a little epic from the city of Corunax far away to the east on the coast of the Aulorad. He began with the ancient formula of the prologue, singing, "O! muses, sing to me of Corunax, and of Thersiteos' evil deeds therein; and tell how he, a poor man of the town, by merely donning kingly purple robes, became at first an one of ancient line, and presently a tyrant slaked with blood;

and how Aristeus, a noble son, would no more bide Thersiteos' falsehoods crowned, but killed the tyrant with a dagger's death—and though the slayer by a mob was slain, Aristeus' virtues into stars were made, a constellation bright; now to my lied…"

The Mansa listened intently as Draba continued into the first book, which concerned Thersitios' less-than-honest acquisition of purple aristocratic robes. His eyes closed as Draba's strong voice rolled through the courtyard, and a smile crossed his face.

As the Mansa's eyes closed, one of his wives turned her eyes on Draba, and flashed a smile his way. She was not the youngest, yet possessed a self-assured beauty that shone brighter than the fresh faces of the two younger wives. Her eyes met Draba's but a moment before she looked away and stilled her smile, but for that moment it seemed to Draba that a fire was kindled between them, and it burned under his skin. Nevertheless, he continued his song.

But Draba had not made it far beyond Aristeus' disgust at the proclamation of Thersiteos' kingship, when Idwara slammed a hand down on the table, upsetting the yams there and interrupting Draba midstride.

"How can you listen to this liar's verse?" Idwara cried out, his eyes sweeping over all those assembled there before looking finally to the Mansa himself. "See what a poet's silver tongue he has, that he recites his song from lifeless words, scratched out in ink on his papyrus scrolls! Just like a child, he has no grasp of verse, but epithets recalls from written cues."

"And see the adder all puffed up with pride, insulting others' songs with venomed stings." Draba turned from Idwara toward the Mansa and continued, "Great Mansa, but a moon ago I heard this song, out on the sea of stretching sands—shall I be faulted, knowing not each line?"

"A moon ago! How many weeks is that? And I could sing of ancient Sundi's deeds, and not a week had passed since first I heard."

The Mansa raised his hand, and silence fell again over the court. "Be still— let's hear no more of this tonight. Ye jalis, sing one song before I rest." Servants returned to collect the platters and remaining food, while the jalis sang a mournful song about a lost hunter.

Draba rolled up the papyrus and returned it to his belt, while Bukra trembled at his side, and Idwara smiled to his fellows. But Draba affected stoic indifference as he glanced toward the Mansa's third wife and wondered after her smile.

VI

"We are finished!" Bukra cried in the Koine when he, Draba, and their entourage returned to their apartments. He cast himself down on some cushions on the floor. "Idwara has rebuked us, and the Mansa agreed with him." He jabbed one jeweled finger at Draba. "And you said that we should write it all out, the better to remember it!"

"It seemed prudent at the time," Draba rumbled. "And the Mansa would have listened, if not for Idwara. Damn that man!" Draba began to pace through the room, while Bukra sat, hunched over on the floor. The six young men of Draba's retinue watched him in silence, while Bukra's servants lay down to rest.

"All my money is wasted," Bukra said. "You will pay me back everything— all the silk, all the rings on your hands, and these slaves too."

"Be quiet and let me think," Draba barked back, and Bukra before him. "We are not finished," Draba continued as he resumed pacing. "We need only present a better case in court on the morrow. And deal with Idwara, somehow." His eyes narrowed.

"Why do you argue in a foreign tongue?" one of Draba's six slaves asked suddenly in Asongan. "Are you plotting against the Mansa, and afraid that he will hear?" He turned to Draba. "Or is it because you are not really Asongan?"

Draba and Bukra fell silent and turned to regard the former warrior, who looked back without fear. His name was Iyawasu, and he had taken it on himself to act as chief of Draba's servants.

"Am I not of Gaoa?" Draba finally replied, in Asongan.

"The tongues of Gaoa and Asongai are the same," Iyawasu said. "Yet your accents are stranger than mine, though I am of Makesh. You are playing some trick on the Mansa, aren't you?"

"Perhaps," Draba said. "Does it matter to you?"

"What do I care for the Mansa of Asongai?" Iyawasu said. "He is not my mansa. I was only curious."

"We should have him killed," Bukra said in the Koine, pointing at Iyawasu with a trembling hand. "He is too clever for a slave!"

"Don't be an ass," Draba replied. "What does he care for the Mansa?"

Turning back to Iyawasu, Draba said in Asongan, "Say nothing of this to anyone, and perhaps I will buy your freedom from this goldmonger."

Iyawasu nodded. He and the others murmured to each other in their own tongue, and then fell silent again, wearing expressions of stoic disregard.

Draba turned back to Bukra. "We will work out our arguments for the morning," he said. "And we will stay up all night to perfect them, if we must. You must also speak!"

Bukra passed a hand over his face, and when he looked back to Draba, greed shone in his eyes again. "It is good that I found you," he said. "You are like a bulwark against my fears."

"There!" Draba said. "Already, he speaks in metaphor—now he only needs a sense of meter."

Then he and Bukra began to work on their arguments, and stayed up late into the night. Draba demanded the details of Bukra's claims, and the history of the mines, and how they had fallen out of the possessions of the Idrash tribe, to be farmed by the Mansa alone. All this, Draba wove them into metaphors and verse. Then he had Bukra recite everything back to him, over and again, until Bukra could intone everything from memory, however slowly.

But at last, Bukra began to yawn, and could no longer recall more than two lines for weariness. He lay down to sleep, as the slaves had already done, ignoring Draba's protests as he did.

Only Draba remained awake, reciting endless variations of verse to himself in Asongan. But he started from this reverie at the rattling of the beads that hung as a curtain across the open doorway of the chamber. Draba saw that a small woman stood with her head poked through the beaded archway. She wore the simple robes of a servant of the palace, and as Draba looked up, she beckoned to him silently.

Draba arose and followed her into the corridor beyond, where they stood together in the night's darkness. "My mistress Belecane, third wife of the Mansa, wishes to see Camba of Gaoa, and to test his tongue," she whispered to Draba through the shadows.

A close-lipped smile, invisible in the darkness, curved across Draba's mouth. "Lead on," he said.

She led him through a maze of corridors until they passed finally into the cool of a courtyard open to the night sky, but unlike the Mansa's royal court. Trees with the sword-like leaves, and other local plants filled the space. A musky-sweet scent on the air suggested flowering blooms under the boughs of the trees, but none could be seen in the night. Clouds had filled the sky since the evening feast, and they shrouded the stars and the moon in darkness.

"Belecane awaits Camba there, under the locust trees," the servant whispered to Draba. Then she slipped from his side and faded into the night, leaving Draba alone at the edge of the garden.

Draba entered slowly. He felt at his side for his kopis out of habit—but the Mansa allowed none but his own guards to come armed into his palace. Draba was naked, except for the knives he had smuggled in with his baggage, but which remained in the apartments he shared with Bukra. His skin prickled as he stepped out into the shadow of the trees, remembering other secret meetings that had turned out to be ambushes.

A light rain began to fall, rattling on the leaves around him. Yet, despite the darkness, Draba didn't fail to see the figure that arose in the shadows under the locust grove, a slim feminine figure.

"Belecane?" Draba asked quietly. Even half-whispered, his deep voice carried through the night.

"Is that Camba of Gaoa?" a woman's voice returned.

"It is he," Draba said.

The shadowed figure stepped from under the trees, and Draba recognized the third wife of the Mansa through the dim night. But he also saw another silhouette move behind her, someone as tall and as broad as Draba.

Draba stiffened, and recoiled as Belecane's hands reached out for his. "Who else is here?" Draba asked.

"My eunuch, Feiraz," Belecane said, and Draba heard amusement in her voice. "My will is his will. He is only here to ensure your good behavior, Camba."

"Is that so?" Draba said. He relaxed somewhat, and let Belecane take his hands. Hers were cool and soft, and he felt her fingers touching his calouses in wonder. But he kept his eyes on big silhouette behind her. "Why have you sent for me, Belecane?" Draba asked.

"The Mansa will not speak to me," Belecane said. "My own husband will not even embrace me, because I cannot sing to him in verse!"

"Surely you know some songs," Draba said.

"But none are my own," Belecane said. The rain began to fall more heavily, splashing through the canopy and flecking cold water on her face and Draba's. She pulled Draba under the locust trees.

There, she continued, "I can indeed sing others' songs to the Mansa. But I want to tell him my thoughts in my own words." She pressed Draba's hands in hers. "I have heard you sing. I have heard your silver tongue. Will you not teach me how to sing to my man?"

Draba listened to the rain's increasing patter in the leaves above and around them, and to the excited breathing of the woman before him. He could feel her quickened pulse in the fingers that grasped his, and wondered if the sweetness he smelled was her breath, or a flower's.

"How beautiful is night, how dark her face, while in her eyes is silver light of stars," Draba said. "And o! how sweet her breath, how cool her touch, though in her fingers burns a fire white. I think that I might burn away, beneath the moon's cold tongues of beauty's fire."

Belecane's fingers tightened around Draba's broad hands. "Go on," she breathed.

Draba grinned. "I thought you wanted to learn poetry, not to hear it," he said. "Why don't you try a verse or two?"

She took a deep breath. Silence stretched between her and Draba, and he saw her eyes searching out his features through the gloom. Suddenly, lightning flashed, illuminating everything in a stark white moment—Belecane's fine high forehead, her thick lips parted for quick breaths, and how her close-cropped hair accentuated the graceful lines of her cheeks and neck. The torcs of gold around her neck were all bleached grey by the stark flash.

Then all was darkness again, and thunder's drums rolled across the sky.

"His voice is like thunder," Belecane began slowly. "He comes like a storm—

his eyes flash like lightning, and his touch tingles, like the charge in the air. The strength of the strong winds moves in his limbs, and to be loved by him is like— Like to be struck by a thunderbolt."

Draba laughed, and Belecane wrenched back her hands.

"You don't have to make fun," Belecane said.

"I'm sorry," Draba said, stilling his laughter. "It was not bad. The words were good, but not the cadence. Have you no ear for meter?"

"I don't know," Belecane said, a little stiffly.

"Here—listen," Draba said. As the rain drummed around them, increasingly steady, he canted, "I take her trembling hand, I kiss her palm; the softness of her skin, her fingers slim, are wonders like the thistle's silken bloom, and yet, they prick me with a nettle's pains."

"I take his strong right hand in my fingers, and feel the strength of their calouses, rough like the rocky pillars of a high cliff-wall," Belecane replied, feeling his hands with hers.

Draba shook his head. "Not quite," he said. "But a good metaphor!"

Then Belecane let go his hands, and reached up to draw Draba's face to hers. Their lips met, and Draba felt the cool rainwater on her face and his as they pressed together.

"It has been so long since I felt the touch of the Mansa, or any other," Belecane whispered when they parted for breath.

Draba drew himself up to his full height and crossed his arms over his breast. "What of Feiraz, and good behavior?" he asked in a low voice.

"My will is his will," Belecane repeated. She reached out to Draba again. "Camba, Camba of the silver tongue—will you not come to me?"

Draba gathered her up in a close embrace, feeling her warmth against the cold night. Lightning flashed again, and Draba glimpsed Feiraz over Belecane's shoulder, as impassive as the tree against which he stood.

Belecane's fingers scrambled at Draba's robes to pull them from his shoulders. Draba swept her hands aside and shrugged his broad shoulders from the silk with ease. He shuddered slightly as the night's chill suddenly touched his skin, and shivered again as Belecane's fingers traced his huge frame, while he worried at her dress.

But as Belecane traced his body, he felt her fingers run over the scars that criss-crossed his back. She stiffened in his grasp as she felt them. "Are these the scars of a warrior?" she asked quietly as Draba bent his head to kiss her neck.

"Yes, each one a reminder of a man I've killed," he growled. "Each one a reminder of my survival in the fighting-pits."

Belecane recoiled suddenly from Draba. She clasped her dress close about her breast and looked up at him, while disbelief and outrage mingled in her eyes. "You were a slave of the fighitng-pits?" she hissed.

261

Draba drew himself up again, half naked in the night. He laughed and flexed his massive arms. "I killed every man I faced," he said. "And many more since."

"Feiraz!" Belecane gasped. "Kill this impostor—this liar. This slave has tried to seduce the Mansa's wife!"

Draba's laughter darkened, but the huge figure of Feiraz sprang at him, and Draba felt as if he had been tackled by a leopard. Just like a pard, Feiraz went for the throat, locking his hands around Draba's neck, and he bore Draba down in surprise.

But Draba's neck was thick and corded with muscle, and though tenacious, the eunuch wrestled without technique. He relied on size, but had never had to reckon with a man as powerful as Draba.

Draba broke the hold and threw Feiraz to the ground. Feiraz seized something from his belt—a long knife glinted suddenly in his hand. But Draba laughed, and he seized Feiraz's head where he sprawled in the mud, and with a savage wrench of his hands, he snapped the eunuch's neck.

Lightning flashed as Draba stood over Feiraz's corpse in the mud, and Belecane cowered back against a tree. She tried to run, but Draba leaped out and grasped the back of her dress with his hand. Thunder rolled over them as he hauled her back.

"Not so fast!" Draba said. "Now that we've come to this pass, I might as well take what I want."

"The Mansa will kill you," Belecane spat. "His warriors will skin you alive, and nail your bleeding corpse over the Stone."

He gripped her shoulder in one hand, and held out the other before her, palm open. "Give me those torcs at your neck, and those bracelets too."

When Belecane had delivered into Draba's hand all her torques and gold bracelets, he thrust her away. He barked laughter into the night, echoed by peals of thunder. "Go on and weep to your Mansa!" Draba cried to Belecane as she fled. "Go and sing through your tears that Draba the Hilakkian has stolen your gold!"

VII

Draba burst through the beads of his apartments, startling awake the six youths of Makesh, while Bukra and his slaves continued to snore. The six watched in silence as the half-naked Draba, with a heavy knife bare in his hand, leapt to his bundle of belongings under the wall and deposited a pile of golden torcs and bracelets in his lion-cloak. Nor did they make any noise when he produced two other blades, hidden in the bundle.

"Weapons are not allowed in the Mansa's court," Iyawasu observed.

"I go nowhere unarmed," Draba answered. He turned to the Makeshi, holding two of his three knives out, hilts first. "Do you wish to be warriors again?"

262

"We are your slaves," Iyawasu replied slowly.

"You were warriors of Makesh, captured in battle," Draba said. "Against whom did you fight?"

"Against Asongai," Iyawasu said.

"Will you fight Asongans now?" He fell silent, and cocked his head toward the doorway. "They are coming. Do you hear?"

They listened, and past Bukra's heavy breathing, all could hear dimly the tramp of the feet of many men in the corridors.

"The Mansa's warriors are coming!" Draba said. "They will kill us."

Iyawasu pointed at the gold torcs and bracelets piled on the cloak at Draba's feet. "Because you are a thief," he said.

"I am a captain of Hilakkia!" Draba returned straightening to his full height. "I take what I want when I want it, and only pay when I wish. I'll have you on my ship, if you wish—slaves no longer, but earning a share of every venture."

Iyawasu explained in the Makeshi tongue, and the others muttered quietly, as Draba looked on. The shouts and the tramp of feet grew louder in the corridors.

"We have no weapons," Iyawasu said. "But we are with you."

"Good!" Draba said. "I have only two knives to spare. The rest may have to use their hands. Gather all the gold you can, and we will flee from here!"

Iyawasu directed the other Makeshi to do as Draba asked, and one man hoisted the bundle Draba had made in his cloak, while others rummaged through Bukra's baggage.

"What's going on?" Bukra mumbled, coming slowly out of sleep, while his slaves roused themselves and crouched back against the wall with their arms crossed, watching the banditry before them.

"Will you not also join us?" Draba asked them as they glared. "I will make freedmen of you if you come with me."

"We will remain loyal to our master," their chief replied, shaking his head, and though the others looked between themselves, none moved to join Draba and the Makeshi.

"Suit yourselves," Draba said. He poked his head out the doorway, and saw the glow of torchlight around a corner farther down the corridor. Drawing back into the room, he growled, "They are almost upon us! We must go."

"Who are upon us?" Bukra cried suddenly, starting fully awake.

"The warriors of the Mansa!" Draba said. "They are coming to arrest me. You must go and beg mercy, or they will kill you too!" He pointed down the corridor to his right, towards whence the torchlight and the tramp of feet came.

Bukra stood, with as much dignity as he could muster in the loose robe he had donned for sleep. "They have discovered your ruse?" he whispered in the last grasp of sleep's delirium.

"Our ruse!" Draba growled. He thrust a stiff finger into Bukra's breast. "You are as much to blame as I. You will also be hanged—or worse!"

"No!" Bukra cried. "I am a citizen of Asongai. The Mansa will grant mercy to me." He turned to his slaves. "Come!" he cried, beckoning them, and they gathered around him. Then, all together, they stepped out into the corridor, and started off toward the oncoming troop of warriors.

"Now! Quickly!" Draba hissed to Iyawasu and the Makeshi. They poured across the threshold into the nighted corridors beyond, with the clatter of beads behind them. Draba went first, feet pounding out a cadence matched by his breath as he led the Makeshi down a corridor opposite the light of the Mansa's coming warriors.

"Please!" they heard Bukra pleading behind them. "Mercy—the man deceived me!"

"Arrest him!" a deep voice cried over Bukra's supplications. "And arrest his slaves." And then, resounding down the corridor, the same voice boomed, "Lo! I am Ezana, the Executioner of the Mansa of Asongai, and I conjure Camba of Gaoa to surrender himself to me, or to suffer the displeasure of the Mansa!"

Draba led his troop of six around a corner just as the warriors behind them arrived at the still dancing beads of the curtained doorway. "There's no one here!" one of the guards called back to Ezana.

Then Draba ran, swiftly traversing corridor after corridor, with the six Makeshi warriors behind him. He sought a threshold between palace and city, or a courtyard with a wall that could be scaled to the world beyond. The Makeshi ran at his heels, bundles of gold jangling at their shoulders, followed through the halls by the shouts of Ezana and the Mansa's warriors.

After several false findings, they found such a courtyard, long and nighted, and Draba thought that the far wall, unbroken by any doorway, must be an outer wall. He thought too, that the trees that lined it would make fine stairways to freedom.

But it was already occupied. A host of tribesmen crouched in the night's rain, faces turned toward the outer wall. The driving rain drowned out sound in the court, and the tribesmen were focused on the tall idol of twisted black wood before them, and the ancient man dressed in shamanistic fetishes who stood shaking at its feet. He sang as he trembled, limbs shaking feverishly, but the tongue was an ancient tribal dialect. The only sound that cut through the rain was the rattling of the ivory bracelets clasped around his wrists and ankles.

"It is the god of the thunder-madness, and the storm-terror," Iyawasu declared in awe. He and the Makeshi hid their faces behind their hands, but Draba laughed and stepped boldly into the rain.

He went alone at first, but the Makeshi saw him go between their fingers. He went like a lion in the night, advancing alone in disregard against a pack of hyenas between him and his goal. And the Makeshi followed, though they shook with terror in the face of the god.

Draba made for the outer wall, but several of the tribesmen saw him, and they raised a shout and pointed. The heavy knife dripped with rainwater in his hand.

They leapt to their feet and gathered in a knot between Draba and the outer wall, where the shaman continued to chant before the idol. Draba recognized them as Onga-men, and one stood above the rest, with scars on his right arm, and none on his left.

"Do not let them pass," a familiar voice cried. "Do not let them live—they will speak of our sorceries, and we will be hanged over the Stone!"

"Idwara!" Draba cried through the rain. "I only wish to pass! Let us climb the walls, and we will be gone from your life forever."

"The coward comes to run away across the courtyard's walls, a crow who flees the hawk," Idwara returned, and his clear voice rang through the night. "Bold Camba fears to lose his dignity, and so he flees through darkness of the night, and hopes to hide the rot within his heart."

Draba laughed. "The monkey stands before the lion bold—he chatters on as if his insults cut, but in his flesh the pard will sink his teeth." He and Idwara advanced against each other, and Draba raised the knife in his right hand over his left shoulder for a heavy blow, but Idwara's fist struck out like a viper, and smashed the blade from Draba's hand. Draba shouted as the knife spun away through the night.

Behind Draba, the Makeshi advanced, while the Onga-men approached from behind Idwara. The tribesmen were unarmed, and wary of the two knives held forth by Iyawasu and his Makeshi companion.

Then Draba and Idwara rushed against each other, clasping hands around waists, seeking wrestlers' holds with their strong grips. They strained against each other like dark gods from the dawn-age, who could crack mountains with their struggles, while around them boiled a melee between the Makeshi and the Onga-men.

Muscles bulged and tendons creaked. Draba found that his weight and strength were greater, but that they availed him nothing against Idwara's skill. The man writhed out of every lock and armbar, and pressed Draba where a man's strength could not resist. But Idwara's hands did not have the breadth to grip Draba, and every time he barred him, Draba broke forth like a lion bursting its fetters.

Back and forth through the night rain they rolled, throwing each other to the mud and churning it up with their feet. They lost sight of the world around them—to relax a guard at any moment invited defeat, by a broken back, or even something as little as a snapped finger. They breathed mud and rain, and felt each other's heartbeats hammering through their breastbones, and still they writhed, each trying to pin the other to the earth and to crush the life from him.

Then suddenly Idwara cried out and went limp in Draba's hands. The huge Hilakkian stood, dropping the dying Onga-man to the mud, and saw Iyawasu with a bloody knife clasped in his young hand. The five other Makeshi stood around him, alone. The tribesmen had fled, leaving their idol, and the shaman who lay collapsed from exhaustion at the feet of the wooden god.

"I'd have had him," Draba growled through the rain.

"We must go!" Iyawasu cried. "Can you not hear the shouts of the Mansa's warriors?"

Draba heard their shouts through the rain, echoing out of the corridors of the palace. "Over the walls," he said. "That tree! Send the gold up first, and I'll come last."

They stepped over the fallen bodies of several tribesmen, and clambered up the sturdiest tree, one by one, to the top of the courtyard's outer wall. Beyond lay freedom in the vast city of Asongai. When Draba reached the top, he turned to the Mansa's warriors behind him, and laughed. Then he dropped to the ground beyond, and led the Makeshi youths through the benighted city toward a secret cove on the western coast, beyond the river Ambla.

The bundles at their backs jangled with gold.

VIII

Draba's ship, a lean black galley with a bronze ram like a falcon's beak, already rocked in the shallow waters of the cove as Mendax approached. Its sails were still furled, and its oars still shipped, while men worked to load it through the surf.

Mendax came brazenly down the beach, his black cloak billowing behind him, sword belted at his right side. Watchers caught sight of him as he came around the bluff and looked down into the cove. They demanded the watch-words, and threatened to kill him when he could not recite them.

But he said, "I am a friend of Draba's—do you think he would be glad to see me killed?"

So they took his sword, and led him to Draba to ask their chief if they should kill him.

"Mendax!" Draba cried when he saw Mendax approaching between the two watchers. He leapt to his feet from under the shade of a pavilion where he had been surveying his crew as they loaded stolen wares and fenced wealth onto the ship's boats to carry to the galley on the waters. Six young Makeshi stood among the men below, strapping amphorae of wine, oil, and garum into one of the boats. The other was already loaded down with gold and bundles of ivory tusks.

Draba stepped out from under the pavilion's shade. "Give him his sword back," he said, and the watchers did. Then Draba turned to Mendax. "What brings you here? It is too late for our deal with Aska—I had other help."

"I heard a strange rumor that a thief attacked the Mansa's wives and made off with a great deal of his wealth," Mendax said. "He was said to be killed—funny thing, but the Mansa said it in prose!—but I wanted to be sure of the truth."

Draba laughed. "He must be dead," he said. "Unless he was as good a fighting-man as Draba."

Mendax nodded, a crooked smile crossing his lips. "Indeed! It seems that Camba was not a nephew of Bukra after all! A pity he was killed—he sounded an interesting fellow. Also unfortunate for Bukra, as he was sent to the salt mines he coveted, for bringing a criminal into the Mansa's presence."

Draba drew himself up. "Enough gossip-mongering," he said. "What really brings you here? And how did you manage to find my cove?"

"Some of your men are talkative after a krater of wine," Mendax said offhand. Draba glowered, but Mendax forestalled any complaint, continuing, "As for me, I am unemployed, because the Hunter's Girdle was wrecked in the great storm a few nights back."

"So you have come to ship with me!" Draba said, grinning.

"Not as one of your crew," Mendax returned. "But as a mercenary, I'll fight for anyone who pays."

Draba laughed and drew one of several gleaming golden torcs from his neck. He threw it to Mendax. "Here's your first payment," he cried. "Now get down there and load the boats, you weasel—we're off to the Aulorad to sell this loot!"

CULLEN GROVES *lives in northern Idaho, where he studied philosophy at the University of Idaho, and now aspires to be a court poet and polymath. He has had a handful of poems published, mostly by* Heroic Fantasy Quarterly *(including the short rhyming epic "Lethe's Cup and the White Sword"), but also in* Asimov's Sci-Fi Magazine *and online at* Apex. *Alas, his writing has been somewhat put on hold of late to free time for his quest to learn Ancient Greek.*

THE REEDS OF TORIN'S FIELD

BY ANDREA G. STEWART

Torin's Field stretches before me like a reedy ocean, the hills forming the crests of waves. I take a swig of wine from the pouch at my side, and it slides past my tongue, rich and astringent. My former comrades liked to proclaim wine akin to courage, but it does nothing for me now except settle, warm, into my stomach. Or maybe I'm too much a coward, past any help, 'cause all I can do is sit here on a rock, my bum scorching, watching the wind weave in and out of the reeds below. It's a bleeding waste of time, but I only come here when I'm looking to waste it.

"Come to take the long road, good sir?"

An old man strides up the path beside me, leaning on a walking stick, his sandaled feet the same dusty brown as the earth. He's got the air of a pilgrim—pack strapped to his back, two pans jangling at his side, a bedroll tied on underneath. He looks worn; they all look worn. His voice wavers a little when he talks, though I can hear him trying to make it steady.

Funny how someone else's fear can make yours feel a little less real.

I shake my head and put a hand on one of my daggers. "Hunting quarry." I spit into the dirt beside my rock, trying to clear my mouth of the sour aftertaste. "Just waiting for nightfall. I got no reason to speak to dead children." It's a lie, but I've grown comfortable with lies. "You'll have to take the road alone."

I watch them sometimes. Don't know why some people insist on taking company. There's a thousand reeds below—a thousand-thousand. They never find the ones they're looking for right next to each other. I'd bet my bleeding life on it that no one ever does.

The old man doesn't say anything. He just stares at me, his dark eyes reflecting the sunset, his lips pursed. And then, bit by bit, his face crumbles, like a cliff side falling into the sea. "I had a daughter," he says. "She drowned. She—"

"Keep it to yourself," I snarl.

He sucks up his tears, his mouth closing, his eyes blinking like I just pulled back the curtain in a dark room. He gives me a terse nod before starting down the road again. I watch him as he wades into the waist-high reeds, as he starts bending his head, whispering to them, trying to find that one reed—the one that'll let him talk to her.

It's near night by the time he finds it. He falls to his knees in the field, so I only see the top of his balding head amongst the plants, like he's drowning. The wind carries his sobs back to me on my rock. They always weep, and I'm sure I'd do the same, but for different reasons.

Doesn't last long. The reed dries up, its magic spent, and the old man is clutching it to his chest like the withered thing is his daughter, and not just a plant. Don't much see the point, dredging up past pain like that. Or maybe that's the fear talking. I take another pull of wine, then stretch out my legs and hop off my rock. I got murderers to catch, and a sorceress to kill, and a life to keep on living, no matter how tired of it I am.

* * *

I track the murderers to the flats outside of Vedas, the cracked earth spotted with twisted trees and thorn bushes. They've been killing any they can get their hands on, and taking the bodies away. Rumors in the city say they're working for a sorceress.

I kneel, checking for footprints in the dust. Not sure why I keep going back to that bleeding field of reeds. I'm like a man poking a viper with a stick. There's no point in it, and it'll only lead to pain and disappointment. Not like anyone leaves the field smiling; I've watched them.

But the gods take me for a fool. Just being there makes me remember Lytash.

A click sounds and before I can think, I'm sprawled on my back, pain spreading out from my shoulder like its taking root. Crossbow bolt, digging into my left shoulder. I roll onto my side, spitting dust from my mouth as I grope for my daggers. Thinking about the past always fogs up my killing edge, makes me miss things I might have otherwise noticed.

When I get my feet beneath me, I see five men stalking toward me, fanning out so they can surround me. Must have been hiding in the thorn bushes, and me too caught up in thoughts of Lytash to look for them. I got one dagger in my right hand, but my left fumbles at the hilt of the other, pain tingling to my fingertips.

None of the men say a word as they approach, their blades out, their expressions dark. The man who shot me calmly pulls another bolt from the quiver at his side and begins reloading, like he's just getting ready to put down an animal. He lingers behind, but the other four keep coming, one from each side—North, West, East, South—and I'm the center of the compass, the needle.

I back up a little, try to get a thorn bush behind me and make things more difficult for them. The space between my shoulder blades itches, like South's marking it with his eyes as a place to sink a sword into.

Finally manage to get a grip on my other dagger, though pain shoots up my arm as I draw it. I'm a bleeding idiot, letting myself brood. Just as I lift both blades, the four of them rush in.

My heartbeat quickens, my senses sharpen. I hear the brush of their feet against the ground, feel the rush of air as South lifts his blade to strike. I slip to the side to avoid the blow from behind, lift a blade to block the one from East. Just as quickly, I slide my left blade across his throat.

East staggers back, hand to his neck. Not a clean cut; my arm's too weak for that. But I've no time to lament poor work. South's now tangled up in the thorn bush, but he won't be for long.

West attacks, and I block with my uninjured arm. For a brief moment, we stand locked, and all I can see are the rugged mountains and valleys of his face; all I can smell is his rotten breath.

He lifts a leg to kick me, but I'm quicker. I get my other blade between us, cut the artery in his thigh. No one tells you, when you sign up to kill other men, that they all look the same when they die. The wide, startled eyes, whitening face, parted lips. Lytash looked the same, yet I still rushed him to the city healer. Took my eyes off him for one moment too long.

Lytash passed before I could even knock on the healer's door. My son.

I whirl to avoid an attack from North, but his blade catches the bolt in my shoulder. All the breath goes out of me; my vision goes red. My foot slips in the dust.

I slide to the ground, get my blades above me in a guard position. I'm almost disappointed when North's sword strikes my daggers and not my flesh. Never can seem to get a clean death. Been too long I've been fighting, too long I've been living.

Another click sounds and a bolt whizzes past my ear. A rustle of brush as South untangles himself. Three left.

I get a firmer grip on my left dagger, and shove it into North's gut. His sword lowers and cuts my scalp, but then he loses his strength, his face pale.

Two.

I barely get my feet beneath me when South attacks. He's got his sword in one hand, but he uses the other to grab the bolt in my shoulder. He yanks on it, his teeth clenched.

Pain blazes across my chest and down my arm. Can't breathe. If the man with the crossbow hadn't already fired and missed, I'd be dead. Try to cut South with my left dagger but lift my hand to find it empty, the dagger gone from my grip. His sword comes down.

I hold my breath, tighten my muscles, and jerk to the side.

I wrench the bolt from his grip, and it feels like I've been shot all over again. But I manage to keep my head as he overbalances. His sword strikes the dusty ground and my dagger strikes his back.

He lets out his breath in a moan. None of us are swept away by the gods. None of us die with such comfort. We are creatures of flesh and bone, here one moment, winked out in the next.

The ratcheting of a crank sounds as I yank my blade out from between the murderer's ribs. The last man stands across from me, fumbling to get another bolt into place. I stride toward him, and blood trickles from my scalp and into my brows. He slides the bolt into place and starts to lift the crossbow. I dart in, slash at his arm. He drops the weapon and cradles the wounded limb to his chest. I whip the dagger about, settle it right up against his neck.

He swallows. "Who are you?" His gaze flicks to my right wrist and then back to my face.

I let him look, 'cause I have questions to ask, and the more afraid he is of me, the better. "Just a man trying to scratch a living from the hides of criminals," I say.

Sweat beads on his forehead, bright as jewels. "Lutarian," he says, his gaze flicking, again, to the tattoo on my wrist.

"Nope. Left the company eight years ago."

"But you fight with them until you die."

I am dead. Dead to my wife, to my former comrades, to the great city of Nimera itself. "Yes," I tell him. "But that doesn't matter if you kill everyone who thinks you're still alive, does it?"

He's pissing himself, I'm sure of it. Didn't actually happen that way. I told my captain I wanted to leave, and they all turned their backs on me, like I wasn't there any longer. Spoke not one word more to me. You can leave the Lutarians and break your oaths, it's just not pleasant.

"The sorceress," I say. "Where does she live?" You can't go about terrorizing the countryside, abducting and killing people, and expect no one will notice. I wish I could say I do this all for Lytash, to make the world a better place for him, but he's dead and gone and I'm just eager to follow.

The man snorts a laugh through his thick, black beard. His face is rough-hewn, his eyes large and bright. Probably has some Gorak blood in him, in some unspoken part of his lineage. Nobody likes to admit their ancestors once lay with cave-dwellers. "You think I'll tell you?" he says. "What do you think she'd do to me if I did?"

"You'll tell me what I want," I say.

"You'd go after her alone? She'll kill you."

"Maybe that's what I want." Please, yes.

"There are easier ways to die." His hand snakes to a knife at his belt, but I catch his wrist, squeezing until he gasps in pain.

"Yes," I say slowly, letting it sink in. "Yes, there are." I twist the hand, and then he's on his knees, mouth agape, eyes wet with unshed tears. "Tell me where the sorceress lives."

"In the foothills," the words trip over one another, "north of Vedas. A hut. No path to it 'cept one that's used by animals. Off the main road to Nimera. Oak stump, split in two at the trailhead."

"You have my thanks."

He knows I'm going to kill him. I know it. And, like so many others before him, he slides in a few last words.

"She's bringing them back, you know," he says, with the tremulous smile that only deranged fanatics seem capable of. "The Silent Ones. The Watchers."

And then I slit his throat and he's got nothing left on his tongue but choked gurgles.

What he said: it means nothing to me, but I've never known a lot about the occult. I like not knowing.

* * *

Takes me an entire day to bind my wounds and collect the bounty, and another day to get provisions and get on the road. I got money enough for a horse, but I swore I'd never ride again, not after what happened to my son.

So I set out on the road from the city, horsemen and wagons kicking dust in my face, my armor and my boots going the same even brown as that pilgrim's. Been a lot of times I've set out after quarry, thinking they were my last days, only to have my training come through, to save me with the slice of a dagger, the slide of a foot. This time, though, I think I've found quarry I can't kill. Hasn't been a sorcerer round these parts for a hundred years. I can't say my like is as rare.

I'm tired and hungover by the time I find the split oak stump, my wounds weeping through their bandages.

Four days on the road and I'm finally out of wine. No use wishing for more, either, not in the middle of bleeding nowhere, with the sun beating down on my neck with all the heat of a blacksmith's forge.

The split in the path is easy to find; it's following it that proves difficult, especially once the sun starts to go down. I should wait until it's light out, until I can see the path better and check for sentries. But I don't.

The hut's a thing of weathered wood and thatch, barely held together. Not a sound comes through the wood, not even the crackling of a fire. My head pounding, my mouth dry as the dusty earth coating my leather armor, I push open the door and step inside.

My sweaty hand slips free of my dagger's hilt soon as I do. It's not a hut on the inside—it's a bleeding palace, all black stone with veins of silver. My single footstep seems to echo a thousand times off the walls, off ceilings and pillars that climb into the sky. Two sets of stairs hug the walls. Suppose I should have expected this, fighting a sorceress. Not sure which one's real: the hut or the palace.

Doesn't matter. I've killed hundreds of men these past eight years; if a sorceress can't put an end to my misery, I'm not sure who can. Time was when I'd have prayed to the gods to return me home safe. When I had a wife who loved me, and a son who treasured the trinkets I brought him home. I'd give anything to go back, to have her kiss my cheek and smile, to ruffle my fingers through Lytash's chestnut hair.

My younger self would have jumped at the chance to kill a sorceress, to risk his life for his city, his country. My current self just wants to get the whole thing over with. I got nothing waiting for me on the other side, but I got nothing waiting for me here. So I just stroll on in, brash and bold as you please. If this place is as big as it looks, it'll take me damn near forever just to find her.

A woman appears at the top of the staircase on the right. She drips with gold and silver, the chains like shining droplets of dew against her white dress. She's not beautiful, and for some reason that surprises me. Her face looks as though it's been carved from granite—all sharp cheekbones and chin, with eyes the same golden-brown as her skin. She's tall, perhaps even a bit taller than me, and when she moves to descend the stairs, her shoulders do not shift at all.

"So you've come to kill me." Her voice fills the room.

"Yes."

She keeps walking down those steps, her blonde hair floating after her, as if she's underwater. She tilts her head to the side, like a bird looking for a bug on the ground. "No. You've come to die."

"Yes." Not sure why I tell her the truth.

"Why?"

I expected a fight, not a conversation. I keep my hands away from my daggers. "It's my own bleeding business."

She stops at the foot of the steps and neither of us moves. "I suppose that it is. But you don't have to die, Philos."

I know it's sorcery, but hearing my name on her lips sends prickles of ice climbing up my spine. "Could just kill you."

The corner of her mouth quirks upward. "Could you?" She lets that hang in the air for a moment. If she's bluffing, it's a damn good bluff. Her gaze drops. "I don't want to kill you. I could use you."

"Like those men I took for bounty?"

She throws her head back and laughs. "No, not at all. They served me well, but you and I both know that you're different. Do you think just anyone could walk into my home?" She beckons to me, the bracelets on her arm clinking together. "Come, follow me. I will show you."

The woman turns her back on me and glides between the two staircases, into an area with a lower ceiling, closer walls. I could strike her now, have done with it, move on to the next bounty, the next fight, the next day. One sunrise after the next.

I keep my hand on my dagger, but don't draw it. I thought I'd barge in, she'd summon demons, and I'd be a goner. Instead, I'm walking through her palace like she invited me here. Maybe she did. Maybe that's how magic works, I don't know.

She leads me to a door at the end of the hall. With a wave of her hand, the lock clicks and the door opens. The room inside is vast, as large as Suncourt Square in Vedas. Torches line the walls, and they burst into flame with another wave of the sorceress' hand.

"I'm bringing them back," she says. "The Silent Ones. The Watchers."

I'd have pissed myself if I had a drop left in my bladder. Men and women stand, shoulder to shoulder in the room, lined up evenly, like pieces on a chessboard. None of them so much as blink, but they breathe together, as one, and each breath stirs the papery skin around their noses and mouths. Their breathing fills the room with the faint sound of waves against the shore. Each stares straight ahead with clouded eyes.

The Silent Ones. The Watchers. I suppose all these dead people, together, are very silent, and they do look like they're watching. What they're watching, I've no idea.

My mind rambles along in disconnected lines, trying to keep the fear from rising. Must be a thousand of them in here. A thousand-thousand, just like those reeds in Torin's Field. "What do you mean to do with them?"

"Take Vedas. Make it my own."

"And what do you want with me?"

"You've the sorcerer's gift, Philos. Why do you think you've lived so long without intending to?"

All of a sudden, my mouth's as wet as the space behind a farm boy's ears. I want to vomit, but instead I speak. "Can you teach me this, bringing back the dead?"

She smiles, and it softens all the crags of her face, makes her look like a cat, purring in the sunlight. She touches the side of my head, a sharp tingle runs across my forehead, and then something in my mind clicks together, like a door closing. "Yes. But then you must do something for me."

Should ask what it is she wants, but she's holding all the cards. "Anything. I swear it."

* * *

Lytash's death was my fault. I dream about it nearly every bleeding night, except here in the sorceress' palace. Eight days and the place already feels familiar. Eight days and I'm forgetting that wide-eyed look on Lytash's face. Not sure if I'm grateful or sad, 'cause that's the last time I saw my son alive.

Trampled. By my own bedamned horse.

I rise from my cot, trying not to think about what I'm doing, why I'm here, but the question rises to the surface as it does each morning: what in the nine pits of hell does a sorceress want with an entire city? I shove it to the back of my mind. It's her bleeding business, and I've got my own concerns. Even if I could bring Lytash back, what's the difference between that and the reeds? He must hate me. I'd hate me.

My heartbeat quickens as I rest my callused feet on the cold stone floor. But this way, I'd have the time to explain. I'd get to tell him how my horse trampling him wasn't my intention. He'd get to know how hard I tried to save him, how if I could go back, I'd never have trained the beast to stomp on those that raised a sword against him. Never would have brought back a wooden sword for Lytash from Kaliphar. Never would have gotten a horse in the first place.

Just as on the first day, the sorceress appears in my doorway, like she didn't walk there at all, just flew. "Good. You're awake. We have fresh bodies."

She takes me to another room down the hall, with four bodies laid out on the floor. They're freshly dead, still stiff, wounds still weeping blood. Two men and two women, three old and one just barely out of childhood. I wonder if that one's got a reed in Torin's Field.

At least I was defending people when I was a mercenary. At least I was killing murderers. But I do as the sorceress bids, kneel, and place my hands on the cold cheeks of the woman nearest me.

If I got a chance to bring Lytash back, I got to take it.

"Take in a breath," the sorceress says above me. "Gather it in your belly, think of Nestor the Dead, then breathe it out onto the corpse. Will her alive again."

The stone floor makes my knees ache, and I'm reminded again of how old I am. The breath I take pops my shoulders and ribs.

I think of Nestor the Dead, with his lapis-tipped staff, his black eyes, his ragged gray robes. And I actually say a little prayer in my head, that's how bleeding desperate I am.

Heat gathers in my belly. It's pleasant—a bit like a good swallow of soup after a cold day. When I breathe it out, I can see it; it shimmers through the air as it travels into the body of the woman on the floor. It settles over her graying hair, her chapped fingers, the crow's feet at the corners of her eyes.

"Good," the sorceress purrs. "Now you will help me finish my army. It will go faster with the two of us."

Wish I could shake off her praise. I don't want it. Shouldn't care, but I always saw myself as something of a hero.

But I'm sure of this: raising the dead is villain's work.

The woman's wounds close, her eyes open—gray, like her brethren. There's something between me and her, I can feel it in my head, like there's a rope between our minds, stretched taut.

Before I can explore it, or even do anything with it, a sharp pain hits the back of my head, and then dissipates.

"Go downstairs," the sorceress commands. "Join the others."

The woman rises and strides away, silent as a ghost.

I rub the back of my head, trying to find the spot where the pain hit. It's gone. Can't rise to my feet yet 'cause I'm suddenly tired, my limbs weak and shaking. "So I get to raise the dead, but I don't get to control them?" I ask.

She lifts an eyebrow at me. "Do you hand a child the reins to a stallion?"

I flinch. Too close to my own situation. "What do you want Vedas for anyways?" I wave my hand at the walls of her palace. "Just stone and mortar— don't you have plenty of that already?"

She lifts her chin. "Perhaps I wish for more power."

There's a quiver in her lip, a shine in her eye—tells me she's not saying everything. "Does someone say 'perhaps' in front of something they actually mean?"

Her lip firms up, and the shine in her eye is gone. "Perhaps."

The floor chills my fingers as I push myself to my feet. "Why don't you tell me the truth?"

"We all make mistakes, Philos. Some of them, we spend the rest of our lives trying to fix." And then she's moving from the room, her hair waving a farewell.

* * *

Twenty-eight. That's how many people I've raised from the dead. Makes me feel sick each time I think about it. I've tried talking to them, and sometimes I think they're listening, but mostly they just stare straight ahead. Maybe if the sorceress didn't wrench away the connection each time, I'd be able to make them understand me. They understand her well enough.

Whatever power we've both got in our blood, she's got it stronger. Raising the dead doesn't seem to wind her at all.

"Philos," her voice cuts through my thoughts. "The next one."

I've changed in my armor for robes, and I can feel my muscles shriveling, day by day. This sick and weakly thing isn't me. Or I thought it wasn't. I put my hands around the forehead of the next body in line, the skin cold and dry.

We buried Lytash in the fields outside Nimera. He would have wanted his bones to nourish the earth—that was the sort of child he was. I only remember bits and pieces of that day, my memories fractured as I was. My wife's hair catching on my stubble as she wept into my shoulder. The brown of the earth as Lytash was placed in the ground, dark and endless as the ocean at night. The hollowness inside me that grew with each passing moment.

The man on the floor rises, the sorceress cuts my connection with him, and the pain strikes the back of my head.

"The next one," she says.

"How many?" I ask, and my voice is just as rusty as that murderer's by the fire. Seems a lifetime ago. Only I'm the murderer now. I don't kill them with my own two hands, but I might as well have. "How many do you need?" What I meant to ask was: "When can I leave? When can I raise my son from the dead?"

"As many as we can get," she says. "We're close, very close."

I crawl to the next body in line—my pride's gone the way of my strength. Somehow I know: I'll do whatever she says. I swore to it. How much can I truly complain? She's giving me the chance to fix my life's greatest mistake. But my mouth runs off on me. "Half of the dead below would get you Vedas. Why do you need so many?"

She approaches, feet near sliding across the floor, that's how graceful she moves. When she kneels next to me, I catch a whiff of jasmine and sandalwood. She stares into my face just above my eyes, and I'm not sure whether she's figuring if she should confide in me, or if she should kill me. She takes three even breaths before she speaks. "I don't need to just take Vedas. I need to own it—to control it."

Maybe I was mistaken, and all she wants is power. She takes another breath, as if she's about to say more, but then she stops herself, reaches over, and presses her own hands to the dead woman's forehead beneath me.

In the next moment, the woman is breathing, moving.

"I'll take care of the rest. Go. Get some sleep."

* * *

I don't sleep, even though my eyelids grow heavy.

There's no window in my room, but I know it's night. How many days have I been here? Fourteen? Thirty? My shoulder has healed into a reddened scar. Each time I try to count the days, even lying still in my bed, the numbers slip away from me. Other than my room, the room where we raise the dead, and the big room below, I haven't seen the rest of the palace.

"What are you hiding?" I whisper into the darkness, and as the words slide from my mouth, I realize I don't even know her name.

With shaking fingers, I find my armor and daggers on the floor next to the bed. I touch them, run my fingers over the hilts of my daggers. It's like that door in my mind opens a crack. I am—was—a Lutarian.

Putting on my armor is a struggle. My hands don't want to obey. They fumble at the straps, making threading the buckles an exhausting chore. But with every step I manage, that door opens farther—it feels like I'm pushing it open against a strong wind.

It isn't until I've strapped on my daggers that I realize she's put a spell on me to keep me complacent. And with that realization, the door opens the rest of the way, and my fingers can move again, of their own accord. Maybe I'm a sorcerer now, but I was a fighter first, a hero.

I make my way into the hall. Moonlight creeps in from the window at the end, as though afraid to venture too far into the sorceress' home. I wait for a moment, but hear nothing. She might be asleep, or she might not be.

The first door I open reveals only an empty room. The second one reveals some sort of alchemical operation—bottles and bubbling concoctions, pipes and tubes. The third one is a study, books lined on the shelves and papers spread across a desk. Here, I linger.

With a wave of my hand, the torches on the walls light up. A map of Vedas is painted on one black wall, the details too small and too accurate for human creation. If I squint, I can make out tiny, individual cobbles on the streets. She must know everything about the city.

A quick glance at the desk confirms this. Page after page of genealogies, of all the families in the city—from noble to common. Lines and letters drawn off the pages, connecting lineages. Some of the names are marked with red dots and neatly-written numbers. "3.125" "25" "6.25."

In the top drawer of the desk, I find more pieces of paper, all of them with the names marked in red. New genealogies.

Breeding papers.

Don't even realize I'm sweating until I lift a hand to wipe it from my forehead. This is why she needs to control Vedas: to make sure that no one enters and no one leaves. To make sure they heed her every command. Even who they will marry, who they will have children with.

"I told you to sleep."

I got both my daggers in hand before I can remember touching them. She stands in the doorway, her gown draping from one shoulder, her face hard and craggy as stone. No cat-softness to it now. She's carrying a small skeleton in her arms. Another one of her exhumed dead. Another to join her army.

"Didn't much feel like sleeping," I say. If we were to fight, which magic would win out—hers or mine? I wave one of my blades in the direction of the open drawer. "What's all this about?"

"Power," she says.

"You're lying." I want to throw a dagger at her, just to shake her off balance, just to get her to talk. "You said you made a mistake. What kind of mistake requires taking over a city to fix it?"

She sweeps a hand and the torches flare higher, hotter. Bright as day inside the room, and just as warm. "I am one thousand, fifty-six years old." If she meant to silence me, it works. "If you think you've been living for too long, Philos, think how I must feel."

"But why the city?" She starts to stride closer, but I lift the dagger in my right hand as if to throw it, and she stops. "Tell me. Please."

It's that last word that does it. Her eyes shift, from deadly anger to grief. She clutches the skeleton to her chest, the dusty bones smudging her white dress with gray. "When I was young, and just discovering my gift, I killed an entire species. One of them hurt me, so I wished a pestilence upon her entire race." Her eyebrows lift in the way one might shrug—a helpless gesture. "It worked. I didn't know then, the extent of my power, or what would happen. I acted thoughtlessly, without contemplating the consequences.

"The few who survived interbred with the humans in Vedas. I've tried offering them money to marry one another; I've tried offering them power. I've even tried casting my spells on them, as I have with you, but I can't make them do things they were never inclined to do in the first place. In the end, the only thing people respect is fear. If I conquer the city and breed their descendents, just so, I can bring the Ilyanoras back. I can fix the wrong I did, all those years ago."

How can she not see? "Do you think that's what they would want? For you to control their few descendents, to force them to interbreed?"

She shakes her head at me. "It doesn't matter."

What have I done, helping this woman, all on the promise of being able to raise my son from the dead? "Then it isn't about them, it's about you. You made a mistake. You're the one that's got to live with it. Not everyone else."

"Is that so?" Her mouth breaks into a sneer, turning her face into a landscape of jagged cliffs. "You and I are the same, Philos. I thought to bring you a gift, while you slept. Foolish of me, I suppose." She proffers the skeleton and dread sinks its claws into my bones, locking my joints. I thought the skeleton just another desecrated corpse, but from the look in her eye, I know who it is.

Lytash.

I forget about my dagger and take an involuntary step forward. "Don't—" Too late. Always too goddamned late.

She presses a hand to his forehead and breathes out.

Dry, papery flesh winds around his bones, filling out the space, and dry, papery skin covers it. He's missing the chestnut hair, but it's him all right. And then Lytash opens eyes gray as the ashes in a fire, and I can't think at all.

The sorceress sets him on his feet.

"Papa?" The voice that emerges is thick and raspy, as though he's swallowed cobwebs.

I'm kneeling, I'm opening my arms, my heart fixing fast and hard as a thousand feet rushing into battle. Don't care that his skin doesn't look quite real. It's my boy. "I'm here, Lytash."

"You," he looks at me but doesn't move. "You killed me."

All the explanations I've had holed up in my chest pour from my throat, overflowing. "I tried to save you. I tried so hard. I've wished every day that I never got a horse, that I never got you that wooden sword."

"Stop."

I do.

Lytash tilts his head, and the motion jerks and stutters. "It was your fault. You did this to me."

"I know, I know." Tears choke my voice. "Please, son. Forgive me."

He takes a step toward me. "Forgive you? Do you know how much it hurts to die? You could have stopped it. You should have latched the gate tighter, should have taught me never to raise the sword against your horse. I thought you were supposed to protect me."

Each word he speaks feels like a hammer, and I'm the nail, being pounded into the ground. Never welcomed death quite like this. Wish I could take a dagger to the heart, right now. It's what I deserve.

The rustle of skirts sounds from behind me. The sorceress. She's whispering something beneath her breath. The whole place trembles. And then I hear the march of a thousand-thousand feet, all in time.

My breath catches. The connection—that thing that binds her to the dead, that makes them do her bidding—it's still there between her and Lytash. It's not my son I'm talking to. It's her. The hiss of a blade sounds in my right ear.

My hand's on my dagger, the blade drawn before I can remember reaching for it. I whirl, and my dagger clashes against hers.

She's got her teeth bared, her eyes wild with anticipation for the kill. I'd tell her I'm sorry to disappoint, but she bears down on me, her strength more than I expect, and mine waned more than I'd like.

"Papa," Lytash's plaintive voice echoes from the walls. "You murdered me."

It makes my hands tremble, and she pushes me back. She lashes out and scores a stinging cut across my chest. I leap back just in time to stop her from gutting me. The pounding feet grow louder, as the dead climb the stairs—toward where we're fighting.

A thousand fifty-six years is enough time to learn a lot, it seems. The sorceress moves with the grace of a hunting cat—silent, liquid. I draw my other dagger, but then she's on me, all glinting blade and teeth and eyes. My arms are heavy; my breathing aches past my throat. Can barely block her attacks, much less fight back. Might as well just give in, get that death I've been waiting for.

And if I die? She'll still have Lytash, bound to her, his old bones doing her bidding. I cast out a hand and close the door with the force of my will, holding it shut. It won't keep the dead out for long, but maybe it'll keep them out for long enough.

I push past the pain, the weakness, find that reserve of strength burning in the pit of my belly. She can have me, but she won't have him. I've failed him enough in one lifetime. Won't let him down in the next. My blade locks with hers.

"You can't win this," she says.

I kick at her belly and she whirls away from the blow, taking her dagger with her, leaving me stumbling.

"Papa," Lytash says. He's reaching for me, fingers curled, nails long as claws, and my lips go numb.

"Not this." The words escape my mouth in a moan. "Please."

"Not what?" the sorceress says, her voice mocking. Lytash's cold hands paw at my armor, his feet tangle with my own. I'm helpless to stop him.

The dead begin to pound at the door, and my will is barely strong enough to hold it shut. I imagine the door bursting open, the dead flowing over me like a wave, drowning me. The sorceress, sensing my weakness, circles, seeking an opening to plunge her dagger into my neck. I'm trying to keep my guard up, but Lytash sinks his nails into my leg, and they're sharp as daggers. It would be fitting for me to die because of my son, when my son died because of me.

My will slips, just a little. Gray fingers squirm into the gap between the door and the wall, writhing like so many worms.

"Your fault," Lytash mutters, plaintive.

I squeeze my eyes shut for just a moment. The sorceress darts in, and her blade scores a deep gash across my collarbone. I try to move away, but Lytash is ripping into my arms; each wound burns and weeps trails of blood. The sorceress aims again for my neck, and I barely block her blow. I shove her away, as hard as I can. "Yes," I gasp out. "It was my fault." I know it's the sorceress speaking through his mouth, but maybe he can still hear me. "But this isn't you."

My heart clenches as I strike my son's gray face with the back of my hand. His nails scrape at my skin as he falls. And then I'm kicking him, sobbing, wishing this wasn't my life, that this wasn't me. I feel bones crack beneath my feet, but he keeps coming, fingers outstretched and red with my blood.

In my mind, I'm watching my horse rear up again, hooves glinting in the sunlight. Lytash beneath him, hands upraised, wooden sword still in his grip, too small and frail to stop what's happening. And me, running, screaming words I can't even hear because I know what's coming, because I can't do a bleeding thing about it.

Fists pound at the door, louder, like the pounding of hooves against hard-packed earth.

Today is not that day. That day is dead and buried. Like my son.

I trample him one last time, pray that he stays down, and then whirl to find the sorceress crouched and ready to leap. It happens quickly. I catch the sorceress' dagger beneath the hilt, send it skittering across the floor. I have my other blade at her neck before she can draw her next breath.

"If you kill me," she pants, "you lose him, all over again. You can't raise the dead twice."

I want, so badly, to look back at Lytash, to take in the sight of my son— gray-eyed and thin-skinned, and some semblance of alive. But I won't take my eyes off the sorceress. "It's my mistake," I say. "I'm the one that's got to live with it."

She relaxes and closes her eyes. Been too long she's been living. She knows it and I know it too. I draw the blade across her throat.

Behind me, Lytash falls into a pile of rattling bones. Just outside the door, I hear a rumbling like thunder as the sorceress' army crumbles.

No one's going to take Vedas. No one's going to breed its people to bring back a long-forgotten race.

And no one's going to bring Lytash back to life.

I know I've done hero's work, but I'm too bleeding sad and tired to care.

* * *

I get my two hundred gold slips, from a man in Vedas who barely even glances at my face as he pays the bounty. He doesn't know what it's cost me, or what the sorceress had planned for his city. To him, it's just one more villain dead and gone, and more gold leaking from the city's coffers.

Lytash's bones rattle a bit when I move, though I got them packed up nice and tight. Sometimes I think he's trying to tell me something, but I know it's all in my head. It's ten days by foot back to Nimera, and if there's one thing left I got to do, it's to bury my son's bones where they belong.

Sun's starting to set by the time I leave Vedas, glazing the fields with orange and pink. I got a lot of ground to cover, but when I reach the first dusty fork in the road, I stop. The way straight ahead leads to Nimera, and so does the path to the right. But the path to the right is the long road, the one that curves past my rock on the hill, the one that cuts through Torin's Field.

Now I swear, by all the gods above and below, that I'm standing stock-still in the fork, so still I don't even breathe. But something in my pack rattles a little. Two dirt-smudged bones, clanking against one another.

Those accusations, the terrible words coming from Lytash's mouth? They weren't his. I wish I could say that Lytash would never say those things, that he was a sweet boy who would forgive anyone, even his papa for causing his death. But the truth is, I don't know what he'd say to me if he had the chance. That's what scares me, more than anything else.

I reach, reflexively, for the wine pouch at my belt. It's empty, and I've been so preoccupied I didn't think to get any more. If I do this, I got to do it alone, no wine in my belly and no other pilgrims to keep me company.

I shift my pack, whisper a prayer, and set my feet toward Torin's Field.

Been a long time coming.

ANDREA G. STEWART *is the daughter of immigrants, and was raised in a number of places across the United States. Her parents always emphasized science and education, so she spent her childhood immersed in Star Trek and odd-smelling library books. When her (admittedly ambitious) dreams of becoming a dragonslayer didn't pan out, she instead turned to writing books. She now lives in sunny California, and in addition to writing, can be found herding cats, looking at birds, and falling down research rabbit holes.*

Shamans

by David Farney

Countless tribes speaking countless tongues
frequent xanthous shores of a long-burning lake.
Come hunters, come nomads, come fishers too—
unlikely neighbors enthralled by songs of shamans
through whose lyrics tribesmen discover discourse.

But soon it seems the shamans sing too loudly—
this common tongue strips mysticism and melody from words
such that fishers and nomads hear only shouting
and prophecies of good harvests while facing full baskets,
begging them ask: "What good are these shamans
with uncallused hands and songs grown harsh?"

"Useful," shamans chant, "for the coming drought—
which burns field and fish and fauna
just as surely as it withers the soul. Can't you see?
The lake already burns hotter with high-spiraling flames;
you need us to lead you across, to yon sulfur-less shores."

The fishers, though, with their steely nets
cast keen eyesight upon fiery water, saying:
"The lake burns no more than it did before.
Indeed red seems blue with louder songs from shamans;
noxious vapors and fires intensify only upon their breath."

The nomads, what with their wandering ways
say, "Going downstream to avoid a drought makes no sense.
We'll back-trace rivers to find clearer-seeing shamans—
perhaps they yet sing beautifully, and intelligibly.
But if not, this fiery lake glows to show us home."

The hunters, though, envision thick herds, as of old.
"We trust the shamans to guide us through fire and flood
toward temperate shores against verdant fields and woods,
toward fewer tribes and constant use of this common tongue.
You fishers and nomads are doomed damnable fools!"
To which the fishers reply:
"If this drought comes upon us, driving inferno higher,
yonder down the shore we'll join a tribe who
legend says never once has seen the lake afire.
Go, obnoxious hunters and ill-convincing shamans—
we are staying."

"And so too now are we," the nomads say, "for fishing with
cold-questioning eyes seems a more sensible plan than
traveling upstream with hearts hoping to find
simple-singing shamans enjoining tribes around a lake,
instead of coaxing from it flames."

Co-founder of Heroic Fantasy Quarterly, DAVID FARNEY'S *creative juices have been sorely marginalized by his employment in medical sales, as well as by the never-ending demands put upon him by his money-pit of a house. But he still enjoys writing and editing when he can. His poetry has appeared in* Aiofe's Kiss.

About the Artists

ROBERT ZOLTAN has done work for a wide variety of clients, including Simon & Schuster, and Disney. He is also an award-winning music composer, graphic designer, owner of Dream Tower Media (https://dreamtowermedia.com/), host of Literary Wonder & Adventure Show, and author of *Rogues of Merth: The Adventures of Dareon and Blue*, *Tomorrow Girl and Other Tales*, *Betting On the Shadows*, and the upcoming novel *The Long Long Long Long Rescue: A Tale of the Incomparable Quill*. He holds a Bachelor of Fine Arts Degree in Illustration from Washington University in St. Louis, and currently lives in the Silver Lake neighborhood of Los Angeles.

JUSTIN PFEIL is an IT Guy, draws a Webcomic, and fences with Medieval swords. He's an Old-School RPG player and has been married to his wife for 22 years. Check out his website at https://justinpfeil.com/ for more!

SIMON WALPOLE has been drawing for as long as he can remember and is fortunate to spend his freetime working as an illustrator. He primarily uses pencils, pens and markers, and a bit of digital for tweaking. In addition to interior illustrations for various publishing formats, he has also drawn a lot of maps for novels. His work can be found at his website, http://swalpole6.wix.com/handdrawnheroes.

KAROLÍNA WELLARTOVÁ is a Czech artist and painter creating images predominantly with the wildlife themes, nature studies and the literary characters. She's inspired by the curious shapes and a materials from the nature, but the main source still comes from literature. Check out more of her work at website https://carolwellart.com/galleries.

MIGUEL SANTOS has years of experience illustrating for RPG's, magazines, books and comics. Major themes are Sci Fi, Fantasy and Horror, he has done multiple illustrations for *Heroic Fantasy Quarterly*.

RICHARD HARTLEY is currently working in the field of graphic design, but his first love has always been illustrating. He was weaned on comic books and fantasy art at the wee age of 4 by his uncle, who would bring over stacks of magical books filled with page after page of art and would read them aloud. As Richard grew older, his uncle taught him about the greats: Kirby and Ditko, Buscema and Romita, and his favorite artist, Frank Frazetta. The sheer action and bold lines hooked young Richard. He considers himself light years away from the skill these giants had, but they continue to inspire him. And, perhaps, one day his work will inspire another little kid somewhere.

GARRY MCCLUSKEY has been a professional artist for more than 15 years. He's done book covers for every genre imaginable (such as the memoir of a coma survivor's trip through the afterlife), as well artwork for comic books, children's books and RPG games. Recently, he completed five ebook covers for Roger Zelazny's Amber series and several interior illustrations for a new hardcover version of Edgar Rice Burroughs' *The Oakdale Affair*. He's currently working on a comic book about a vampire-shark. (http://garymccluskey.carbonmade.com/)

About the Founding Editors

ADRIAN SIMMONS is a Norman, Oklahoma, based reader and writer. His short fiction has appeared in *James Gunn's Ad Astra Magazine*, *Giganotosaurus*, *Lackington's*, *Cirsova*, *Heroic Fantasy Quarterly*, and *Weirdbook*. His essays and reviews have appeared in *Black Gate* and *Strange Horizons*.

DAVID FARNEY studied architecture and science in college before earning a journalism degree. He works in medical sales, and enjoys writing epic and historical fantasy, as well as speculative poetry. He lives in Oklahoma City but dreams of living farther north — which might explain his fascination with Norse and Viking lore.

About the Designer

KEANAN BRAND has been a proofreader and an associate editor for indie presses, and has served on editorial teams for ezines (such as *Fear & Trembling* and *Ray Gun Revival*). An amateur photographer and occasional wanderer, Keanan is also the author of several award-winning short stories and a novel, *Dragon's Rook,* the first half of an epic fantasy duology. He is at work on its companion, *Dragon's Bane*, among other novels.

Kickstarter Contributors

Keith West
Troy Chrisman
GtheStalker
David Tonzola
Barbara Barrett
Pegana
Joshua Hampton
John O'Neill
Derrick Eaves

Benefactors

Ernie Batten
Eric Lentz
Mark Hall
Gerald P. MacDaniel

Advanced Retail-Level Backer

Ken Boorman

Help Support Us Through Patreon!
https://www.patreon.com/HFQezine

Made in the USA
Monee, IL
27 January 2020